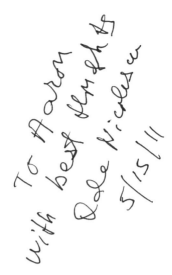

To Aaron
with best thoughts
Ada Nicolescu
5/15/11

PRELUDE IN BLACK AND GREEN

A Novel

Ada Nicolescu

Order this book online at www.trafford.com
or email orders@trafford.com

Most Trafford titles are also available at major online book retailers.

Note for Librarians: A cataloguing record for this book is available from Library
and Archives Canada at www.collectionscanada.ca/amicus/index-e.html

Printed in Victoria, BC, Canada.

ISBN: 978-1-4251-8931-0 (sc)
ISBN: 978-1-4251-8933-4 (e)

*Our mission is to efficiently provide the world's finest, most comprehensive book publishing
service, enabling every author to experience success. To find out how to publish your book, your
way, and have it available worldwide, visit us online at www.trafford.com*

Trafford rev. 7/27/09

 www.trafford.com

North America & international
toll-free: 1 888 232 4444 (USA & Canada)
phone: 250 383 6864 ♦ fax: 812 355 4082

To the memory of
my Parents and my Sister, Catlia.

ACKNOWLEDGMENTS

I WANT TO THANK MY MENTORS and guides, CAROL EMSHWILLER and MARTHA HUGHES, whose help was essential for the completion of this book. I was also blessed with the intelligent, warm and patient support of my fellow writers and friends, GABRIELA CONTESTABILE, BARBARA FLECK-PALADINO, IRENE GLASSGOLD, FLORENCE HOMOLKA, MARGARET SWEENEY, MARIA TAMICK and GAY TERRY. And I am grateful to the loving encouragement of my husband, LAWRENCE L. LE SHAN.

INTRODUCTION

T HIS BOOK IS A NOVEL about a Jewish family in Bucharest, Romania, in the 1930s.

It is a time of unrest and transition. Life is still enjoyable, but clouds are gathering at the horizon.

This is a work of fiction, inspired by historical events. All characters are imaginary, and any resemblance with real people is coincidental.

TABLE OF CONTENTS

THE LIST OF CHARACTERS

The Stein Family

Adrian Stein .... Electrical Engineer, 39.

Nina .... His Wife, 36.

Suzy .... Daughter, 13.

Nadia .... Daughter, 8.

Nina's Relatives (all maternal)

Uncle Ariel Geller .... Her mother's oldest brother, 80
Chief Rabbi of London
Famous Linguist and Zionist.

Clara Geller .... His youngest daughter, 21.

Aunt Josephine Gold .... Uncle Ariel's youngest sister, 64.

Uncle Leon Gold .... Her husband, 70.

Joel Gold .... Their son, Pediatrician, 28.

Mathilda Gold .... Joel's wife, 22.

Stella Frühling .... Nina's sister, 32.

Sorel Frühling .... Stella's husband, Pediatrician,
35.

Theo Frühling .... Their son, 9.

Corinna Frühling .... Their daughter, 11.

Emil Regen........................ Construction Engineer, Nina's
oldest brother, 41.

Dora Regen .... His wife, 36.

Liviu Regen....................... Nina's middle brother, Internist,
40.

Bea Regen .... His wife, 33.

Others

Silvia................................. Governess, 23.

Dr. Victor Georgescu........... Psychiatrist, Director of the
Mental Hospital, 54.

Dr. Eugen Milo .... Psychiatrist, Assistant to Dr.
Georgescu, 27.

Charles Kass....................... Electrical Engineer in Switzerland, 41.

Edward Stiller .... Representative of the International Red Cross at the Swiss
Embassy, 43.

Fräulein Lilly..................... Governess, the Stein children,
28.

Domnişoara Braunstein....... Adrian's Secretary, 27.

Skender.............................. Tartar boy at the Black Sea,
Theo and Nadia's friend, 14.

Fritz.................................. Adrian's chauffeur, 41.

Marish .... Maid, 25.

Ilona .... Cook, 37.

PART I

PREPARATIONS—BUCHAREST 1936

I N HIS OFFICE ON THE quiet street, Adrian stands near the window and waits for the secretary to bring him the letters to sign. One is for General Electric in the U.S. regarding an order for household appliances he has made for his neighbor, Doctor Ionescu, and the other is addressed to the Barclay Bank in London.

While he is waiting for the secretary, Adrian is examining the large frosted glass pane of the window, engraved with the image of a tall devil—a naked and hairy creature endowed with horns, hooves and a bushy tail, who is covering, with his large hands, the chimneys of two factories. The smoke, which cannot escape through the chimneys, is now billowing out of the buildings through broken windows and narrow doors, through which a frantic crowd of workers also streams out on the street. The devil is taller than the tallest chimney and he grins with delight as he watches the tiny creatures scramble on the ground. His bushy tail whips up the smoke like a whirlwind, choking the workers below.

Adrian had this scene copied from a drawing which had appeared in a German satyrical publication a few years ago and was entitled, "The Ugly Face of Industrialization." He had liked the cartoon because he found much truth in it. An artist friend, who had studied glass engraving at the Bauhaus in Germany, had enlarged it and engraved it perfectly onto the frosted window pane.

As an electrical engineer in charge of the construction of the first electrical plant in the heart of the Carpathian mountains (and also as a representative of several important foreign electrical companies), he had no doubts about the superiority of the clean, electrical energy over the toxic, dirty and polluting use of charcoal.

As he stands by the window, his secretary, Domnişoara Braunstein, enters the room and hands him the two letters to sign, adding that the letter for Baden near Zürich in Switzerland has already left.

"Would that be all for today?" she asks, looking at him with her clear blue eyes. She holds the letters in one hand and arranges her bun with the other. Even though her hair is always tidy and neat, she is always worried about her bun. "I understand there is no English lesson today?"

"No, not today. Nina, my wife, expects you tomorrow. Today is the family party for her uncle who is arriving from London. She hasn't seen him since 1924, when he came to Bucharest for his father's funeral. And I have never met him, since this happened before our wedding. Now he has announced his arrival with a telegram addressed to Nina, and she has decided to celebrate this visit with a family party to which she has invited all her siblings and their spouses. I must be off to get special treats for this occasion. Is the car waiting outside?"

Before he steps out, the secretary hands him a new letter from Switzerland which has just arrived in the mail. He puts it in his briefcase and takes his leave. "I'll see you tomorrow. Don't forget: the English lesson of today has been postponed for tomorrow at 5."

"I know," the secretary nods. "We're still doing Mrs. Dalloway. Your wife is making good progress." As she goes back to her desk, Adrian watches her walking away in her flat, manly shoes and her gray skirt with deep pockets in which she carries all kinds of office knickknacks—pencils, pens, erasers, pencil sharpeners, even letters and envelopes. She is a practical person. Everything is practical about her— her hair gathered in a bun at the back of her neck, the lack of jewelry, even the absence of makeup. She would look plain and mousey if it weren't for her intelligent, luminous eyes. Adrian shakes his head and thinks that it is a shame that Domnişoara Braunstein must work as a secretary and cannot use her real skills. She is well overqualified for this job! Her doctoral thesis on Mark Twain which was partly published in a prestigious literary magazine should grant her a teaching position at the University. But Domnişoara Braunstein, who is Jewish like himself and lives alone with her old and sick mother, cannot teach at the University because of the anti-Semitic laws of the country. Fortunately, Adrian can pay her a good salary and augment it with the English lessons she gives to his wife, Nina.

"The car is here!" says the secretary, poking her head through the open door. "I'm coming!" Adrian walks toward the vestibule and catches a glimpse of himself in the tall mirror which hangs in the entrance hall. He is surprised how much he resembles his Uncle Bernard, his father's brother, now that he has shaved his moustache, as Nina had asked him to do. He has the same long, bony face, tall forehead and big teeth as his uncle. He has deep set dark eyes, sallow skin and thinning hair. Even though he is of medium height, his long legs and erect posture make him look tall and athletic.

As a child, his brothers and sisters called him "The Horse," because of his long face and big teeth. Later, when he developed a taste for American cigarettes and American cars, and particularly since he started doing business with American firms, he was nicknamed "The American."

In the summer, he always wears comfortable but elegant clothes—silk jersey shirts with short sleeves and open collars, light "shantung" suits and a panama hat.

He now says goodbye to Domnişoara Braunstein, takes his briefcase in one hand and his hat in the other, and walks out the door.

It is warm and sunny outside, the beginning of June. Women are wearing light, summer dresses and men have abandoned their jackets and ties. A glimmer of summer vacation is in the air.

Adrian takes a few steps and sees the car parked under an old linden tree. The engine must have been running, for the air near the car is reeking of fuel. Nevertheless, Adrian can still smell the fragrance of the linden blossoms. Yes, he thinks, if we could only keep the world unspoiled by the new, developing industries!

He has now reached the Dodge, and Fritz, the blond chauffeur greets him bowing lightly and touching his gold trimmed cap with his index finger.

"Quickly, to Leonida's!" says Adrian, as he climbs in the car and sits on the velvet covered banquette. "We need to buy gourmet treats for the party tonight!" The car starts with a jolt, but Fritz stops soon in front of a gas station. While he is waiting, Adrian keeps meditating about the pitfalls of technical developments.

He agrees with the artists and writers who are warning the world about the dangers of growing pollution and industrialization! Adrian loves the trees, the forests, and the waterfalls, and doesn't want to harm them. But is this possible? He remembers that the Swiss have done it. They have built electrical plants in the heart of their mountains, hidden behind the trees. You can take a cable car or an electric train to the peak of the Mönch or the Jungfrau, and never dream that an industrial plant is hiding in the thick of the forest!

Switzerland! How much he had liked studying and working there, in Baden, near Zürich! And he would have kept on staying and working there much longer, if his aging mother hadn't written and asked him to come home immediately and get married! "*This* is your country. Here is your family! What are you doing so far away from us all? I am growing older and sicker... Come home and get married before I die!" she had pleaded.

He couldn't say no. She was sick. She had developed severe Parkinson's disease and could barely eat, his brother Tobias had written. Adrian bought a ticket, boarded the first train, and came home. Then he got married, as she had asked him. What else could he do? But maybe... maybe he shouldn't have listened, he sometimes wonders.

When they finish at the gas pump, Fritz starts the car again. They leave the quiet streets behind and turn into a noisy boulevard jammed with rattling trams, honking buses, cars and horse-drawn carriages. They pass a wagon filled with watermelons, with a gypsy family asleep on the mound of fruit. They pass a shiny black carriage decorated with ribbons and red carnations, and a milkman riding his two-wheel buggy drawn by a rickety donkey.

Everything is covered with dust: a white layer of powder has settled on the street and on the trees. A big truck hurtles past them, whipping up a cloud of dust which chokes them and makes them cough.

They follow the Brătianu Boulevard, rolling by the elegant movie houses, ARO and SCALA, and past the new hotels AMBASSADOR and LIDO, with its flashy ice cream terrace from which one could watch the marble swimming pool with its artificial waves.

On the roof of the newly built high-rises, the neon signs in blue, red and orange glitter even in daytime, advertising luxury products and companies: Fernet Branca, Du bon... Du bon... Dubonnet, Crema Nivea, Vagons Lits Cook, Galleries Lafayette, Astra Română. And on the sidewalks, young women with their little hats, high heels and silk summer dresses and men with panama hats mingle with the vendors of *rahat lokum*, of *mititei*, and *porumb copt* (grilled corn on the cob), who advertise their wares at the top of their voices. There are also blind fiddlers and organ grinders, many with noses eaten by syphilis or pellagra. Mutilated World War I veterans with decorations pinned to their tattered uniforms crawl in the dust and beg.

When the car finally stops in front of Leonida's and Adrian steps on the curb, he is immediately surrounded by gypsy women selling flowers. They stand barefoot, with long, flowery skirts and wearing shiny necklaces made of gold coins. Their arms are full of baskets of flowers.

"*Garoafe! Garoafe!*" yells one woman, one arm filled with red and white carnations, the other holding a crying baby.

"Gladiole! Gladiole! *Să-ți traiască Franțuzoaica!*" (Long live your French sweetheart!), yells another, trying to hand him a long stem with yellow blossoms.

"*Lalele! Lalele! Hai la lalele!*" cries an old gypsy woman, her parched face furrowed with wrinkles, offering him a fat bouquet of tulips.

They are forming a closed circle around him, their almost naked children pulling at his arms, his sleeves and his briefcase. Adrian struggles to free himself from their hold. As soon as he steps out of the circle, they run after him and the toddlers wind their brown arms around his legs. When he finally walks into the store, he has to stop to catch his breath and smooth his shirt and pants.

Leonida is a large hall with a high, vaulted ceiling and walls covered with tiles. A young sales boy with rolled up pants scoops water out of a bucket splashing it on the floor, trying to make the place feel cool, but getting the cement floor slippery. Other salespeople in white aprons rush back and forth between large barrels filled with black olives, pickles and sauerkraut, and the counters and shelves loaded with mountains of fish of all size and colors, mounds of goose pastrami, smoked ham and bacon and garlands of long sausages. Crowds of shoppers stream into the store and gather in front of the counters, pushing and shoving each other.

Adrian stops by the door trying to get used to the sound of the many voices and to the mixed smells of smoked sausages, salty fish, sharp cheeses and garlic. Then he walks to the back of the store and stops in front of a counter where a stocky woman with short cropped hair and knotted eyebrows is arranging chunks of halvah on shiny copper trays.

"Welcome," she says as she steps forward. "What can I do for my favorite customer!" She is cross-eyed, her right eye always wandering toward a hidden, mysterious destination.

"Hello, Sofica! It's good to see you again!" says Adrian. "I need a whole variety of gourmet treats for a family party of about 15." He hands her a bill of 100 lei and pulls out of his pocket a piece of paper folded in two. "I need black and red caviar, *batog*, olives, smoked sturgeon, pickled cucumbers, hard Romanian salami, goose pastrami, paté de foie gras... and so on and so forth. It's all written on this paper!" he says as he hands her the list.

Sofica takes the paper, steps into the middle of the store and claps her hands. In a minute, a young man with a long apron, his face covered with pimples, and his hair, shiny with brilliantine, comes running and takes the list from her. In about 15 minutes, all the delicacies Adrian had ordered are wrapped in wax paper and neatly packed in two cardboard boxes.

Adrian takes hold of the lighter box, while Fritz carries the bigger box. The young man follows them with a case of old wine of Cotnari.

Back in the street, they open the car's luggage compartment and place the boxes inside. Sofica has offered them a chunk of ice for the fish and the caviar, but Adrian refuses, saying that it is a short ride and they're going to be home in no time at all. Besides, he knows that Fritz doesn't want to have his luggage compartment flooded with melting ice!

"All right? Ready? Let's go!" commands Adrian when they're seated inside the car. He is watching the group of gypsy women, who are now pestering a distinguished looking old man with a cane. He is bending down... He is actually buying a large bouquet of carnations from the woman with the crying baby!

The car starts slowly, turns around, and follows the boulevard in the opposite direction. Soon they turn left and follow another tree-lined boulevard toward the residential part of the city. The streets are just as noisy and crowded, and the white blanket of dust seems even thicker than further downtown.

"It hasn't rained in a long time. There isn't a cloud in the sky," says Fritz. "I'm afraid we're in for a drought!"

"Yes, I'm afraid so!" Adrian scans the glazed sky in search of a cloud, but there is none.

The car swerves and stops abruptly. Adrian starts and becomes aware of the noise which comes from outside. There are drums beating, people chanting, pots and pans being slammed against each other... The *paparude*! The rainmakers! Adrian looks out the window and sees, right there, in the middle of the road, in front of the car, a group of *paparude* singing and dancing to gather the clouds and make the rain pour down. They are five—two boys and three girls, all very young, barefoot, wearing nothing but skirts made of palm leaves, garlands of willow branches and wreaths woven of leafy twigs in their hair. One boy holds the pots and pans which he slams rhythmically against each other. The second carries a tin watering can from which he pours water on the others, simulating rain, while the three girls, holding long grasses in their hands, dance and chant, "*Udă, udă, paparudā!*" (Wet, wet, rainmaker). They raise their eyes and arms toward the sky, imploring it to send rain over the plains and the forests...

Fritz makes the sign of the cross and so do other people in the street. Whatever God they're praying to (Greek Orthodox, Catholic, Protestant, Jewish or even Muslim), let Him hear their prayers and send plenty of rain very soon, thinks Adrian. For the drought is a real danger. It can become a serious calamity for his work. It can affect the water level, just now when measurements have to be taken at the electric plant. And in that case, it can interrupt or slow down the whole operation, God knows for how long! And if the drought is so severe as to leave the villagers at the foot of the mountains without water, they could become very angry and take it out on the new installations! Their water had already been slightly reduced since the dam had been built. And if things would get worse, they could climb the mountains armed with pitchforks and clubs and destroy whatever stands in their way!

They could even fall prey to the agitation of the Iron Guard, the Romanian Fascist organization that preaches that "all modern industrialization is nothing but a foreign, Jewish invention to exploit the Romanian peasants."

"We want to live like our ancestors! We want to respect their traditions. We don't want any changes!" the Iron Guard leaders proclaim. Yes, things can really get messy if there is a prolonged drought!

The boy with the watering can pours the last drops over the hood, making Fritz smile. "I hope this is a good sign for us!" he says.

He starts the car, drives a few blocks further, and soon turns into the narrow street with many gardens, where Adrian lives. They stop in front of a wrought iron gate and climb out of the car.

Across the street, opposite the house, stands an elderly man, smoking a pipe. It is Dr. Ionescu, a retired physician. He is shaking ashes into a bed of roses, inside his garden and when he sees them, he waves and rushes across the street. Adrian frowns, wishing to get out of his way.

"A new princely carriage you've got there! Bigger than the old one!" he says, walking around the car and inspecting it from all sides. "Not bad, not bad. Business doing well, I guess?"

He stops face to face with Adrian and lights his pipe. His moustache, his teeth, the tips of his fingers and even his lips are yellow from smoking. He draws on his pipe, and then goes on.

"Say, when will I get my new American fridge and gas stove? Tell them to hurry. With this heat and the lack of rain, soon there won't be any ice left for the ice box and we'll die of heat before the shipment arrives!" He is poking his finger at Adrian's face and flashing his yellow teeth, laughing at his own joke.

"Soon, soon," says Adrian. "I've written again to General Electric in America, urging them to hurry up with the delivery. Your new appliances should be here any time soon."

Adrian is very serious. He takes business matters very seriously.

"No need to worry," he adds. Then he turns toward Fritz, telling him to take the packages upstairs, or to call Ilona, the cook on the intercom and ask her to come down and help him with the parcels and boxes. But Dr. Ionescu posts himself at the gate and continues his monologue, as if nothing else is going on.

"Your fruit trees are beautiful," he says as he looks up a tree. "They're doing better with you than with me. The pear tree here by the entrance and the apricot tree by the stone bench have more flowers this spring and are more lush now, than were ours. What are you doing with them? Magic?" The doctor is squinting behind his bone-rimmed glasses and is pulling at his moustache.

Adrian shrugs. "No magic at all. These are just wonderful trees. We give them plenty of water and prune them when needed. But please excuse me now, I must be going." He nods, turns around, and walks into the garden. It seems to him that Dr. Ionescu is always complaining, always competing and comparing Adrian's house and garden, as well as possessions with his own. Does the doctor still resent the fact that two years ago Adrian bought a piece of land from him that he had been forced to sell?

This stretch of land had once been part of the beautiful orchard owned by his family. But they have lost their fortune, partly due to poor estate management, but mainly due to heavy gambling at the Casino in Monte Carlo. This had forced the doctor to sell a large chunk of their last property in Bucharest, many acres of lush orchard which occupies more than six city blocks.

Adrian had paid the whole sum of money in shiny gold coins, packed in a heavy coffer, so that the doctor could settle the family debts. But he still feels that his neighbor resents the deal and considers that the land still belongs to him. He looks at Adrian as an unwelcome intruder.

When Dr. Ionescu and his wife decided to install new utilities in their home, they asked to see Adrian's own American made appliances. He invited them to the house and showed them his modern gas stove, refrigerator and heating furnace, all made by General Electric. As a representative of GE in Romania, Adrian often used his home as a showroom. They went down to the basement to look at the new furnace, and when they came upstairs, Nina surprised them with homemade apricot preserve from the garden and Turkish coffee, which was served on the terrace.

"The trees, our beautiful trees! They're doing so well now in our orchard!" the doctor's wife said, staring with eyes full of tears into the garden.

Adrian feels angry when he remembers this scene. He tells himself that it isn't worth being so solicitous with these neighbors: they'll never really appreciate his efforts! But now it's too late: the order for their appliances has been sent out whether he likes it or not.

Adrian walks through the garden toward the stairs which lead up to the wraparound terrace. He picks up the pruning scissors from a garden bench, and cuts a large bouquet of lilies and peonies from the bushes which surround the swimming pool. He will bring them to Nina, as a centerpiece for the dinner table tonight. As he approaches the stairs, he can already hear the clatter of plates being set up on the terrace and in the dining room.

Nina stands in the middle of the room holding a telegram in her right hand. She gives a last glance to the telegram before folding it and slipping it in her pocket. "Arriving June 15th, Orient Express. Keep confidential—Only family. Uncle Ariel."

The telegram announces the arrival of her mother's oldest brother. He lives far away, in London, with his wife and 13 children. Nina barely knows him. He left the country in 1885, long before she was born. But his father, her own grandfather, and his brothers and sisters, her uncles and aunts, often speak of him. Her mother has told her many stories about him.

Uncle Ariel is now Chief Rabbi of the Spanish Community of London, even though he himself, like the whole family, are Ashkenazim. Nina has trouble understanding the situation, but she tells herself that she doesn't have the facts to understand the circumstances.

She has seen the Uncle only on two occasions: once, in 1921, when she was 22 years old. He had been invited by the King to receive two gold medals. It was a belated reward, a late recognition of his work on Romanian Popular Literature and Folklore, which he had published in Leipzig thirty years earlier.

He came again in 1926, for a short visit, to see his 94-year-old dying father. And on that occasion, King Ferdinand gave him another gold medal and made him an Honorary Member of the Romanian Academy. Every time, as soon as he arrived, he was whisked away by some important literary or political personality. At every visit, Nina only managed to see him from a distance. Even when he came to see his father, he paid no attention to her: he placed a fleeting kiss on her forehead, while continuing his conversation with his brother Max. This is the first and only time that he has addressed a telegram to her and only to her. Is this to be a personal family visit? Is it a response to her sending him a package of Romanian stamps that she had learned he wanted? Yes, of course, this is the only reason, her sister Stella said.

But now Nina is all nervous about his visit. She has so many questions in her mind: What kind of food does he eat? Is he kosher? Does he eat regular food? Nobody in her family in Bucharest eats kosher food now. But how about her grandparents' house, before the war? Nobody remembers. And how about Uncle Ariel today, as the great leader of the Jewish Community in England: has this elevated title made him revert to kosher food?

Since she hasn't been able to find the proper answer, Nina decides to prepare two kinds of food: a kosher meal of chicken soup with matzo balls, followed by gefilte fish with boiled potatoes, beets and horseradish, and a dessert of kiegel and baked apples with honey and cinnamon. All this will be served in the dining room, in the Passover dishes and glasses. And out on the terrace, there will be a buffet of non-kosher cold cuts with caviar and other gourmet treats which Adrian is bringing from Leonida's. The non-kosher food is going to be served outside, in the open air, so nobody should feel guilty of having sinned at the table!

Nina catches her reflection in the terrace door, and brushes a silver-gray lock of hair out of her face. Even though she is only 35, a strand of hair has turned gray after the birth of her second child. It had been a long and difficult labor, with wrenching pains, and times when she almost lost consciousness—a delivery which arrived three weeks earlier than expected, surprising her in the middle of spring cleaning. A short time after the child was born, she had noticed that a strand of her hair had turned gray and she now suffers from migraine attacks.

But this is not the time to brood about her gray hair! She tightens the belt of her house dress and adjusts her wire-rimmed spectacles. She is grateful to Adrian who, on their honeymoon, bought her a gold-rimmed pair of glasses as soon as she told him that she was nearsighted. For her parents and her sister wouldn't allow her to wear glasses before she got married, saying it made her look unfeminine.

Nina stares at her narrow hands with long, delicate fingers and wonders what ring she should wear tonight. Maybe the one with the red ruby stone which she has inherited from her grandmother and was said to be a present given to her grandmother by her children, Uncle Ariel and his brothers and sisters, at her 40th birthday! Nina wonders whether the Uncle would recognize the ring after so many years!

It is time to prepare for the evening. She takes a few steps toward the door but stops by the breakfront, looking at her grandparents' family picture, with portraits of her mother, her uncles and aunts when they were young.

The picture must have been taken in the early 1880's, with Uncle Ariel sitting between his two parents. He is the oldest of their eight children and here he looks handsome and dark, with thick, wavy hair, a carefully trimmed beard and a fashionable pince-nez. He is smiling at the photographer.

His younger sister, Ruth, a skinny teenager, stands next to her father. Ruth is Nina's mother. She has told Nina that the Uncle had a brilliant start in his career as a linguist, critic and writer, and a passionate collector of Romanian folklore. At the same time, he obtained a rabbinical degree from a famous seminary in Breslau.

Nina remembers how proud her mother and uncles were when they spoke about Uncle Ariel's successes, such as obtaining a chair at the University in Bucharest and being invited to join the most prestigious literary society of Romania which counted among its members the prime minister, a few other ministers and the King himself. These were exceptional accomplishments for a Jew in those years.

Nina is both flattered and intimidate by the Uncle's visit, and she wonders how Adrian will react to him. They have never met, and she cannot tell whether they will get along. The Uncle has a reputation of being arrogant at times and quick tempered at others. There was a mysterious turn of events in his life. In 1886, long before Nina was born, Uncle Ariel was suddenly expelled from the country and forced to leave within 24 hours. Nobody knows exactly why he was banished this way.

But the expulsion promoted much speculation. Some people said that Uncle Ariel was officially accused of agitation on behalf of the persecuted Jews, while others claimed he was thrown out of the country for challenging the prime minister on a philological matter, making him lose face in front of the King. Be that as it may, the banishment did not break his spirit. He settled in England and lectured at Oxford. Later he befriended Theodor Herzl, travelled to Palestine, and organized an early settlement of Romanian Jews in the Holy Land.

Nina remembers that Adrian was shocked when he learned that the Uncle never saw his own mother and his sister Ruth (Nina's mother) again. His relations with the Romanian authorities remained poor for many years and his banishment continued until the end of the war.

Nina remembers the war—Bucharest occupied by the enemy German troops... her family's escape from the burning city in an armored train... Nina, her mother and her younger sister Stella traveling East toward the Russian border into territory as yet unoccupied by the Germans. It is said that their train was carrying the Romanian National Treasure, several cars filled with gold, diamonds, artwork and precious stones. They were at risk of being attacked at any minute.

But they reached their destination safely and spent the rest of the war in a small border town, afraid of the revolutionary Russian gangs.

At the end of the war, her father and two brothers were expected to return from the Front. Any day... in a week... but just then her mother came down with the Spanish flu. They tried whatever they could to save her, but nothing helped. She died a few hours before her doctor husband and two sons arrived home from the Front.

Everybody was heartbroken. But it was too much for Nina. She ran into the kitchen and took a carving knife to her throat. How could she go on living without her sweet, loving, and always cheerful mother?

Fortunately, her father and brothers rushed her to the nearest hospital and her brother, Liviu, himself a physician, sewed the deep slashes on her throat.

Nina raises her left hand to the scar and touches it gently. Yes, that's how it was. Did Uncle Ariel know anything about this? Did he know what they went through during the war? Did anybody write to him? He was so far away!

Her eyes are tearful and she dries them with a handkerchief, just as Adrian walks in from the terrace. He stops in front of her, his hat in his hand, making a deep bow.

"À votre service, Madame. Comme toujours, à votre service. Your wishes are orders for me." He makes a sweeping gesture with his hat which he then presses against his heart, while he offers her the bouquet of lilies and peonies. Nina takes the flowers and tries to smile.

Adrian gives her a worried look. "Not feeling well? Or did someone upset you? Tell me what's wrong? I don't like to see you this way!"

Nina shrugs. "Nothing. A bout of headaches. I'll take a Nanu Muscel. I didn't sleep very well. You know these gatherings are always a bit hard on me!"

She doesn't want to tell Adrian what she is thinking of. He wouldn't understand. He always says: Let the past be the past. Look at the present. Think of the future!" Besides, it is a sad story and it would make her feel worse if she talked about it. Other unhappy events would come to mind, and this is not the time to brood over sad memories.

"I'll get a vase for the flowers, then I'll take my pills." Nina walks toward the bookcase where a vase and a few knickknacks are displayed among the books.

"Well, if that's what you want..." Adrian keeps watching her. He is not convinced by her words.

"Don't worry about me. I'll be all right. The flowers are beautiful. They'll make the table look so elegant!" Nina puts the bouquet on the table and takes the tall crystal vase from the shelf. She blows on it to make sure that there is no trace of dust and arranges the flowers in the vase.

THE UNCLE

I T IS AFTER SEVEN WHEN the guests start ringing the doorbell. The first to arrive is Aunt Josephine, Uncle Ariel's youngest sister, with her husband Leon, their son Joel and his wife Mathilda.

"Is Uncle here? Did he arrive?" they ask, all at once.

"He's on his way. Emil and Dora are bringing him in!" Nina kisses her aunt on both cheeks.

Aunt Josephine has the same rich, wavy hair, the same broad forehead, lively eyes and white, transparent skin as Uncle Ariel used to have. But she is hard of hearing and has to be spoken to loudly, through an ivory horn which she wears suspended from her neck with a silver chain. Sometimes she speaks loudly and sometimes softly, like most people who are hard of hearing and cannot adjust their voice.

"Good to see you on happy occasions!" says Uncle Leon, shaking Adrian's hand. He is a short, fat man of about 65, with red cheeks flushed with perspiration. Uncle Leon is an oriental rug dealer, and his handwoven carpets come from Persia, Bokhara, Isfahan, and sometimes from India and Afghanistan. Many are old and have belonged to the richest princes of the world. Now he sells these carpets to wealthy Romanian princes, and even to the King himself, a great collector of oriental rugs.

Next to Uncle Leon stands the young couple, Joel and Mathilda, holding hands and smiling at each other. They look more like romantic lovers than a married couple and have been nicknamed Romeo and Juliet.

Joel's unruly dark curls frame his face like a halo and fall over his forehead, while his clothes look slightly rumpled and too large for him. With her free hand, Mathilda tries to smooth out his open collar. Even though she is in her twenties, there is something girlish about her. She laughs and blushes easily, and covers her mouth with her hand when she does so.

"How is medicine?" asks Adrian.

"Fine!," Joel smiles and pushes his curls out of his eyes. "Sorel promised me his old X-ray machine. I can't wait to get it!"

Adrian remembers that Joel has recently finished medical school and is in the process of establishing a pediatrics practice at home in his living room. The large foyer can serve as a waiting room. Adrian also remembers that Joel would have liked to do pediatric surgery, but, as a Jew, he cannot work in a hospital.

"Is he here?" The question is asked again, this time by Stella, Nina's sister and her husband, Sorel, who have just arrived.

Sorel, Nina's brother-in-law, also a pediatrician, has deep set blue eyes which are always smiling. His head is perfectly round and totally bald. His features are fine and smooth as if chiselled in marble. He has rolled up his shirtsleeves and has opened his collar. During the summer he never wears a tie or a jacket.

Stella, his wife and Nina's sister, follows him, her face half hidden behind a large black fan of feathers and lace from Barcelona. She is batting her large brown eyes with their long lashes. A tortoise shell comb gathers her hair in a bun, while her large bosom makes her look voluptuous, not only exotic.

"Is he here?"

"He's on his way. Emil and Dora are bringing him over." Adrian compliments Stella on her new fan and her French perfume, but is interrupted by a loud curse which explodes behind his back.

"Du-te la dracu! Du-te la dracu! Go to Hell! Go to hell!" screams a high pitched voice. Adrian turns around and sees a large green and red parrot in a cage, flanked by Liviu, Nina's brother, and his wife Bea.

Liviu's gold-mounted pince-nez glitters in the half-light, partly hiding his protruding eyes. His big, handle-bar moustache covers his mouth and his cheeks. Like usual, the stethoscope is draped around his neck. Nobody should ever forget that he is a doctor. Now he steadies the metal cage with both hands.

"My patient is too sick to take care of his parrot. He had to go to the hospital. So I did what had to be done: I took the bird, and here it is!" Liviu lifts the cage for all to see. His wife Bea, who is taller than him, helps him lift it up. Her grey eyes are highlighted by her lavender dress. She wears a long string of pearls and matching pearl earrings.

"I hope you accept this uninvited guest at your party!" she asks Nina and Adrian.

"Du-te la dracu!" curses the parrot. Then it starts to whistle the aria of the Torreador from Carmen and everybody whistles along.

It is then that Uncle Ariel arrives, accompanied by his daughter Clara who travels with him, and by Nina's oldest brother, Emil and his wife, Dora. They had picked him up from the Gara de Nord train station at 1 p.m., arrival time of the Orient Express from Vienna, and took him first to their apartment.

Uncle Ariel is tall and walks very erect. His well trimmed beard and his hair have turned gray, almost white, but it is still wavy and thick. His face too is still handsome and smooth, his dark eyes still full of sparks. He is wearing an old fashioned stiff collar and a black "lavalière" like in Nina's old family picture. Only his pince-nez has been replaced with gold-rimmed spectacles with thick lenses. In his hand he carries an ebony cane with a silver handle. He is flanked by Emil and Dora.

Watching them, Adrian is always struck by the resemblance of the two brothers. They have the same protruding eyes, regular features and pale, transparent skin. But Emil's moustache is small and smoothed with pomade and he always wears a monocle. His summer suit is perfectly tailored and a starched handkerchief decorates his breast pocket. His patent leather shoes are shiny and polished like a mirror. His wife Dora who is holding onto Uncle's arm, has straight black hair and dark, almond-shaped eyes, which make her look oriental. If she wore a kimono, she would be taken for a Japanese woman.

"Hooray! Here they are! Welcome home! Welcome to your old family!" Everybody screams, as they all run to the entrance to hug Uncle. Sorel and Adrian have to stop the others from knocking him over in their enthusiasm.

"Welcome! Welcome home!" they keep shouting and clapping their hands. Joel and Nina help Aunt Josephine get close to her brother. As she stands on the tip of her toes and kisses him on the cheek, tears run down her face and she reaches for a handkerchief. "I thought I will never see you again!" she whispers.

"I would never let this happen!" says Uncle Ariel, stroking her hair.

"Everybody please come to the table!" Nina says after a while. "Let's sit on the terrace!" she adds, as she takes Uncle's arm and leads him out on the terrace, while the others follow.

"Take a seat! You must be tired... the long trip from Vienna, and then the walk here... You didn't get any sleep and you must be exhausted!" Nina is pushing a chair toward him.

"No, no," says Uncle Ariel. You are mistaken. I always sleep on the Orient Express. I sleep even better than in my own bed at home! I always loved trains. As a kid I even wanted to become a stationmaster and signal the trains in and out of the station with the red and green semaphore. Sometimes I still dream about it and think that it would be fun!"

"Well, you slept on the train... But then you walked..."

"So what's wrong with that?" It is healthy to walk. Even though I am 80 years old, I walk every day, summer or winter, for an hour on the banks of the Thames. And then here, I was eager to breathe again the familiar air of Bucharest. I missed it. I missed its dusty smell and I wanted Clara to feel it too!"

Clara, Uncle Ariel's youngest daughter nods and smiles. "Yes," she says. "Tata told me so much about Bucharest, that I had to come and see it myself!"

She speaks Romanian with a strong English accent which delights everybody. She too has the same broad forehead and pale skin as her father and Aunt Josephine, but her hair is reddish-brown, her eyes are green and her face is full of freckles. She is in her twenties, but since she wears no makeup she looks like a teenager.

"Don't move! Stay still everybody! I want to take a picture before the sun goes down!" Adrian whips out his camera and takes pictures of all of them together. He is a skilled photographer, focusing quickly and snapping the shots without wasting any time.

When he has finished, they all sit down at the round table on the terrace, under the blooming wisteria. A cool breeze reaches them from the garden, and they can hear the twitter of young birds in a nearby nest.

Marish, the Hungarian maid from Transylvania, brings up a crystal bowl with black caviar and passes it around. It is followed by a tray of smoked whitefish with black olives and slices of lemon.

"Are you eating this food? It isn't kosher!" Nina asks Uncle Ariel while Adrian is pouring old tzuică into small crystal tumblers.

"Oh! yes, I know. But even I can sin once in a blue moon! I will do *kapuras* and ask for forgiveness at Yom Kippur." This is worth it! A real treat! I haven't eaten these things in a very long time. And the English fare! I can tell you their cucumber sandwiches are no French cuisine! And English kosher food is an abomination I wouldn't wish on my worst enemy."

Everybody laughs, and after they finish with the whitefish, other trays with gourmet appetizers and treats appear on the table.

Now Joel keeps refilling the tumblers with tzuică, and, after replenishing Uncle's glass, he asks him what brings him to Bucharest this time and how long he is planning to stay?

Uncle Ariel looks at him thoughtfully and strokes his beard. "I've been invited to a Philological Conference in Warsaw and I've decided to stop here and see all of you. I'm not coming this way very often, as you well know. And besides, Nina has sent me a gorgeous selection of stamps for my collection," he adds. "Tomorrow I want to see the Geller Temple, the family temple and the Moria school, if they still stand?" he asks, raising his eyebrows.

"Yes, they stand," Joel answers.

"And I will meet with Professor Popovici to coordinate our presentation on Romanian folklore. I see him more often than any of you, since he attends all International conferences. I also wanted Clara to meet the family and see the place of my birth." He turns toward her, waiting for an answer, but she has gotten up and has walked to the other side of the table. Nina too is standing by the door. Her two daughters, Suzy and Nadia, are coming to meet Uncle Ariel. They are accompanied by Silvia, their governess. For a moment, Nina is resting her hands on the girls' shoulders, then she pushes them gently toward Uncle Ariel.

The two children, Suzy 13 and Nadia 8, advance slowly, intimidated by Uncle Ariel and by so many guests. Their faces are red. Suzy is biting her lower lip while Nadia is pulling at her skirt. They are both wearing white sailor dresses, with striped collars and ties. But here the similarities end: Suzy is tall, with long legs and arms, straight brown hair, green eyes, and the white, transparent skin of the Gellers. By contrast, Nadia is short for her age, with wavy dark hair tied in a bow, brown eyes, buck teeth, and Adrian's bronzed skin.

The girls have eaten dinner separately, in the children's room, with the governess, for Nina, who is following the fashion of the day, doesn't allow the children to eat at the parents' table when there are guests.

Now they stand in front of Uncle Ariel and say: "Hello! How do you do?" and "Welcome home!" in English. After he kisses them on the forehead and pats each of them on the shoulder, they walk around the table and greet everybody. When they finish, they stop near Silvia, their governess. After Nina signals everybody to be quiet, they start singing "My Bonnie lies over the Ocean," accompanied by Silvia on her guitar.

"My Bonnie lies over the ocean,
My Bonnie lies over the sea
My Bonnie lies over the ocean
Oh! bring back my Bonnie to me!

Bring back, bring back
Oh! bring back my Bonnie to me, to me
Bring back, bring back
Oh! bring back my Bonnie to me.

They sing while Adrian is watching them. Why does Nina make the children perform in front of guests? They're neither clowns nor circus animals, he has told her. Let them be themselves and have a good time. This will only make them hate parties and company!

But Nina couldn't be convinced. She said that this provides good motivation for the girls to learn English and is also a perfect opportunity to show the girls off in front of the family. Adrian thinks that this "showing off in front of the family" is Nina's main reason to make the girls sing. For rivalry is fierce between his wife and her three siblings, and they always manage to involve their children in this competition.

Adrian turns to the girls' governess, Silvia, who is playing the guitar, touching the strings lightly with her long fingers and who sings with an American accent. Silvia was born in Iowa, where her father, a German farmer from Transylvania, had emigrated after the Great War. But when the Depression came and he lost his livelihood, he packed up his family and his belongings and came back to Transylvania. That is why Silvia has an American accent.

Silvia is tall and slender with blue eyes and blond braids which she wears wrapped around her head. But today, as he is watching her, Adrian is struck by her sickly appearance:

her face is pale and drawn, with lines around her mouth. Her forehead is damp with perspiration and her glazed eyes stare fixedly in front of her. Her hands shake when she is not touching the strings. Adrian has never seen her like this and he wonders whether she has the flu or an indigestion. Hopefully it is nothing serious.

When they finish with the first song, the children sing Frère Jacques and everybody chimes in, clapping their hands and laughing. After the French version they sing the Romanian, and then the German and English versions of the song. They are clapping and singing and making so much noise, that the parrot becomes agitated and starts to scream and curse at the top of his voice. Liviu has to get up, take him away with his cage and lock him in the pantry, far from the commotion. When he returns to the terrace everybody has calmed down, and Uncle Ariel surprises them with a Gypsy version of the song. He has a deep, melodious voice and it is easy to imagine him preaching in the synagogue as a Rabbi, or singing like a cantor, which he sometimes does.

He finishes singing and the guests cheer and applaud again, while the girls and the governess say good night and depart.

"Dinner is ready! Please come in everybody!" Nina stands at the door of the dining room. "Please come in! Uncle Ariel with Clara and Aunt Josephine with your family, come in first!"

Clara follows her father into the dining room. He makes a few steps to the left and stops in front of a richly carved sideboard. "Our old sideboard from home! Look, here is the mark I carved out of the wood to test my new pocketknife!" Uncle Ariel points to a corner of the chest where the eye of a wooden dragon has been scooped out with a knife.

"And here are mother's old candlesticks," he adds, touching the silver candlesticks which stand on top of the sideboard. "Mother always lit the candles on Friday nights and on the holidays! She knew all the songs and the prayers by heart. It wasn't easy to keep up with her, even after I became a Rabbi myself." Uncle Ariel raises his hands over the candles like in a blessing, and looks up toward the ceiling. "And here is the oil painting which hung in the foyer!" he says, looking at a large painting hanging over the sideboard, which shows a few shabby peasant huts and a primitive fountain in the middle of an empty field. "Look, Josephine, see this mark on the frame? You were about 6 when you threw a ball at the picture, and you got a good spanking for that. You cried the whole day, remember?" He points at a black stain on the gilded frame. "I hated that painting. It was so depressing. You must have hated it too, Josephine, otherwise you wouldn't have thrown the ball at the picture!" says Uncle Ariel.

"Maybe... You're right... You're always right!" Aunt Josephine nods and smiles. It isn't clear whether she's actually heard her brother's words.

They finally sit down for dinner. Uncle Ariel at the head of the table, flanked by Aunt Josephine, Clara and Uncle Leon to the right, and by Joel and Mathilda to the left. The table is covered with a starched damask tablecloth and in the middle stands the bouquet of lilies and peonies from the garden.

As soon as they have finished the borsht with sour cream, Marish fills their plates with gefilte fish with horseradish and boiled potatoes. Adrian pours old wine of Cotnari in their glasses and Uncle Ariel gets up to make a toast for Nina:

"Your food, this meal of tonight is really food for the soul. It refreshes my heart because it tastes just like the food I ate in my mother's house. It always had a special taste, just like this. But, after I left, it was never the same any more..."

"By the way Uncle, tell us how it was when you left," says Joel, when Uncle Ariel has finished speaking. He bends over the table, trying to get closer to him.

"Yes, yes, tell us how it was when you left," everybody now wants to know.

"Oh!" says the Uncle with a sigh. "October 22, 1885. I'll never forget that day!" He falls silent for a minute, collecting his thoughts. "It was a beautiful autumn day, with bright sunshine and a blue sky... My whole family and all my friends came to the train station to see me off. I was wearing the gold medal, the Order of Merit First Class the King had given me... There were eleven of us expelled on that day, all writers, teachers, intellectuals. Outside, people were screaming and yelling... The police had to come and keep order. For all the streets leading to the train station were filled with crowds. On one side stood my friends, my colleagues and my students, all those who mourned my departure and, on the other side, stood those who hated us and were happy to see us leave. They were carrying banners with the words: "Hooray! Hooray! Dr. Geller is finally leaving with his friends!"

"But your family, your parents, they must have been upset with this forced exile?" asks Joel.

"Yes, but they never showed it. My mother didn't allow it! On the day before my departure she took me into the living room, sat me down on the green couch, and told me this story.

Once upon a time there was a couple. The man tried many trades, but was never successful, and gave up in despair. One night he heard his wife crying.

'What is the matter?' he asked.

'I had such a frightening dream, I don't even want to tell you.'

31

But he pleaded until she finally told him that she was in heaven and there she saw some angels mourning and crying. When she asked what was the matter, they said: 'Don't you know? God is dead!'

When she heard these words, said the wife, she got such a fright that she woke up crying.

'How can you believe such a thing? God never dies,' said the husband.

'Oh!' answered the wife. 'If God never dies, why do you despair? God is everywhere! You need not despair. Wherever you go, God will protect you.'

"What an extraordinary woman!" says Mathilda.

"Yes," nods Uncle Ariel, as he takes off his spectacles and wipes them with his handkerchief. "This was my mother, your grandmother, the daughter of the Rabbi from Berditchev in the Ukraine. She was a descendent of the famous chassid, Rabbi Levy Yitzhak of Berditchev who lived in the late 1700's, an exalted, fearless and inspiring man, who fought with God, insulted Him and made angry demands.

"My mother, your grandmother, was strong and just as fearless as the Rabbi—and willful. She only listened to her own ideas. Once she almost got us in terrible trouble because she agreed to hide, in our house, a young Jewish woman, a Nihilist refugee from Russia, who was hounded by the Police after Tsar Alexander II was killed by a bomb in 1881. The bomb was set up by six Nihilists, one of them a Jewish woman. These revolutionaries crossed the borders illegally into Romania, where they were also chased and arrested by the local gendarmes. I remember my mother hiding the young woman in the attic, and even though there were threats from the Police and even though our street was swarming with informers, she didn't give up. She kept the woman in the attic, until she got help from other Russian refugees. One night she was able to leave and escape, hidden in a carriage, and dressed like a man. The woman and her companions took the train to Giurgiu, near Bulgaria, and on a moonless night she crossed the Danube into that country."

"A frightening story!" says Bea. "I wouldn't have the courage to get involved. Didn't the police also arrest the Romanian accomplices of these Nihilists?"

"Yes, you're quite right," says Uncle. "As a matter of fact a number of people were arrested and accused of complicity, particularly if they were Jewish. But my mother was not..." The rest of his words are lost in a sudden commotion.

"Come on, everybody! We'll have dessert and coffee in the living room! The chairs are more comfortable, and it's much cooler there!" says Nina.

They file one by one into the large, high-ceilinged living room, where platters of camembert and other French cheeses and baskets of cherries and apricots are waiting for them.

The room is cool and breezy with a large window reaching from floor to ceiling open toward the garden. There is soft, indirect lighting which makes it feel cozy and intimate. Marish, the maid, brings cups of Turkish coffee, while Adrian pours French cognac in their glasses.

They pull the deep armchairs in a circle around Uncle Ariel.

"Go back to your story, Uncle!" says Joel, bending toward him.

"I don't understand: you had a gold medal, the highest decoration, given to you by the King. How could they expel you? What right did they have?"

Uncle Ariel looks at him stroking his beard. Then he adjusts his glasses and says: "I know it's hard to understand, but the Prime Minister and his friends accused me of being an agitator against the government, a troublemaker who

33

was spreading denigrating information about the country abroad..."

"Was it true? Did you do that?" asks Stella, looking up from behind her fan.

The Uncle stares at the big, black feathers and keeps silent for a minute. "Maybe I did," he finally says. "From their point of view, you see, I did fight for the rights of the Jews and against anti-Semitism. I had become a militant Zionist when they threw me out."

"But why? What was going on?" Joel is sitting on the edge of his chair. "After all, you were so involved and so successful in matters of Romanian language and folklore. When did you get mixed up in Jewish problems?"

"You're wrong: I was always concerned with Jewish problems! That was the tradition of the family. Remember that my father's father had built the Geller Temple and a school for Jewish children. And when I came home from Breslau, after finishing my rabbinical studies, I saw that all of us Jews of Romania were in trouble: we had no citizenship, so we had no rights! Even though we were born in this country for many generations, we were *not* Romanian citizens. We were considered 'foreigners,' and were not protected by any government. This meant that we couldn't go to a public school or university. We couldn't own land and we couldn't work in any public institution. Also, at any time, any of us could be ordered out of the city or even out of the country in less than 24 hours. The mayor, the police chief or any public authority could give such an order. And when this happened, everything was lost. The people had to leave behind all their belongings, their houses and their furniture. They suddenly became beggars with no place to go!"

The uncle's hand trembles as he speaks, and he wipes his forehead with a handkerchief.

A really tragic situation! thinks Adrian. "And was there no hope for change?" he asks.

"Yes, there was. Under the pressure of the Western countries, we were supposed to receive citizenship around 1880's. But there was so much corruption and so much anti-Semitism that only a few very wealthy Jews succeeded in getting their citizenship. Most of us, including my family and myself remained 'unprotected foreigners' like before."

The Uncle stops and strokes his beard, while Dora, Bea and Uncle Leon who are sitting further away, pull their chairs closer to him. And nobody stirs when Marish brings in a large tray with plates of strawberry parfait and a carafe of ice water. Trying to make as little noise as possible, Nina gets up and helps Marish distribute the plates of ice cream to everyone and to fill their glasses with water.

Uncle Ariel eats a strawberry and goes on: "But that wasn't all. At about the same time, there was a sudden wave of official anti-Semitism, supported by the government itself."

"So what could be new?" asks Sorel who has grabbed Stella's fan and is sweeping the air with it. "It seems to me that the government has always been anti-Semitic!"

"Shhh!" says Stella. "You and your anti-government obsession! Shut up and listen. Maybe you learn something new!"

Adrian watches Sorel with some apprehension. He knows that his brother-in-law is both opinionated and short tempered. But Uncle Ariel is not disturbed.

"Well, there was something new," he says. "It was the time of the big pogroms in Russia, and many Jews escaped to Romania, and the Government didn't like it. There were big riots here, and those who started them were not punished, not even brought to trial.

"In one case the attacker was actually promoted to the position of mayor of Bucharest! In our city, too, gangs of students stormed the Great Choral Temple, breaking the sacred ark with the Torahs inside. They also ransacked the entire Jewish neighborhood, looting and setting fire to houses and stores. But after they tried to set fire to the Geller synagogue and broke our windows, we organized a fraternity of young Jews who were so tough that they broke the bones of our assailants. The police had to come to their rescue!"

Adrian shakes his head and smiles, imagining the gangs of students beaten to a pulp by a group of angry Jews!

Then the Uncle tells them how, about the same time, bands of hooligans started attacking Jewish funeral processions on the way to the cemetery. "I was walking in Aunt Rebecca's funeral cortege on Calea Griviței when the goons came out of the pub armed with sticks and rocks, and attacked us, yelling, "One today, tomorrow a hundred!" After several such incidents we decided that every procession should be protected by a few strong Jewish men armed with iron bars. This plan was successful. After several bloody encounters, the attacks ended."

"And," asks Adrian, was that all?"

"No," says Uncle Ariel, "it wasn't all."

"During all this time, I also wrote and published articles and letters of protest about these violent attacks. After a while, I noticed that I was followed and watched very closely. Every word I said was recorded. I felt hounded like a felon obsessed by his crime." Uncle Ariel's face turns somber and tense. He looks in all directions like a man in imminent danger.

Adrian keeps staring at him. What courage! What iron determination! These are the people who make history, who make things happen. He understands Nina's veneration for this uncle and he is proud to have him as a guest. But at the same time he feels that, in his youth, he must have been reckless, even provocative.

Adrian's thoughts are interrupted by Nina and Marish who come to collect the empty plates of parfait. Uncle Ariel has barely touched his own, and it has melted down to a pink, sticky liquid. Nina lifts his plate carefully so as not to spill the pink sauce on his pants.

As some guests get up to stretch their legs and to help themselves to fruit and cheese, Sorel and Joel pull their chairs closer to Uncle Ariel.

"You were followed and watched, all right, but I heard that in spite of this, you organized the first group of Jews to emigrate from Romania to Palestine. Am I right?" asks Sorel.

"And you also had a hand in setting up the first colony of Romanian Jews in Palestine!" adds Joel. They both stare at the uncle with much admiration.

"Yes, it is true!" says Uncle Ariel. "But I became a Zionist only after I saw that things went from bad to worse. After 1879, when we couldn't become citizens, there were many bad laws against us. People who had lost their livelihoods because they were Jews couldn't even be street peddlers. They were arrested and expelled from the cities. But they were not allowed to use horses, or travel by wagon or train. They were forced to walk, escorted by police, even if they were old and sick. And only after I saw friends and neighbors breaking down on the road, without any hope, I decided to do anything I could to help them go to Palestine."

"It must have been quite difficult to set up such a program?" says Adrian.

"It wasn't easy," says the Uncle with a sigh." And to tell you the truth, we were often accused of leading these poor souls to starvation and catastrophe!"

"How discouraging! Nothing seems so bad as making efforts and sacrifices which are not recognized," Adrian concludes.

But he cannot hear Uncle's reply because he must rush to the other end of the room, where there is unusual agitation: people are laughing, chairs are pushed around.

Remembering that the parrot hasn't received any food, Liviu has brought the cage into the room and has put it on a table. Then he opened the door of the cage and lured the bird outside with a slice of apricot. The parrot hopped out, took the fruit in its beak, and flew to the next table, where he ate it. When it came back for more, it glimpsed Clara's small diamond ring which she had taken off to show to Bea, holding it loosely on the tip of her finger. It is a small ring with a bright stone which she had received from her father on her 18th birthday.

As quick as lightning, the parrot picked up the ring in his beak and flew with it up to the curtain rod near the ceiling. Now he is sitting there, perched on the metal rod, ruffling its feathers and staring at the people below. What will he do next? Will he fly out the window? Will he swallow the ring? Will he drop it in a hidden corner—behind a couch or the bookcase? Everyone is holding his breath.

Adrian quickly closes the window, and tries to think of a strategy. He .knows that, if they come chasing after the parrot and scare him, he will either swallow the ring or drop it in a hidden place. Finally, he has a plan: "We must leave a plate of cherries and apricots on the table and pay no mind to the bird. We must ignore him. Pretend that he doesn't exist. Sooner or later he will get hungry again and feel tempted by the fruit. Then he will return to the table, hopefully bringing the ring in his beak."

Everybody is happy with this plan. For a while they are quiet and speak in a low voice, even though they feel tense. And, just as Adrian has predicted, a few minutes later the parrot is back on the fruit dish. It drops the ring on the table and snatches a cherry. Instantly Liviu throws a big napkin over him, crying "I got you! I got you!" Then, holding the bird with both hands, he slips it inside the cage. And, when the door is locked, the stunned parrot explodes in a torrent of curses: *"Du-te la dracu! Du-te la dracu!"* which forces Liviu to take the cage back to the pantry and soothe the bird with more cherries and apricots.

Meanwhile Clara is stupefied. She is pale and can barely move. Slowly, as she recovers, she slips the ring back on her finger, and turns to Adrian, asking him not to say anything to her father. "I don't know what he would do if I lost the ring. He might never speak to me again!" Her eyes are larger and greener than ever.

"I won't say a word!" Adrian promises. Then he rushes to the other end of the room, where a heated discussion is going on. It involves the Uncle's forced banishment.

"About this expulsion, didn't you also have some personal troubles with the prime minister?" says Emil.

Uncle Ariel raises his eyebrows. He takes off his glasses and polishes them with his handkerchief. "You know more than I wanted to tell! The prime minister, who was also a linguist, strongly disagreed with me about the origins of the Romanian language. He tried to convince everybody that the Romanians are descendants of the Romans who colonized the country in ancient times and occupied Transylvania. This, in his political mind, justified the annexation of Transylvania to Romania. But I gave a talk that summer, and I showed that the names of many cities are not Latin at all. This made his theory weaker and weaker.

"The King was there, as well as many important people. They all agreed with me and the King thanked me for my speech. The prime minister turned pale when he heard that. And three months later he expelled me with eleven other Jewish intellectuals."

Uncle Ariel stops and takes a sip of cognac. Then he goes on. "But I met him ten years later in Paris at an International Philological Conference over which I was presiding. He came to greet me and said that I should thank him for my fame and success. Because, if it weren't for him, I would still be sitting in Bucharest, and I would have never become the famous scientist I am today! I looked at him and I replied that I was not going to thank him because this was not what he had in mind when he threw me out of the country." Uncle Ariel pounds the floor with his cane and smiles triumphantly.

"We should all go to Palestine!" cries Sorel. His face is flushed and his eyes are shining.

"And be killed by the Arabs or die of malaria!" says Stella, pointing an accusatory finger at him.

"Why leave? Why go to Palestine?" asks Emil. "We are all citizens now, we have equal rights since the Great War!"

"Equal rights my foot!" grumbles Sorel. "It's only on paper. You're the only Jew I know with an executive position at a State Agency. And it's all because of that strategic bridge you built over the Danube. But I still can't work in a city hospital and neither can Liviu or Joel." His eyes are flashing with anger.

"Things will get better. Be patient. The Western powers—France, England and America--have invested in our oil fields in Ploeşti. They won't let us down. They care about our rights!" Emil makes big gestures with his hands, trying to convince Sorel.

"So how long should I wait? When will they show me that they care?" Sorel shouts at the top of his voice, getting up and advancing toward Emil.

"Enough, enough already!" cries Stella, covering her ears with her hands, while Nina is watching them anxiously. Adrian tries to step between Emil and Sorel, only to be pushed aside.

"Do something! Don't let them kill each other in front of Uncle Ariel," Nina whispers to him. "Turn on the radio... Give them some music... I don't want Uncle to see them like this!"

Adrian walks quickly to one corner of the room and winds up the Victrola, while Marish and Nina roll up the carpet, exposing the shiny parquet. In the next minute, the saxophones of the orchestra invade the living room.

> You leave Pennsylvania Station at a quarter of four
> Read the morning paper and you're in Baltimore...
> The Chattanooga Choo-Choo..."

roars the voice from the record player.

Adrian walks over to Clara, bows deeply in front of her and takes her hand, inviting her to dance. She gets up, her eyes smiling in her blushing face. At some distance, Sorel and Emil keep arguing, but their words are soon drowned out by the beat of the drums and the sound of the trombones.

> Nothing can be finer
> Then to have your ham and eggs in Carolina...
> The Chattanooga Choo-choo..."

Liviu turns to his wife Bea, takes her arm, and they both follow Adrian and Clara to the improvised dance floor. Soon, all the young people turn and twirl in the living room. Some are dancing a classical foxtrot, while others experiment with a free-style of dancing.

After the "Chattanooga Choo Choo," Adrian plays the hit of the season, "Alexander's Ragtime Band," which is repeated several times . While the music is still playing, Liviu steps out of the room and comes back immediately wearing a black top hat and an old-fashioned ivory handled cane. He takes Bea by the hand, and together they start tap dancing, performing a flawless imitation of Fred Astair and Ginger Rogers. Liviu is light and graceful, his feet rhythmically touching the floor. Bea is matching his movements, pirouetting in and out of his arms, as if she were Ginger Rogers herself. Everybody stops dancing to make space for them and watch.

"To Hollywood! You must go to Hollywood where you belong!" All the couples are shouting when they have finished. Even Uncle Ariel is applauding and agrees that that's where they belong.

Liviu bows, takes off his hat, clicks his heels and kisses Bea's hand escorting her to her seat. But he still has boundless energy and now invites Clara to dance. "Let's do the rhumba!" he says, standing in front of her and taking her hand, while the gramophone is playing the fast dance.

"But I don't know the rhumba," she says, her cheeks on fire.

"It doesn't matter. I'll teach you the steps. When you go back to London, you'll tell your friends that you learned to dance the rhumba in Bucharest."

Everybody is dancing now—those who know the rhumba and those who pretend to know. Adrian and Nina, too, are turning quicker and quicker, while the saxophones sound louder than the trumpets of Jericho. Only Uncle Ariel, Aunt Josephine and Uncle Leon are left in their seats, watching the dancing couples.

"I bet this music is too loud for the old folks and the drums must drive them crazy! But I didn't want Uncle to see them fighting like cats and dogs!" Nina whispers to Adrian.

After the first rhumba they dance another one which is followed by a hot foxtrot with a loud beat. They sway and turn and laugh happily, and just when they are at the height of merriment, there is a shrill ring at the door. Who could it be? Everyone freezes.

Adrian walks to the door and opens it. In front of him stands Mrs. Segall, the neighbor from downstairs, blinking her eyes. She wears a pink robe and large paper curlers in her hair.

Adrian takes a step backwards when he sees her. "Why... what brings you here?" he stammers. But she pushes him aside and runs into the room. The paper curlers in her hair look like a flock of butterflies ready to take off.

"Shhhhh! Listen! Don't you hear anything?"

Nina has stopped the record player. In the silence, they can hear the high pitched scream of a child.

"Nadia!" yell Nina and Adrian at once, as they storm out of the room.

"This has been going on for fifteen minutes!" says Mrs. Segall, shaking her head.

Liviu and Sorel follow their hosts on the long corridor. As they approach the children's room, the shrieks grow louder and louder.

Adrian turns on the lights and sees Silvia, the governess, sprawled across Nadia's new bed. A blue silk scarf is tightly wound around her neck, and purple splotches have appeared on her face. Her breathing is shallow and rasping. One hand is pulling at the fringed end of the scarf, while the other is clasping a small black and white photograph. Adrian comes closer and sees that it is a photo of Joel with his bicycle. The picture has red stains of lipstick, which look like traces of kisses.

In her bed, Nadia has tried to get away from the governess. She is curled up near the wall, screaming in terror, her face buried in her small hands.

Nina quickly scoops her up in her arms, and together with Suzy, takes her into another room. At the same time, Adrian and Liviu try to unwrap the scarf which is wound around Silvia's neck. But as they touch her, she scratches and bites their hands and pushes them away,

"Hold her arms and her legs," says Liviu to Adrian and Sorel, while he unties the long scarf.

As soon as he is finished, her breathing becomes more regular and the purple patches vanish from her face. Liviu places a towel soaked in cold water on her temples. The wet compress makes her open her eyes, but at the same time, throws her into new convulsions and inarticulate shrieks.

"I have to give her a calming injection!" says Liviu, shaking his head.

He rummages in the leather briefcase which Bea has brought over after they ran out of the room. He pulls out a shiny metal box and a vial of Luminal. Inside the metal box is a sterile syringe and two needles.

"It's a miracle that I had no time to go home and change. I wouldn't have brought my medical kit with me, and a sterile syringe in the bargain. Hold her arm so I can give her the shot!" He breaks the vial with his hand and fills the syringe. Then he soaks a ball of cotton in alcohol which Nina has prepared and wipes a spot on Silvia's arm.

"Hold her down!" he says to Sorel and Adrian.

With her eyes closed, Silvia moans and tries to move out of his reach. But Sorel and Adrian are holding her tight and Liviu plunges the needle through her skin. Silvia gives a short cry, opens her eyes and stares at the men. Then she closes them again, takes a deep breath, and goes to sleep.

"We'll have to take her to the Mental Hospital!" says Liviu. "We can't leave her here with the children, nor can she be alone without supervision. It's too dangerous!" He pauses for a moment, watching Silvia.

"But we can't use my car. It's too small and it's an open convertible—not recommended for driving a crazy woman who tries to commit suicide. I had enough trouble driving through town with the parrot. He screamed and cursed all the way, and people laughed and ran after us as if we were the Klutsky circus!" Liviu shakes his head and runs his fingers through his thin strands of hair.

"We can use my car!" says Sorel. He is tucking his shirt in his pants and wiping his bald head with a blue handkerchief.

"It's all right! Besides, Stella and I know the doctor who works there tonight. Our children are friends. He'll be helpful to us."

For a moment, they stand near the bed, watching the sick woman. Her crisp uniform is all creased now and her blond braids are in disarray, with locks of hair escaping in all directions. Her face looks pale and drawn; her eyes are closed. Adrian sees her lips moving as if calling a name, over and over again. He bends toward her and hears that she is calling Joel's name. He picks up the small photograph and wipes the red stains with the palm of his hand. He remembers taking this picture at Joel's 18th birthday, when he had received from his parents a new bicycle and a fashionable English sport suit. In the photograph, Joel is smiling broadly, and looks very proud.

Adrian remembers that Joel often came to play with the children. On their birthdays he always had unusual surprises: he would bring Charlie Chaplin or Mickey Mouse movies, which he showed with his own small projector. The screen was a white wall or a bedsheet stretched over the armoire. Other times he improvised an elaborate puppet theatre with lively shows.

Silvia always helped him on these occasions. She knew how to pull the strings of the marionettes, how to animate the puppets which were moved by the fingers and how to speak in different voices, or bark, meow, crow or roar like an animal. In return for her help, Joel brought his harmonium and accompanied her when she played her guitar and sang songs with the children.

Had there been a romance between them?

Joel had often visited the family during their summer vacations in Sinaia, the fashionable mountain resort with the King's summer palace, where he taught the children how to ride their bicycles. For several years, Joel, Silvia and the two girls, Suzy and Nadia, seemed to have a great time together.

Had there been anything? Adrian winds his watch back and forth as he often does when he is perplexed by something. It is true that, after he met and married Mathilda, Joel barely spent any time with the children, and last summer he didn't come to Sinaia at all. Come to think of it, in the last few months, Silvia had become absentminded. She had lost her appetite and the glowing color in her cheeks. Her uniform now seems too large for her.

As he stands near the bed, Adrian picks up the blue scarf which had slipped to the floor. He and Nina had bought it in Paris for Silvia because it matched her blue eyes. She was happy and thankful for it, and wore it with her best outfits on special occasions. He had never expected what was happening now.

"Ready?"

Nina walks in with a small valise in which she has packed a few of Silvia's belongings—her green toothbrush, her soft slippers, pajamas, her comb, her hairbrush and a bar of soap.

"Yes, we can go."

Liviu and Sorel wrap the governess in the blanket and carry her out of the room. Liviu supports her head while Adrian and Sorel hold her feet. They walk through the corridor and through the pantry, where Marish and Ilona, the maid and the cook, make the sign of the cross as they pass. The parrot has been moved away to the terrace, so as not to scream with excitement. Behind the doors of the living room, the guests speak in soft, muffled tones.

The three men carrying Silvia slowly descend the marble stairs and stop near the waiting car. It is decided that Adrian, Sorel and Stella will drive her to the hospital, while Liviu and Bea will stay with Nina and the other guests. Later, they will drive Uncle Ariel home.

DR. VICTOR GEORGESCU

A S SOON AS THEY ARE seated in the car—Sorel and Stella in front and Silvia and Adrian in the back seats—Sorel starts the engine and they're off. Sorel has arranged Silvia in the car. As he lifted her, she was like a limp doll in his arms. He settled her in the back seat and told Adrian to watch her.

They head toward the outskirts of the city, since the hospital is a good distance away. It is a warm night with a full moon and thousands of cicadas are singing in the courtyards which border the streets.

They turn left and pass a church with a round dome. The church is surrounded by a large garden filled with roses and fragrant *regina nopţii* (the queen of the night), which blooms only at night. They turn left again and keep traveling south. The streets become narrow and narrower; the houses grow smaller and smaller and the cobblestones larger, making the road very bumpy. Several times they have to drive around enormous potholes filled with black water which reflects the moon and a few weak gas lamps which light the streets. The dark houses seem to sleep behind wooden fences bordered by sunflowers and trees.

Soon they reach a small garden restaurant with garlands of colored lanterns strung among the green vines. Two gypsy musicians are playing the fiddle and the "țambal" but the place is almost deserted. A young couple is sitting at a table in a tight embrace, and a waiter is leaning against the gate, smoking and watching the road.

Sorel presses the pedal to get away from the music, but the sounds follow them a long way. Adrian closes the windows to protect Silvia's sleep.

They drive at full speed and, as they turn a corner, the sky suddenly grows burning red and gold in the distance, and a vague clamor fills the air. They are nearing Tirgul Moșilor, the greatest fair of the city. Sorel tries to make a detour to avoid it, but there are no side streets in view. In front of them is a big fair, which resembles a Turkish bazaar.

Under an incandescent cloud of dust, which fills the horizon, they can distinguish the silhouettes of the peasant carts, horses, cattle and sheep which surround the fair. Next to them are huge stacks of barrels of wine and beer.

Adrian knows that inside the fair there are giant displays of everything: mountains of fruits and vegetables, heaps of shiny but cheap jewelry, slippers embroidered with gold and sequins, shimmering silks and brocades, polished brass pots, pans and samovars. They can smell the garlic from the grills of *mititei* (spicy Romanian sausages) and the sweet grease of the *gogoși* cooking in cauldrons filled with oil. But it is the loud music of the gypsy bands and the screams of the children riding the merry-go-round that they are trying to avoid. But even though the windows are closed, the noise is still deafening. It gets worse as they come nearer to the fair.

"*Fire-ar a dracului!* We have to get out of here, or she'll wake up!" says Sorel under his breath. To their surprise, a narrow street which they had taken for a courtyard opens to the right. They drive quickly away, but the noise follows them. Silvia starts moving and talking in her sleep.

What if she wakes up and tries to jump out? Adrian worries. He makes sure that all the doors are locked. How about this business of getting her into the hospital? He has heard all kinds of rumors about the Mental Hospital. It is a miserable, even dangerous place, people say. Old women say it is possessed by the devil and cruel things happen there. They always cross themselves when they hear someone went to *Mărcutza*! There is even a rumor that young people have died there mysteriously. Their flesh was chopped up into meat patties and served to hungry patients and staff!

Adrian doesn't believe these wild tales, but he is suspicious. He would like to learn more about the hospital, but he doesn't know anybody connected with it. People keep silent about it, like about something mysterious and dangerous. He has to trust Sorel and Liviu, who are physicians.

Nevertheless, he keeps worrying about Silvia. The thought of this hospital is like a dark cloud on the horizon. Have they made a rash decision? Should they have waited? But then, who could have treated her? Who could have watched her 24 hours a day? And where could she have stayed? Nobody knows how to reach her family in Transylvania. She has never given them their names and address. And here in Bucharest, everybody has young children who need protection.

Adrian would like to have more information, to talk to Sorel and Stella, but he can't do it with Silvia asleep next to him. She keeps mumbling for a few more minutes, then she yawns and is quiet again.

They're back on the highway now, with the fair and the noise behind them. They drive along the city dump, where the gypsy ragpickers live in their hovels of cardboard and refuse. The stench is so overwhelming, they cover their noses with their handkerchiefs.

"If we don't get out of here fast, I'll need smelling salts!" says Stella. "I hope you have some with you!" she adds. She is fanning herself, pushing the foul air toward Sorel.

"Stop that! You make me dizzy and I can't see the road!" he snaps. He raises his right hand ready to grab the fan.

"Sshhhh! Don't get excited. We're almost there. It's no big deal!" Stella shrugs and slips the fan to the other hand.

They're silent as they ride along the narrow Dîmbovița River. The water is low because of the drought. The bank of the river is overgrown with poplars and weeping willows, over which bats are flying in circles.

Adrian looks back toward Tîrgul Moșilor and toward the city where the sky is aglow with thousands of lights. It looks like a huge aurora borealis. Then he stares at the lush trees and the dark fields beyond, under the moonlit sky.

The car turns right, and the breeze brings a strong fragrance of linden trees.

"We're very close," whispers Stella. "We'll be there in a minute. Can't you smell the linden trees of the Domeniile Coroanei (The Royal Estate) which lies beyond the Mental Hospital? Look, here is the wall!" she adds, as they drive along a thick wall topped with barbed wire which encloses the grounds of the hospital. She has barely finished her sentence, when they stop in front of an iron gate flanked on each side by a watchtower.

Immediately after their arrival, Sorel, Stella and Adrian are taken to Dr. Georgescu's office, while Silvia is wheeled away on a gurney. They are accompanied by an orderly in felt slippers, wearing a faded hospital coat. The dimly lit hall stinks of urine and phenol disinfectant.

The doctor's office stands opposite the entrance door. It is a large, high-ceilinged room, with thick iron bars at the windows. A naked bulb hangs from the whitewashed ceiling. Tall bookcases crammed with books line the walls, and a large chart of the brain and the entire nervous system is attached to one of the shelves.

Dr. Georgescu, a tall, slightly hunched man with graying hair, stands near his desk, talking to a young man. The young doctor is smoothing his white lab coat with one hand and holding a few charts in the other. On the wall behind them hangs a faded portrait of King Carol II in military uniform. A red, blue and gold Romanian flag is draped around the picture.

"Welcome to my office!" says Dr. Georgescu walking toward his visitors. "This is Dr. Milo, my assistant."

"Good evening!" says the doctor turning his black eyes toward them and pushing his rich curls away from his forehead. He bows, picks up a few charts from the desk, bows again, and walks out of the room.

"Sit down, please have a seat!" Dr. Georgescu makes a broad gesture with his arm, inviting Stella and Adrian to sit on a low leather couch and pushing an armchair toward Sorel.

"Your brother-in-law, Dr. Liviu Regen, called to tell me that you were on your way. Your children's governess has tried to strangle herself? But you stopped her? You were able to stop her? That's very good. Still, it's very good that you brought her here."

"Where is she?" asks Stella. She is sitting on the edge of the couch, fanning herself nervously.

"She is in the next room, being prepared for admission."

Adrian turns toward an open door which leads to a short corridor and then to another room. The doors are open and people are speaking softly.

He sits very erect, with Silvia's valise on his knees. Next to him stands a glass cabinet filled with straitjackets and various patient restraints. A shudder runs down his back when he sees them, again remembering all the rumors about the hospital. If you're not sick, they make you crazy so they can experiment on you or use your blood for all kinds of tricks. They shouldn't have brought her here—to this place with locked doors and iron bars at the windows.

"She will be well taken care of," says Dr. Georgescu, as if he has read Adrian's mind. He takes a cigarette from a lacquered box which stands on the desk, squeezes it into an ivory cigarette holder and lights it with a silver lighter. He then offers cigarettes to his three visitors, but only Stella takes one from the box. The doctor bends toward her with the lighter, and when their hands touch, Stella blushes under her makeup.

Dr. Georgescu leans back in his chair and stares at Adrian with his unblinking eyes.

"Tell me more about the governess: did you see any changes lately?"

"Some, and only recently," says Adrian.

"Like what?"

"She seemed less cheerful, somewhat absentminded."

"Did she cry a lot?"

"I didn't see her cry, but she seemed nervous."

"Did she eat properly? Did she lose weight?"

"Yes, it seems to me that she looked pale with rings under her eyes. Her uniform was hanging loose. It looked too large on her."

The doctor turns to a potted plant which stands on the desk near him. He picks a wilted leaf from the stem and rubs it between his fingers.

"How long was she in your house?"

"About three years. Nadia was still a toddler when she came."

"Did she ever behave strangely before?"

"I don't know. But I don't think so." Adrian puts the valise on the floor with a thump and starts shifting on his seat. He is sweating. He feels hot and starts fussing with his watch, winding it back and forth.

"Anybody sick in her family?"

"Not that I know of."

The doctor stands up and goes to the window, clasping an iron bar with his hand. Next to him, on the window sill, stands a row of potted plants with delicate, pale flowers. Orchids. I bet they are orchids! Adrian remembers Stella talking about Dr. Georgescu's famous orchid collection. In a competition among orchid breeders, he has won Romania's first prize and is now competing with the champions of other countries—even America—for the world title! People are saying that the same mysterious magnetism which makes him able to reach the sickest, craziest patients, is also at work with the orchids. It is a great puzzle for everyone how delicate plants which barely survive in special greenhouses around the world come to thrive wildly on this windowsill and even on his busy desk.

Dr. Georgescu turns around suddenly and stares at Adrian. "Well, what do you think brought this about if she never had symptoms before?"

Adrian shrugs. "Is it... love? Is she, maybe, in love? Was she rejected by someone?" Dr. Georgescu concentrates his dark eyes on each of his visitors.

"Hmm," says Adrian, clearing his voice. "I don't know, but I found this picture in her hands."

He reaches into his pocket and pulls out the photo of Joel with his bicycle. A few red marks of lipstick are still visible in a corner. As he hands the picture to Dr. Georgescu,

Stella also gets up to look. She folds the fan and throws it on the couch before taking hold of the picture.

"Yes, yes, I see," she mumbles, as she pores over the photograph.

"Yes, yes, I see is not enough! What else do you know? Did your sister perhaps tell you more? Some secrets we don't know yet?" Dr. Georgescu narrows his eyes as he stares at Stella.

"Who is the young man with the bicycle?"

"Joel. Joel Gold," stammers Stella, blushing.

"Who is Joel and why is she holding onto his photograph?"

"Joel is Nina and Stella's youngest cousin and a good friend of our family. He used to spend much time with our children and the governess," says Adrian, as he stops winding his watch.

The doctor nods.

"Is she pregnant?" he suddenly asks, staring at each of his visitors. Everybody is silent and looks around.

"Pregnant?" repeat Adrian and Stella in disbelief.

"Yes," says Dr. Georgescu matter-of-factly. "It would explain her desperate gesture." He puts out his cigarette and starts cleaning the ivory holder with a toothpick he has pulled out of his pocket.

Adrian is watching him in silence. Silvia pregnant? Nina would die if it were true! She would die of shame! It would ruin the family's reputation, she would say. The neighbors would gossip and laugh, and no other nanny would want to work for them. God forbid! They could even suspect him of being the cause of the trouble. And Silvia, how about her future? All alone, without a job, but with a child. What would her family say? Would they take her back?

Adrian sighs, as he stares at the tip of his shoes.

"No, no. she can't be pregnant!" Sorel finally says. "Not from Joel, in any case!"

"How do you know?" snaps Dr. Georgescu.

Sorel shrugs. "I can't guarantee, but I'm pretty sure Joel got married just about nine months ago. He is much too involved with Mathilda!"

"Who is Mathilda?"

"His young wife. She is the one who would love to get pregnant!" Sorel smiles and rubs his large, hairy hands.

For a few minutes, it is quiet in the office.

Adrian feels somehow relieved. If Sorel is right, there is more hope for Silvia and Nina would not have hysterics. But he cannot shake the load off his chest. A suspicion, a vague fear without name is still nagging at him. He cannot describe it. But it reminds him of the fear of the dark he knew in his childhood.

He looks up and sees that, behind the doctor, on the wall, a few inches below the King's portrait, hangs a reproduction of a painting showing a professor demonstrating a medical case to his students. In the large auditorium, the scientist is talking to his audience, pointing his hand toward a young woman who is the patient.

With her eyes closed and seeming unconscious, the patient or the young woman is collapsing into the arms of a young assistant. There is something romantic and exalted in the painting, thinks Adrian. It is hard to define: maybe it comes from the abandonment with which the young woman collapses in the arms of the young man, maybe it comes from the arrogant self-confidence of the professor.

The title of the painting reads: Professor Charcot presenting Hysteria at the Salpétrière. Adrian notices that Dr. Georgescu wears his graying hair long and tucked behind his ears, just like Charcot. And, just like the French professor he wears a stiff white collar, a bow tie and an old fashioned black frock with a small gold medal in the lapel.

Nobody speaks in the office, but they can hear people moving about in the next room. Silvia moans and says a few unintelligible words.

"What will you do with Silvia? What kind of treatment do you have in mind?" asks Sorel.

Dr. Georgescu gets up and makes a few steps through the room.

"I don't know yet. I'll have to examine her when she's awake. I'll have to see how she behaves. How she responds." He picks another dry leaf from one of the pots.

"I bet you'll hypnotize her or analyze her! It's so fashionable these days!" Sorel points to the painting which hangs behind the doctor's desk. "The great Charcot! And there, the famous doctor Freud," he adds, turning toward a photo of Freud which stands on a bookshelf and has a handwritten dedication.

"You know him personally! He even gave you a signed photograph!"

Sorel walks to the bookcase and takes the picture from the shelf: "*Für meinen geherten Kollegen, Doktor Victor Georgescu, mit besten Wünschen, signed Dozent Dr. Sigmund Freud,*" reads Sorel. "Don't tell me you believe in these charlatans!" he adds.

"And why not, may I ask? They have cured a fair number of cases!" Dr. Georgescu gives Sorel an amused look. "Why shouldn't I trust them?"

"For my part, shock treatment is more reliable, more *medical*, and more scientific," says Sorel. "Insulin… camphor… Metrozole are more familiar, more *chemical* and more dependable than all this magic and abracadabra!"

"Stop! Stop that right now!" Stella covers her ears and turns to Sorel. "Who are you to teach Victor Georgescu how to treat his patients? That's out of your depth! You wouldn't let him meddle in your pediatrics, right? So drop the whole thing! Besides, it's getting late. Much too late for scientific debates!" She yawns and covers her mouth with the fan.

Sorel looks at her with irritation. "You must have the last word! Even in medicine!" he mumbles and shakes his head.

"It's not medicine. It's common sense," Stella says quickly. "But I must ask Victor a favor, before we leave," she adds, turning to the doctor. "Could you find a private room for Silvia, even a small cubicle where she can be alone and safe, not exposed to—how shall I put it—to other dangerous patients?" Stella looks at Dr. Georgescu with her big, shiny eyes and joins her fingers in an imploring gesture.

"Well, I'll try. I've never done this before..."

The doctor keeps pulling a strand of hair forward from behind his left ear, and chewing the end of the empty cigarette holder.

"I'll try the guest room off the corridor... It's usually empty, unoccupied."

"And here are a few small things for Silvia, which will come in handy when she gets her own room!"

Stella takes the valise from Adrian and sets it on the desk, between a potted orchid with golden flowers and a pile of medical charts.

"No, no! You can't leave it here!" Dr. Georgescu is pushing the valise back toward Stella. "Patients are allowed only a few private belongings: their toothbrush, toothpaste, hair brush and comb. Maybe a bar of soap and some toilet paper. Only as much as can be contained in a night stand drawer. Everything else—a nightgown, slippers, a robe (actually a hospital coat), she'll get from here. This is a Mental Hospital, not a private sanitarium, and we have very strict regulations. But if you want to, you can go and see her before you leave," he adds in a softer tone when he sees Stella's long face.

"Yes, yes, I'd like that," she nods, as they all walk into the next office.

This room, which serves as the Admissions Office, is also lit by a naked bulb hanging from the ceiling and has the same iron bars at the windows. The picture of the King in military uniform is decorating one wall, while a red oil lamp is burning under a crucifix. The air smells of strong disinfecting alcohol.

Eugen Milo, Dr. Georgescu's young assistant, sits at a wooden desk, writing notes. Next to him, a fat nurse with thick spectacles and greasy hair bends over the stretcher.

Silvia is still asleep, but something about her has changed: instead of her striped nanny uniform, she is now dressed in a coarse hospital gown and wrapped in a faded hospital coat, like those worn by the orderlies. Her face too looks strangely anonymous, as if she has turned into a cheap mass-produced mannequin.

The fat nurse with greasy hair seems impatient and irritable. She is stuffing Silvia's clothing and shoes into a large bag which she has to take to the Administration.

But, at Dr. Georgescu's urging, she gives Stella all the clothing. On doing so, she drops Silvia's silk stockings into a jar filled with green alcohol, which is crammed with syringes and needles for disinfection.

"La naiba!" she curses. "Too many things to do at once! What ward is she going to?" she asks in an angry tone.

"To the guest room!" orders Dr. Georgescu.

"To the guest room?" ask both the nurse and Dr. Milo at once. The nurse turns the stretcher toward the door, while the young doctor stands motionless, his eyebrows raised.

"You must be joking. You can't be serious!"

"Well, call it an experiment," says the older man. "And you'll be in charge. So take the necessary precautions."

The young man shrugs. There is a puzzled look on his face as he pulls a bunch of keys from his pocket, goes to a glass cabinet which stands in a corner, unlocks the door, and takes out a folded straitjacket which he throws on Silvia's gurney.

"He has the same curly hair and the same broad forehead as Joel!" thinks Adrian. "I wonder whether they know each other?"

Dr. Georgescu props the door open for the gurney to pass.

"We'll have to watch Silvia when she wakes up!" he says to the nurse and to Dr. Milo.

Adrian stands next to him and follows Silvia with his eyes. It is the best solution which could be found, he tells himself. Nevertheless, he is not at peace: the load is still on his chest and a strange restlessness is mounting inside. He looks at Sorel and Stella. They too keep silent and thoughtful as they walk to the door.

"Well, we should be off, and many thanks!" says Adrian.

Dr. Georgescu accompanies them to the main staircase, where he clicks his heels, bows stiffly and kisses Stella's fingertips, before letting them go.

They walk in silence through the avenues of the hospital garden. The wards and pavilions are separated from each other by patches of lawn planted with chestnut trees and bushes of lilac and jasmine. When they step out from under the trees, they can see the full moon in the sky. The whitewashed pavilions are gleaming in the moonlight, and it seems to Adrian that he can see pale faces pressing against the iron bars. Then, suddenly, halfway toward the entrance gate, they hear a distant howl, like that of a hungry wolf, coming from the far end of the garden.

Sorel, Stella and Adrian freeze and listen. The howling becomes louder and louder and it grows closer, as it is picked up by the inmates of one pavilion after another. And, in addition to howling, they also start hitting the iron bars of the windows, adding the hard sound of metal to the animal howls.

One by one, all the pavilions around them are caught in the frenzy. Sorel, Stella, and Adrian stand frozen and look at each other. A deep, primitive fear takes hold of them. Finally, Adrian is able to move. Seizing the others by the arm, he drags them toward the entrance.

It is not long before they reach the car and climb inside. As Sorel starts the engine, Adrian takes a long look at the full moon.

"Luna... Luna," he sighs. "She reigns supreme over this world!"

THE OLD SYNAGOGUE

E ARLY NEXT MORNING, JOEL GETS up and dresses quickly, grabbing the clothes within reach, forgetting to brush his teeth and to check himself in the mirror. He hadn't set the alarm the night before, and now he rushes downstairs and hurries toward Adrian's house. They're going to pick up Emil, Uncle Ariel and Clara and take them to the old Jewish section of the town. Uncle wants to see the house where he was born on Glazier's Alley, as well as the Geller Temple.

Later in the afternoon, Uncle Ariel has been invited to Professor Popescu's home to discuss their forthcoming presentations at the Warsaw Linguistic Conference.

Joel is tired. He has barely slept during the night. He is worried about Silvia. After Nina told him about the photograph with the bicycle, he felt even worse. He is embarrassed, in addition to being worried. Uncle Ariel and Clara are going to think that he led her on or that there had really been a romance between them. Even Mathilda might suspect him of having carried on with Silvia! It might be difficult to persuade her that nothing had happened between them.

He has a great desire to close his eyes for he had slept fitfully. When he had closed his eyes, he dreamed that he had been arrested and dragged to a trial in handcuffs.

He didn't know what crime he was accused of, nor did he know his accusers. They were unknown people who vaguely resembled Mathilda, Uncle Ariel and Clara. The judge and the prosecutor were the same person. They both looked like his father, only they had enormous heads like balloons and pointed fangs.

He walks quickly toward Adrian's house, for he wants to find out more about Silvia's condition. The night before he had to take his parents home before Adrian's return from the hospital, while Mathilda had stayed overnight with Nina to help her with the children. What had gone wrong with Silvia? What had upset her so much? How much did he contribute to all this?

It is true—they had spent a lot of time together, singing and playing with the children. But in the last year, after he married Mathilda, he had seen much less of the children and of Silvia. He never thought that it would matter to her.

He reaches the last corner and, as he is crossing the street in front of Adrian's home, he is almost run over by the milkman's cart.

"Watch where you're going, *idiotule*! Ho! Hrrr!" shouts the milkman as he pulls the reins of the horses. "The streets are full of *bezmetici*!"

Joel climbs the stairs to the second floor and finds Adrian dressed and ready to leave. Mathilda and Nina are still sitting at the breakfast table. A basket of buttered rolls, plates of cheese and jars of honey and jam are scattered on the embroidered tablecloth. The women are drinking hot coffee with steamed milk. The whole room smells of freshly brewed coffee and toast. Sunshine is streaming in from the terrace. The dishes from last night's dinner have been washed and are piled up on the sideboard, waiting to be shelved.

As Joel walks into the room, Mathilda gets up and greets him. She wears Nina's blue housecoat, which is too big for her. She smiles when she embraces Joel, but she looks tired. Nina, too, is tired, with dark circles under her eyes. She says that neither of them had had a full night's sleep. The children were too frightened to go to bed. Everybody had been up, waiting for Adrian's return. It was after one when they finally switched off the lights.

"How is Silvia? How did it go last night?" Joel asks. He pays no attention to the cup of Turkish coffee Marish brings in for him.

"She was asleep the whole evening," says Adrian. "I don't know how she will be when she wakes up! Dr. Georgescu put her in the guest room and promised to take special care of her. I hope she'll be all right!" he adds, as he folds the linen napkin which lays on his knees.

"I hope so too."

Joel's words are drowned out by the parrot's shrill curses in the pantry. "*Du-te la dracu! Du-te la dracu!*" accompanied by childish laughter. Nadia and Suzy are up and are playing with the bird, which Liviu has left behind for another day.

"Fritz is here and the car is ready!" announces Marish as she brings in two cups of coffee with milk for the children and two buttered croissants.

"All right then, let's go!"

Adrian quickly hugs Nina and the girls, while Joel barely has time to kiss Mathilda goodbye. But just before he turns to go, she points to his feet and starts to laugh.

"Look! Look! You're wearing a brown slipper on your left foot and a black shoe on the other! Scatterbrain! You've done it again!" She is wagging her finger at him.

Joel turns deep red, peering at her and Nina. "I'm sure I have an identical pair at home!" he manages to say before running out the door to catch up with Adrian.

At Emil's house, Uncle Ariel, Emil and Clara are waiting for them. Even though it is hot and both Adrian and Joel wear sport shirts with open collars, Emil has put on a navy tie with very thin white stripes. His carefully trimmed moustache, his delicate pince-nez, his silk tie and the snow-white handkerchief in his breast pocket give Emil a serious and distinguished look. But today his face is tense. He paces nervously back and forth.

Uncle Ariel stands near the door wearing a black fedora with a broad rim and dark sunglasses, so that half of his face remains hidden.

Joel is surprised, but before he can say anything, Uncle tells them that he doesn't want to be recognized by anyone.

"I don't want people to know who I am!" he says.

"But tata, nobody here still knows you. You left so long ago. You'll be dying of heat with the black fedora," says Clara. "Better put on a light straw hat, the kind Adrian is wearing!"

But Uncle pounds the ground several times with his cane and says, "One never knows. You're too young. You have no experience. Better safe than sorry!" And with these words, he is pushing the hat even deeper over his forehead.

Adrian, Clara, Joel, Uncle Ariel and Emil squeeze into the car. Adrian and Clara sit in the front seat. Joel, Uncle Ariel and Emil climb in the back.

Clara is wearing an off-white shirt dress with short sleeves, a jade necklace and earrings. The green stones make her red curls look richer and shinier and her eyes greener and more transparent. Fritz starts the engine and the car takes off.

The day has grown hazy with the sky hidden behind a misty veil. In front of them lumbers a heavy truck and they are swallowed by a cloud of dust. When the air finally clears, they have reached Hala Trajan (Trajan Market Hall). This is a large, squat building with a glass roof, housing innumerable stalls of all kinds of produce. Housemaids and peasant women in their flowery skirts walk in and out through the packed gates. The clamor of voices as well as the mixture of odors is almost solid and tangible. But it doesn't disturb the mangy dogs sleeping on the pavement under the swarms of flies, nor the crowds of shoppers gathered in front of mountains of melons and eggplants and the huge piles of live chickens with their legs tied which surround the building.

"Here are the sweetest and the cheapest melons in town and the fattest chickens," says Adrian. "We'll send Fritz later to buy some," he adds, as they continue their way past low houses guarded by stray cats and dogs.

At the end of Trajan Street stands a hundred-year-old mulberry tree with gnarled branches. At its foot sits an old gypsy beggar with a white beard and wrinkled face.

"I think I remember this old man, or maybe his father or grandfather from my schooldays!" says Uncle Ariel.

When they reach this corner, they turn into Calea Dudești, a busy thoroughfare with narrow sidewalks and a dizzying stream of packed tramways and horse drawn carts.

The street is lined with small shops and is very noisy, with merchants doing business at great speed and at the top of their voices. The narrow shops are shabby and dirty with walls covered with peeling paint and falling plaster and tight entrances to half-basements. The small windows are dusty and splashed with caked mud. Joel explains to Clara that families with as many as eight or ten children live in these cellars, behind the stores, and that the faded yellow signs which hang above the doors advertise the goods one can buy inside: buttons, underwear, galoshes, wedding bands, umbrellas, costume jewelry, pills for impotence, cooking oil, and many other things.

"As you can see, we're in the heart of the Jewish section," Joel says as they drive past bearded men with sidelocks, wearing black hats or skullcaps and dark, greasy caftans. They are rushing in all directions speaking in loud Yiddish sing-song and moving their hands incessantly.

To the right, they now pass an assemblage of low hovels, where agitated Jewish men with skullcaps and black caftans are bargaining over a million different objects—some haphazardly strewn around, others neatly piled by the hovels.

"This is Taica Lazār, the greatest secondhand store in the City," Joel tells Clara, "and here you can find anything you want from rusty bathtubs, cracked mirrors and scrap metal to old shoes, used furniture, and secondhand clothing and underwear." Clara nods and buries her nose inside her handkerchief because of the smells which hang in the air.

"Follow the tramway line to the Mămulari Station," Adrian tells Fritz.

Suddenly, the car has to stop behind an oxen cart. At the same time, a small boy with reddish sidelocks, wearing a dirty caftan and a skullcap, comes running toward the car. He stops short by the backdoor and flattens his hands on the window. A greasy smudge is left on the glass.

"I hate these religious Jews and their children!" says Emil, waving the boy away. "They're trouble for all of us! They're good for nothing: only for prayer and sitting in shul."

There is an edge in Emil's voice and a nervous twitch in the white hand with which he picks up a speck of dust.

"Why do you hate them so?" Uncle Ariel takes off his sunglasses and stares at Emil.

"Because... because... believe me, in this country, they're only trouble!" Emil passes his fingers through his thinning hair. "They're useless parasites. They don't work and they can't work because they have no trade. They don't even speak Romanian properly. Their ugly, outdated appearance, with their sidelocks, their skullcaps, and their caftans make them repelling. Not to speak about their lack of cleanliness and their general shabbiness. They sit in shul because they don't want to work. They do harm to all of us!"

Emil closes his eyes briefly with a grimace and adjusts his pince-nez. Then he shrugs. Joel is struck by the tension in his movements, but his words make him think of his father. He remembers that more than once, his father had spoken the same way about the religious Jews. He couldn't stand them and he was convinced that they were causing much trouble.

Joel looks out the window and sees the smudges left by the boy's hands. He remembers how, as a first grader in a Romanian public school, the teacher seated him in the same bench with a Jewish boy who wore a caftan and a skullcap. He had long, greasy sidelocks. His face and hands were unwashed and his hair unkempt. Two days after the beginning of school, Joel came home with lice.

His mother had to go to the teacher and bribe her with an expensive bottle of Arpège perfume to convince her to move Joel to another seat. The teacher told his mother that she thought Joel would enjoy the company of another Jewish boy "just like him!"

But how much was this boy "like him"? Joel couldn't tell. It was the first time in his life that he had encountered Jewish Orthodoxy. It had confused and upset him.

"How are the religious Jews making trouble for everyone else?" asks Uncle Ariel. He takes off his glasses, wipes them with his handkerchief and then puts them on again.

"How? Simply by refusing to work and to dress properly. They refuse to adapt and to assimilate to the Western world. This makes all of us look bad, as if we're all incapable of adapting and keeping up with the modern world. It throws suspicion even on the best of us, on those of us who are patriots and have risked our lives in the Great War, and have received gold medals for our courage!"

"Like your father, your brother, and yourself. Right?"

"Yes," Emil nods and blushes. "But you must remember that in this country there is a hierarchy, a classification of the Jews according to their *quality*. There is a small, elite group made up of war heroes and assimilated Jews who resemble the Gentiles. On the other hand, there is a large mass of useless, backward, unadaptable Jews, the mass of Religious Jews, who live here and in the *shtetls* of the North of the country. They are hopeless, the real scourge of the land and of Jewry!"

"Yes, yes," says Uncle Ariel, as he keeps stroking his beard. "It's an interesting point. But not everybody accepts this classification: some officials in the army, for instance, have other opinions. Do you remember your cousin Dov? He was a decorated war hero, who had received a gold medal for luring a German unit into an ambush. He was shot in his left foot during the battle, which earned him the medal. But when he recovered and returned to the Front, things changed: there were secret orders to place the Jewish soldiers in the front lines, have the Romanian soldiers shoot them in the back and accuse them afterwards of being deserters.

"That's exactly what happened to Dov's company. Fortunately, for him, a Gentile officer told him about these secret orders. Dov listened and the man helped him escape across the Danube into Bulgaria. From there he went to Palestine where he got married and lives to this day." Uncle Ariel takes off his fedora and starts fanning himself with it.

"That may be true, but it didn't happen to anybody I know, including my father and my brother," says Emil. "We all got back safe and sound, proud of our decorations!"

"But it happened to one of my neighbors," says Adrian. "He and his Jewish comrades were sent on reconnaissance in the first lines, and were shot in the back on the last day of the war!"

Emil shrugs with impatience and inhales deeply from his cigarettes. "Still, these are exceptions," he says. "All war veterans I know have been well treated, and their courage has been rewarded."

Adrian tries to say something, but the car stops in front of a tall gate crowned by the Star of David. Fritz opens the door and lets them off. They have reached the Geller Temple.

Joel recognizes the squat building decorated with marble plaques and surrounded by a paved courtyard. The temple has stained glass windows. The gold inscribed tablets of Moses with the Ten Commandments guard the doorway.

A few bearded men, wrapped in their white and blue prayer shawls, sit on stone benches in the courtyard talking to each other. Others are walking in and out of the building. Joel is surprised at their continuous comings and goings.

"Let's get in while the morning service is still on!" says Adrian, leading them through a high-ceilinged hallway into the sanctuary.

Emil and Joel put on the black skullcaps they carry in their pockets, while Adrian and Uncle Ariel keep their hats on. Clara ties a green scarf over her red curls and climbs a rickety stair to the women's section.

It is hot and stuffy inside the sanctuary. Only a handful of men are dovening. But on the *bima*, Rabbi Naftali and Cantor Israel dressed in their flowing robes perform the morning service. They bow their heads repeatedly as they recite the sacred lines.

Joel watches the service and joins in the prayers. He knows all the words. He also knows the temple very well. Each member of the Geller family has his own seat, marked by a bronze plaque. But they can't reach their seats now. They are too far away and trying to do so would disturb the service. They all sit down at the farthest corner of the sanctuary, trying not to draw attention to themselves.

Joel listens to the prayers and keeps staring at the front seat near the *bima* which is now empty. It belongs to his father, Leon, who is the oldest member of the family and who always sits in that spot when he attends services. It had been the seat of his great-grandfather, Simon Geller, the builder of the temple. Then, after his death, it traditionally became the seat of the oldest member of the family. Now it is the place of honor where his father sits, even though he attends services only on the High Holidays. But here, at the Geller Temple, nobody cares that he is only a "Holiday Jew." Nobody questions his religious beliefs. All that matters is that he should occupy the family's traditional "Ancestor Seat."

The service goes on for another half hour. When the prayers are finished, the visitors stand up and turn toward the aisle. But before they can get out of their seats, the Rabbi and the Cantor join them.

"Welcome to Bucharest!" says the Rabbi, grabbing Uncle Ariel's elbow. "I know who you are. You're Ariel Geller, the Chief Rabbi of London! Once again, welcome to our town!"

The Rabbi shakes hands with Uncle Ariel, smiling broadly. He has a dark, pointed and wiry beard and very small, piercing eyes, surrounded by countless wrinkles and creases. He is a short man, but his long, black robe and very erect posture make him look tall.

Cantor Israel stands next to him, grinning and nodding. His face is round and clean shaven. He has a double chin and dimples in his cheeks. His ears are bright red and stick out from his head.

"I couldn't have missed you!" says Rabbi Naftali, as he keeps shaking his head. "You look so much like your grandfather, Simon, who built this temple. I'm sure you've been told this before. Besides, I couldn't fail to recognize these gentlemen," he adds, shaking hands with Adrian, Joel and Emil. "You, too, welcome to the temple. Please, come into my study and be my guests. You can't leave the shul without stopping at my office."

"Gladly! But just for a few minutes." Uncle Ariel signals to Clara to join them, as she climbs down from the women's section. After she is introduced to the Rabbi and Cantor, they all walk through a dark corridor into a small room filled with bookcases and thick Hebrew books.

In the middle of the room is a table covered with a flowery oilcloth. In the corner stands a stove, made of blue-green ceramic tiles. Next to the stove is the window which opens onto the backyard of the temple, a small garden, overgrown with poison ivy and weeds. A strong smell of fried fish comes from the kitchen window across the yard, where the Rabbi's family lives.

"What a pleasure to have you here! I thought I would not live to see that day!" says Rabbi Naftali, as he pushes chairs toward his guests. "We are trying to build a collection of your work," he adds, turning to Uncle Ariel. "We have all your old publications, but the current ones are hard to come by." He points to a narrow bookcase which is filled with pamphlets and magazine articles written by or about Uncle Ariel. On the top shelf is a large photo of Uncle, presiding over the Tenth Zionist Congress in Basel. "I hear so much about you, particularly as the Rabbi of the Geller Temple. But I still remember the day when you were expelled from the country," he goes on. "What a sad day it was. I was only ten years old, but I wanted to go with my father and brother to the train station. I will never forget how frightened I was by the mounted police with their bayonets and horses, and by the shouting crowd which filled the streets. I can still see you standing there so proud and courageous with your gold medal. My father who was a learned man, a *zadig*, always spoke with great respect about you. It was your example which made me think of becoming a Rabbi. Then, it was such a lucky break to get this position at your family's temple! It was the best thing that could have happened to me." He is smiling and stroking his beard.

As he finishes speaking, he opens a compartment at the bottom of a bookcase and brings out a bottle of kosher wine, a few glasses, and a honey cake wrapped in a kitchen towel.

Cantor Israel moves a pile of papers out of the way, smoothing the oilcloth with his hand and picking up a few bread crumbs and pencil shavings with his thick fingertips.

As soon as they are seated, the Rabbi slices the honey cake with a knife, while the Cantor pours wine into the glasses.

"*L'chaim!* I wish to return this *mitzvah!*" says Uncle Ariel. "I'll send you the new publications as soon as they come out!" He raises the glass and inhales the fragrance of the wine. Then he takes a long sip. He weighs the glass in his hand, and strokes its surface with his finger.

"These are the same cut crystal glasses and plates which were used at my Bar Mitzvah. My grandfather gave them to the temple for *kiddush* on that occasion. You still have the same chairs, table and lamp from that time. I recognize all of them," he says, pointing to the chairs and to the brass chandelier which hangs from the ceiling. "Only then it was a gas lamp and not it works with electricity. Otherwise, it's all the same."

"And we still have the same prayer books, only older and greasier." The Cantor is licking a crumb from his fingertips. "But... fewer congregants are coming to services!"

"That's right!" The Rabbi turns toward Emil, "I haven't seen you since the High Holidays!"

"Too busy. If you earn a living, you can't spend your days at temple," mumbles Emil.

The Rabbi gives him a doubtful look, but makes no comment.

"And you, Joel? I haven't seen you since your Bar Mitzvah!"

"Since my wedding!" Joel corrects him and blushes.

"Are you sure?" The Rabbi raises an eyebrow, teasing him. It was only during that time that you came regularly to temple!"

The Bar Mitzvah. How well Joel remembers those days. He takes a sip of wine and, in spite of the smell of fried fish which fills the room, it tastes as fruity as on that day. How stormy those months had been back in 1922, shortly before his 13th birthday. He remembers the endless fights and discussions between his parents.

"A Bar Mitzvah? Who cares about a Bar Mitzvah! It's pure nonsense. A waste of time, effort and money!" his father had said. "A return to the old gobble-de-gook, to the old superstitions! I want my son to grow up a modern man, intelligent, educated, emancipated, free of the old-fashioned beliefs and foolish traditions!"

But to his mother, this was unacceptable.

"In our family, every boy was Bar-Mitzvah'd. How can Joel, a descendent of the great Chassid, Rabbi Isaac of Berditchev not do it? It would be an unforgivable blow to the tradition of the family! What would the Community say? How can we ever set foot in the Geller Temple, if our son has no Bar Mitzvah."

"I don't care about the family tradition and about the Community!" shouted his father. "To hell with them! I'll stick to my guns!"

But later, just before Yom Kippur, when his wife Josephine turned pale and couldn't sleep because she feared the wrath of God and of her dead parents, and when the Rabbi confirmed the seriousness of her condition, Joel's father finally relented. But he wasn't pleased. "It's so much simpler to be a Gentile today and not be faced with these decisions," he sighed at the dinner table.

Soon after the High Holidays, Joel started going to the Temple every morning to put *teffilim* and to study with the Rabbi. Not only did he learn the prayers he was going to say, but he also studied Hebrew with a young, tanned and muscular school teacher, Professor Jakubow. The professor was a militant Zionist. He always wore open collar shirts, knickerbockers and hiking boots. He never owned a winter coat.

He spoke to Joel about Palestine, the land of "Sunny Oranges," brought him books and photographs of young *Chalutzim* ploughing the earth in sun-drenched colonies. By the time Joel finished with his Bar Mitzvah, he had told his father that he was going Alyah to Eretz Israel.

"You're not going anywhere!" his father thundered, pounding the table with his fist. "You stay right here with us. I haven't been wounded and spilled my blood in the Great War for you to run to Palestine and become Lawrence of Arabia, roaming the desert with camels and Bedouins. Do you hear me? You don't go any place! This is where we belong. This is where we'll stay!"

After that Joel avoided discussing the issue of Palestine with his father.

"Have some more wine!" The Cantor raises the bottle and grabs the nearest glass. His face and his ears turn even redder than before.

"And try some more cakes!" The Rabbi cuts another slice and places it on Uncle's plate.

"No, no, thank you!" Uncle Ariel pushes the plate away. "Emil is right: time is short and we mustn't waste it. We're off to my parents' old house on Glazier Alley. It's just around the corner, if I remember well."

He gets up and they all join Emil who is already standing by the door. They file quickly through the narrow corridor and the entrance hall. When they step into the courtyard, they are suddenly faced with a crowd of onlookers.

"Welcome back to Bucharest, Rabbi Geller!" they shout and clap their hands. Then they step aside, letting the visitors walk to the gate.

They spend no time at all at the old house since the garden gate is locked and a big wolfhound keeps barking viciously at them. But next door stands the Moriah School, which had been founded by Uncle Ariel's grandfather and where Joel completed his elementary classes.

The school is a gray, two-story building, with vaulted windows, and a red sloping tile roof. The walls are thick and massive. The entire structure reminds Joel of an armory. He hasn't visited the school in many years. This makes him feel guilty, like when you neglect to visit your grandparents for a long time.

They climb the stairs to the entrance hall and are greeted by a tanned young man in a white shirt with an open collar, who takes them to the office of the principal. The door is open. From the entrance hall, Joel can see the principal standing in front of a large map of Palestine. He has rich, wiry silver hair. He wears the same open collar, sport shirt and knickerbockers as he did many years ago.

They shake hands and introduce themselves to Professor Zeev Yakubov, and Joel remembers how, during the time of his studying for the Bar Mitzvah, the young teacher had taken him to a farm near the city, where young Zionists, young *Halutzim*, were training in agricultural work before going to Palestine.

The professor's enthusiasm and the work in the open air with other young people at the farm had awakened in Joel a great desire to go to Palestine. But he had had to abandon this dream when his enraged father refused any discussion on the subject.

Joel remembers an earlier event, when, for his ninth birthday, his Uncle Sorel, the pediatrician, had brought him a book called *Benny Flies to the Promised Land*. It was all about a little boy's trip to Palestine in a small plane constructed by himself. Indeed, attached to the book was the folded model of a cardboard and canvas plane which could easily be assembled.

Joel read the book and constructed the plane which was big enough to let him sit inside. Then, starry eyed and very proud of himself, he called his father to show him what he had done. He announced that he was going to Palestine with his new plane. But his father flew into a rage and broke the toy plane.

"You're not going to Palestine to be killed by the Arabs! You stay here and finish your studies. Then you'll decide what you want to do."

Joel was so angry at his father that he didn't talk to him for almost a month. It was the first of many arguments with his father in connection with emigration to Palestine.

Now Professor Jakubow takes his guests on a tour of the school with its many classrooms and workshops. When they return to his office, they are treated to rose petal preserves from the Zionist farm.

Joel takes his small plate of preserves and is immediately reminded of an old incident. Many years ago, during his Bar Mitzvah studies, he too brought home two jars of preserves—one cherry, the other apricot. They had been prepared with fruit grown on the Zionist farm. His mother had been delighted and had immediately served them for dinner. But not so his father. As soon as he learned where the sweets came from, he took the two jars, threw them in the garbage and smashed them. He was red in the face and yelled that he didn't want any Zionist propaganda product in his house.

"Jew hater! Anti-Semite," Joel had screamed, which made his father run after him with a leather belt. He would have received a serious beating if his mother hadn't stepped between them.

Joel remembers now that on that very evening his father had been invited to a great reception at the Royal Estate which was not far from the Zionist farm. It was his father who had bought the priceless oriental rugs which decorated the new palace. He had travelled to India to make this deal. The rugs had never even been delivered to the store. They had traveled directly from the palace of the Maharajah of Sultanabad to the Royal Villa near Bucharest. That evening his father was eager to see them in their new home. His elegant white tuxedo was hanging in the corridor. He had gone to the barber that morning for a special haircut and shave.

After so many years, Joel finally understands that in his desire to be accepted and respected by the King and the Court his father had come to reject Jewish things.

Now Joel eats the rose petal preserves absentmindedly, without being aware of its taste. Then he looks at the others who are eating slowly, taking small sips of water.

After they finish their treat, they say goodbye and thank the host for his hospitality. They wish him an enthusiastic "Next Year in Jerusalem" as they file out the door. They walk back toward the Geller Temple, where Fritz is waiting with the car.

As they turn the corner, they come face to face with two gypsies and a bear on a chain. Adrian and Joel try to avoid the gypsies, but the men stop in front of them, blocking their way.

The gypsies have long, dirty hair and shiny teeth. They wear torn rags. The bear sports a small red fez with a half moon and star. One man plays a gold tambourine while the other makes the bear dance on his hind legs by pulling the chain attached to its nose and poking its ribs with a stick.

> *"Joacă bine Moş Martine*
> *Că-ti dau pâine cu măsline!"*

> ("Dance well, Mr. Martin
> And I'll give you bread with olives!")

sings the man with the tambourine, while his companion holds out an old military cap to collect money.

Adrian drops a few pennies into the hat. When the bear finishes dancing, Clara strokes his head, talking to him in her soft voice. The bear turns its small eyes toward her and licks her hand.

"Never do that again," says Fritz, who has stepped out of the car and is wiping his face with a rumpled handkerchief. He has taken off his driver's cap with the gold trimmings.

"Bears are treacherous. They seem friendly, but they can maul your hand and arm. It is said that they carry rabies. There is no cure for that!"

Clara says she is sorry. She didn't know about the rabies. Fritz nods with satisfaction and opens the door of the car.

They settle inside, Joel and Clara in front, next to Fritz, and Emil, Uncle Ariel and Adrian in the back seat.

"To Professor Popovici on Berzei Street, just beyond the Law School," says Adrian.

As they ride again through the dusty streets, nobody speaks. Soon they leave behind the shabby and crowded Jewish section and turn into a tree-lined boulevard. The old chestnut trees make the air feel cooler and they roll down all the windows.

"We'll be there in no time." Adrian checks his watch as they speed by the bronze statue of Ion Brătianu, an important liberal statesman. After they pass the Cişmigiu Garden, they have to slow down. By the time they reach the Law School, all traffic has stopped. They too have come to a halt behind a big yellow bus and cannot see what is blocking the road. They only hear a clamor of voices and songs coming from the University building.

When the bus finally drives off, they find themselves surrounded by a large crowd of demonstrators. They are all young men, many bearded with shaggy hair, all wearing green shirts, black pants and black leather belts with pistols tucked in their holsters. They are singing an anthem about the "Awakening of the Romanian Nation" and "Freedom from the Tyranny of the Kikes." When they finish singing, they raise their right arm in the Fascist salute.

"The Iron Guard!" Adrian sounds alarmed. "We have to get out of here!"

The car cannot move. A solid wall of screaming, green-shirted demonstrators carrying heavy clubs and large slogans with the words: "ROMANIA TO THE ROMANIANS! THE KIKES TO PALESTINE!" is pressing against the car, almost crushing it.

"Close the windows and lock the door!" orders Adrian.

As they huddle inside the car watching the frenzy outside, they notice a tight knot of screaming and club wielding men on the sidewalk, right in front of the Law School building. Then, as the crowd shifts and some demonstrators step aside, they can see a man lying in a puddle of blood. His leather briefcase and a newspaper lay next to him.

"THE KIKES TO PALESTINE! ROMANIA TO THE ROMANIANS!" the crowd is still screaming, shaking their clubs.

"Quick! Let's take him to the hospital!" Clara opens the door, trying to jump out of the car.

"No! It's too dangerous! Lock the door!" Adrian and Joel pull Clara back in and lock the door.

"We have to get out of here before it's too late!" Adrian is bending so deeply forward that he almost tumbles into the front seats.

Fritz honks a few times and by surprise the demonstrators part enough for the car to turn into a side street and speed toward Professor Popovici's house.

As they drive away, they sit in the car stunned and speechless for several minutes.

"What a scare! Those brutes should be punished. They shouldn't get away with this! They should be shot!" Adrian keeps twisting his hat in his clenched fists.

"And their hands should be chopped off before their execution." Uncle Ariel is pounding the floor with his cane.

Joel doesn't say anything. He keeps looking back, as if trying to catch another glimpse of the poor man sprawled on the pavement. He feels bad that they had abandoned him. There should be something they could do, not just run away like hunted animals.

He keeps turning his head and looking back. Even though he can't see anything now, the image of the wounded man remains engraved in his mind. After a while it changes and is slowly replaced by the image of Silvia, unconscious, being carried to the waiting car. Then, too, he had felt guilty from his inability to help.

FROM THE PRIVATE DIARY OF DR. MILO

6/17/36: YESTERDAY I STARTED TO work with a new patient, Silvia N. She is a 23-year-old, unmarried woman, who was brought in last night for a suicide attempt in which she tried to strangle herself with a scarf.

The Jewish family for whom she works as a governess said that she was in love with a young man, a relative of the family, and she was unhappy because he had recently married someone else.

Dr. Georgescu wanted to give her shock treatment with insulin or Metrazole, but I reminded him of all the accidents we had had because of the strong convulsions—broken arms and legs, fractured spines, swallowed tongues which made patients choke, and loss of memory which turned patients into zombies, not to mention the angry families. I convinced him to let me try Charcot's hypnosis. I reminded him how much he admired the French neurologist, which was not difficult since he has a large painting of Charcot called "Le Maître à la Salpêtrière," hanging in his office.

I am interested in this young woman because I suspect that she is an excellent candidate for hypnosis and also because she could be a good subject for the forthcoming public demonstrations at the end of the month.

So, once I had Dr. Georgescu's permission, I set to work and this is what I found:

When I entered her room early yesterday morning, she was in bed with the covers pulled over her head. Even though Rita, the nurse, had brought her breakfast and left it on the table, the patient had ignored it and had not moved from her bed. Even when I walked in and called her name, she still did not respond. She only turned her face to the wall and pulled the blanket even higher over her head.

I made a sign to Rita to come out of the room and told her to leave the stale bread with jam and the tea, which was cold by now, on the table. I also instructed her to leave the patient alone and just watch her from time to time. She should only remove the breakfast plate when she brought the lunch tray.

Rita didn't like that. "Who does she think she is?" I heard her mumble as she walked away.

I went twice back to Silvia's room, once at four in the afternoon and then late, before leaving, but nothing had changed. The soup from lunch and the bean *iahnie* from supper were still untouched on the table. Both times, she turned her face to the wall as soon as I walked in.

6/18/36: Yesterday was a repetition of the first day. The patient stayed in bed all day without eating or getting up and refused to look at me or to answer my questions, even though I went three times to her room. Rita told me that she only drank a little water and used the bathroom once, late at night, when she thought nobody was watching.

6/19/36: Today, Dr. Georgescu said that we could not continue this way. The family keeps asking about Silvia and wants to know whether she is improving and how we are treating her. They even want to come for a visit.

I am not surprised by Dr. Georgescu's comments. I have also decided that we must start doing something and move toward treatment.

I went to the patient's room. Even though she turned away from me and hid under the covers, I told her clearly and firmly that from now on she would have to get out of bed, wash her face and eat. Her present behavior would not be tolerated.

When I finished, there was a moment of silence. Then she sat up in bed and burst out screaming that "all she wanted was to die and she hated us because we stood in her way."

First I let her scream. Then I said firmly that this was not a subject for discussion. Finally I ordered Rita to hand her the tray with the breakfast.

Rita gave me an angry look, but did as I said. Silvia howled furiously and threw the tray across the room. We had to duck behind a chair to keep from being hit.

This was what I was waiting for. The patient's angry outburst was a good opportunity to have her packed in a straitjacket and wheeled to my quiet office at the other end of the pavilion. I told Rita that this was what I had expected and suggested that she call an orderly for help. I then walked out of the room. I don't like to see patients forced into straitjackets. I could hear her screams way down the hallway, as I passed the women's ward.

Later on, I stopped in our library and looked at Charcot's *Leçons du Mardi à la Salpêtrière*. I couldn't remember whether he had ever hypnotized a patient in natural sleep? I looked at several chapters, but found no reference to this subject.

Finally, I returned to my office. I walked in on tiptoe and, as expected, found Silvia tied in her straitjacket, asleep on the couch. Her eyes were closed. Her face was relaxed and she was breathing deeply and regularly.

If I could only hypnotize her without her waking up. I sat behind her, where she couldn't see me in case she opened her eyes. Then I started the induction process, speaking in a whisper.

I used Charcot's method and I told her, "You are deeply asleep now and you're breathing regularly. Your body is totally relaxed, all your muscles are very relaxed. Your eyes are shut; your eyelids are heavy. They are ten times as heavy as before and your eyes are shut so tightly that you cannot open them. All your muscles are limp and pliable. Your arms are getting heavy and limp."

All that Charcot said worked perfectly. I told her to raise her left arm very slowly and let it drop to her side. "Very slowly... that's very good. Now do the same with your right arm. Very good, very good." And in no time she raised each arm, one after the other, letting it fall heavily to her side. This showed me that she was hearing my commands and following them. So I continued the process:

"From now on you will get out of bed every morning. You will wash your face and your body and brush your teeth. Every morning, you will get dressed and eat your breakfast, and your other meals, later in the day. Now, too, you will eat your dinner when you go back to your room.

"And every day you will meet me here in my office, but you will never remember that I spoke to you here. Now they will take you back to your room and you will wake up when you're in your bed."

I called Rita and Sandu, the orderly, to take Silvia back to the guest room.

That evening, she ate her dinner and did not complain.

6/20/36: Today Silvia was brought to my office early. She was still wearing a straitjacket, but Rita told me she had eaten her breakfast and brushed her teeth without any opposition. It was only when they put on the straitjacket that she had started to fight them. But Rita told her that she had to wear the straitjacket to come to my office so then she gave up her resistance.

As soon as she lay on the couch, I ordered her to close her eyes and let her body go limp. "Breathe deeply and regularly and go to sleep," I said.

She did as I told her and slipped into a trance before I could count to three. I tested her by ordering her to raise her left arm and let it fall limp along her side.

"Somebody hurt you and upset you before you were brought to the hospital? Who is it?"

She mumbled a word which sounded like "Joel," but immediately her breathing became shallower and she started to toss and turn. One more minute and she would have fallen out of her hypnosis. So I had to deepen the trance in order to stave off the emotion which could have woken her up. I counted very slowly to 20, telling her to keep breathing deeply and to relax her muscles. She calmed down and I ordered her again to tell me about her and Joel.

"I cannot remember!" she whispered at first.

"You will think about it under the pressure of my hands," I said, as I held her head nestled between my palms. She then started speaking.

She told me how they spent much time together, during the summer in Sinaia, preparing all kinds of shows and celebrations for the children. They had sung songs and played music. She played the guitar and Joel played the harmonium. Once they had taken a long walk and sat in a clearing in the woods composing and rehearsing skits for Nadia's upcoming birthday. On that occasion, they had spoken about the opera. Joel had said something about taking her to *La Traviata* when they returned to Bucharest. After that, she had waited for his invitation. She had secretly sewn a lamé evening dress and bought silver pumps for the occasion. But instead, the other woman, Mathilda, had appeared from nowhere. Joel had forgotten about the children, the shows, and Silvia. "He and Mathilda got engaged and married, which was bad enough, but the worst was when they went to the opening of *La Traviata* and told everybody how much they had enjoyed the show. This was too much. I couldn't take it any longer."

As I listened, I applied more pressure to her forehead and told her to go on breathing deeply and regularly. Then I commanded her to let go of her passion for Joel. "You will stop yearning for Joel. He is now gone from your life and your mind like a shadow dispersed by the sun, like mist scattered by wind," I said. I repeated it several times.

I closed the session by instructing her to keep eating her meals, wash regularly and comply with the rules of the hospital. "You will wake up in your room and you will forget that *I* gave you these orders." I then called Rita to wheel her away.

I am sure she will be cured with this treatment, and she will certainly help me demonstrate the power of hypnosis.

6/21/36: This morning Silvia was calmer and even smiled when they brought her in. She was still wearing the straitjacket, but Rita had braided her blond hair and she looked really pretty. She tried to get off the gurney and onto the couch by herself so I rewarded her by untying the straitjacket. Then I placed her in a deep trance. I had decided to ask about her past and her childhood. (By now she slips very quickly into hypnosis, as soon as I start the induction.)

This is what she told me:

She was born in a small village in Transylvania, not too far from the village my parents come from. When she was three, they moved to America, where her mother died in a car accident. Her father started to drink and, for a few years, ran around with other women. When she was 7, they came back to their village in Transylvania. There he married the mother's sister, Aunt Dorina, who turned into a wicked stepmother, just like the ones in the fairy tales. She pretended to be Silvia's birth mother and asked her to call her "Mama." She made sure that there were no pictures of her real mother anywhere in the house. Nevertheless, Silvia found one in a forgotten drawer and kept it hidden under her mattress.

She hated the aunt and couldn't wait to leave home. She did just that as soon as she could by coming to Bucharest to work as a governess. This didn't sit well with her father and stepmother who thought that her work in the City, for Jewish families, was too degrading and shameful. They told her never to come back to the village unless she was married.

During this session, I had to intervene several times and deepen the trance. For every so often Silvia would stop talking and say that she couldn't remember. It was always a painful incident which made her fall silent. Every time this happened I pressed my hands on her forehead and said, "Concentrate now and you will remember!" In a short while she answered, "It comes back to me" and went on with her story.

My plan is to take Silvia back to these episodes and drain them of emotion. Then she will become a stronger and less vulnerable person. She will become "my new creation," a challenge fit for a Pygmalion of modern times.

In the meantime, I am also preparing her for the Big Meeting at the end of the month. I think this is very promising, since she is an exceptional candidate.

Two weeks later. Silvia is doing much better now. A few days ago she started walking and sitting alone in the garden. In our sessions, too, she is doing remarkably well. I am still working at freeing her from her infatuation with Joel. She slips with great ease into trance and never resists the "regression in time" which I use for her treatment. I make her go back in years and remember in detail the first time she met Joel at a family dinner, then the birthday and other occasions when they made music or worked together. At every point in time I make her aware that Joel is gone for good from her life and order her to let go of her passion for him.

"He has vanished like air from your life and your mind, and you have buried your feelings for him." I repeat firmly again and again.

I also had to ask Dr. Georgescu to stop the Stein family and the others from visiting her, since their presence would certainly have rekindled her obsession with Joel. It was not easy to convince the old fox. He gave me a suspicious look, even though I had made it very clear that total distance was essential for her cure.

Ten days later. The Medical Meeting on Hypnosis was a great success. It was held in the great auditorium and was attended by at least 200 people, doctors and students alike.

Dr. Georgescu presided and at the last minute Rita told me that Silvia's "Joel" and the Stein family were in the audience. Fortunately, it was dark in the lecture hall and only the dais was lit.

There were many reports and boring papers. I had the only "live" demonstration.

Silvia looked very pretty. She wore a beautiful dress provided by the family at Dr. Georgescu's insistence. Rita had braided her blonde hair and made her wear some lipstick.

When she first appeared on the platform, people wondered whether she was an actress and whether this was a "con" act, particularly since she was not intimidated in front of such a large audience. (It is true I had prepared her for this event under hypnosis, making sure that I erased her fear.) I sat behind her in our usual way. As soon as I started the induction, she fell into a trance, which I had to deepen only twice by placing my hand on her forehead and pressing lightly.

I ordered her to sit up and I started with simple tests, such as the arm weight test, in which I ordered her to stretch out her left arm at right angle in front of her. Then I told her to place the forefinger of her other hand directly under the palm of the outstretched hand. I told her that this arm was totally limp, paralyzed, and supported by one finger. As proof, I instructed her to withdraw the supporting forefinger. The outstretched arm fell down instantly and without hesitation, as if indeed it was limp and paralyzed.

In another test, I made her stand up, with her eyes closed, her hands at her side and her feet together. I told her that her body was a plank of wood. I asked somebody from the audience to come up, stand behind her, and place a finger on the back of her neck. I told her that this finger was supporting her and, if it were withdrawn, she would fall backwards, just like a plank of wood. Then I signaled the person to withdraw his finger. Silvia swayed backwards and tumbled into his arms for all to see.

But the last two demonstrations had the greatest success. With Silvia still in trance, I pulled a pencil out of my pocket, telling her that this was a red hot poker and that it would produce a blister if I touched her with it. Then I quickly touched her left arm with the pencil in two places. Immediately, a big red blister appeared in each spot.

This provoked great excitement in the audience. People rose to their feet, trying to get a better view of the blisters. It took a big effort to make them sit down again. For a minute I was really afraid that Silvia would wake up from her trance and the rest of the demonstration would be ruined.

But the audience calmed down and I could proceed with my last experiment. Now I was going to apply an "anesthetic" solution to Silvia's skin and insert a needle in her arm, telling her that she wouldn't feel anything.

In reality, I rubbed her skin with an alcohol swab, having displayed the bottle of alcohol for all to see. I inserted a thick needle into her arm. She didn't move and didn't react, as if a real anesthetic had been rubbed into her skin.

At the end of the meeting, before the lights went on, I had Silvia wheeled back to her room. I didn't want her to be awakened by the applause and I didn't want her to see "Joel" and the Stein family in the audience.

After she left, many people came up to congratulate me. Dr. Georgescu made me shake hands with his Jewish friends. I recognized Joel Gold. He had been two years my junior in medical school. Colleagues and friends had said that we resembled each other and had asked me whether we were related. This had upset me greatly because I didn't want to be confused with any Jew. Nevertheless, I shook hands with him in order to please Dr. Georgescu. I wish that he himself would drop this unsavory association.

SILVIA

SILVIA IS SITTING ON A bench in the hospital park watching the birds. It is warm and sunny. Now and then a slight breeze moves the leaves in the trees and ruffles the locks of her hair. She has gathered a small bouquet of daisies and snapdragons which she holds in her hand. She feels at peace, much more so than ever before.

The day she was brought to the hospital seems far away. It seems as if it happened in a dream or to somebody else. Since her treatments with Dr. Milo and even though she remembers a great deal, everything seems distant. It feels like watching a movie: everything is out there, behind a curtain of fog. Nothing is touching her now. She doesn't ruminate about the past. She lives day by day in the hospital the way Dr. Milo has taught her. She trusts the good doctor. He knows everything and he promises her that she will be all right.

She catches herself thinking about him during the day and wishing to give him the flowers. What would he say if she brought him the daisies and snapdragons? She isn't quite sure. But she can't wait to meet with him in the morning.

In the beginning of her hospitalization, things were different. That very first night she was awakened from deep sleep by loud howling and a deafening noise, like metal bars hitting on metal. She didn't know where she was. She thought that it was the end of the world and the beginning of the Last Judgment. She ducked under the covers and prepared herself for Hell and its cauldrons of boiling pitch.

Fortunately, after time that seemed endless, the howling stopped and she went back to sleep until morning. Then, too, she was scared. She still didn't know where she was and it took some time until Dr. Milo explained to her that she was in a Mental Hospital receiving treatment.

This place is still frightening at times, even though she has her own room. She knows this is a special favor and she is grateful to Dr. Milo for placing her there.

But even though her room is separated from the big wards, she quickly learned what was happening there. One night, a young woman escaped from the ward and ran into the corridor without wearing any clothes. Her thin body was covered with dirt, and she was screaming and cursing.

When the nurses and orderlies caught up with her, they threw her against the wall banging her head and hitting her with their fists, until blood was streaming out of her mouth. Finally, two orderlies pinned her to the floor and Rita, the fat nurse, gave her an injection with a long needle and a large syringe. Then they strapped her into a straitjacket and wheeled her away, without wiping the blood from her face.

After this, Silvia didn't dare walk alone outside her room for several days. But she couldn't avoid seeing what was going on inside those wards for she has to pass them on her way to Dr. Milo's office.

In the morning, the doors stand ajar. She first reaches the hall of the syphilitics, the men suffering from progressive paralysis, the last stage of the disease. The stench in that room is unbearable. The thirty rusty beds without sheets are occupied by thirty shapeless, moaning human hulks. In the middle of their faces, where their noses should be, is a gaping black hole since the tissues have been eaten away by the deadly bacteria.

Further down is the ward of the severe schizophrenics, where half-naked, wild-looking men with bloodshot eyes are cursing and raging. Others are giving fiery sermons and calling themselves God, Messiah or Napoleon. When she is wheeled past that ward, Silvia shuts her eyes and covers her ears.

For ten days now, she has been allowed to walk in the garden after her session with Dr. Milo. This morning, as she sits quietly on the bench, arranging her wildflowers, an old woman in a tattered hospital coat stops next to her. On her head she wears the remains of a once magnificent straw hat—a wide, yellow brim, to which she has fastened a wilted rose.

Her thin face looks like a dried prune and her mud-caked feet are stuck in old slippers. From her right hand dangles the greasy skeleton of a dead fish.

"Princess," she says, as she raises the fish toward Silvia's face, "this sacred relic, the holy bone from the body of Saint Sisoe, knows everything about you. It tells me that you took a long boat ride over the ocean when you were very young."

Silvia listens to her in amazement. She is spellbound by this woman. How does she know these things? Is she a mind reader? Does she get messages which Silvia cannot hear? Or is it the illness which makes her so sharp? She would like to ask these questions, but before she does, the woman goes on: "You also dreamed of marrying a man whose name started with "J", but the Saint is telling me that this is changing now. Sssshhhht! Wait, I can't hear what he says!"

The old woman lifts the fish to her ear, trying to listen. To hear better, she takes off her hat. Now Silvia can see an army of lice crawling in her hair and in her sparse eyebrows. She feels sickened by what she sees, yet she is still fascinated by what she hears. "Yes, yes, that name, that letter is changing now. The Saint is telling me about your future!"

In her excitement, the old woman takes a step toward Silvia and throws her hat in Silvia's lap. This makes Silvia jump to her feet and let the yellow brim with the rose slide to the ground—her terror of lice being greater than her wish to know the future.

She turns around and runs toward the far end of the garden, following the path, until she reaches what looks like a small vegetable garden. Here she plops herself on a green bench and starts watching men working in the beds of lettuce, tomatoes, eggplants and cucumbers. They are all hospital patients. They are probably "chronics" who have lived here for many years and have been forgotten by their families. They are all very thin, disheveled and dressed in hospital robes which have turned to rags.

As she is watching them troweling the earth, weeding and watering the plants, she hears footsteps behind her. She turns around and sees a small man with a large fedora and a gray beard. His glasses are broken and his silk tie is badly frayed. He wears a torn jacket and no shirt. In one hand, he carries a pile of papers covered with musical notes and, in the other, a conductor's baton. He stops in front of Silvia's bench, bows deeply touching the fedora with the baton, and says, "With whom do I have the honor? But first, let me introduce myself: I am Tchaikowsky, Pyotr Tchaikowsky, and I have just finished the Overture 1812. You see, here it is on these pages, the entire Overture." He leafs through the pages and pushes them under Silvia's nose.

"His Highness, our Great Tsar Nicholas I, has commissioned this piece. He is a very wise man and God has blessed him to have me as his advisor! It was I who organized his campaign against Napoleon and made him victorious. I advised him to chase the French Army back over Europe and into France. Our troops could have occupied Paris, but I told the Tsar to stop them, for fear of destroying that marvelous city!

I want to tell you that the premiere, the opening of my Overture 1812 will be this Sunday at the Winter Palace, and I will ask the Tsar to send you a special invitation. A beautiful lady like you belongs in the Royal Box.."

Silvia listens to him and smiles. Even though she knows that he is not really Tchaikowsky and the invitation to the Winter Palace is only fantasy, she can imagine the splendor of this unique theater. She hears the sounds of the overture with the broken fragments of the *Marseillaise* and pictures herself sitting in the Royal Box. Her face is hidden behind a shimmering fan, leaning toward the Tsar, whose broad chest is entirely covered with medals.

"This is how it goes," says the little man. "First, the violins, then the cellos and now the trumpets and the flutes." In his excitement, he jumps on the bench, stands on his toes, and conducts a large, invisible orchestra.

After about ten minutes he stops, Silvia applauds and laughs. "Bravo! Bravo!," she cries, as the man bows deeply and salutes, touching his hat with his baton. Then he shuffles the sheets of music and starts humming another composition. He moves his body and his arms slower and gracefully. Silvia recognizes the Swan Lake Ballet. She remembers that as a schoolgirl she wanted to become a ballerina and practiced in front of the mirror of an old armoire. She nods thoughtfully, claps her hands again. Finally, he sits next to her on the bench.

"Domnița," he says as he gathers his papers. "It is a great pleasure to rehearse the orchestra with you. Had I met you earlier, I would have certainly dedicated the Swan Lake to you! Soon I will tour Europe and conduct my greatest compositions, including the *Symphonie Pathétique* in Vienna, Paris and London. I know it will be a great success. All the kings and princes of Europe will invite me to their table and shower me with gifts. When I come back, I will..."

But he cannot finish his sentence. Rapid footsteps accompanied by loud panting are approaching. An agitated haggard-looking young man comes running around the corner. His face is dark purple and swollen. His unkempt hair is drenched with sweat. His eyes are red and have no focus. Froth has formed around his mouth and drips down his chest. He looks ready to attack anybody who crosses his path.

As he comes running—unsteady on his feet, he bumps into one of the inmates who is pushing a wheelbarrow filled with rocks. The wheelbarrow turns over and all the stones spill out.

"What the hell are you doing?" yells the man with the wheelbarrow. Then he sees the other man's red face and the froth at his mouth and screams, "Beware! Rabies! Rabies! A rabid man! (*Atenție! Un turbat!*) and starts hurling rocks at him.

The word spreads quickly. From all directions, pale figures in torn pajamas and hospital robes come running and aim stones at the intruder.

The man stares at them without understanding what is going on. His face turns more purple and more froth keeps dripping down his chest. The rocks come flying from all directions, and the man tries to protect himself by raising his arms and hiding his face. Then, suddenly, a heavy rock hits his skull. He gives a cry, loses his balance and sinks to the ground.

Meanwhile, Silvia covers her eyes, while Pyotr Tchaikowsky watches the whole scene perched on the bench.

"What are you doing?" he yells at the men. "Stoning an innocent? You're killing him! Who among you isn't a sinner? Who has the right to throw a stone?" He drops the sheets of music and runs to save the fallen man. But the inmates cannot stop: they keep hurling rocks, as they encircle the men.

"Pyotr Tchaikowsky" picks up a handful of rocks and throws them at his attackers, but he is met with a shower of stones. He reaches the other man, crouches near him, and tries to pull him from under the heap of rocks. He doesn't succeed. So as he starts removing the stones, a few men with wheelbarrows—advancing among the others—sneak up from behind. They turn over the wheelbarrows and empty the entire load on top of him, burying him underneath. And even though the two victims lie now motionless under the stones, the attackers continue hurling rocks and screaming.

When the guards and the orderlies finally arrive at the scene and subdue the inmates with hoses of cold water, they find Silvia lying unconscious under the green bench. They carry her to the main building where Dr. Milo listens silently to their report.

The next morning, before being taken to Dr. Milo's office, Silvia covers her face with her hands and doesn't want to talk. Like on the first day at the hospital, she refuses to eat, to drink her tea, and to wash. They have to strap her into a straitjacket to bring her to his office. It is only there that she can be untied.

Even though at first she refuses to open her eyes and to speak to him, Dr. Milo coaxes her to cooperate by telling her that she is his best patient ever and he knows he can rely on her more than on anybody else!

Silvia listens to him. After she calms down, he puts her in a trance by ordering her to relax her whole body—her arms and her legs—until she goes totally limp. Then he deepens the trance progressively by laying his hands on her forehead and pressing gently against her temples.

In her sleep, Silvia tells him what happened the day before and how frightened she was. "I was sure they had stoned me, too. I thought I was dead. But when I opened my eyes and saw that I was still alive, I became very scared. I kept seeing them and hearing them everywhere. They are watching me, following me all the time, day and night."

Dr. Milo reinforces her trance, telling her again to relax all her muscles, until she feels totally limp. To shut her eyes slightly and let go of the fear. "Imagine that you are Joan of Arc and you are leading an army into battle. You don't know fear and pain! Just like Joan of Arc at the head of her army, all you know is the victory for a holy cause. Pain, death, even danger—don't matter to you. You rise above them in your quest!"

After this session, Silvia, is still withdrawn and agitated. She sleeps better at night, but she still refuses to eat her meals, drink her tea or walk in the park. It takes about ten sessions of deep hypnosis for her fears to diminish.

When she is finally well enough to venture outside, she is still too afraid to pick flowers. She sits on a bench close to the Administration Building. She gets up and walks away as soon as another patient sits next to her or starts a conversation. Whenever the old lady with the straw hat and the dead fish appears in the distance, she jumps up in terror and runs to her room.

The days go by and she slowly continues to improve—little by little she spends more time in the garden. One morning she makes herself a small wreath of daisies and wild snapdragons. She even starts exchanging a few words with the orderlies and the nurse's aides. It is in the middle of this week that Dr. Georgescu decides to discuss Silvia's discharge from the hospital with Dr. Milo and Stella, Nina Stein's sister.

They are all sitting in Dr. Georgescu's large office, sipping hot Turkish coffee and smoking. Like usual, the doctor's desk is littered with patients' charts and medical journals squeezed between large pots of orchids in bloom.

"But where can she go?" asks the doctor, while picking a wilted flower from one of the pots. "Certainly not back to the Stein family nor to her father and stepmother's village in Transylvania. Yes, where can she go?"

"The best would be a furnished room in somebody's..."

"...in a widow's apartment!" Dr. Milo finishes Stella's sentence. The lab coat which he is wearing over his bare torso is unbuttoned, showing his tanned, hairy chest. With one hand he is leafing through Silvia's chart and with the other he is brushing his curls from his forehead. "But who will pay? She cannot work yet!"

"That's no problem," says Stella.

Adrian wants to pay all her expenses at least for one year. Here is the money for the next three months."

She puts the silver cigarette holder with the lit cigarette in an ashtray, folds the fan in her lap, and takes an envelope out of her purse. Her fingernails are as red as her lips and the roses on her summer dress.

"My sister Nina has also given me Silvia's belongings." She points to two bulky valises an orderly has brought into the room. "Everything is in here. Even her winter coat and her snow boots. Only her guitar is still at the house. We all felt it was too fragile and too precious to be dragged around. Well, any suggestions as to where she might go?"

"Give me some time to think." Dr. Georgescu is pulling distractedly at a strand of long hair behind his right ear, while inspecting another flower pot.

"Come to think of it, I have an aunt who could rent Silvia a room with access to kitchen and bathroom. Let me check with her," says Dr. Milo.

Dr. Georgescu nods.

"Alright, speak with her and I'll wait."

He finishes his coffee and turns the cup upside down on the saucer. Stella smiles, takes her cup and does the same thing. Then she says, "Here we are intelligent, educated people behaving like ignorant peasants who have faith in the magic of coffee grounds!"

Dr. Georgescu makes the cup spin in the saucer, without lifting it. He shrugs. "We scientists have no clues about the future. Anything can happen! Tea leaves and coffee grounds are just as good as our learned projections!"

He gives his cup another spin, then he stands up and paces around the room.

"However, speaking about the future, the near future, I mean, even though we allow Silvia to leave the hospital, she still needs treatment. Will you go on seeing her in the clinic?" he asks Dr. Milo.

"Yes, of course," the young man nods and his curls again fall on his forehead.

To Stella, he looks familiar. "Just like Joel," she thinks, as she turns toward the doctor.

"And don't worry about payment. Adrian will take care of it, for as long as it's needed."

A few days later, after Dr. Milo has checked with his aunt, Silvia moves into her apartment.

AT THE BLACK SEA

W HEN NADIA OPENS HER EYES, the sun is squeezing through the blinds, throwing patterns of light on the opposite wall. Swallows are chirping outside, and the regular rhythm of the sea sounds like the deep breathing of a large animal.

Nadia opens her eyes just a crack and watches the sunlight glide through her eyelashes and break into thousands of rainbows. She cannot sleep anymore, so she watches the moving patterns the sun paints on the wall. It makes her think of the movies of Charlie Chaplin and Laurel and Hardy. With her two hands, she now projects shadows on the wall: the head of a barking dog, a bird in flight—tricks Joel and Silvia have taught her.

She gazes at the bed to her right and sees that Mathilda is still sound asleep. In the bed to her left, Fräulein Lilly, the new governess, is snoring away.

At the foot of the bed are two large valises, covered with many colorful labels of foreign hotels, such as Hotel des Bains (Lido), Hotel Danieli (Venezia), Baur au Lac (Zürich), Beau Rivage (Geneva) and many others. Even though she cannot see the labels now, she knows that they are there and they illustrate places and hotels her parents have visited. She knows that when she leaves this resort, a new, colorful label with the words, "Hotel-Pension Perla Mării, Eforie" will be added to the others.

Nadia also thinks of the newer, more elegant valises her parents and Suzy have taken on their trip to Paris, to Italy and to Switzerland. Yes, her parents and Suzy have left on their trip just one day before herself. When Fritz and Marish carried the bags down to the waiting car which was to take them to the train station, Nadia's eyes filled with tears. "They're always going away and leaving me behind... and they're taking Suzy with them. It's even worse now since Silvia has vanished. Last year at least Silvia had been with us and had brought her guitar to the beach. But this year everything is so different," she thought.

After the night Silvia had tried to strangle herself, she never came back. Nadia had missed her and had hoped that Silvia would return. She was angry at her parents who were always vague about Silvia's whereabouts and changed the subject when Nadia asked too many questions. For some time, the guitar had been left in the room. Nadia had hoped that Silvia would soon be back. Even when her mother started interviewing other governesses, Nadia still secretly hoped that Silvia would show up again.

But one day the guitar disappeared: Aunt Stella and Uncle Sorel said that they were going to return it to Silvia. Then Nadia understood that she would never come back.

About this time, her mother hired Fräulein Lilly, a friend of her cousin's governess. She was a small, mousy looking woman with bad skin, black teeth and a sad look on her face. She talked very little and didn't like to sing. She spent most of her time fixing runs in silk stockings and crocheting woolen socks.

It wasn't only Silvia's absence and her parents' trip that upset Nadia. After the frightful night of the suicide attempt, she was plagued by nightmares. She would wake up screaming every morning at two, asking for the lights to be turned on.

For a short while, her mother allowed her to turn on the night light. But soon she stopped it and went back to "normal," saying that the child should not be too much indulged. Even though Nadia was still crying in the dark, her parents stuck to their plan for their trip abroad, hoping that this "unpleasant phase" would vanish with time.

So before she went on vacation, Nina and her house staff packed up the whole apartment to protect it from the sun and from dust. The carpets were rolled up against the wall. The couches, armchairs and the large paintings were covered with white bedsheets. All the lamps were packed in gauze. The whole apartment took on a ghostly air of desertion. The naked floor creaked at every step. This was a haunted house, Nadia thought.

Now, at the seaside, she looks through the cracks of the blinds at the golden light outside. She remembers that yesterday, just one day after her parents left, it had been her turn to take the Orient Express and travel to the Black Sea resort, Eforie, accompanied by Mathilda and Fräulein Lilly.

This trip by train always fascinated her. She loved the excitement of the big train station in Bucharest with the colorful crowd of passengers running in all directions, the porters with their red wagons filled with shiny trunks— shouting at the top of their voices, and the train conductors standing at attention in their navy-blue uniforms with gold buttons and braids. Stopping just under the train windows, peasants in their white, homespun pants and embroidered vests were selling pink lemonade and paper bags filled with popcorn and sunflower seeds. The whole station smelled of popcorn, charcoal and smoke.

Fritz had driven them to the station and had handed their valises to a porter with a red wagon. Then they had climbed onto the train and made themselves comfortable in a large compartment with lush velvet couches. Nadia loved the softness of these seats. She chose the spot near the window and nestled in a corner. But after a moment she stood up, made a few steps and ran her finger along the brass lighting fixture, the luggage rack, and the marquetry panels that lined the walls of the compartment. She loved the coolness of the metal fixtures and the smoothness of the paneling. Then before going back to her seat, she took off her sandals and buried her big toe in the soft carpet which covered the floor. Finally, the whistle blew and the train started to move.

As soon as it left the station, the passengers were invited to the dining car.

She now smiles when she thinks of how happy she felt sitting at the table covered with the starched damask tablecloth and the white linen napkin spread out on her lap.

A young waiter in a black jacket and white gloves poured chocolate in her gold-rimmed cup and added a helping of whipped cream from a crystal goblet. Then he placed a buttered croissant with wild cherry preserve on her plate. He made her feel very important. She fancied herself to be a young celebrity, fussed over by adoring fans.

While she was eating her breakfast, the train gained speed. Even though it swayed from side to side in the rhythm of the *Blue Danube* waltz, which filled the air, the young waiter kept perfect control of his heavy tray and silver teapots. "He must be a ballet dancer or an acrobat!" Nadia thought full of admiration.

She ate her croissant in tiny bites. She was in no hurry to return to her compartment. They were rolling through green cornfields dotted with red poppies, along village roads covered with dust and crowded with sheep, chickens and donkeys, as well as swamps teeming with wild geese and storks. In the distance she saw a long row of poplars and willows, announcing the presence of a river. Soon they thundered across the metal bridge which spans the Danube at Cernavodā.

On the far side of the river, there were no more cornfields or groves of green trees. The hilly land was hard and dry, covered with pale sand and dust. At the end of the road glimmered the black and silver line of the sea.

After a while, the train slowed down and stopped just long enough in the small station of Eforie to allow them to get off and unload their luggage. They were met by a bearded man with a red fez who carried their valises to a carriage decorated with garlands of blue paper roses and drawn by two donkeys. Their reins were also decorated with paper roses. As soon as they climbed in the carriage, the coachman cracked his whip and the two donkeys started to trot.

A mild breeze stroked their face and ruffled the leaves of the wild olive trees which bordered the street. The leaves shone like silver.

They passed a row of whitewashed villas surrounded by narrow flower gardens and hidden behind the trees. They reached a dirt road leading to the old Tartar village with its clay huts dug into the hills. A few Turkish and Tartarian fishermen watched them from their coffeehouse, while smoking their *norghilea* or sipping *braga*.

The carriage kept descending toward the sea until it reached a pension called *Perla Mării*—the Pearl of the Sea, an imposing, gleaming white hotel with many balconies overflowing with geraniums and petunias. They stopped here, and the coachman unloaded their luggage.

"*Am ajuns cu bine!*" (We made it in one piece!) said Aunt Mathilda as she powdered her nose. "It was a good trip!" she added. Then they all climbed down from the carriage and walked to the reception area. She gave the coachman five lei tip, after which a bellboy in a white uniform with gold trimmings—just like a steward on a steamship—took their valises and carried them up a carpeted stair.

Now in her room, Nadia sits up in her bed and stares out the window. She hears wings fluttering and loud chirping. The baby swallows are learning to fly. But in the room, both Aunt Mathilda and Fräulein Lilly are still asleep. Nadia wants to cry out, clap her hands, whistle, make noise to wake them up and get going. But she doesn't dare because she doesn't know what time it is. As she watches them, she remembers yesterday and bites her lip so as not to laugh. As soon as they were in their room and the two women were busy unpacking, Nadia tore open her own small bag, hid in the bathroom and put on her yellow swimsuit. Then she raced down to the beach. She was so eager to get to the sea that she dashed out without saying a word. All year long she had dreamed of this moment. She ran down the wide staircase and the long corridor which leads to the courtyard, then followed the garden path, opened the wooden gate, and, after crossing the street, she rushed down the steep wooden stair which led to the beach. She almost flew over the burning sand and jumped into the waves.

She swam a few strong laps away from the shore, then turned on her back and floated motionless, staring into the sky. Her entire being was becoming one with the sea and the air, dissolving into weightlessness. She forgot about Aunt Mathilda and Fräulein Lilly, about her parents and Suzy. All she could think about was the sea and the sky. Weightless. Transparent like the air.

But soon the shrill whistle of the *Salvamar* (Lifeguard) and his red boat speeding in her direction startled her out of her dream. She swam back toward the shore, keeping the hotel in direct view. She reached the beach and stepped out of the water. She saw Aunt Mathilda waiting for her, with a large blue towel in her hands.

"She is going to scold me and punish me," Nadia said to herself. "She looks very angry!"

But Aunt Mathilda neither scolded nor punished her. She only wrapped her in the blue towel. Nadia remembers how much she hated the towel ordeal. It made her feel like a baby.

After they finish breakfast, they head for the beach. Aunt Mathilda and Fräulein Lilly wear big straw hats and carry bags filled with large towels, reserve bathing suits, swim caps and suntan lotion. They walk down the wobbly stairs very slowly, holding on, with one hand, to the broken railing. Nadia, who has run ahead, waits for them at the foot of the stairs. She looks up and realizes again how steep this cliff top really is—a ravine of calcareous stone, with the sea at the bottom.

Here, the beach is not very wide—a long strip of sand dotted with rows of colorful tents and umbrellas. As they walk, they are met by naked toddlers armed with toy pails and shovels with which they are building sand castles at the edge of the water. They shriek at the top of their voices whenever the waves swallow their constructions and drown them in a whirlpool of foam.

Mathilda stops to lease a tent from a boy who wears a fez with a crescent moon and a silver star. He looks about 14 and stands barefoot in the burning sand. A torn shirt tucked in his striped pants covers his tanned arms and shoulders. He has short black hair, narrow eyes with long lashes, high cheek bones and shiny white teeth.

"*Salaam Alecum!*" he says to Mathilda. Nadia recognizes Skender, the fisherman's son from the nearby Tartar village.

"Where is your father?" asks Mathilda. Skender shrugs.

"He isn't here. He went fishing with my uncles. But I take care of business when he's not around."

Nadia keeps looking at Skender. She remembers him well from last year when he was friends with her cousin Theo. She would like to talk to him, but doesn't dare.

When their tent is set up, Mathilda and Fräulein Lilly take off their dresses and lie down on the large beach towel they have spread on the sand. They rub their bodies with suntan lotion. Fräulein Lilly tries to put some on Nadia's shoulders.

"No! No! I don't need that! I hate this greasy stuff!" she cries, pushing Fräulein Lilly's hand away so forcefully that half the bottle spills in the sand. Then she feels upset about her clumsiness, but she does not apologize to Fräulein Lilly.

They all lie motionless on their backs. Nadia gazes into the burning sun listening to the shrieks of the seagulls and the rhythmical sound of the waves. But after a few minutes, she becomes restless. Something inside her forces her to get up and wander along the water's edge toward the jetty where the old lighthouse stands. She follows the shoreline until it makes a turn and she can see the long, gray jetty with the lighthouse standing at its furthest tip.

Nadia steps on the pointed rocks and then follows the path to the building. She opens the rusty gate and climbs the winding stairs. She has been here before with Theo and Skender. She knows this old tower very well. It is always deserted during the day, except for the small creatures who live in the cracks of the walls and the swallows who nest under the eaves.

Now, a frightened lizard runs over her bare feet, stops, looks at her with beady eyes and vanishes in the dark.

She goes on climbing the stairs. When she reaches the top, she steps out on the narrow terrace wrapped around the tower. From here she can look in all directions. She sees the yellow hills which border the subterranean Tartar village with its dwellings dug into the earth or hidden behind tall walls of clay, the mosque with its pointed minaret, and the ancient cemetery at the edge of the cliff.

On the opposite side of the lighthouse is the *ghiol*, the lake celebrated for its healing powers—its thick and foul smelling waters are rich in sulfurous mud. Further in the distance, perched on a rock like on the promontory of a ship stands the casino with its bulbous roof. To Nadia, it looks like a witch's castle.

She stares far away at the horizon, wonders what lies beyond the sea? The sky and water look endless, yet at the same time, they seem to melt into each other. Cousin Theo has told her that you can climb into the sky on an invisible stair.

But where is Theo? Will he join them this year? Things were always so much more fun with him! Together they could go to the end of the world. He always had so many ideas and knew so many stories. And then, he was also friends with Skender. Nadia remembers the good time the three of them had together when Skender showed them the old subterranean tunnels of the Tartar village, which go back to the time of Genghis Khan.

As she stands on the terrace, a warm breeze is touching her face and stirring the water. In the whistling of the wind and the drone of the sea, she seems to hear human voices and the gallop of horses. She checks to see where they're coming from. When she doesn't see anything she remembers the stories about the Island of Leuce—that mysterious island which, it is said, was hidden far away in the Black Sea and where the ghosts of ancient Greek warriors are still frolicking and singing. Theo and Skender have told her many stories about the ghosts of these heroes who were in exile and forced to live on this island.

There are other tales: the old widows of fishermen who have drowned at sea swear that the rocky island is inhabited by mermaids and nymphs who sing sweetly to the boatmen, tempting them to come to the island until their boats shatter on the rocks. They say that the island is always shrouded in fog and the sailors can never tell when they're nearing the cliffs. Nobody has ever seen the Island of Leuce. Theo said that it becomes visible only once in a hundred years and that whoever sees it is struck with blindness for the rest of his life.

Nadia looks into the deep waters and remembers all the stories Theo and Skender have told her about the kingdom of Poseidon and the strange beings who lived under his rule. They told her that there were monsters with six heads who were barking like dogs, others who were half women and half serpents who dragged men into caves and devoured them raw, and still others who had a hundred eyes and whispered in human voices. But scariest of all was the "Killer Octopus," the giant creature who attacks shipwrecked sailors, pulls them apart with its tentacles and sucks the flesh from their bones.

"This monster can come ashore and attack people during the night," Theo said. "It can climb over fences and into trees. It is frightfully ugly and it smells so bad that it can kill its victims with its breath."

Nadia didn't know whether to believe him or not. But these stories always scared her and made her shudder. Now she keeps on scanning the water. Some place, not too far from the lighthouse, lies the "Shining Rock," submerged under the sea. It can be seen sometimes, on moonless nights, people say. Nadia keeps searching the water, even though it is bright sunlight now. For Theo and Skender have said that it marks the spot where a pirate ship sank a long time ago. The ship came from Turkey or even from further East. It carried large coffers of gold, silver and diamonds. The captain's quarters were richly decorated with brocades and silk. "It was a slave ship!" Theo said. "These pirates caught and abducted young girls from these shores and took them to Istanbul, where they sold them to the Sultan and to his pashas for their harems. Only the most beautiful girls made it to Istanbul. The others were pushed into the Black Sea before they reached half the trip. I think we should try to look for the rock," Theo added. "Can you get your father's fishing boat so we can get near it?" he had asked Skender. "That would be a fine adventure."

At first Skender didn't answer. He didn't say no. He had only scratched his head. "I'll see what I can do," he had said in the end.

"Yes, it would be a fine adventure," Nadia is thinking now. But she needs Theo to do it. Will he join them this summer? She doesn't know and couldn't find out. His parents didn't say anything. It would be a sad summer without him, a very sad, boring summer just with Fräulein Lilly and Aunt Mathilda! Nadia sighs as she stands on the lighthouse terrace and scans the crowded beach, trying to find the green and yellow tent. But the air is so hazy and the white glare so strong, every color is bleached out. The sun burns like fire.

She finally turns around and starts climbing down the narrow stairs.

THE BIRTHDAY PARTY

S HE WALKS QUICKLY ALONG THE beach and when she reaches the tent, things don't go as smoothly as yesterday. Aunt Mathilda is both worried and angry. Her face is deep red under her large straw hat. She takes Nadia under the tent for a serious grownup talk in all privacy. Sweat is dripping down her face, but she doesn't take off her hat.

"You cannot do this," she tells Nadia, "disappearing like this for hours without asking permission or telling us where you're going. I was so worried that something had happened to you. Fräulein Lilly said we should call the police." Mathilda's eyes are very dark and her face is stern. "I've promised your parents that I'll take good care of you, but you have to cooperate." Mathilda bends her face toward Nadia and speaks in a low voice: "I'm afraid Fräulein Lilly won't stay with us if you don't behave, and then good-bye Eforie! We'll have to go back home."

Nadia looks at Aunt Mathilda's nose which shines in the dark and says, "She can go if she doesn't like it here, but we don't have to leave. We can stay here without her!" She smiles thinking how nice it would be without Fräulein Lilly.

"That's not what I mean." Aunt Mathilda frowns as she speaks. "If she goes, we go. It's as simple as that. So you better behave! By the way, this afternoon you're invited to Anca

Georgescu's birthday party. You'll go there with Fräulein Lilly at 5 o'clock. I might come by in the evening."

Nadia stares at Aunt Mathilda and nods mechanically. Then she turns away and sighs. She looks at her knees all covered with scratches. Here and there is a dried blood stain. She knows that going to that party means scrubbing away the blood from her skin, washing the salt out of her hair, shaking the sand out of every skin fold and hiding place. As much as one showers and scrubs, it's never enough. Nadia doesn't really want to go to this party because she knows she will have to be on her best behavior and watch her dress, her shoes and her socks.

When they go home they have lunch in the garden shaded by colored umbrellas and potted palm trees. Then it's up to the room and under the shower.

At four-thirty, Fräulein Lilly pulls the white organdy dress with pink roses over Nadia's head and slips on her white socks and white patent-leather shoes. Nadia could have done all this by herself, but Fräulein Lilly doesn't want her to rip or stain the new dress.

She felt all tingling and cool after the shower, but now the stiff fabric scratches her skin and the shoes are too tight and too warm. When she is ready, Fräulein Lilly tries to place a small straw hat on her head. But this is too much for Nadia. She pulls it off and throws it on the floor. Aunt Mathilda comes to the rescue, and they compromise on a silk bow in Nadia's hair.

They arrive at the party ten minutes later than planned, because the silk bow didn't sit right and had to be adjusted a few times.

Dr. Georgescu and his children, Anca and Paul, live in an elegant villa, not too far from the promenade on the way to the casino. The villa has its own swimming pool and tennis court. Chauffeured cars with fashionable people are constantly coming and going. Aunt Mathilda has told Nadia that Dr. Georgescu has to stay in this villa to be close to the Queen, who is his patient.

When they arrive at the villa, a few guests are already there. Anca, who has just turned 11 and has blond, curly hair, large teeth and a dimple in her chin, quickly tears the wrapping paper and opens the big box Nadia has brought. Inside is a toy loom made of wood with all its miniature parts and the beginning of a red woolen scarf for a doll. Paul and his friend try to snatch the loom out of Anca's hands to see how it works and how it is made. This scuffle almost turns into a fist fight, but it is interrupted by the arrival of other children with gifts. They all carry big boxes wrapped in colorful paper. As soon as they enter the house, the girls run to look at Anca's collection of dolls and her new dollhouse with bedroom, living room, kitchen and bathroom, while the boys rush to see Paul's kites, toy guns and Swiss Army knives.

But the greatest attraction this year is Paul's new dynamo, a system of steel wheels linked to each other, which is set in motion by electricity. The wheels of the dynamo make a lot of noise and send off as many sparks as a firecracker. The boys gather around it and marvel at its technical intricacies. Paul, in particular, has been so fascinated by it and has handled it so many times, that he has ended up cutting his hand at the fast turning wheels.

"You're lucky you didn't lose your finger!" said his father, Dr. Georgescu, as he wrapped his hand in a white bandage which Paul now proudly displays.

Nadia has no enthusiasm for the dynamo, nor does she like to play with dolls. She misses Corinna and Theo, her cousins, who are also friends with Anca and Paul and were here last year. She stands on the terrace and stares into the garden with the pool and the high diving board flanked by the swing and the parallel bars. If Theo were here, they would certainly run downstairs, try the parallel bars and dive into the pool. She can see herself swooping down through the air and hitting the water with a big splash. But her thoughts are suddenly interrupted:

"Come on everybody. We're going to play a game!" shouts Schwester Karla, Anca and Paul's governess. "Everybody in the garden! We'll draw lots to see who is the first player!"

Schwester Karla is tall and bony with big hands and feet and the voice of a bullhorn. Her blond hair is short and neatly held in place by two shiny pins. Her sharp eyes never blink, and her unsmiling face resembles a mask. People listen whenever she speaks. "Let's go now!" she says, as she points toward the garden. Everybody starts moving in that direction.

The children draw lots and the first chosen is Nicu, Paul's best friend, a short, fat boy with a high-pitched voice who is shy. He turns deep red as he is being blindfolded with a green bandana.

Schwester Karla spins him around a few times while the circle of children moves around him in the opposite direction. He stumbles helplessly in the middle, making the others giggle. But as he trips around, he manages to catch onto Anca. Now it is her turn to stand in the center.

After a few more rounds, the lots fall on Nadia and she steps in the middle of the circle. Like before, everybody cheers and applauds. But she feels suddenly frightened. She is the youngest here and doesn't even know all the other children. Schwester Karla's bony hands fasten the bandana tightly over her eyes, and then spin her around, faster and faster. She feels dizzy and wants to stop, but she can't. If she falls, all the others will laugh and make fun of her. She must keep her balance and steady herself on her feet. Now blindfolded and with closed eyes she stretches her arms as far as she can, but catches nothing but air. She hears laughter at her right, then whispers to the left. But when she turns in that direction, there is nobody there. It feels as if the circle is moving away and out of her grasp. She wonders whether and how she'll catch onto them. She strains to listen, then she suddenly tenses her muscles and jumps like a cat. Now she grabs Paul's bandaged hand in her own.

"Au! This hurts!" he screams as he pulls out his hand, leaving the bandage hanging from Nadia's fingers. He scampers away while she tries to get rid of the clinging gauze. People laugh. What should she do next? Untie the bandana? Run after another player? The children keep laughing and screaming.

"It's Paul's turn!" shout the girls.

"No! No! Nadia must stay for another game!" yell the boys.

She raises her hand to the kerchief and tries to move it or open the knot, but the more she tries, the tighter it gets. Then, in the general confusion, she is suddenly saved. A loud gong sounds on the terrace and Schwester Karla calls everybody to come up and eat. At the same time, the bandana finally loosens up and she joins the others in the big dining room.

The round table is covered with a starched damask tablecloth, on which gleaming crystal platters are set. Some are filled with devilled eggs; others with small sandwiches of beluga and salmon caviar. Others have goat and Swiss cheese or sandwiches of liverwurst, salami and ham in aspic—all decorated with black olives, red peppers and thin, almost transparent slices of cucumbers. Nadia plops herself in a chair next to a round platter filled with caviar sandwiches. She is so fascinated by their sight and smell, she piles her plate high with the black and red sandwiches and wolfs them down with her eyes shut. She stuffs her mouth full. When her hands are all smeared and sticky with caviar, she lets them drop in her lap, ready to wipe her fingers on her dress before helping herself to more.

But at the same moment, Fräulein Lilly swoops down on her like a bird of prey, grabs her wrists and hisses: "No! No! not on your organdy dress!" as she pulls Nadia out of her chair and rushes her toward the bathroom.

When they're inside and after the door is closed, Fräulein Lilly scrubs Nadia's hands in the sink with a heavy brush, making sure that no drop of water or soap splashes onto her dress and white shoes.

"Shame on you! I can't believe your bad table manners!" she says, raising her voice over the running water. "A girl like you should be more careful and more delicate, not wild like a gypsy or a red Indian! Schwester Karla is right," she adds as she wipes Nadia's fingers with a terry-cloth towel. "You're so wild because you're always with Corinna and Theo, mostly with Theo. Schwester Karla won't let Anca and Paul spend time with them. They're too wild. They're not good for you either!"

"That's not true!" says Nadia, pulling her hands so quickly out of the towel that it falls to the floor. Nadia stamps her foot and clenches her fists. "I don't care what Schwester Karla has to say. She's not my friend, but Theo is my friend and my cousin. I will not give him up!" Then she storms out of the bathroom and slams the door.

She runs back to the dining room, just in time for the big chocolate cake with the burning candles which is brought from the kitchen.

After they finish the last bite of cake and the last sip of hot cocoa with whipped cream, the children decide to play a word game known as "*Telefonul fără Fir*" (Wireless Telephone) in the garden.

Everybody sits on a long bench, next to each other, and whispers a complicated word into each other's ear. The last person in line has to repeat the word aloud. If the word is distorted or incorrect, the last person remains in the same place until a word makes it correctly to the end. Then the last person in line moves to the head of the group and starts with a new word.

The children sit on a long wooden bench under the wisteria bower and are ready to start, when Paul suddenly stops them:

"Nadia shouldn't play with us. She is too young and won't know all the words! This is no Kindergarten!"

"If it's no Kindergarten, Nicu shouldn't play either. He isn't older than Nadia!" says Anca.

"He is good with words, so he can play!" says Paul.

"But today is my birthday, so I decide," shouts Anca who has climbed on a garden chair from where she surveys the scene. "When it's your birthday, you decide. So, in conclusion, no Nadia, no Nicu. All right, girls?" She asks her girlfriends, making a wide gesture with her arms.

"Yes, yes. No Nadia, no Nicu. All the girls shout and clap their hands.

"*Bine, bine* (All right, all right), we'll see in the end who is the winner!" Paul shrugs and raises his newly bandaged hand like a white flag of surrender. Then he joins the others on the wooden bench. Anca, who is the first in line, whispers a word in the ear of her neighbor, who passes it on to the next person.

"Milan!" cries the last in line.

"No, no, it was marzipan!" says Anca.

They go on playing, and many more words get distorted: Constantinopol becomes Xenopol, salamander turns into oleander, and Hortansa into Constanța. When it's Nadia's turn to be last in line and to say the word aloud, she doesn't wait for the whispered word to reach her. She bends over, watching the first person's lips, reading their movement, so that, even though the word which reaches her is distorted, she can repeat the original, correct word. She does this several times and she always wins.

"How do you do it? You must have magical powers!" says Anca, shaking her head. "From now on, you'll always play on my team, particularly when we're playing to score."

Nadia smiles. She feels very proud, almost like a grownup. There are always surprises and often when you least expect them, she thinks, as she moves to be first in line for the next game.

It is late when they leave. A large, orange moon hangs over the sea, and small blue and yellow lights flicker here and there in the Tartar village. Fräulein Lilly stops to admire the moon and to listen to the sound of the saxophone which comes from the terrace. Her face has a calm, dreamy expression which makes her look like a different person—somebody Nadia has never seen.

They both watch a few couples dancing in the moonlight, and Nadia wonders whether Aunt Mathilda is among them? She looks for her, but doesn't see her.

Nadia is relieved that the party is over. She would like to run to the lighthouse and check whether the burning rock is gleaming tonight. But Fräulein Lilly has stopped dreaming in the moonlight and is now marching next to her like a prison guard, poking her in the back with the tip of her bony fingers and directing her straight to the pension. Fräulein Lilly walks with jerky little steps which make her look like a big bird hopping along the road. Her limp curls and everything she wears—her little summer hat with the transparent voilette, the lace collar, her thin silver bracelets, bob up and down as she walks.

When they reach the corner of the promenade, Nadia sees a shimmering firefly in the dust. She stops and bends down to catch it, but it flies toward the grassy border of the avenue and Nadia runs after it. She bends down trying to catch it again, but the firefly vanishes among a swarm of other flickering bugs. She is so fascinated by this, she gets down on her knees and doesn't notice when her silk bow gets caught in the thorns of a rosebush. It slips out of her hair and trails in the dust.

"What are you doing here? Playing or praying in the dirt?" asks Fräulein Lilly who stands next to her. "Get up immediately and let's go!" She grabs Nadia's shoulder and tries to pull her to her feet. But Nadia pushes the nanny's hand away and mumbles under her breath. She is too fascinated by the dance of the fireflies to pay attention to the Governess and to the white bow.

Fräulein Lilly untangles the silk ribbon from the thorns of the rosebush, folds it carefully and slips it inside her purse. "All right, are you getting up? Are you coming? No? Very good. I'll tell Aunt Mathilda to come and get you herself. Goodbye!" she says as she snaps her purse shut and starts walking away with her small, jerky steps.

"Wait! Wait for me!" shouts Nadia, suddenly aware and frightened of the Nanny's departure. The thought of Aunt Mathilda coming down to get her is very troubling. It surely means leaving the sea and the beach and returning to Bucharest in no time at all.

"Please wait for me!" she begs again, as she gets up and runs after the Governess. But Fräulein Lilly keeps walking and pays no attention to her. She doesn't even turn her head once to check whether Nadia is coming. In the darkness, she can imagine the blank face with the tight lips, the blotchy skin and the black teeth. It is only when they pass the last corner before the pension that Fräulein Lilly finally breaks the silence.

"You should be ashamed of your reckless behavior! I have no words to describe it. But I promise you that you will be a different person when your parents come back from vacation. As a start, tomorrow afternoon, we'll go to the promenade and you'll play hoops with Anca and Paul. You can wear your white sailor suit with the navy stripes on the collar. It's the right dress for the promenade. Besides, there won't be any caviar sandwiches or hot chocolate with whipped cream to drip on your clothes," she adds as a joke.

Nadia cannot believe her ears: running after a hoop on the promenade, under the watchful eye of Schwester Karla and Fräulein Lilly! What a bore! What a humiliation! If Corinna and Theo would see her, they would make great fun and call her a baby." They may even stop playing with her.

She stares in silence at Fräulein Lilly and suddenly notices a dark, round chocolate stain on the front of her elegant blouse. It should be funny, but it doesn't make her laugh. She feels half avenged for her sufferings at the hands of the governess.

NADIA DREAMS...

T HAT NIGHT NADIA DREAMS THAT she is a circus acrobat. She is standing in the middle of the ring, dressed in her white sailor suit playing with a pink hoop. She cannot see the spectators, because the spotlight is focused on the center and the surrounding space is dark.

As the orchestra plays a march, she circles the arena, following closely a large lion who runs in front of her.

In the center of the ring stands the lion tamer with a whip, black leather boots with spurs and a black top hat. The lion tamer is a woman, and under her tailored jacket she wears a white lace blouse, just like Fräulein Lilly. When she comes closer, Nadia sees that she is indeed Fräulein Lilly. She stands erect and looks very tall. She holds a burning hoop in her raised hand.

The lion in front of Nadia advances toward the hoop, and as he does so, the drums beat louder and louder. Finally, at a few feet from the lion tamer, he slows down and then stops briefly. In the end, he tenses his muscles and jumps through the flames. The audience applauds, and now it is Nadia's turn to jump through the hoop. As she gets closer, she feels the heat of the flames. The blaze frightens her and she looks for an escape, but she doesn't find any. With every step the heat becomes more intense; the flames look more threatening.

Nadia closes her eyes, starts running, and jumps through the fire. The audience applauds. It sounds first like thunder and then like rushing water. The noise wakes her up. When she opens her eyes, she finds herself in bed, bathed in perspiration. It is morning and Aunt Mathilda is taking a shower. The door to the bathroom is open and the rushing water sounds like the applause in her dream.

On the other side of the room, near the armoire, Fräulein Lilly is busy preparing the white sailor suit for the afternoon, checking it for wrinkles and stains, and getting the matching white socks and shoes. When Aunt Mathilda steps out of the shower, Nadia watches her face in silence searching for a frown and wondering whether Fräulein Lilly has complained about her? But Aunt Mathilda smiles and asks her whether she had a good time at the birthday party. This convinces Nadia that she knows nothing about yesterday.

Later, while they are having breakfast on the terrace overlooking the sea, hundreds of swallows and their young fly around chirping. Fresh sparrows hop on the table nibbling the bread. From time to time Nadia sneaks a suspicious look at Fräulein Lilly.

"Eat your croissant and stop feeding the birds!" says Aunt Mathilda, as Nadia throws crumbs at several sparrows.

"Yes. Yes!" she nods, but she throws two more pieces of crust at her guests. Then she gets up and follows the two women inside the corridor and down to the street. They stop briefly for Fräulein Lilly to buy a bowl of creamy yogurt from the café next door, and start climbing down the rickety stairs which lead to the sea. In the distance, the fishing boats are already returning with their morning catch. High above the houses, from the top of the minaret comes the voice of the muezzin calling the faithful to prayer.

"Allah! Allah!" he calls, but the rest of the words get lost in the cries of the seagulls.

Down at the beach, Aunt Mathilda and Fräulein Lilly settle in front of their tent. Aunt Mathilda strips to her bathing suit, rubs her skin with suntan lotion and arranges her straw hat firmly on her head. Then she lies down on the large beach towel with "CHÉRI," the popular French novel by Colette.

Fräulein Lilly also takes off her dress and remains in her bathing suit, then she covers her face, her body and her shoulders with yogurt. She also wears a large straw hat, with an artificial red rose tucked into the ribbon, and she hides her nose under a large grape leaf which she has picked on the way. She sits up straight on the beach towel, pulls out the crochet needle and a ball of wool from her bulky handbag and starts work on a new pair of socks.

Nadia goes for a quick swim. The water is clear and calm like a big mirror and so transparent that she can see the countless schools of small, silvery fish, the water bugs, and the shimmering jellyfish floating by. She can count every pebble and shell on the bottom. When she has finished swimming, she stops near the water's edge and plunges her hand in the sand to scoop out a fistful of pink, white, and gold pebbles and shells. She takes them to the tent and returns to the water for more. She goes back and forth several times. When she has gathered a small heap, she sorts them by color and size. She then starts arranging them in a picture: a tall lighthouse appears in the sand and, next to it, a boat with billowing sails, surrounded by several large fish—all made of pebbles and shells. Nadia is so engrossed in her work that she tunes out everything around her—the shouts of children, the whistle of a train in the distance, even the calls of the birds circling over her head.

From the air, a few seagulls are watching the fish she forms on the beach. One bird drops a rock on the fish, trying to kill it; another one swoops down fiercely, attempting to catch it in its beak. Then all is quiet and she goes on setting the pebbles on the sand. But suddenly she starts and listens: a deep and joyful voice is hovering over her.

"Get up! Get up, lazy bones. Let's go swimming!"

Nadia looks up and, to her surprise, she sees Uncle Sorel's figure silhouetted against the sky.

"Uncle Sorel! Where are Corinna and Theo?" she jumps to her feet and runs to him.

"How come you're here? Where are the others?" asks Mathilda as she sits up and shields her eyes from the sun.

"Emergency. We had an emergency cable from Dr. Georgescu which made us pack and come right away." Sorel takes off his summer shirt and pants and remains in tight swimming trunks.

"Stella will explain!" He turns and looks toward his wife who is approaching in the distance. She waves at them as she steps carefully on the hot sand, moving her wide hips and full bosom voluptuously, like a belly dancer. She is barefoot and has lifted her flowery skirt above her knees, gathering it in one hand, while she carries a basket filled with towels, suntan lotion and a paper bag chock full with cherries and apricots in the other. As she comes closer, she trips, the paper bag falls and breaks, letting the cherries and apricots spill on the sand. She bends down to pick them up, but Theo and Corinna, who follow behind her, are faster. They pick up the spilled goodies and start a fight over them.

"You've got all the apricots!" shouts Theo.

"And you have all the cherries!" says Corinna.

"It's not fair!" they both scream. Theo clenches his fists and makes a step toward Corinna.

"Stop that at once!" orders Sorel. "Give me the fruit, both of you. You just had breakfast one hour ago. You'll eat the cherries and apricots after your swim. Now, ready everybody?"

"No, wait," shouts Corinna. "I have to pin up my braids!"

"You girls with your braids. You're always busy pinning them up or pinning them down!" says Theo. "I'm glad I don't have to bother with braids." He scoops water in his cupped hands and splashes Corinna who shrieks and runs after him.

"Enough already. Let's go!" Sorel darts into the sea, followed by Nadia, Corinna and Theo.

Sorel swims with strong strokes dipping under water and then coming to the surface again, his bald head gleaming in the sun. At first, Theo keeps up with him, but then Nadia overtakes Theo and swims next to her uncle. The water feels cool and soft like silk, and Nadia again thinks that she would never tire of this. Maybe she isn't even a regular human, maybe she is a kind of water creature, some sort of fish made to live in the sea.

Uncle Sorel is in no rush to return to the shore. He glides smoothly through the waves, as if he too were a prince of the sea. Nadia wishes that they could swim on and on, without ever stopping.

Meanwhile on the beach, Stella strips to her bathing suit and takes a stroll at the edge of the water with Mathilda.

"So how did you convince Sorel to give up his practice and come to the sea?" asks Mathilda as soon as they are alone.

"It all happened because of Victor Georgescu. He sent us an urgent cable asking Sorel to bring him a very special orchid which had just arrived from abroad, and which he had promised to give to the queen. Sorel immediately decided to leave his practice in the hands of Joel, and asked me to quickly pack all the bags. So here we are!"

"He certainly wouldn't have done this if you, or Joel or anybody else had asked him to!" Mathilda is shaking her head. The white foam of the surf is whirling around her ankles.

"You're right!" says Stella. "But Victor Georgescu and his orchids are a different matter."

They walk a little further in silence, watching the bathers play in the waves, and trying to find Sorel and the children among them.

"When are you bringing the orchid to Victor Georgescu?" asks Mathilda.

"This afternoon Nadia is invited to play hoops with Anca and Paul, the Georgescu children, on the promenade. Of course, Corinna and Theo can join them!" she adds.

Stella starts to laugh: "Corinna and Theo play hoops on the promenade? They will never do such a thing! They hate the promenade and they hate playing hoops. First, we have to bring the orchid to Victor's house. After that we can come back to the beach to swim or play volleyball. Or we can play ping pong in his garden! That will free the governesses, Fräulein Lilly and Schwester Karla, who will be delighted to sit on a bench on the promenade without the children!"

"A good idea!" nods Mathilda, as they turn around to go back to the tent.

But when they arrive, to Mathilda's surprise, Fräulein Lilly objects to the new schedule. She explains that Schwester Karla won't accept these last minute changes.

"She is a real German Junker for whom all planned programs are commitments graven in stone, which can never be altered."

But her words are lost in the general confusion: the hungry swimmers are back on the beach, devouring cherries and apricots and throwing the pits at each other.

THE GOLDEN ORCHID

A FEW HOURS LATER, THEY ALL go to Dr. Georgescu's villa. The three children run ahead, followed by Stella, Mathilda, Fräulein Lilly and Sorel, who carries the new orchid in a large cardboard box, wrapped in brown paper and tied with a cord. Everybody wears shorts and light sandals on their feet, except Fräulein Lilly who is dressed in an ivory lace blouse, a linen skirt, long silk stockings and suede pumps.

Stella wears shorts, sandals and a thin, sleeveless blouse, but she has spent more than half an hour in front of the mirror, brushing her long, black hair, putting on makeup and trying a new lipstick and a French perfume called "Orchidée."

"Do you want to seduce Dr. Georgescu?" Corinna has asked her, as she watched her mother trying to match a pair of silver earrings with a coral and silver necklace.

"Mind your own business and don't be fresh!" Stella has told her, only to hear Corinna snicker behind her back.

In truth, Stella is very excited by this visit. She has been thinking of the doctor and missing him for a while. It even looked as if they weren't going to meet this summer, even though he had promised to find a way to bring them to the sea. "It is all Sorel's fault!" Stella tells herself. Her husband,

Sorel, the pediatrician, was so busy with his practice and his Zionist meetings, he had made no vacation plans. At the same time, he didn't let Stella make separate plans with the children, since he wanted to take their vacation as a family.

But then, when the cable from Dr. Georgescu arrived from Eforie, asking him to urgently bring the new orchid for the queen, everything changed. Sorel immediately decided to leave his practice in the hands of Joel, Mathilda's young husband, and postponed all his meetings. Stella was delighted. The doctor's promise to bring them to the sea was being fulfilled. Providence, in the guise of a rare plant, was conspiring to bring them together.

In her room, Stella finishes putting on her jewelry and then joins the others on the way to the doctor's villa. In spite of the heat, they're all walking fast. Only Stella is limping and falling behind because of a blister on her big toe. She looks forward to this visit and remembers how she first met Dr. Georgescu at the Army Hospital in Bucharest. It happened twenty years ago in 1916 during the Great War.

Dr. Georgescu was the Chief of Surgery, while she was volunteering as a nurse's aide. He looked so handsome and so dapper in his army uniform with all the gold buttons and trimmings. He remained her dream hero for a long time, even though he was married to a beautiful woman from the nobility. Only after she got engaged to Sorel did Stella stop dreaming about him—for a while.

But then Victor Georgescu and Sorel started working together during a polio epidemic and became close friends. Soon after that, in 1930, Dr. Georgescu's wife died in a car accident.

Still, nothing would have happened between Stella and the doctor, if they hadn't met, unexpectedly, one stormy night at a mountain refuge at Babele. Stella had hiked from the little resort without Sorel, who was still busy with his practice in Bucharest. Dr. Georgescu was there all alone. This accidental meeting was the beginning of a special romance between them.

"It's not fair to Sorel, your loving husband," Nina, her sister scolded her. "Leave the poor man alone. Get out of his life so he can find a spouse!" she added.

Stella listened to her and broke up the relationship. But, at the end of a miserable year, they ran into each other on the bus. Stella was loaded down with household packages and the doctor helped her carry them home. This time she let things run their own course. Now she shrugs when she thinks of all this. Maybe she should listen to Nina, but ...

The villa is quiet when they arrive. Only the doctor is waiting for them on the terrace, smoking a pipe. When he sees them, he runs down the stairs to the garden, skipping two steps at a time, like a youth. He is tanned and looks younger and stronger than usual.

"Welcome to Eforie, and thank you for coming so quickly!" he says kissing Mathilda and Stella's fingertips with a gallant bow. He cradles Stella's narrow hand in his own and looks deep into her eyes. "So happy to see you!" he whispers in a low voice, before taking the big box from Sorel. Then he steps into the dining room, followed by all the others. He places the box on the table, while everybody gathers around him and watches in silence.

"A kitchen knife! I need a sharp kitchen knife!" he says. When Schwester Karla hands him the knife, he walks slowly around the table, as if ready to perform a sacred rite. Everybody is silent, watching him.

He clears his throat and turns to the children who have been joined by Anca and Paul and who are huddled together.

"This is a gift from the jungles and rain forests of South America," he says. "It comes from far away, near the end of the world, where wonderful flowers and birds still live in the wilderness. Many wise and courageous men have paid with their lives for the discovery of these flowers. To find them, many have wandered up to thirty-five years through the jungles and have crossed the ocean up to forty times before dying of malaria and yellow fever. Others have been killed by local tribes or ruthless adventurers. These sacrifices have shown real passion!" he concludes.

And, as if driven by the same passion, the doctor raises the gleaming knife in the air, like a sword. Then, with a bold swing, he brings it down and cuts the cord of the package with a single blow. He tears the wrapping paper, letting it drop to the floor. With a concentrated look he opens the lid of the box and clears his throat again, as if preparing for another speech. Stella thinks that he is pompous with these theatrics, but she loves him for it. A touch of Charcot, the Maître of La Salpétrière.

He is now bending over the crate and plunging his two arms inside. Everybody is waiting, breathless and tense. Finally he straightens up and brings to light a cascade of golden blooms which shine with a magical glow.

Nobody moves, nobody speaks. Everyone is bewitched by the flowers. The children too stand in awe, while the doctor's face beams with pride.

"*Odontoglossum crispum* from Colombia! The most beautiful orchid in the world!" he says, bowing with reverence in front of the flowerpot.

"Wow! What perfume! What flowers!" says Sorel, the first to break the silence. He inhales deeply, with eyes closed. "Aaaaah! I never knew that I was carrying such a unique and precious treasure!"

"Precious, indeed, because it comes from so far away, and unique, because, as far as I know, this is the only specimen of its kind in this part of the world," says Dr. Georgescu. "The Queen will be delighted and will boast to her entire court and to the neighboring kings of Bulgaria and Yugoslavia! I'm sure that none of them possesses such an orchid. But we must celebrate this special event. Let's have some țuică and salted fish from the Royal Estates!"

He winks quickly toward Stella and turns toward Schwester Karla who gets up and disappears in the kitchen in search of the bottle of brandy. A few minutes later they all sit around the table and savor the fiery drink and the pungent fish.

"I love this. The fish tastes much better with țuică!" says Stella passing her tongue over her red lips. "What a treat for a gourmet like me!"

"A treat to be continued on the beach, by the sea!" says Sorel, getting up. He explains that the promenade program for the afternoon has been cancelled, since Corinna and Theo don't like to play with hoops. "Instead," he says, "I will take Mathilda and the children for a swim and a ball game on the beach. Then Fräulein Lilly and Schwester Karla will be free to go to the promenade and enjoy the brass band by the casino with all the handsome young musicians." He nods toward the nannies and goes on. "Only Stella will stay at the villa because of her foot."

Everybody is pleased with the new arrangement except Anca who wanted to show off the new dress she had received for her birthday and Schwester Karla who, just ad Fräulein

Lilly predicted, wants to stick to the old program. "Always changes, changes, changes... What is this crazy world coming to?" she mumbles, as she carries the empty glasses and plates back to the kitchen.

When everybody has left and Dr. Georgescu returns to the terrace, he goes straight to Stella and takes her hand. Then he draws her close to him.

"I missed you so much! I'm so happy to have you here!" he says as he takes her in his arms and walks her into the bedroom. The air is cool here and the shades are drawn. There is a subtle fragrance of fresh lavender in the room. The bed is soft as they lie down.

Soon their clothes are scattered on the floor at the foot of a bookcase.

"You are my softest, most velvety orchid maiden!" Victor Georgescu whispers into Stella's ear, as he keeps caressing and kissing her.

"Make me drunk with your kisses, your kisses are sweeter than wine!" she mumbles, laughing softly, as she quotes from King Solomon's *Song of Songs*.

The call of the muezzin for afternoon prayer startles them out of their dreamy haze. They slip silently out of bed.

"I wish we could spend nights and days on the Riviera, just you and me!" she says as she combs her hair in front of the mirror.

"Or take a long trip on a fishing boat!" he replies, watching her. They are silent for a while, even after they step out of the bedroom. Stella puts a new cigarette in her cigarette holder and lights up to smoke, while the doctor makes coffee in the kitchen.

"You know what?" she says after they finish their coffee. "We should take your new plant to the greenhouse, where it belongs. Sorel will surely ask me whether I saw your orchid house, and what I think about it!"

"Good thinking! Let's go" He picks up the large flower pot and they walk through the kitchen onto a winding stair which leads to the roof. Here a spacious, glass enclosed greenhouse has been built.

As she steps inside, Stella is blinded by the brilliant colors of the blossoms and stunned by their fantastic shapes. Some flowers are large and velvety, with pink, violet or gold petals. Others are burning orange or blood red, covered with a tracery which looks like a silver arabesque. There are tall, bizarre flower spikes and blossoms whose colors are changing by the hour.

It is warm and humid here, and the heavy perfume of so many flowers makes her feel dizzy and faint. As she is struggling to catch her breath, she imagines that she has been transported into the middle of a jungle teaming with monkeys, parrots, giant fireflies and bats. Mysterious shining eyes are lurking in the dark. Strange tales about orchids come to her mind.

"So much has been told about orchids," she says, as she ducks away from a garland with flashy red and black spotted flowers. "Tales about orchids which can roam freely in the jungle or which can make themselves invisible at whim... or stories about giant flowers which are so murderous and blood thirsty that they lure innocent travelers close to them. They put them to sleep with their perfume and, when they're unconscious, they pull them inside their chamber and crush them to death!"

"And what else?" The doctor has set the yellow flower on a table and looks at Stella with an amused smile.

"Yes," she says frowning and trying to concentrate. "I have read that some orchids are inhabited by demons, and others by naked, seductive women. This is why they are called Flowers of Evil. I remember now—there are orchids which change at night into exalted maidens and engage the men they encounter in orgies of dance and lovemaking. Is this why you love the orchids? Because of their secret perversity?"

"No, no!" he laughs. "Of course not!" I told you before: you are my one and only orchid maiden!" He takes her hand and kisses her fingers. "But let me show you my most secret project. You are the only one with whom I can talk about it."

Dr. Georgescu leads Stella to the far end of the greenhouse, where blinds made of reeds protect the orchids from the sun, and a small fan produces a slight breeze. They stop in front of a row of plants with clusters of light purple flowers.

"My project deals with these wild orchids, called *orchis*, an ancient plant which grows around the Mediterranean and here, near the Black Sea. It is from its lower parts or "tubers" that the native people made a drink called "Salep." I think they still sell this drink today in some villages. But in my childhood, it was very much sought after. Since it was made from the tubers of the plant which look like human testicles, it was thought to give great sexual powers to man. This is an old belief which goes back to the Greek legend of Orchis, who gave its name to the whole class of orchids."

The doctor waves away a large bee which buzzes around Stella's head, and then goes on, "Do you know the legend of

Orchis? No? He was a wild youth who, during a festival for Bacchus, tried to rape a priestess. The Fates punished him for this and had his body torn apart by wild animals. But the gods took pity on him and changed his remains into a flower, to whose lower parts they attached his own testicles. Orchis in Greek means testicles. Here, let me show you."

He points to a picture which hangs on the wall which shows a plant identical with the ones they are looking at. It has the same flowers and leaves, but at its lower parts, near the roots, are two bulbous lumps which look exactly like testicles.

"This is a picture of Orchis and here are its tubers or testicles from which Salep is made," says the doctor. He pushes a watering can out of his way and leans against the shelf, as he speaks. "I remember that, in my childhood, my grandfather who was a pharmacist in Constanța used to prepare Salep from these orchids. Peasants and folks from the outskirts of the town or nearby villages brought him the plants after the flowers had died. My grandfather peeled the bulbs and dried them in the sun or in an oven. Then he crushed them to a sort of flour which he would mix with water, with milk or with wine and sell it to his clients. Salep was very much in demand in those days, mainly as an aphrodisiac. Street vendors were also selling it in the marketplace and in the streets. I saw that it also stimulated physical and mental energy and I thought that it might be used for depression and other nervous illnesses. So now I want to try to cultivate enough of these wild orchids to be able to produce some Salep. It may turn out to be a real good medicine for my patients. You never know!"

Stella nods as she looks at the small purple flowers.

"You're right. One never knows. You can even try to give some Salep to Silvia, Nina's former governess. Together with hypnosis, it may help her get better faster than with hypnosis alone."

"If I can only convince Eugen Milo to cooperate! You don't know how headstrong he can be when it comes to hypnosis. But you don't even know how right you are!" They step out of the greenhouse and sit on a bench on the roof terrace.

"No, you don't know how right you are! I keep thinking of this all the time. Remember the Great War of 1916 when we were treating the shellshocked soldiers at the Army Hospital? I hypnotized them. Since I still had a small supply of Salep, I tried it with them. I gave them a daily amount in addition to the hypnosis. They seemed to be getting better much faster. But just when I thought that we were getting somewhere, I had to interrupt the whole experiment. We had to evacuate the hospital because the Germans had started to bomb it."

"Oh, yes, I remember," says Stella. "It all happened when the Zeppelin was bombing Bucharest and the hospital. It was pretty bad. A bomb fell in our courtyard and wrecked the whole house, so we had to leave the city and travel North to Moldova. We traveled with the same train which carried you and the Military Hospital."

"Did you know that the train too was in danger of being bombed by the Germans? We escaped only due to that terrible storm with thunder and lightning because their planes couldn't fly when there was a major storm!"

"Yes, yes, I know!" says Stella. Then she sighs and adds, "We go back many years with our joint memories."

The big bee has returned. The doctor is chasing it away with his hands. "I never told you, but I was drawn to you from the first day I saw you at the hospital," Stella goes on. "I was all intimidated because you were the big chief of the military hospital, and you looked so important and so handsome in your uniform with all those gold buttons and braids. I was just volunteering as a nurse's aide."

"But you looked so young and so pretty, I thought you were somebody's kid. It was hard to believe that you were working with the dying soldiers."

Stella nods. "It was long ago, but it still feels like yesterday. I had a small picture of you in your officer's uniform. I carried it for a long time, hidden in a silver locket." Stella raises her hand to her necklace, as if searching for the locket. "I fell in love with you long before I ever met Sorel. But you were freshly married to a beautiful woman. Too bad she died so young!"

"Shhhht! Don't talk about these things. They're too sad. Let bygones be bygones. We cannot change the past. Let's enjoy what we have—our own secret happiness. When I'm with you I think that Beaudelaire's poem, *L'Invitation au Voyage* was written for me.

> Là, tout n'est qu'ordre et beauté,
> Luxe, calme et volupté..."

This is what you make me think of."

Stella smiles and puts her hand on his knee. "I know what you mean, and I feel the same. But when you're not around, or near me, the whole world is deserted. In the words of Lamartine,

> Un seul être me manque
> Et tout est dépeuplé!"

> (If only one person
> Is missing, the whole world is deserted!)

The doctor looks at her and says, "I know... I too feel that the world is deserted when you are not around! But enough of these lamentations!" He gets up and walks toward the table with the golden orchid. "Isn't she gorgeous? I think she is one of the seven wonders of the world!"

Stella follows him with a puzzled look on her face. "Isn't there any work you have to do? Make some cuttings for yourself before giving the plant to the Queen?"

The doctor laughs. He leads Stella back to the wooden bench. "Now listen, I have to tell you a secret. There's no urgency with the cuttings. The Queen doesn't even know that the plant has arrived! I concocted the telegram because I needed to see you. I wanted you here with me."

"Naughty, naughty! That's lying, concealing the truth!" She laughs flattered by his words, her eyes shining. "Aren't you afraid of punishment for the sin of deception?"

"Look who is talking!" says the doctor, wagging his finger at her.

Stella blushes. She stops laughing. She frowns and is suddenly very serious. Dr. Georgescu puts his arm around her and whispers, "I'm sorry. I didn't meant to upset you." He is stroking her hair.

They stand like this for a while, gazing in the distance, where the sun is starting to set. The sea is turning purple, and a rose colored sailboat glides across the horizon.

The scent of lilies in the nearby garden mixes with the perfume of the orchids. Moist air rises from the evening sprinklers which shower the flower beds with coolness. The sounds of an Argentinian tango rises from the promenade.

"Let's dance!" The doctor takes Stella in his arms and holds her tight, moving slowly in the rhythm of the tango. "I wish we would go downstairs again, like earlier this afternoon," he whispers. But his words are drowned by the loud bang of the garden gate and the children's voices calling them from below.

THE BLUE CAVE AND THE OLD CEMETERY

O N THIS CLOUDY AFTERNOON WHEN the wind is stirring up spiral columns of sand on the beach and the fog is hanging over the sea, Nadia and Theo walk briskly along the water.

"Faster, faster, walk faster," says Theo, "or we'll never get to the Blue Cave!" He takes a big stride as he steps over a rock.

"Stop pestering me! Your legs are much longer than mine. It's hard to keep up with you."

Theo looks at his legs and at Nadia's, as if he sees them for the first time. He nods, then pushes his pith helmet to the back of his head and checks the compass which hangs from his neck.

"South-West. We're walking in the right direction. Soon we should be at the jetty and meet Skender. He told me that the Blue Cave is not far from there and that it's easy enough to catch the pink salamanders. If it weren't for this damned wind and sand!" They both stop and turn their back to the onslaught of the storm, which whips up big wheels of prickly sand. "Ptiu! It gets everywhere—in your mouth, in your eyes... and then it's so hard to get rid of it!"

When the wind calms down, Theo blows his nose and spits out a mouthful of saliva speckled with sand. "But I must get to the Blue Cave and bring a salamander home. Otherwise, Corinna will never stop teasing me and making fun of me. She calls me a balloon full of hot air who will never discover anything new. Well, these salamanders haven't even been classified yet, Dr. Georgescu has told me and I can't wait to see Corinna's face after I put one on her pillow! She'll have a fit. After she recovers, she'll have to recognize that I'm an explorer in my own right."

"Of course, she'll have to recognize you! But to tell you my secret, I have always dreamed of checking out the sunken ship which lies off the old lighthouse. I can't wait to dive and explore it. I'm sure it is a pirate ship, and I always wanted to be a pirate! But not a simple, regular one. I want to be the captain of a pirate ship and spend my life on the water."

"Vorbeşti prostii! You're full of nonsense. You can't be a pirate. Girls can't be pirates."

"Then I'll be the first one. I will dress like a man, wear a red bandana, and a black patch over one eye."

"Prostii. Nonsense. Girls can't be pirates."

"They can, if they want to. My ship will have a black flag with a white skull and crossbones. We'll hunt for treasures on far away islands and on sunken ships."

Theo shakes his head and gives her a superior look. "You don't know what you're talking about. A pirate ship must be armed with guns and cannons and shoot at other ships. Girls don't know anything about shooting."

"Big deal! So I'll learn. And I'll shoot much better than any man!"

"Nonsense again. You may lose an eye, or a hand, or a leg. You don't know what you're talking about, nor do you know what you want." He makes a dismissive gesture, waves her away, and turns up his nose. "I at least know very well that we must get to the cave and catch at least one salamander. I only hope that we meet Skender at the old jetty because only he knows the way to the cave."

Theo stops talking and turns around, as they are again trapped in a whirlwind of sand. The wind roars in their ears and the fine sand pricks their skin. After a few moments, it is quiet again.

They have walked away from the colorful tents of the tourists, in the opposite direction from the lighthouse. The beach here is a narrow strip of sand squeezed between the rough sea and the steep wall of the cliff. High waves break against the sharp rocks which are the landing site of innumerable seagulls. Their shrill calls are the only noise piercing the thunder of the surf and the roar of the wind. In the distance, heavy clouds and fog are gathering over the sea.

Theo and Nadia have to wade into the water and climb over slippery boulders before reaching the old jetty.

The place is deserted, except for the birds perched everywhere. In addition to the seagulls, a few egrets and cormorants are also resting on the ruins of the old pier.

Heaps of rusty metal and crumbling blocks of cement lie near the rocks covered with seagrass, and a deep crater filled with dirty water opens at the foot of the jetty. It is flanked by a faded sign with the words, "*Trecera Oprită—Pericol de Explozie*" (Passage forbidden, danger of explosion). There is a skull and crossbones painted under the inscription.

"Bombs from the Great War," says Theo. "I thought they had removed them by now. We must be careful. But where is Skender? I hoped we would find him here!"

Theo looks in all directions, but nobody is in sight. He cups his hands in front of his mouth like a bullhorn and calls, "Skendeeeer! Sken... deeeer..." Then he sits on a block of cement, opens his explorer bag, and takes out a Boy Scout whistle. He whistles three times, but there is no answer.

"Where can he be?" he asks. "He will be here soon," he reassures himself. But he cannot sit still. He picks up a handful of stones and hurls them at the birds perched on the jetty. Even though he doesn't hit any, the seagulls take off shrieking and wheeling through the air. Then he takes aim at a large bird still floating on the water. The stone flies past it without touching it and falls into the sea with a big splash. The cormorant takes off, flapping its large wings.

"If I had a gun, I could shoot them like the explorers did. Captain Cook wrote in his memoirs that they shot the albatrosses which followed their boat. Some we could cook and eat for dinner. The captain wrote that their meat was tasty. Some we could take home and have stuffed. That would be great fun!"

"How cruel!" says Nadia. "You have no heart."

"Look who is talking! You, the queen of the pirates, who is ready to attack ships and plunder them, shoot their victims with cannons and guns. You get upset about killing a bird or stuffing one which is already dead! "

"Wait a minute. Don't go so fast. Let me explain. I will shoot at people, but only if they attack me and I must save my life."

"So what kind of a pirate will you be? Do you think that ship captains and their crew will hand you their gold and their diamonds just for fun? For your looks? I said it before and I'll say it again, 'Girls are too dumb to be pirates!'"

"You're wrong. You're wrong. Just let me tell you." Nadia tries to explain, but Theo doesn't listen to her. He is too busy picking up rocks and throwing them at the birds.

Meanwhile a new gust of wind comes from the sea, stirring whirls of sand, forcing the children to crouch near the ground and to fold their arms over their heads. They can barely breathe. The roar of the storm is deafening. They close their eyes and sit motionless. When the wind dies down, they get up and shake the sand from their skin and their swimsuits. Then Theo climbs to the highest point of the jetty to scan the horizon for Skender. But as he doesn't see him, he returns to Nadia, who has remained at the same spot on the beach.

"Let's do it alone, just you and me," he says. "We can't sit here and wait forever. I know there will be trouble if we're not home in time. I know my father. He lets us play and go wherever we want as long as we're home for dinner. But if we're late, he'll take it away. He will ground us for good, and we won't be allowed to go any place. Also, I can't go home without the salamanders. I must stop Corinna from making fun of me. I have to show her who I am. I have sworn that today is the day!"

Theo taps his foot and fingers his compass full of impatience.

"So, are you coming?"

"But we don't even know how to get there. You've never been to that cave."

Nadia clenches her fists and bites her lip. She is frightened. "We'll get lost. Skender will be here any minute. He won't let us down."

"Alright then. *Bine, bine.* You sit here and wait for Skender. *La revedere!*"

Theo stands up. He shakes the sand out of his explorer hat, closes his canvas bag and puts it on his shoulder. He checks his compass and marches off toward the jetty.

Nadia watches him until he disappears behind the pier. Then she stands up and scans the horizon, searching for Skender or his fishing boat.

Only when the next gust of wind blows the sand into her face and hair does she run for cover and duck down at the foot of a block of cement. The wind is roaring like a hundred demons, forcing her to close her eyes and cover her head with her hands. Her hair feels sandy, sticky and tangled up and she can imagine Fräulein Lilly's frustration when she'll have to wash it. What great punishment for Fräulein Lilly! Nadia smiles, even though she knows that washing this hair will be a very painful ordeal.

Aunt Mathilda will threaten with an immediate return to Bucharest. But she knows that nothing will happen as long as Uncle Sorel and his family are here with her. She feels protected and she thinks again of her secret plan to explore the sunken ship and find the pirates' treasures hidden in its hull.

Skender will help her. He is the only one who knows the exact location of the shipwreck. He'll be here any minute. He must have had trouble mooring his boat or coming into the harbor with this great storm. Theo should have waited and not hurried off all by himself. He doesn't even know how to get to the cave.

When the storm calms down and Nadia opens her eyes and looks in the distance, she sees thick clouds and fog sweeping toward the beach. The clouds are very dark, almost black, and threaten to engulf everything—the pier and the beach. It is almost night suddenly, and Nadia feels so alone and so frightened that she gets up and starts running after Theo, calling his name. She forgets about Skender. She has no more time to think. All she wants is to reach Theo. She keeps calling. But he doesn't answer her calls.

As she runs, the strip of sand almost vanishes and she is forced to climb over slippery rocks. She calls Theo's name, but there is no answer.

After a while, the way is blocked by a large tumbled rock. When she stops to catch her breath, a trickle of pebbles rain down on her from above. Nadia looks up, but all she can see is a steep wall of stone. With determination, she starts climbing the slippery wall. It is a hard climb. She grabs the few ridges and bumps she can reach, pulling herself up, then sliding down again until she arrives at a small, flat plateau, flanked at one end by the wall of the cliff. She is out of breath and her hands are numb. Then she hears Theo's voice.

"Look who is here! And Skender? Not waiting for him any longer?" He grabs her wrists and helps her to her feet.

"But this is *not* the Blue Cave! Where are your salamanders? We are too high, too far from the water." She points in the distance through a narrow rift in the fog.

"So, you too gave up on Skender! You were too frightened to wait there all alone. Great pirate you are."

"That's not true. You are too scared to go home to Corinna."

"*Prostii!* Nonsense. I am an explorer." Theo pulls out his compass and examines the needles. "This is a scientific expedition."

"*Da! Da!* Great explorer you are. You don't even have a map of the place, and you don't know how to get to your cave!"

"Nonsense—map or no map, I'll find a way to the cave," Theo says, looking down at her with contempt.

But Nadia has stopped listening. She stares at the calcareous wall behind Theo, pockmarked with round holes in which scores of birds have made their nests. They slip in and out of these tunnels calling to each other with high pitched voices. Here and there long and dark rods stick out of the holes. Nadia pulls out one such rod and examines it.

"It's a bone. It's a bone!" she screams. She lets it drop to the ground with revulsion and takes a step back. What on earth is it doing here? And why so many bones?"

Before Theo has time to answer, she picks it up and thrusts it inside other holes, like a shaft, emptying them of nests, feathers, broken eggshells, and bunches of long and short bones.

"Why so many bones?" she asks again, as a white jaw crowned with a row of teeth and a round skull tumble out of a deep burrow.

Finally, as she cleans out the last hole, among small twigs and feathers, two shiny coins roll to the ground. She picks them up and rubs them between her fingers, then she examines them carefully, noticing that they are incised with the picture of a warship under full sail with many seamen at the oars.

"Look at this! I bet these coins come from the treasure of the sunken ships. This must have been an old pirate cemetery, and these are the pirates' graves. I must check out the sunken ship. I must dive and see what's left in the hull. Where is Skender? Only he knows where to find the wreckage. Where is he? Why did he let us down?"

"Here I am. I just made it up here. What do you want to know?" a voice says behind her.

"Skender! You frightened me!" Nadia turns quickly and finds Skender standing at the edge of the plateau. He has tied his fishing rod and the handle of his bait bucket to his belt.

"Where were you? Why didn't you meet us at the jetty?"

"Too much wind. Too much fog. I couldn't get into the harbor and moor the boat."

"And how did you find us here?" asks Theo.

"That was easy. I walked toward the Blue Cave, but then I ran into the large rock which blocks the road. From there, all I could do was to climb the wall and end up here."

"All right, then, let's go to the cave. We must catch those salamanders today! I can't go home empty-handed." Theo stands erect and fires his words like bullets. He turns around ready to march off.

"Well, I must disappoint you." Skender touches Theo's shoulder. "We can't go to the cave. The road is closed. There is no way to get there."

"No way? I don't believe you. This can't be true." He has turned pale and takes a step toward Skender.

"Stop this. Leave him alone!" Nadia pulls Theo back, grabbing his bathing trunks. "Let me ask Skender some questions. Where are we? And what are these?" she asks, as she shows him the coins. "Is this a pirates' old cemetery? Do these coins come from the sunken ship?" She stares at him with big eyes and holds her breath.

"Well, let me see." Skender turns the coins around with his fingers. "Hm! Let me see. My father told me that long ago it was said that a bunch of pirates lived around here and this was their cemetery. It reached much farther into the sea. The coast was much wider than it is now, but it was all washed away. That's why the graves are open today and the long bones stick out of the holes. It was also said that the sunken ship was a Turkish pirate ship, which carried beautiful slave girls and treasures of gold and diamonds plundered from other ships and that it belonged to the pirates who lived on this coast.

"I once dove under the water there and tried to get inside the hull where the treasures were kept. I went down all the way, but the only opening which led inside the ship was too narrow for me. So I came up empty-handed. Only Nadia is small enough to slide through that narrow hatch!"

"That's great!" Nadia shouts, clapping her hands. "When are we going? Now? Now! Let' go right away!"

She is skipping on one foot, knocking over Skender's fishing gear and Theo's explorer bag. "Let's go! Let's go!"

"*Stai! Linişteşte-te!* Stop, stop. Take it easy! We can't go today! It's too late. But maybe tomorrow or the day after. Anyway, before next week when the summer regatta will start."

"Wait. Wait a minute. Before we make any plans," Nadia yells. "We can't tell anybody about this. This is our deepest secret. Theo must promise he won't say a word to Corinna or Anca or Paul."

Nadia holds a long bone in her hand and raises it like a magic wand. "Do you promise to keep this silent as our greatest secret?" she asks Theo, while touching his forehead with the bone like in a sacred ritual.

"I promise," says Theo with a sour voice, "but only if you give me half of what you find!"

"That's not fair!" Skender steps between Nadia and Theo. He makes a quick calculation. "Nadia should keep two-thirds of what she discovers in the ship and we should split the other third. If she dives and does the work under water, she should have most of what is there. We can split the rest. That would be fair!"

"I don't know. I don't know any more what is fair! If I can't get my salamanders, that isn't fair!" Theo opens his Swiss Army knife and hurls it toward the wall of the cliff.

The knife zooms through the air and buries itself in the earth near Nadia's foot.

"Stop this nonsense!" Skender orders. He pulls the knife out of the earth and slides it into his pocket. "Let me think! We'll find a way to get to your salamanders one day soon. You must be patient now!"

IN SKENDER'S BOAT

FIVE DAYS LATER, SKENDER'S FISHING boat glides silently on the quiet sea. It is two o'clock in the afternoon, a glorious day, without a breeze or a cloud, with transparent air and a hot, burning sun in the sky. The beach is deserted. The crowds of bathers have withdrawn to the coolness of their rooms. Even the birds are quiet. The swallows are hiding in their nests under the eaves; the seagulls are dozing, perched on rocks and wooden poles.

The children—Skender, Theo and Nadia—have left the pier near the old lighthouse at the North tip of the beach. They are headed toward the rock with the sunken ship. First, they have to reach the last buoy beyond the fishing nets, then they have to sail in a straight line toward the horizon—a good distance out of the bay. Only Skender rows. He sits in the middle of the boat. Only he knows how far they have to go.

He has repainted the boat white, with a blue stripe on the side and on the bottom. The freshly painted oars and the whole inside of the boat and the benches feel somewhat sticky. A bucket of paint, two long ropes and a fishing net are tucked under the last bench where Theo sits now. He frowns as he concentrates on his compass. He wears small, dark bathing trunks and has propped his bare feet on Skender's middle bench. His pith helmet rests on the floor.

Nadia, who sits in the front of the boat, wears her yellow bathing suit. She can't keep still for two minutes. She stands up and sits down and then stands up and sits down again.

"I can't wait to get to the rock and dive for the ship. I'm sure it hides a treasure and we'll be rich, rich, rich!"

"*Uite le ea, Regina Piratilor!* (There she goes, Queen of the Pirates!) Already boasting of riches she may never have."

"That's not true. I will make it. I'm not a loser like you, who can't bring home even one salamander. You should collect squid or jellyfish. Squid—you can serve for dinner, marinated or broiled."

"Stop that, or you'll get it now!" Theo gets up and starts toward Nadia.

"Easy now, or you'll capsize the boat!" Skender extends his left arm, letting go of the oar and stops Theo in his tracks. "You know very well it wasn't Theo's fault that the salamander cave didn't work out," he says to Nadia.

She sits down with a grimace. She hates to admit that Skender is right. Only two days ago, on a beautiful afternoon just like today, they set out for the Blue Cave by boat, not by land like they had tried the first time. The sailing was smooth and they were all excited, particularly Theo, who was telling them about Corinna and the pink salamanders. "I'll show you who is right in the end. She'll have to stop calling me a balloon full of hot air!"

But as they approached the old jetty, they saw many boats and many people. They heard military commands shouted through a bullhorn. They saw gray army boats swarming with soldiers. Then, all of a sudden, a string of loud explosions rocked the air and the sea, while clouds of black smoke and flames covered the beach. A smell of sulfur and burnt rubber filled the air. Nadia and Theo closed their eyes and covered their faces with their hands.

"The bombs! They're exploding the old bombs left from the Great War!" said Skender. "I'm afraid this is the end of the Blue Cave and the pink salamanders!"

Nadia remembers that last time. Theo didn't say anything, but he grabbed Skender's oar and almost capsized the boat.

Later, after they sailed away from the old pier, Skender invited Theo to come fishing with him, one early morning. "You never know what you'll catch!"

"Perhaps a big fish who has swallowed a gold ring, or a precious pearl, or even a diamond necklace," teased Nadia.

"You bet! Then I'll be richer than you!" Theo was ready for combat again.

"No, you can't be richer than me. I'll be a real pirate and find all the sunken treasures!"

Nadia had trained for swimming under water for a long time. It was her greatest passion. She was very good at it. She was so obsessed with it that during the last few nights, she had constantly dreamed about diving and finding the treasure. Aunt Mathilda and Fräulein Lilly told her that many times she had gotten out of bed during the night, sleepwalking through the room with open eyes, trying to pull them out of bed and inviting them to come diving with her.

She had practiced swimming under water whenever and wherever she could—at the beach in the summer, at the public swimming pool in Bucharest, and in the small garden pool at home. In winter, she even tried diving under water in the bathtub. This made Fräulein Lilly very mad because she ended up with wet hair full of soap.

But what would Fräulein Lilly do if she were caught on a pirate ship? Nadia has to laugh when she imagines this scene.

She sees Fräulein Lilly's horrified face, since the pirates never shave their beards, wash their hair and their ears, or brush their teeth. All they're doing every day is making merry and drinking, singing and dancing. Fräulein Lilly would surely hide her face in disgust. If she were too upset, she might even jump into the sea and drown.

"And what will you do with the treasures you'll find? How about your captives? Will you slaughter them all?" Theo and Skender are asking.

"Of course not! I'll set them free as soon as I can. The most precious treasure I'll keep for myself. The rest I'll share with the poor people who need my help."

"Then we should be poor, too, to benefit from your kindness," scoffs Theo. "But if you think that your good heart will keep you safe, you're wrong. All pirates end up on the scaffold and you will, too!"

"That's not true!" Nadia starts to reply. But she cannot finish. The boat turns sharply to the left, making her slip from her seat. There is a strong smell of fish all around them.

"The fishing nets! We can't get entangled in them," yells Skender. He rows quickly away from the cork-stoppers which float in the water and hold up the fishing nets. If we get caught in them, it's hard to get out. He gives a few hard strokes with the oars and the boat heads straight toward the last orange buoy, then out to sea in the direction of the sunken ship.

As they get closer to the buoy, Skender stops rowing and pulls out of his knapsack a tin box filled with tobacco and thin white bits of paper. He rolls himself a cigarette and slips the tin box back into his knapsack.

"You must have heard about the curse of this shipwreck, the curse which claims that anybody who dives down and reaches the sunken ship is doomed never to come back alive?" says Skender. "Many people believe this and stay away. But I don't think it's true. I think the fishermen invented it to keep strangers away from their catch. I myself swam down to the sunken ship to inspect it. Here is a drawing of what I saw."

He pulls a stained sheet of paper out of his pocket and pushes it under Nadia's nose. It is a pencil drawing of a large ship.

"Here is the deck and here is where the masts were. This is the Captain's cabin. Here, halfway between the stern and the masts is the little hatch which leads inside the hull. I tried to get inside, but the opening is too small for me. You'll have to do it now!"

As she bends over the drawing and studies it, Nadia hears loud splashing right near the boat. When she looks down she sees a couple of glistening forms arching out of the sea and then diving down into the waves. They are followed by other fish, then by others and others.

"The dolphins!" yells Skender, as he pulls in the oars. "Now if our boat capsizes and we fall into the water, they'll rescue us and bring us back to shore." He folds the piece of paper and puts it back in his pocket.

The dark and shiny animals circle the boat and make joyful summersaults.

"They can swim with the speed of light!" says Theo, who has let go of his compass. Now the dolphins move in circles around the boat—small circles and then larger ones, turning so fast, as to fill Nadia and Theo with thrills. There are six or seven adults and two babies, and they jump out of the water.

Nadia is fascinated by them. They look so happy and so friendly as they come closer and closer to the boat. They then align themselves at its stern, trying to push it to make it move faster. But when they don't succeed, they swim away as suddenly as they had appeared.

Nadia looks back to the shore. The old lighthouse has become smaller and smaller in the distance. A single white seagull follows the boat without moving its wings. The water is dark here, almost black, because of the tall seagrasses which reach just below the surface. Schools of small red and silver fish, gray turtles and jellyfish dart to and fro, hiding in the throbbing sea-forest.

Nadia and Theo stare into the water, watching their busy comings and goings. Skender is the only one rowing, taking the boat toward the sunken ship. Nadia thinks of the many riches which lie forgotten on the bottom of the sea.

If only she had Aladdin's lamp to rub and to polish and to say the magic words. The hidden treasures would pop out of the water and lie at her feet.

"We're getting close to the sunken ship!" says Skender. "Time to prepare for your dive!"

He bends down and pulls the two ropes from under the bench, unwinding them first, and then tying one around Nadia's waist and her shoulders, while Theo helps with tying the knots. The second rope, Skender fastens to the handle of the bucket in which he has placed a rock from the shore. Then he sits down facing Nadia, rolls himself a cigarette, and tells her what to do.

"When we reach the rock you'll dive and descend all the way until you find the hatch which leads to the hull. You slide inside the room, locate the treasure, and fill the bucket with what you find. Then, when you're finished, you swim out of the hull with the pail and pull three times on the ropes. We will immediately bring you up.

Nadia is very quiet as they row toward their destination. She stares into the water which is light and transparent here.

The dark grasses are behind them now. The rock with the sunken ship is surrounded by clear, silvery waters.

"Ready? *Ești gata?*"

They have arrived. Under the boat, the water which covers the rock with the shipwreck is deep and dark, with a thin shaft of light.

Skender stops rowing.

"Are you all right? *Gata?*"

He gets up and gives Nadia a hand, helping her climb on the edge of the boat. She takes several deep breaths.

"*Unu... doi... trei...* Jump!"

Nadia holds the bucket in one hand and dives into the sea. The water is cold and it gets colder as she descends. But she keeps moving in the bright shaft of light. She stares at the bottom where she can clearly see the craggy outline of the rock and the steel carcass of the ship.

She swoops down quickly and smoothly, holding the bucket in one hand. On her way, she encounters blue and yellow fish, which stare at her with their round eyes. Then she is surrounded by a school of transparent jellyfish, who come dangerously close. She is frightened for she knows that they are poisonous and could paralyze her. She stays still and doesn't move and the jellyfish disappear in the depths.

As she continues her descent in the shaft of light, she can clearly see the stern of the ship and the narrow hatch which leads inside the hull. But suddenly she hears strange moaning sounds, accompanied by clicking, puffing and whistling. "What could this be?" Nadia wonders, as the sounds come closer and closer.

And then, the graceful bodies of the fast swimmers surround her in a loud frenzy: the dolphins are back! With their moaning and clicking, whistling and clucking, they talk to her and to each other. Are they welcoming her under water? They whirl around her, darting upwards then shooting down, swimming above her and under her, making summersaults, then tumbling around in the water and floating belly-up. They stare at her with small, beady eyes—moaning, groaning, whistling—inviting her to play with them.

Nadia feels dizzy from their noise and frolicking. She tries to swim out of their way, pushing hard with her legs. She feels the heavy pressure of the depth.

Now she is hovering right over the deck, almost touching the hatch with her hand. But a large, spotted dolphin darts toward her and bumps into her temple, pushing her sideways. Nadia feels the blow, her strength starts fading and she is out of breath. The heavy pressure of the water is almost unbearable. But she comes back to the hatch and grabs hold of a hook. She is ready to slide inside, when she feels a sharp pain in her ear. Like a needle, it pricks through the ear and bores into her brain.

She is overwhelmed by this pain. She cannot think. Automatically, she covers her ear with one hand, letting go of the hatch. All she knows is the sharp needle-like pain inside her head.

In the next second, she exhales quickly. The bucket tumbles out of her grasp and, without moving, she lets the sea bring her up to the surface.

PART II

HOTEL BAUR AU LAC, ZÜRICH

IT IS A CLEAR SUMMER day in the ancient city of Baden, near Zürich, where the sun makes the old spas and hotels sparkle with the same glow as the ultramodern industrial buildings. Richard Wagner came here often 100 years ago to drink the waters and take the healing baths while he was writing the libretto for *Der Ring des Nibelungen* and composing the music for *Das Rheingold* and *Die Walküre*. One hundred years before him, Wolfgang Goethe tasted the same waters as he wrote his sad love poems to his adored Lili Schonemann.

Now, Adrian Stein sits in an elegant office at Brown Boveri Corporation and has a lively conversation with Charles Kass, the Director of the Department of Electrical Turbines.

"Your electrification project at Grozăvești in Romania is impressive: ingenious and outstanding, I would say. The last model turbines you have chosen and installed should solve the complex problems of that location, and will surely work perfectly for many years to come. As always, your scientific judgment and expertise have done wonders. Bravo!"

The Swiss official nods approvingly and takes Adrian's hand.

"Congratulations! *Dazu soll'n wir doch etwas trinken!*"
(We should drink to that!)

Without waiting for Adrian, he gets up and grabs his jacket and his pipe. Adrian gazes at the golden hunting horn embroidered on the breast pocket of his blazer, and then at the three deer heads with their crown of antlers which adorn the walls.

"It's a pity you have to leave so quickly and can't join in our *Jagdpartei* by the Rhein Fall," says Kass, smoothing his blond hair with his large hand.

"But I am not a hunter. I wouldn't know what to do with a gun."

"Too bad! You should take advantage of those Carpathian mountains in your country and those dark woods. I should come and teach you some time; in three days you would be a perfect *Schütze*, I promise."

Kass opens the door and leads the way out on the corridor, where they are greeted by a marble bust of Nicola Tesla, the father of all electrical and steam turbines. They descend the shiny steps of the grand staircase, walk through the rock garden with its dark pine trees and splashing fountains, and step into a boulevard buzzing with traffic. Kass is a tall man with long legs and walks quickly, with large steps. Adrian has trouble keeping up with him, and is out of breath when they turn into a narrow street bordered by small hotels— each of them a spa of carbonic or sulfurous springs. These are ancient spas with warm waters, famous for the treatment of rheumatism and various women's diseases. They sit down in a *"Gemütliche Bierstube"* called "3 Könige" and Kass orders *"Eine Halbe und Würstli"* for each of them.

"Schade dass du nicht mit uns auf die Jagd kommst, und nochmal schade dass du nicht hier mit uns arbeitest! [A pity that you don't come with us hunting, and even more of a

pity that you don't work here with us.] But even this can be corrected: we are expanding our section of electric turbines and we need somebody with your expertise to manage it. The job involves both theoretical research and practical applications, which may also require travel to conferences and to various locations. I cannot think of anybody more qualified for this position than you." Charles Kass stops eating his *würstli* and looks at Adrian, who also stops eating. "How about my papers... my passport and my naturalization papers? I understand that this can be a problem for a foreign citizen?"

"Mach dir nichts aus!" [Don't worry about this!] shrugs Kass. "We can take care o f you and your family's papers. And, sincerely, if I were you, I would start liquidating my assets and property in Romania and move them to Switzerland. The sooner, the better. I wouldn't waste any time. Opportunities have to be grabbed when they come. They may never knock again."

Adrian looks at Kass, but doesn't see him. Is it true that opportunity knocks only once? he wonders. He remembers when a similar offer was made to him in the same place, 25 years ago... It was Charles Kass' predecessor, his uncle Richard. They were sitting at the same table under the cuckoo clock and they were drinking *eine Halbe*. Like Charles, his uncle Richard was also a passionate hunter, proud of his gun collection.

Adrian was just ending his apprenticeship at Brown Boveri after finishing his engineering studies in Düsseldorf. He liked living in Switzerland and working for Brown Boveri. He was proud of the offer he had received, and wrote home about his decision to remain and establish himself in Switzerland. But his mother would have none of it and begged him to come home. He listened to her, and soon after he went back, the war started, and his oldest brother was killed on the front.

After the war, by the time he reconnected with Brown Boveri, Richard Kass was gone. In Romania, his own parents were old and sick and needed his support. In addition he was newly married and had a small daughter.

"Yes, yes, you shouldn't miss this opportunity under any circumstance," says Charles Kass, as he signals a waitress in a *dirndl* to bring another round of beer. "Things don't look too good in your part of the world with your new government. Constant violence and unrest. You would be much better off here." He lights his pipe and draws a few puffs. "By the way, I have opened an account in your name with the Schweizerischer Bankverein in Zürich. It has 10,000 Swiss Francs, and, if you want, you can add to it as much as you wish."

Adrian is so pleased, he blushes and stutters a little as he thanks Kass.

They sit at the table for a while longer discussing various projects in the field, and when the cuckoo comes out and calls five times, Adrian gets up and says that he has to return to Nina in Zürich.

"I'll see you to the *Bahnhof*," (train station) promises Kass.

He pays the blond waitress with the *dirndl* and steps out with Adrian. "I almost forgot: my wife Brigitte wants to meet your wife and your daughter. We'll have a small party Saturday, at the end of this week," he says as he flags down a taxi.

On the express train to Zürich, Adrian is all excited about his discussion with Kass. He watches the mountains covered with snow in the distance, and thinks of his future career and of all the possibilities which have suddenly opened: opportunities of research and discovery in the new field of electricity, trips to conferences and modern labs all over the world. Today he is working with electrical generators and power transport, but tomorrow it could be radar, or nuclear energy, or electromagnetic radiation. His head is full of ideas for new projects, and he is eager to start new things. For his children, too, moving to Switzerland would be an excellent solution: the schools and "pensions" in this country have a great reputation. Sorel, Stella's husband and Nina's brother-in-law, had been in a Swiss boarding school since the age of six and has studied medicine and pediatrics at Zürich University. He has told Adrian that the Swiss schools—particularly the Montessori system—are the best in Europe. Not to speak about growing up healthy, so close to nature and to clean mountain air!

All this reminds him of the "Dream House," the plan he and Nina have made on their honeymoon when they traveled from Zürich down to the South of Switzerland and stayed in an inn in Lugano, by the Great Lakes. They had never imagined anything as beautiful as this strip of land, part Italy, part Switzerland. Here it was always spring—in the groves of orange, fig and lemon threes which grew at the foot of snowcapped mountains and at the edge of the blue lakes. They were so carried away that they made a vow to buy a villa by the water and grow a garden of Mediterranean trees and plants around it. Could this dream become reality now?

Adrian knows the answer is yes.

He rushes off the train to share his news with Nina. He has only a short distance to walk on the exclusive *Bahnhofstrasse* with its elegant stores. When he reaches "Türler Schmuck und Juwellen" he stops in front of the window. He looks for one piece of jewelry—and yes, it is there—the gold and diamond brooch which Nina so admires because it is identical with the one worn by Marlene Dietrich.

Adrian rings the doorbell and then enters the store; he will surprise Nina, by bringing her the brooch.

A thin girl with a shy smile is ready to help him, but when Adrian shows her the brooch he wants, Herr Türler himself comes up from the back room and hands Adrian the jewel. *"Eine wunderbare Brosche. Ihre Frau wird sich sehr freuen."* (This is a wonderful pin. Your wife will be very happy.") He packs the jewel in a black velvet box.

A few minutes later, Adrian stops at "Sprüngli Schokoladen." The boxes in the window and on the shelves look just like a display of precious stones from the jewelers.

Adrian chooses a large box of truffles, assorted chocolates and marzipan for Suzy. He knows the chocolates she likes. Then he hurries down the tree-lined boulevard, impatient to share the good news with Nina and Suzy.

He can already see the squat three-story hotel, the Baur au Lac, surrounded by its private park. When he reaches the gate, he stops to admire the balconies embellished with gilded wrought-iron balustrades which overlook the lake. Every room in this hotel has a view of the lake. Johannes Baur, a Swiss farmer who built the hotel in 1844, was smart, and particularly lucky, for in the fall of 1912, Kaiser Wilhelm II of Germany vacationed here with his entire court. Since then, the hotel has become the world's most famous vacation and meeting point in the century.

From his vantage point at the gate of the park, Adrian looks up at the roof. He sees, with shock, that next to the Swiss flag which was always there another red and white flag with a fat swastika in its center has been raised. It was not there when he left the hotel. He suddenly notices that the parking space in front of the hotel is filled with shiny black Mercedes, all adorned with the red, white and black Nazi flag. For a moment, Adrian believes that he is in the wrong place and wants to run away. But then, when he thinks of Nina and Suzy, he walks through the palatial entrance, crosses the lobby, and starts climbing the grand staircase. Under his feet, a soft oriental carpet. Against the wall, flush with the stairs, marble statues of naked goddesses set in niches painted with trees and river views. Everything bathed in a sunny glow.

On his way he crosses stern-looking men with swastika armbands around their sleeves. But he pays no attention to them, and hastens toward his room. He can barely wait to get there. He imagines Nina's face, red with pleasure and her eyes growing big and shiny when he'll give her the brooch. He hopes that she and Suzy are getting ready for dinner and for the concert that follows afterwards.

"Be home for dinner at 7, so we get to the concert before 9," Nina had warned him.

When he reaches the room, Adrian opens the door and says *"Am Sosit. Sunteţi gata?"* (Are you ready?) But he finds himself in a dark room, with the shades and the curtains pulled shut.

"Nina, what's wrong?" he asks, as he turns on a small night light. An ominous feeling takes hold of him. "What's wrong, Nina? What's going on?" He can make out her head—buried between the pillows. Her left arm covers her face.

"I can't go... I have a terrible migraine... Take Suzy and go with her." Her voice sounds muffled and weak.

Adrian stands by the night table with the velvet box in his hand. Should he give it to her? Would it lessen her pain?

No. Not now. He knows Nina too well. It wouldn't do any good. He takes a deep breath, which turns into a sigh. All his joy has suddenly vanished. He feels like a child whose new toys have been broken.

But it's not the first time this has happened. Nina had a migraine attack last year in Venice, and before that—in Rome, in Paris and London. The attacks are always the same: severe throbbing pain in one eye and in one half of the head. Sometimes there are flashing lights in one eye, before the pain starts.

"Take some medicine, just a 'Nanu Muscel.' And I'll call room service for a cup of tea."

"No, no!" Nina moans. "You know it won't work." She moves the pillows under her head. Then she again covers her face with her arm. "Just take Suzy and go. And switch off that light."

Adrian shrugs. He covers the night light with his pajama top and puts his packages in a drawer. He goes to the armoire and takes out a dark suit, a white shirt and a tie. Then he tiptoes to the bathroom to change his clothes.

"There are always surprises with Nina! Hope she'll be fine by tomorrow... Sleep has always worked," he tells himself as he stands in front of the mirror ready to shave.

WAGNER AT THE BAUR AU LAC

A T SEVEN O'CLOCK SHARP, ADRIAN and Suzy walk into the elegant terrace restaurant which is located in the park of the hotel. From their table they can see the glowing geraniums and the hibiscus plants which surround the restaurant and the stage with its little band.

"Look at the gorgeous flowers!" says Adrian. "I wish I could take color pictures with my camera."

He watches Suzy, and sees that she has eyes only for the young musicians in their band uniforms with their shiny instruments. She tries a nonchalant pose as she sits at the table and arranges the pleats of her blue dress with white polka dots.

"Today she looks 16 or even 17 with her rich brown hair down on her shoulders," thinks Adrian. "No trace of the sloppy high-school student with pigtails. Nina would be proud of her. Too bad she couldn't join us."

A waiter in a white jacket with a red carnation in his lapel hands them thick menus inscribed in bold gothic calligraphy. Adrian chooses a salad of fresh endives followed by truffles with venison and a dessert of *crème de marrons* with whipped cream. Suzy is slower to make up her mind; she hesitates between an appetizer of escargots followed by broiled frogs' legs with mashed potatoes and asparagus tips, or a *pâté de foie gras* followed by a roast of wild boar. She settles for the pâté. Tomorrow she might try the other choice. She would also like to taste the cheese fondue, but her mother had told her that it is too hot now for this dish. The dessert will definitely be hot chocolate soufflé with vanilla ice cream.

They have barely finished with the menu when their attention is caught by the people at the next table. This is an American couple with their blond and pudgy seven-year-old son. The parents are tall and slender and speak as if they had *"Prune in gură,"* or "plums in their mouth," Suzy observes. The boy is busy throwing bones and bits if meat to a yellow dog under the table.

"Stop that! Stop that at once!" orders the father. The boy ignores the command and keeps throwing food to the dog.

"Henry, listen to your father, or we'll have to leave the restaurant!" implores the mother.

But little Henry makes a face, and goes on with his game. The father's cheeks are covered with red blotches and he bites his lip. The dog has finished his pieces of meat, and starts growling for more.

Everybody is watching them, when suddenly the sounds of a military band fill the air. The small orchestra has started to play, and a chorus of voices immediately accompanies the band. *"Deutschland, Deutschland über Alles, über Alles in der Welt!"* The words come from a large table near Suzy and Adrian, where a group of young men in dark suits stand at attention and sing the German anthem at the top of their voices.

Adrian recognizes some of the men he has met earlier, when he walked into the hotel. They are all wearing the red and white band with the black swastika around their sleeves.

Everybody on the terrace watches in stunned silence. Only the American family gets up and walks out, the father dragging Henry with one hand, and the dog on the leash with the other.

Automatically—without thinking—Adrian pushes his chair away from the table, ready to get up.

"We're not leaving, are we?" Suzy looks at him with big, frightened eyes. "You promised we'll stay for the concert!"

Adrian catches himself and pulls the chair back to the table. Suzy is right: he has promised her the concert and he can't let her down. She is so in love with Wagner's operas that he must let her see this one where it was first performed.

The band has finished playing the German anthem and Adrian starts nibbling at his salad. The endives are fresh and crisp, and the vinaigrette sauce is spicy and a touch bitter—just right. Nevertheless, he is thoughtful and silent. Everything around him seems to have suddenly lost its sparkle and zest. He should have taken a stand, not just sit here passively like a lump just to please Suzy! Leaving with her, and later explaining to her that it is important to take a stand and to make sacrifices, was the right thing to do. He had behaved like a coward, and now he felt guilty. What would Nina have done? Would she have walked out of the room? Would she have taken a stand? Yes, she did in the past, but for other things. Adrian remembers that she had mixed feelings about the hotel: she admired its stylishness and its elegance, but she resented its snobbery and its high cost.

Adrian recalls an incident which happened in this same restaurant about two years ago. He ordered truffles with pheasant, which was the priciest dish on the menu. Nina got so angry at him for being a spendthrift that she chose a simple fare of macaroni and goat cheese. Soon Adrian got his order of truffles and pheasant and Suzy her plate of veal chops with young asparagus tips. Only Nina's order failed to appear.

It was a long wait. Suzy and Adrian had almost finished their meal when a big commotion took place at the far end of the terrace, near the kitchen door: three waiters came in pushing a gleaming metal cart which supported a large silver tureen. Under the tureen was a gas burner with a lively blue flame. The waiters kept fussing over the cart, while everybody in the restaurant turned to watch this unusual procession. It advanced slowly toward Nina and Adrian's table and stopped right in front of them.

"Gnädige Frau, hier sind ihre Macaroni!" announced the maitre d', making a bow so deep that his nose almost touched the silver tureen.

Nina was embarrassed by this show. Her face turned red. But she ate all the macaroni without saying a word. And in the end the "simple" pasta fare turned out to be twice as expensive as Adrian's fancy delicacy.

They have finished dinner now, and have moved to the concert hall of the hotel. It is a spacious round room, with walls and chairs covered with blue velvet and a dark red stage curtain. The arm- and backrests of the chairs are gilded, and so are the trimmings of the velvet curtain. Crystal chandeliers illuminate the ceiling, which is painted with rosy clouds and flying angels, as if heaven were open overhead.

A note on the program says that this hall has not been changed since the year 1852, when Richard Wagner performed here.

Suzy sits on pins and needles. She can't wait for the concert to start. She loves Richard Wagner's music—his melodious and dramatic tunes, the fresh sounds of water and fire, of wind and thunder, the special magic which suffuses his works. Since Uncle Joel and Aunt Mathilda have taken her to the performance of *Lohengrin* at the opera in Bucharest and since her father has bought her a record album with the prelude and with arias from this work, she is deeply in love with this music.

She now listens carefully to a short, balding man in a dark jacket and striped pants who stands on the stage. He represents a musical organization called "Young Wagner." He speaks about "Young Wagner in Switzerland."

"Wagner arrived here broke and desperate, a hounded political fugitive from his native Germany, whose government sought to arrest and imprison him for high treason. We, the Swiss and our generous country—Switzerland, always a haven for all kinds of fugitives—welcomed him here in Zürich and gave him a new home away from home."

As she listens, Suzy can see in her mind Richard Wagner the "fugitive" dressed as a woman in a long satin dress with a wig and a ribboned hat, stepping into a black carriage pulled by dark horses. It is night, and the carriage rushes through dark, winding country roads. Behind the carriage, several policemen follow on horseback, shooting into the night.

The speaker reminds everybody of young Wagner's important role in the Dresden uprisings of 1849. Of course he ended up a revolutionary on the city's barricades. From the very beginning, his life was full of disasters and suffering. The youngest of nine orphans—Suzy imagines the little boy barefoot, shivering in the cold, hungry and crying...

Then, later, plagued by terrible nightmares which make him scream in the night, he is locked in a dark room, far away from the others.

The world is alien and cruel... He thinks of suicide... In her mind, Suzy can see the image of Goethe's unhappy

Werther shooting himself in the heart with a pistol borrowed from his best friend.

But Richard Wagner does not shoot himself. Music wins over everything else. As he composes new, powerful operas free of old conventions and traditions, he is ready to conquer the world. But Europe is not ready for him. When Suzy learns that Paris rejects him, Vienna ignores him and his own Dresden opposes his innovations, she imagines him wandering alone in the dark, poor, disheveled, dressed in rags and torn shoes, playing his fiddle at street corners, country fairs and backyards reeking of garbage. She is filled with compassion.

But young Wagner is no ordinary musician. When everything fails, he turns to politics. He joins his friend, Mikhail Bakunin, the Russian founder of the Anarchist movement. He writes left-wing articles against the corrupt government. And, to Suzy's surprise and delight, he gets deeply involved in Dresden's social uprising. It is he who plans the burning of the Royal Palace and who orders the ammunition for the torching. It is he who organizes an armed conspiracy. And it is he who climbs to the top of the city's Bell Tower to incite the people to revolution. Suzy can see him running, talking, writing, scheming and planning, tirelessly, without sleep, full of fire and energy.

Nevertheless—it all ends in failure. An arrest warrant—to be followed by a long sentence—is issued against him. Fortunately he manages to get a false passport with a woman's name. He escapes to Switzerland.

What courage! What abnegation!" Suzy is deeply touched by his revolutionary zeal. She thinks this is always neglected by his biographers.

On the stage, the little man is ending his speech. "Tonight," he says as he gathers his notes, "we will watch the performance of *Lohengrin*, which Wagner conducted in this room in 1852. He had never watched a performance of this work before this time."

With these words he takes a deep bow and vanishes behind the curtains. The audience applauds, and the orchestra starts playing the prelude to *Lohengrin*. Suzy closes her eyes, letting herself melt in the spellbinding music of the Holy Grail. When she looks up again, the curtain rises and she is transported to medieval Brabant on the banks of the river Scheldt. Here, Princess Elsa, an innocent maiden, is accused of the murder of her brother, the rich Duke Godfrey of Brabant.

The music carries Suzy deep into the story. She sees herself now in Brabant, and stands near the judge of the trial, King Henry the Fowler. He sits on a throne, under the legendary 1,000-year-old Oak of Justice. The King decides that justice should be done through "ordeal by battle" between the noble Telramund—Elsa's accuser—and her own champion.

Suzy is completely involved with the opera. She is now standing near the young princess who walks in a trance surrounded by her maidens. When the plot thickens and there are signs of danger, she becomes as fearful and restless as the crowd on the stage. She fidgets in her seat, and bites her fingernails. Then, with the appearance of Lohengrin, Suzy is awed by the strange knight in shining armor who arrives on the swan-boat. She has never seen such a handsome youth— tall, with golden hair and deep blue eyes. Her heart goes out to him as he sings a tender farewell to the swan. And, in her mind, while the strings and the woodwinds play—he becomes Wagner himself.

The moments of bliss continue as the knight asks Elsa to be his bride. "All that I have, all that I am, is thine!" Elsa replies, and Suzy nods, with folded hands, holding her breath.

But then she is worried again, as the heroes, Elsa and Lohengrin, face new perils and heartbreak.

At the last notes of the orchestra, Suzy is in tears. She is deeply moved by the unhappy fate of the princess and by Lohengrin's melancholy charm. Without any doubt he is Wagner himself. "What a sad, sad story," she says as she wipes the tears from her eyes. "Richard Wagner must have had a heart of gold to write such a moving opera. And he must have been a real self-sacrificing revolutionary!"

"Well, not quite," says Adrian. His voice is very matter-of-fact. He holds her arm as they walk out of the room.

"What do you mean?" Suzy throws him a sharp look. She is angry.

Adrian shrugs. He still holds on to her arm.

"I don't want to upset you, but if Richard Wagner was a romantic revolutionary in his youth, he certainly changed with the years. He became a fanatical German nationalist and a militant anti-Semite. Also, he was anything but selfless. He liked to live in luxury: elegant villas and fancy clothes. His shirts, his underwear, his bed linen were all made of expensive, imported silk. And he wrote his operas with a golden pen he had received from King Ludwig II of Bavaria. He often ended up with huge debts and had to flee from his creditors. And he hated Jews, he accused them of being an inferior, dangerous race, with a ruinous effect on German music."

Adrian stops at the first landing and rests his back against the banisters. Then he goes on. "He often accused his creditors of being Jewish, and abused them. He also hated the Jewish composers Meyerbeer and Mendelssohn—particularly Meyerbeer—even though he had received much help from him. Wagner got his first opera, Rienzi, performed due to his intervention. But when Meyerbeer refused to lend him money, Wagner started writing hateful articles against him.

"I can't believe all these stories!" Suzy frees her elbow from Adrian's grasp.

"Well, perhaps it all has to do with the question whether Wagner himself was Jewish or not. His adoptive father, Ludwig Geyer, who was believed to be his real father, was suspected of being Jewish. So young Richard changed his name from Geyer to Wagner. But nevertheless, he looked Jewish. He had a big, hawklike nose, for which he was often teased by other children in school, and he was born in the Jewish section of Leipzig... They say that he was so anti-Semitic to prove to everybody and to himself that he wasn't Jewish... And the tale of Lohengrin's forbidden name was directly inspired by his own secret identity!"

"No, no, all this can't be true!" Suzy covers her ears with her hands. "I just don't believe you!"

"But these are historical facts. Even his friend Nietzsche has written about this."

Suzy shakes her head and purses her lips. She has dropped her hands from her ears. "Your historical facts stink. Why should I believe you? Mama and you have always told me that people are jealous of greatness and success, and often invent nasty stories in revenge. Why should I believe this dirty gossip? If Wagner were the way you describe him, he could never create an opera as pure and beautiful as Lohengrin!" She turns a glowing face toward Adrian.

They walk down the corridor toward their rooms. Adrian is silent.

"Your logic is perfect, but your facts are wrong," he says when they stop in front of their doors. "Maybe one day you will understand and you'll change your mind."

"I won't ever change my mind! Don't bet on it!" She replies. She then opens her door, turns around, hesitates, and gives her father a kiss on the cheek.

"Good night. I don't buy your facts. But don't be cross with me."

For a moment, Adrian stands alone in the corridor. "I wanted to teach her how to make a stand. But she knows this already. Maybe I should learn from her!" he tells himself and smiles, as he opens the door to his room.

THE KING AND THE SWANS

N EXT MORNING NINA BRUSHES HER teeth and combs her hair in front of the venetian mirror which hangs in the bathroom. She looks at her pale face, at the gray strand of hair which curls over her forehead—and at her eyes, which still look tired—even though she has slept through the night and the headaches are gone.

The headaches are such a curse! They poison her life and play havoc with all her plans. They are particularly bothersome when she is traveling. Anything can set them off: loud noise, too much heat, poor sleep, or food which disagrees with her. Not to speak about worrisome or frightening events.

The pains usually start on one side of the head and then spread to the rest of the skull or half of the skull, crushing and squeezing it in a vice. No pill or syrup has ever helped. All she can do is lock herself up in a dark and quiet room and sleep. She is ashamed of her headaches and afraid that one day Adrian will have enough and leave. But he assures her that he has no such intentions and that he "loves her too much" in spite of her migraines. Besides, he is used to people with headaches, since his own mother suffered from them.

Nina hopes this is true. She now puts on some lipstick, brushes the gray strand of hair out of her eyes, ties the sash of her Japanese kimono and steps into the room.

It's only 8:30 in the morning, but Adrian sits already on the balcony, fully dressed and freshly shaved. He wears English Leather, a cologne which pleases her and makes her feel good.

"Good morning, my dear. How are your headaches?" he asks.

"They're gone now and I feel fine!"

Adrian smiles, and gets up to give her a kiss.

"You look as if you had a good sleep. Am I right?"

Then, without waiting for her answer, he asks, "Tea or coffee? And an *oeuf à la coque*?"

"Tea, please. And no eggs, thank you. Only cherry preserve."

As she sits down, Nina looks into the distance and is dazzled by the snowcapped mountains glittering in the sun and the deep blue Zürich lake speckled with red, white and orange sailboats. A flock of swans fly gracefully over the water, which reflects their spotless glow.

"I'm so sorry I missed the show yesterday. How was it?"

"Beautiful. A really good performance. A perfect Lohengrin and a charming Elsa. Suzy was bowled over. You should have seen her yourself: she is very taken with Wagner!"

"Yes, indeed! I wish I had been there. But thank you for walking so quietly into the room last night. Were you late? I didn't hear you at all!"

"I'm glad." Adrian stirs the tea with a monogrammed silver spoon. Many things here have a monogram: the silver cutlery, the cups and saucers, the tall crystal glasses, the ashtrays, the damask napkins and tablecloth—even the towels and the bed linen are elegantly embroidered with the initials of the hotel. Nevertheless, objects go missing, as guests pack them in their luggage as "souvenirs."

Adrian and Nina sit quietly in the shade of their striped yellow and blue parasol and Nina spreads the dark red cherry preserve on her slice of buttered toast. She would like to talk more about Suzy and Wagner, but the silence is so peaceful and so refreshing that she doesn't say anything.

A transparent dragonfly alights on her piece of toast, and when she picks up her napkin to chase it away, she discovers the black velvet box tucked underneath.

"*O Doamne, ce-i asta?*" (Oh my God, what is this?) she asks, looking at Adrian.

"How should I know?" he shrugs. "Just open the box and we will see."

Nina takes the box in her hand and examines it carefully. The name "Türler" which appears on the gold label tells her immediately what to expect—and for a moment she doesn't know whether she should get up and give him a kiss or look into the box.

"Open the box! Just open the box!" He laughs and blushes slightly, embarrassed by the desire to please her. Nina turns the box in her hand, caressing the velvet with the tip of her fingers. Finally, when she opens it, she is mesmerized by the sparkling rubies and white diamonds. And there, in a corner of the pin, is the space of the small missing stone, which made Marlene Dietrich sell the pin, after making it famous in *Der Blaue Engel*.

"I can't believe this," she whispers, as she looks up from the brooch to Adrian, and again to the pin.

"Well, you stopped so often at Türler's and admired the brooch, I knew what you wanted: nothing less than Marlene's old pin from *Der Blaue Engel*! How does the song go? *Ich bin von Kopf zu Fuss auf Liebe eingestellt, und das ist meine Welt!*" Adrian bursts out singing, and before Nina can push him away, he takes her in his arms and dances with her around the balcony.

"Spendthrift!" she scolds him. "I will never be Lola!"

"For me you are. More than Lola." He smiles and kisses her hand.

"But where will I wear it? I won't turn into a cabaret dancer just to wear Lola's pin."

"Of course not. I know where you can wear it: Saturday at Charles Kass's party. He wants us to meet his wife Brigitte, and a few other friends."

"Charles Kass? Why? What kind of party?" Nina sounds intrigued, almost suspicious.

"...You can wear your black satin suit and the silver fox if it's not too hot."

"You didn't answer my question. What kind of party? You never mentioned it before."

"Sorry. Yes, Charles Kass's party." Adrian lights a cigarette, clears his voice, and finally tells Nina about his meeting with him and the unexpected job offer which could bring all of them to Switzerland.

"This is more than a dream come true! It opens up so many wonderful opportunities—new developments in turbines and the transport of energy, travel all over Europe and possibly even to America, research projects, meetings with people in the field, to list only a few."

Finally he tells her that Kass has already opened an account in Adrian's name and deposited 10,000 SF with the Schweizerischer Bankverein.

Nina listens to him and sips her tea. She watches a small boat with a golden sail approach the pier. Adrian keeps looking at her as he goes on talking. "It would be good for the children too to study here, in the best schools, and practice sports and mountain climbing in the fresh air."

"When would we have to move?" Nina asks, still watching the boat at the pier.

"Well, of course, the sooner the better." He shrugs and arches his eyebrows. Then he puts down his cigarette and takes Nina's small hand in his own.

"Remember the villa in Lugano? The pink villa which sits by the water's edge?"

"What villa?"

"The villa with the grove of orange and lemon trees, and the white magnolia bush. The villa we discovered on our honeymoon, and which you liked so much."

"What about it?" Suddenly Nina feels the air getting heavier and heavier. Will the headaches start again?

"We could buy that villa now, if we decide to move to Switzerland." Adrian speaks louder and faster than usual. He's full of excitement.

"Let me see: I think I found an old plan of the house in the bottom of my valise. It had two bedrooms and a couple of guest rooms—enough to invite your sister Stella and her family." Adrian looks at Nina with shining eyes. He can barely contain his enthusiasm.

"But we haven't seen that villa in more than ten years. How do you know it is still for sale? How do you know it even stands anymore?"

Adrian shrugs. "I don't know. But we can go there and see. And if it isn't for sale or doesn't exist anymore, we can find another one like it."

Nina looks down and doesn't say anything. She wipes away an invisible crumb from her flowered kimono and bites her lips.

"I'm so overwhelmed by this news—I don't know what to say," she whispers. "I'm so happy for you... and the children, of course. But it's so overwhelming and so sudden... almost shattering. I can't find my bearings. I have to get used to this... plan." She turns toward him with anxious and pleading eyes.

Adrian takes her hand over the table and gives her a worried look.

"It will be all right—you will see. Nothing to be frightened of. Don't you trust me? I'll make sure that everything is safe for us." He winks at her and raises her hand to his lips.

"Well, we'll talk more when I'll be back for lunch. It's getting late now and I must be off to the bank."

Nina follows him into the room and watches him fix his tie and slip on his jacket. Then she sees him to the door and returns to the balcony with her English copy of *Mrs. Dalloway*. It is a small paperback, which Domnişoara Braunstein, her English tutor (and Adrian's secretary) gave her before the trip. She holds the open book in her lap, but she doesn't read. A vague, brooding sadness takes hold of her. Absentmindedly she watches a long procession of ants marching down the side of a stone planter and carry with them the iridescent wing of a dead moth. In the sunshine, the shimmering wing looks like a moving flower. She follows it gliding down slowly until it vanishes inside a crack.

As she watches them, the ants frighten and depress her. She sees them grow large and threatening, with monstrous jaws, ready to devour whatever stands in their way. Nina feels suddenly cold and gathers her kimono tightly around her.

The dark crack in the wall of the planter seems to grow deeper and more cavernous, and its jagged borders remind her of the bombed-out house of her parents in World War I, all fallen in ruin. She then sees one room, where her mother lay, dying. Her mother had caught the Spanish flu and was getting weaker and weaker. But she was restless, and in her agitation said that she couldn't find peace until her four children and her husband were gathered in the room, near her bed. It took a great effort to bring her husband and her two sons back from the front. But even though she was barely breathing, she hung on to life until they stood there, by her.

"Promise me that the four of you will always stay close and keep an eye on each other. You will not scatter away in the world, in the direction of the four winds."

These were her last words, and only after they had all sworn to stay together—holding hands with each other— did she close her eyes and depart.

And indeed, for 20 years they had kept the promise.

No one had moved away from Bucharest! And it felt impossible to Nina to be the first one to break the oath and leave, thus betraying her mother and committing an unforgivable sin.

She shudders again as the old memories come back—her mother's death, followed by her own suicide attempt. For she knew she couldn't live after her mother died. She can still feel the sharp kitchen knife slashing her throat from side to side, driven by the pain and despair of being abandoned. For her mother had taken with her, to her grave, Nina's most loathsome and darkest secret.

From deep down, a dreadful memory now comes to the surface. She cannot control it—she has no power to push it away. It's the shameful attack of her cousin Arnold, when she was 10 and he was 16. It happened on that day, June 30th—Uncle Herman's birthday—when everybody had gone across the street to his house to celebrate, and she was to join them there. She had been late from school and was alone in the house, changing her clothes. The kitchen door was open, to let Tiţa, the dog, run in and out.

Nina was just buttoning her blouse when she heard the door open and close, and then steps in the corridor.

Thinking it was the maid, she stepped out of her room and found herself face to face with cousin Arnold. She still remembers his greasy hair, his bad skin, and how spittle was flying around when he spoke.

"I came to return your brother Liviu's book. Is he here?"

"Nobody's here," Nina said, trying to get back into the room.

"Are you alone?" he asked, with a nasty glint in his eyes.

When she said yes, she was alone, they were all at Uncle Herman's and she was rushing to join them, he suddenly jumped on her and grabbed her. At the same time he made her bend forward and lifted her skirt over her head.

She felt his hands all over her body, and she tried to scream, to fight him, to bite and to scratch him, but he pulled her skirt so tightly over her face that she almost choked. He had also twisted her arm behind her back.

Then she felt sudden pain, helpless rage and waves of nausea—until it all vanished in a dark blur.

When she came to, all she remembered was Arnold zipping his pants and threatening that, if she ever broke the silence, he would tell everybody that she had lifted her skirt and shown herself to him.

After that, her headaches started and she felt really sick. She couldn't eat, she couldn't sleep, she grew very thin and had dark circles under her eyes. She felt so guilty and soiled—she was sure it was something bad she had done which made Arnold attack her. These thoughts made her sleep badly and gave her frightening nightmares.

Her father—who was a doctor—made her drink cod liver oil to improve her appetite, and her mother fed her thick slices of barely cooked calf's liver, dripping with blood.

But in the end it was her mother who noticed that Nina grew nervous and pale and ran to her room whenever Arnold came to the house. One Saturday afternoon when he was visiting and Nina stormed out the door, her mother got up and followed her to her room. Nina remembers her mother taking her in her arms and telling her that she guessed what happened, and that whatever Arnold had done was not Nina's fault.

Nina buried her head in her mother's chest and burst into tears. Then she told all she remembered, and her mother kept hugging her and saying that she was always going to love her, and that she had done nothing wrong. After that, the headaches were gone, and her sleep and appetite were as good as before.

Now, sitting on the balcony, Nina absentmindedly touches the raised scar on her neck. She knows that the old wound is not very visible, but she can feel its hardened borders with her fingertips. Nina remembers how her sister Stella found her slumped to the floor and how she rushed her to the hospital, where she got 12 stitches and where she had to stay for 10 days. To her great disappointment she wasn't allowed to leave the building and attend her mother's funeral. This made her very sad and she cried a lot, even though her father and her two brothers came to see her several times before going back to the front. They brought her apples, strawberry preserve and Turkish delight, which she loved. These gifts helped her bear the heavy stench of pus and disinfectant which pervaded the hospital filled with wounded soldiers.

It was her young sister Stella who nursed her back to health at home and in the hospital. Stella, who had just started working as a nurse's aide with the injured soldiers, was like a substitute mother to her "orphaned" older sister.

Little by little, as Nina felt protected and cared for by her like a "real mother," she trusted Stella and told her her deep secret. After that she felt so tightly bound to Stella, as if they were two parts of the same body which could not be cut in two.

Thus, Nina thinks, the promise made to their dying mother has become reality. And, to complicate matters further, Stella has told her that she would never leave the country because of her great love for Victor Georgescu.

But how about Adrian? How about his plan to move to Switzerland? How about his career? Does she have the right to stop him or slow him down?

And how about the children? They weren't badly off in Bucharest. They went to the best schools in the city and enjoyed wonderful vacations. But life and school in Switzerland would be something else. What right does she have to interfere with their future?

Nina rubs her forehead in confusion. Of course, logic tells her to be sensible and follow Adrian's plan. But deep inside her, her heart tells her something else. She still hears her mother's words and feels Stella's caring embrace.

Nina closes the book in her lap and puts it on a chair. Then she opens the box on the table and takes the new pin in her hand. She turns it around and admires the unusually fine workmanship, the sparkling, transparent diamonds, the fiery rubies nestled in delicate leaves of gold. It is hard to believe that the pin is hers now. She was happy just stopping at Türler's window and admiring it day after day. She had no wish to buy and possess it. She is always happy just contemplating an object of beauty—a flower, a sunny landscape, a sculpture or painting by a good artist. She likes stillness and privacy, a quiet evening with a book and soft music or with a few friends.

Not so Adrian. He likes to do things, meet people and go places. He bought her the brooch as soon as he saw that she loved it. And didn't he give her the silver fox and the black alligator bag with the golden clasp so that they could go to concerts and meet friends at fine restaurants? And now she will have to go to Charles' party and face people she doesn't know. Nina closes her eyes and tries to imagine Charles Kass's home, his wife Brigitte and the guests she doesn't know.

But in the next minute the door flies open and Suzy bursts in, followed by Adrian.

"The flags! The flags!" she screams in excitement. "The Germans have left, and now the hotel is celebrating us! The three of us!"

"What are you talking about? It's all nonsense," says Nina.

"They're celebrating us, I tell you," Suzy insists. "There are Romanian flags all over the place, even on the roof, on top of the building. Come and see, if you don't believe me!"

"What got into her?" Nina asks Adrian. "It all sounds so weird to me."

"No, no, I think it's true. Come down for a walk and you'll see. There are Romanian flags all over the place. They must be celebrating us." He stops and thinks. "It's soon time for lunch, anyway. We can take a walk first, and then a short boat ride on the lake."

Nina dresses quickly, slipping on a light cream color linen dress and a small string of pearls.

"You look lovely. Quite elegant." Adrian nods with approval, while Suzy rolls her eyes and taps her foot with impatience.

They follow the carpeted corridor, and as they walk down the staircase they notice that, indeed, the Germans have left, and that Romanian flags have appeared on the desk of the concierge and at the entrance. They look at each other with a mixture of pride and puzzlement, and smile. Then, when they're out on the driveway and look back at the roof of the hotel, they see that the German flag with the big black swastika has been replaced with a large Romanian flag which flutters next to the Swiss one with its white cross. This makes them feel very important—somewhat like royalty—and they now strut, full of authority, holding their chins very high. "You see, I was right again," says Suzy. "You really should trust me more!"

They cross the park and walk past the pond with its goldfish and its family of swans—two snow-white adult birds and three grey, puffy babies, riding on the back of their parents.

Before long they reach the edge of the water, and they embark on a small steamship which takes them across the lake. They sit on the open deck letting the soft breeze cool their faces, their necks and their arms, and they watch the goings-on around them. Most passengers are tourists like themselves, some carry rucksacks with camping gear, others are fishermen armed with various types of fishing rods, fishing nets, and hooks and worms prepared for catching the 20 pound trouts they dream about.

Not far from them sits a hunting party, all the men wearing green felt costumes and hats decorated with colorful feathers, and carrying hunting guns to shoot rabbits and foxes. Long hunting knives and leather pouches are hanging from their belts, and one man with a red feather in his hat is carrying a hunting horn attached with a silver chain.

Children are running from one end of the deck to the other, screaming with shrill voices, and throwing bits of white rolls and croissants to the swans which follow the boat. There is a large flock close to where Suzy sits, and she throws them pieces of a raisin croissant she has tucked in her pocket. The gracious birds look up with their beady eyes, then they curve their long necks and dip their bills under the water to catch their food.

"They must have been here in Wagner's time, and he must have loved them—otherwise he wouldn't have put swans in his two operas, *Lohengrin* and *Parsifal*," says Suzy. And when three very large white birds fly over her head making a strange singing sound with their wings, she wonders whether they are real swans or enchanted princes and princesses like the ones in Swan Lake.

The little steamship follows them, as it hugs the hilly bank of the lake—all covered with pine forests and linden trees. White villas surrounded by gardens of roses, geraniums and peonies are hiding behind the woods, and an old church tower rises above the trees.

Half an hour later, Adrian, Nina and Suzy get off the ship at a small bathing resort tucked between vineyards, and start home on another boat. It is hot now, not a cloud on the horizon—the air is like a blazing furnace—and there is no bird in the sky.

Back on the shore, on their way to the hotel, they stop on the street, at a bookseller's table, and Suzy buys a book about "Young Wagner" written by Professor Dr. Müller, the man who lectured at the concert the night before. On the cover is a picture of Lohengrin in his shiny armor, traveling in the swan-boat, while behind him a mighty palace is engulfed in flames.

"The King's palace in Dresden, set on fire by Wagner's revolution!" Suzy declares with shiny eyes.

Adrian gives her a worried look. "You're turning into a true revolutionary—if I may say so. I only hope that you don't set fire to the hotel before we leave." He smiles, but worry lingers in his eyes.

"I'll think it over." Suzy is delighted with her father's concern.

At the hotel, they are again greeted by Romanian flags which flutter on the roof and on the desk of the concierge.

"It really makes me feel good to be treated like this." Adrian walks tall and pulls back his shoulders.

"Maybe this isn't for us, after all," Nina whispers in a low voice.

"Nonsense! Of course it's for us. Who else?" Adrian and Suzy say, full of conviction.

Lunch is served on the garden terrace shaded by tall chestnut trees and colored umbrellas. On the way to their table they pass by the pond once again, and Suzy stops by the baby swans.

"Why did Andersen call them Ugly Ducklings? To me they look like adorable little toys."

"Because to a duck they must look very ugly," says Nina.

"That's a duck's point of view. But to me they look very lovely. Can't we take one home with us? I'm sure they'll let us, if we ask the maitre d'. Today, with all the Romanian flags, he'll want to please us."

"Let's eat first, and we'll decide later." Nina is pulling Suzy away from the pond.

They have finally reached their table and are ready to take their seats when a loud commotion of voices and footsteps reaches them from the other end of the terrace.

A tall, handsome and slightly portly young man with blue eyes and a blond moustache advances between the tables, arm in arm with an elegant young woman with flaming red hair and very white skin. They look deep into each other's eyes, and are followed by a host of attendants and waiters, one of them holding big hunting dogs on a leash.

As the convoy advances—led by the maitre d'—the restaurant band starts playing the Romanian National Anthem. Adrian, Nina and Suzy watch in surprise, then: "The King! King Carol!" say Suzy and Adrian at the same time.

"And his mistress, Magda Lupescu!" adds Nina. "I told you, those flags weren't for us!"

But Adrian and Suzy don't listen to her; they don't know what to do, whether they should remain seated, or stand to attention, like the German officials did yesterday, when the band played *"Deutschland, Deutschland über Alles."*

As the king and his companion come close to their table, they notice that he wears a hunting costume with a revolver tucked into a leather holster attached to his belt. The young woman wears an elaborate jade and gold set—a necklace, large earrings, and a fine bracelet. The jade matches her green eyes, setting off her rich red hair.

"I missed you so much—*mi-a fost aşa dor*—I could barely wait to see you again. [*Abia am putut să aştept să te vad din nou.*] It was lonely in London, at Buckingham Palace without you."

The king and the young woman continue their sweet talk as sudden barking and growling can be heard behind them. A baby swan has ventured close to the terrace, and is quickly followed by its excited mother.

In the next minute, the largest of the hunting dogs breaks out of his leash, and bounds with great leaps toward the birds. The other dogs start barking and struggle to join him, so that the man who is holding the leash is pulled along by the force of the animals.

There is a big commotion as the king's attendants and the hotel waiters with white gloves run down the lawn, trying to catch the dogs. But the animals are faster, and cannot be stopped. In the next moment, the king turns around, pulls his revolver out of the holster, and fires three shots in the air. Instantly, the trained dogs give a loud yelp and return to the king, depositing their prey—a half-dead baby swan and its bleeding mother—at his feet.

Out of nowhere—like a *"Deus ex Machina"*—a press photographer appears between tables and starts snapping pictures.

Soon there is chaos: women shriek hysterically at various tables, Magda Lupescu, the king's companion, is given smelling salts while she's stretched out on a lounge chair, and an army of waiters and kitchen help hasten to wash away the stains of blood and the broken feathers left by the wounded swans. During this entire time, the band of musicians goes on playing the Romanian National Anthem.

Adrian, Nina and Suzy have watched the whole scene in perfect silence. Then, when the calm is restored, Adrian points to the photographer, who is still busy with his camera.

"I can see the photo and the caption in the newspapers tomorrow morning. It will probably say something like: Romanian king with Jewish mistress shoots swans at luxury hotel."

"I always said he should abdicate, like his cousin Edward VIII in England, who married Walli Simpson." Nina shakes her head in disapproval, and lowers her voice. "This monarchy is corrupt..."

"Like the monarchy in Dresden, in the time of Richard Wagner," Suzy pipes up. "Monarchy is a corrupt institution!" she adds at the top of her voice, while her parents signal her desperately to lower her tone.

MEMORIES, MEMORIES...

ADRIAN SITS AT A TABLE of the small "Wilhelm Tell" café in the old square, at the foot of St. Peter's Church. He looks up at the steeple, which houses the second largest clock of Europe after Big Ben. It has just tolled 12, and the air still vibrates from its overwhelming sound, which seems to have released a sea of other church bells all around. Adrian covers his ears to avoid being drowned in this cascade of sounds.

When the air is still again, a young waitress with freckled cheeks and blond braids wound around her head like a Gretchen brings him a cup of *"Caffee mit Schlag"* and the *Neue Zürcher Zeitung* of the day.

He lights a cigarette and opens the book he has bought for Suzy at the bookstore near the University. It's a collection of math puzzles for young people. He moves his lips as he reads and turns the pages. It's the same collection of math puzzles he had as a student. He loved them and found them entertaining. They actually helped him learn calculus and algebra. He bought the book for Suzy, because a few months ago he surprised her sitting at her desk, totally absorbed in a page torn from a magazine of math puzzles. He was delighted to see that she was interested in math, so that a career based on applied calculus—such as architecture, engineering or physics—looks like a possibility.

Adrian takes a sip of coffee and keeps browsing through the new book. It reminds him of his student years, when he traveled from Münich—where he studied—to Zürich to attend scientific conferences. It was at one of these special meetings that Nicola Tesla, the great physicist, gave him the autographed photo which he keeps in his office.

The two cities, Zürich and Münich, weren't far from each other: just a few hours by train. Also one summer he took a job as a tram conductor in Zürich. (His mother wanted him to come home for the summer, and when he refused, she stopped sending him money.) The pay from his job was good, and he lived frugally in a small room, right under the roof, in an old house close to this square.

With the money left after he paid his living expenses, he traveled to the most famous peaks in the Alps, and also south, to Lugano and the other Great Lakes. It was then, when he was in his twenties, that the dream of moving to Switzerland and living in Lugano, in the land of eternal spring, took hold of him. Lugano always brought to his mind Goethe's lyrical poem "MIGNON," which he had learned in school:

> *Kennst du das Land wo die Zitronen blühn,*
> *Im dunklen Laub die Gold-Orangen glühn.*
> *Ein sanfter Wind von blauen Himmel weht,*
> *Die Myrtle still, und hoch der Lorbeer steht?*

—the mythical land where lemon and orange trees bloom forever, surrounded by tall and silent bushes of myrtle and laurel. For a minute, the little café and the whole city cease to exist, and he is transported to a shore covered with palm trees and cypresses. But the blond waitress brings him back to reality, when she stops at his table and pours him another cup of coffee. He closes the book, puts it back in its bag, and opens the Real Estate section of the newspaper.

Yes, he thinks, with the money from Charles I can buy a nice villa in Lugano. And if I sell the office and our house in Bucharest, we can also get a decent apartment in Zürich. As he reads the *Neue Zürcher Zeitung*, he starts making marks at certain apartments.

I have to sell my property at a good price, he keeps calculating in his mind. But he suddenly stops when he realizes that he would never again see the rooms in which he has spent so much of his life. He will never again see the engraved windows of his office, on which a naked giant is shown covering, with his hand, a row of tall factory chimneys. This forces the smoke back into the buildings, and then makes it pour out, into the streets, through narrow doors and windows. Crowds of tiny people are running around, trying to escape the deadly fumes. Meanwhile the gigantic devil with his black horns and long tail keeps watching them and grins.

Adrian remembers the original cartoon published in a German magazine which served as a model for this panel and the caption which condemned the evils of industrialization. But to him it represented a condemnation of the "poisonous" coal-burning custom—to be replaced with "clean" and new electricity. But even without its symbolic meaning he has always loved this engraving, which was made for him by a gifted artist. Leaving it behind feels like cutting off a part of himself. Adrian sighs. Sometimes the price one has to pay is very high.

He wonders about Nina. How will she cope with it? How about her ghastly headaches? But then he discards this thought. Right now she has accepted to travel with him to

Lugano, on condition that they continue their trip to the top of the Alps. In two days it will be Suzy's birthday, and they should celebrate it high in the mountains. Suzy always dreamt of going there, but they never took her, and Nina said they were neglecting her.

Adrian puts on his glasses and pulls out of his pocket a folded map of Switzerland. He spreads it out on the table—after pushing aside the cup of coffee—and studies it carefully: Wednesday, the day after tomorrow, they will take the train to Lugano, where they will stay two days, and then they will be off to Interlaken to start their trip to Grindelwald and Jungfraujoch. He can barely wait to watch Suzy's excitement at the sights she will encounter—the bare, snow-covered peaks, the thundering waterfalls, the meadows covered with blue enzian and red Alpenrosen, and, in the cracks between the rocks, the solitary Edelweiss. Then, near the top of the mountain they will stop at the edge of the Eismeer or the Sea of Ice—a frozen ocean of virgin white, sparkling with the cold fires of hidden diamonds. Finally, near the peak of the Jungfraujoch, they will visit the Ice Palace, the fairy-tale castle chiseled in ice, with its turrets, its ballroom and banquet hall, its vast throne room bathed in the blue light of translucent ice.

All the furniture and decoration is made of ice: the slender columns, the couches and armchairs, the vases with exotic flowers, and even the chandeliers. He remembers the trips up there like journeys to another planet. One time, precisely on their honeymoon, it was so cold that Nina had to buy woolen underwear, woolen socks, gloves, a scarf and a hat right there, at the tourist shop on top of the mountain.

Adrian takes a pen out of his pocket, and starts writing notes on a paper napkin. They will travel up the mountain by cable car or *teleferique* and by electric train, and then eat at the rotating restaurant at Schilthorn. Later they will admire the sunset at Wengen, where the entire mountain turns red when the sun goes down, and all the tourists applaud the spectacle.

But what if the day is windy and the cable car shakes from side to side? This could give Nina a migraine headache, and then the whole trip would be ruined. Adrian sips the last drop of coffee. It could happen. It did—in the past. But why worry now? There is no time to be lost. He should hurry home, to the hotel, and make train and hotel reservations.

He folds the newspaper before getting up, and there, on the last page of the Real Estate section, at the bottom, he finds the picture of a house like the old villa they had visited in Lugano on their honeymoon. Adrian has dreamt of it so many times! Now he thinks that he recognizes the front of the villa, the sunny balcony, the palm trees near the wrought iron gate and the climbing wisteria. Everything looks almost alike, only the address is different—two blocks away from the house they had visited. He remembers how they planned to decorate the rooms with rattan furniture and light floral cretonne, and how, for some time after their honeymoon, they put aside prints, watercolors and a few ceramic vases for their "dream house" in Lugano.

Adrian keeps staring at the picture in the newspaper and shakes his head. He is all excited by the unusual resemblance of the two villas. A strange coincidence indeed! He gets up, pays the waitress and leaves the café just as the clock tolls half past one. He rushes home through the narrow streets of the Old City until he reaches the linden trees of the *Banhofstrasse.*

The hotel is quiet now. King Carol and his entourage have left, and the Romanian flags have been taken down. No new famous guests have checked in. Adrian asks the concierge to make train and hotel reservations for Lugano and Interlaken.

"Jawohl," says the concierge. *"Hier sind zwei Telegramme für sie, die sind gerade jetzt angekommen!"* he adds, as he hands him two new telegrams.

Adrian takes the letters and reads them quickly. The first one comes from Warsaw, is signed by Uncle Ariel, and says: "Arriving in Zürich on Wednesday. Urgent Zionist conference. Will meet you at the hotel." The second one is from Sorel, also announcing his arrival for the same day, also specifying "Important meeting." He will also join them at the hotel.

Adrian reads the telegrams a second time and frowns. What is going on? Surely an ad-hoc, unplanned emergency Zionist meeting, since both Sorel and Uncle Ariel are active leaders in the organization. He stands in the lobby and worries about bad news. At the same time he is getting angry. Something important is happening, otherwise they wouldn't be coming to Zürich so much ahead of the Zionist Congress, which is scheduled for early September. But why do they have to arrive just now, at the exact time when he is planning his trip to the mountains? If he were superstitious he would think that the Gods are plotting against him. But no, he is a practical and rational man. He lights a cigarette and tries to organize his thoughts. He is decided to go on with his expedition to the peak of the Alps and the trip to Lugano.

With the letters in his hand he paces the floor, and concentrates on his choices. He could pretend that he has never received the telegrams or that they have never arrived—and thus he can keep up with his travel plan. This would make them miss Sorel and Uncle Ariel, since he, Adrian, and his family would be away.

But in this case he would have to lie to Nina and to everyone else. He could never tell her the truth. And he would have to cut the telegrams in little pieces and burn them or throw them away, in any case make them disappear. And he would have to go on lying to Nina, even when looking into her eyes. But... he shakes his head. He knows he cannot do that. And besides, he would certainly betray himself sooner or later and Nina would never forgive him for the deception.

What else can he do? He stares at the geometric pattern of the wallpaper—interlocked stylized flowers and birds—trying to concentrate as hard as he can...

Then, suddenly he has an idea: why not change the sequence of the itinerary, since they have to change the date anyway? Why not travel first to Interlaken and the mountains and then down to Lugano on the way back? He runs back to the concierge.

When Adrian reaches the desk, the young man in his gold-trimmed uniform stops polishing his fingernails and opens a thick book which contains all the train schedules of Switzerland. He turns page after page and goes down the list with his manicured index finger. Then he arches his eyebrows and makes a clicking sound with his tongue. "No, it can't be done," he finally says. "There are no good train connections on the days you have chosen."

The concierge's German accent reminds Adrian of somebody—but whom? He struggles to remember, and now he has it. It reminds him of Kass. He remembers him saying, "You don't have much time, you must act quickly!"

Adrian walks slowly away from the desk, squeezing the handkerchief in his pocket. He stares at a crystal vase without seeing it. What he sees is a deserted train station, and a train pulling out just as he is walking in. It is dark and cold, and the shrill whistle slices the silence like a knife. He stands alone on the empty platform, clutching the papers in his hands. To his left, the clerk in the ticket booth closes the window and pulls down the blinds. Behind him, the station master locks up the waiting room and turns off the light. There won't be any trains running tonight... and God knows until when. Adrian sighs. His mouth is dry.

But then he rubs his eyes as if waking up from a dream... He straightens his body. A voice repeats in his ear Lugano... Lugano... It gets louder and louder. He knows. He must go there immediately, he can't waste any time. He must do it today, or it will be too late. If he leaves tonight, by wagons-lits, he can visit the villa tomorrow and be back in Zürich by the time Sorel and Uncle Ariel arrive at the hotel.

Later, in the room, Adrian shows Nina the two telegrams and tells her about the problems with the train tickets.

"I'll have to go to Lugano tonight and look up that villa. We could go by sleeping car and arrive there in the morning. Then we'll be back here by dinner time. Will you come with me?"

Nina shakes her head. It's a short trip, she knows. But she's not ready to go. Besides, he'll be back very soon. So she must let him go by himself.

SEARCHING FOR THE VILLA

IT IS STILL VERY EARLY—ABOUT 7 o'clock in the morning—when the express train pulls into the Lugano station.

"Lugano! Lugano! Everybody up!" yells the train conductor.

Adrian is up for a while—he even had a quick breakfast of croissants with wild strawberry preserve, freshly squeezed orange juice and hot *café au lait* with *Schlag* in the dining car. He has slept deeply during the whole trip and woke up only once, when the train whistled as it entered the St. Gothard Pass. He had had to unbutton his silk pajama top and get rid of his blanket, since it was quite warm in the compartment. Crossing this nine-and-a-half-mile tunnel at 10,000 feet above sea level takes about 20-30 minutes, since the engine has to slow down here. And, even though all the windows and doors are tightly closed so that no smoke can get inside the cars, the air still smells of soot when they reach the other end of the tunnel, at Airolo. Surely one day soon these tunnels will be crossed by electrical trains without soot, Adrian told himself as they rolled through the St. Gothard Pass. Then he went back to sleep.

Now as he steps out of the train into the mild morning air, he knows that it is much too early to visit the villa. On the other hand he doesn't want to arrive there too late either, and find that somebody else has just grabbed it away. He doesn't know when the house was put on the market nor how long it was advertised in the paper, but he already worries that somebody else may "steal" it from him. Curious! he thinks. I haven't seen the villa, nor have I spoken to the landlord—but already it feels like mine.

Before leaving the station he stops at a yellow kiosk and buys a small box of hard raspberry candy and the local newspaper. Then, leaning against a lamppost, he consults the Real Estate section of the paper and finds that the villa is still advertised. He sighs with relief and wonders whether he should also buy a map of Lugano. It may be helpful, since so many new buildings and modern hotels have appeared here. But no, he decides he will find his way strictly by memory.

He walks out into the wide piazza, but stops right away, dazzled by the scenery. Down in the valley lies the blue lake, sparkling in the morning sun. The large bay is surrounded by green vineyards guarded by dark cypresses. In the distance he can see the glittering peaks of the Alps.

Adrian starts crossing the piazza, but is stopped by a procession of nuns in their black habits, followed by a horse-drawn cart filled with barrels of wine, and then by a flock of geese watched over by a little boy with a harmonica.

He waits, then finally walks through the piazza, steering clear of the many outdoor cafés. Waiters with white aprons are scrubbing the stone tabletops with hot water and soap. Only a few elderly men—who may be suffering from insomnia—sit there sipping their *café au lait*, reading the morning paper.

Adrian heads toward the promenade which runs along the lake and which will take him to the villa—but reaching the promenade means walking through old and narrow streets shaded by arcades. He is excited and starts to whistle the "Villia" aria from the *Merry Widow* as he thinks of the stores they visited in the past, and the special "treasures" Nina had so much admired.

Will he be able to find these stores again, even though he cannot remember their names and addresses, and even though so many new stores have opened in the meantime? NO! he corrects himself. This isn't a question. It's an order. It is a command. He MUST find the stores of the past, even though he doesn't know their names and their addresses. He lingers a moment at the corner, looking left and right, trying to make up his mind, then he walks straight ahead into the old Via Nassa with its shady arcades.

A few steps and he stands in front of the "Palazzo Vecchio," the antique shop with the inlaid and hand-painted Renaissance chests Nina cherished so much. Now they seem even more beautiful than ten years ago. Adrian feels happy, he keeps whistling, he cannot believe that the store and the chests are still here, as if waiting for him. Further down, beyond the bakery, stands the "Safavid" store, with its luxurious display of oriental rugs and Persian vases. He stands still, glued to the pavement. He knows that he belongs here, he feels that this is his home. It is as if he never left Lugano, as if no time has passed.

When he starts walking again, he recognizes the jewelry store where he bought himself the most beautiful gold cufflinks of his collection. Then, on the next block, he rediscovers the "Brüder Christoph," the store with rattan furniture and floral chintzes which Nina had loved so much.

But where is Nina? Why is she not here with him to savor these treasures? He stops whistling, and sadness grows inside him, like a dark shadow. Yes, she should be here with him, he scolds himself, even though he knows that she wouldn't have joined him now. He sighs. The only hope lies in the future.

He walks faster now, gazing at his feet, avoiding the street cleaners who are hosing down the sidewalk with hot suds. At the corner he turns into the promenade and heads toward the villa. The wide alley is shaded by tall chestnut trees. The lake is at his right, and, as he watches the blue water and the pink water lilies, another lake comes to mind. It is Lake Roşca, back in Romania, formed by the lazy waters of the Danube in the Delta, where his grandfather took him by boat when he was a child. This was an enchanted trip, for he could watch all kinds of flowers and birds. Pelicans, cormorants, white egrets, blue herons and storks strutting majestically among islands of water lilies and tall, blooming reeds. He had sailed by boat from Galați on the Danube, his hometown, to Tulcea, where his grandparents lived. They had told him how they had traveled all the way to Vienna on the Danube. His youngest uncle, Bernard, had sailed from Galați to Tulcea, then to the Black Sea, and then north, along the coast, to Odessa. And his middle uncle, Tobias, had also left from Galați, and, without changing boats, had reached the Black Sea and then traveled south, to the Bosphorus and to Istanbul.

Once, Adrian had seen in the harbor a most beautiful yacht with a large crown on its mast and on its flags, and his grandfather told him that it belonged to Alexander III, the Tsar of Russia. Another time a golden yacht was moored at the pier, with a crescent moon on its flags. It was also outfitted with a heavy shining cannon, and his grandfather told him that this was the personal yacht of Sultan Abdul Hamid, the "Great Assassin" who had massacred thousands of Armenians. Adrian got so scared by this yacht that he had nightmares about the Sultan and his eunuchs coming to fetch him—until his father assured him that, since he was not Armenian, he had nothing to worry about.

It was at the time when he was ten years old and his grandfather took him by boat to the Delta that Adrian became curious about traveling and exploring the world. He swore that he was going to do it, as soon as he could.

Adrian keeps walking along the promenade, watching, at his left, the modern hotels, the new concert hall, the large tennis and sports complex which were built here in the last ten years. Good news for Nina and the girls! The children can play tennis here, and swim further down, at the "Lido" swimming complex, while Nina and Suzy can attend musical events at the Concert Hall in the park. (Adrian has already seen an ad for a concert with arias from *Lohengrin* and *Parsifal*. It would make Suzy very happy.) And then 15 minutes from the Promenade stands the Art Museum and the famous Villa Favorita, Baron Thyssen Bornemisza's unique collection of the best work by the great artists of Europe. There is, right now, a show of paintings and drawings by Dürer. No, certainly, Nina could not complain of lack of intellectual stimulation!

The road turns suddenly left, and Adrian stands at the entrance to the Public Park. It is warm now, and he would like to sit in the shade and drink a glass of cold lemonade. But he is afraid of "missing the train" and being too late at the villa. Maybe he should keep on walking fast, and then wait in front of the house? But no, that's not good. They may think he's a thief and call the police. He looks at his watch.

It's only 8:45, so he decides to sit on a bench in the shade of a magnolia tree.

The air is filled with the chirping of swallows and sparrows, with the sounds of a splashing fountain, and with the perfume of roses, camellias, and palm trees in bloom. He closes his eyes and inhales deeply, filling his lungs with the exotic perfume.

A garden! he thinks. A miraculous, wonderful garden! He remembers that the house they visited ten years ago had a tropical garden descending all the way to the lake. Will this villa have such a garden too? He prays that it does. If yes, he imagines himself tending the fig trees, the lemon and orange grove, and walking along the cypresses. And he would build a rock garden with a real waterfall, cascading all the way into the lake.

Next to him, in the park, a bearded painter with a velvet cap is setting up his easel and his paint brushes. He hesitates between painting the fountain and the children playing with sailboats, or the blooming magnolia with the couple of lovers who lie in the grass. He turns his easel one way and the other and peeks at Adrian, as if waiting for some advice. Then he pulls out a sketchbook and draws a quick portrait of Adrian, who sits still.

"*Fertig!* Here is your portrait. It was easy to sketch you!"

"*Danke!*" Adrian takes the drawing and examines it. He recognizes his long face—like that of the mare "Rosinante," his friends used to tease him—his tall forehead and receding hairline. His twinkling eyes are hiding beneath bushy eyebrows, nevertheless, even in the drawing there is a sparkle of light in their black pupils. Yes, he likes the portrait, but there is something which bothers him. The black moustache. He thought it was stylish a few years ago, but now it makes him look like Hitler. "Adolf!" Nina calls him when she wants to tease him or punish him.

True, he should have shaved it off some time ago. But like most men, he liked the masculine adornment. His father and grandfather had big, bushy, awe-inspiring moustaches. He really would have loved to grow a long, old-fashioned beard—but he knew too well that this was out of the question. So he had settled for a small moustache, which now will require serious reconsideration. But enough rest. Enough philosophizing. It's getting late.

He gets up, shakes hands with the painter and gives him 10 francs. Before leaving, he asks him to sign the drawing. "Nobody knows! Maybe one day your portraits will hang in the Villa Favorita among other celebrities! And I'll be the proud possessor of a famous work!"

THE VILLA

TWENTY MINUTES LATER HE STANDS in front of the villa. He has immediately seen the sign *"Zum Verkaufen"* on the wall, and has recognized the palm trees by the fence, and the wisteria hanging from the balcony. Like the other houses on the street, the villa is built of roughhewn stones and has an orange tiled roof.

He rings the doorbell and is met by a gray-haired giant with an unkempt beard which reaches to his waist. He has a black patch over his left eye and he limps when he walks. One foot is shorter than the other. He is accompanied by a big black dog with red eyes which growls and bares his teeth when he sees Adrian.

"Sh! *Silenzio!*" the giant yells at the dog.

A vague scent of caves, of forests and lakes seems to emanate from the man. Polyphemos? The Wild Man of the West? Rübezahl? Adrian steps back, struck by the resemblance between his host and the ferocious giant of the Schwarzwald who was known to uproot hundred-year-old trees with a finger and to swallow a herd of cattle in one gulp. He is petrified by the tall man.

"Sh! Stop it!" the man shouts at the dog with a deep voice.

The dog stops growling and the man takes a large key out of his pocket and opens the gate.

"Come in, please! Come in!" he says with the same deep voice. And, when he opens his mouth, Adrian can see his single black tooth. But there is a softer glint in the small eye hidden beneath his bushy eyebrows. "You came to see the house."

He stretches out his right hand, which is larger than Adrian's foot.

"I am Giuseppe Pietrofino. I'll show you around." He touches Adrian's elbow, inviting him in. "Just follow me."

He is so tall that he has to stoop at the entrance, even though the door is large. Adrian follows slowly, hesitant at first, but then with more confidence. He has never seen such a big man. He still walks slowly, watching the dog, who is following them, but as he advances into the rooms, he recognizes, he knows, that this villa, this is indeed the dream house he wants. He walks faster and faster, from one floor to the next.

The rooms are light and airy, each one with a fireplace, and the high ceilings covered with wooden beams make the space feel cozy and warm. There are several bedrooms and bathrooms, so that guests like Stella and Sorel or even Charles Kass and his wife, Brigitte, can be invited.

When he looks through the large windows, he sees, to his delight, that a small stream is flowing through the garden. Yes, he will be able to build the waterfall he dreamt about for so long.

But the most beautiful spot, the greatest surprise is the second-floor loggia, all hung with wisteria, with the wide view of the lake, of the silent cypresses, all the way to the distant Alps.

"Kennst du das Land wo die Zitronen blühn,
Im dunklen Laub die Gold-Orangen glühn..."

The song from Goethe's *Mignon* is haunting him. He feels that he is living his dream—and nevertheless a vague, undefined feeling of nostalgia is still filling his heart. Maybe this is the essence of happiness, maybe the longing, the thirst persists, even though we think we have quenched it for good. Or maybe it has only to do with him being alone here, with having nobody to share his happiness. He misses Nina, her absence fills him with sadness and longing. He closes his eyes for a moment and imagines that Nina is here with him, holding his hand. Yes, this is it. It feels good... Surely he must arrange something for her, to come here before they go home... to Romania...

"Where are you?" Senior Giuseppe has caught up with him. He stands at the top of the staircase, panting, and wants to give him details about the villa. But Adrian walks away. He rushes from room to room, opens windows and doors, lightly touches the walls and the wallpaper, looks at pictures and furniture, wondering whether Nina would like them or not. He pauses in the living room, in front of a *tondo*, a round wall painting of angels with flutes and harpsichords. He gazes at them with happiness. He feels protected by the heavenly concert!

Finally, after Adrian has inspected the whole house they sit down at the dining room table to talk over the finances. Senior Giuseppe lights his "Brissago"—a long, gnarled cigar which fills the room with thick clouds of smoke. They go over a heap of papers and documents, and, after the deal is made and Adrian gives him the down payment, Senior Giuseppe gets up and limps to the pantry. He comes back with a bottle of white Lugano wine, two glasses, and a plate with several slices of hard polenta. From a cupboard he fetches fresh local goat cheese and a plate of olives from the garden.

"God bless you!" he says as they clink glasses. "Have some goat cheese and olives!"

Adrian sips his wine thoughtfully. He cannot believe that he is buying the villa. On the wall facing him hangs the picture of a boat named "Giuseppe's Puppet Theater," and behind it he can see the outline of the house with the open loggia. Next to this picture hangs a family photo of a young couple with a little girl standing in front of them. The tall man has a black patch over his left eye, and Adrian recognizes a young Mr. Giuseppe.

They keep silent for a moment. Then Adrian asks, "Why are you selling the house now? Where will you go?"

Senior Giuseppe takes a sip of wine and stares into his glass.

"I can't stay here any longer," he finally says. "Since the death of my wife two years ago, I have no rest. I feel like crying all the time." He takes a large, red handkerchief out of his pocket and wipes his eye. "I can't work anymore. I am a puppeteer, I carve marionettes." He points to a row of puppets—Pinocchio, Punchinello, the Blue Fairy, the Devil—who sit on a shelf, high over the fireplace. "I carved them and Maria, my wife, painted them. She had golden hands; no two puppets looked alike. I think she wanted them to answer her with real words." He blows his nose in the red handkerchief.

"I could swear that you are a fisherman. I saw a boat in your boathouse."

"My father was a fisherman and he left me the boat. I used it to travel to sell my marionettes. Sometimes I took the whole puppet theater with me when I went to a fair or to a show." He turns his face toward the picture on the wall. "But not any more." He shakes his big head with its rich mane of white hair.

"But what will you do now? Where will you go?" Adrian is concerned.

"Oh, not to worry. I have plans. I'll move to Como, near my married daughter. She can help with the puppets. Her mother taught her everything she knew." He pours more wine in the glasses. "Also, Como is a bigger place. More tourists. More fairs and more street festivals. More children... more schools... You have children?"

"Yes, two girls."

Senior Giuseppe gets up, puts down his cigar and limps to the shelf with the puppets. With one big hand he takes down two marionettes—Pinocchio and Punchinello— wraps them in paper and gives them to Adrian. "For your daughters. I hope they will still like the puppet theater."

Adrian thanks him. He has finished the wine and the olives.

Senior Giuseppe takes three sets of keys out of a drawer.

"These are for you: the key to the front door, to the back door and the key to the garden gate." He rubs them with the red handkerchief, trying to make them shine. Then he hands them to Adrian. "Here are good keys for a good house..." he sighs. "After all, we had many good years in this house... My daughter was born here and they [pointing to the puppets on the shelf] were born here, too. No, I must say, all in all it was a good house for us. And it will be a good house for you, too."

As he leaves the villa, Adrian decides not to tell Nina about the down payment he made on the house. He will surprise her: he will lure her to Lugano and make her visit the villa. Only afterwards will he tell her the truth.

On his way to the train station, Adrian chooses to go back with a small steamer which sails across the lake. The train is due at 5, and the trip to the station lasts only a little more than one hour.

He boards the boat at a nearby dock, climbs on deck and takes a seat in the front of the ship, near the prow, where he can watch the scenery. Soon the engines start rumbling, the horn blows twice, and the boat moves smoothly along the shore.

The deck is full of passengers now—to Adrian's left a couple of lovers in a never-ending embrace, to his right a blond youngster in lederhosen with two binoculars and three cameras, and further down a silver-haired grandmother quietly crocheting lace.

As the boat follows the shoreline, they first come across the lakeside view of the villa with the boathouse and the freshly painted boat visible inside. Adrian feels a childish pride at the thought of having a boat of his own: he always dreamt of having one, but of course, this wasn't possible in his childhood! He knows that his daughters will be delighted with the boat, and he imagines them paddling happily on the lake, not too far from the house. Nadia will probably be the most excited about the boat, and Nina will worry a lot. He will have to get involved, negotiate between the two and calm Nina down. He misses her greatly. He wishes she was here, sitting next to him on the boat. He still wants her to come to Lugano before going back to Romania. But how to convince her? She is so stubborn and she hates changing travel plans.

Absentmindedly he watches the shore. The ship docks at Gandria, a small village with old houses of crumbling stones. Fishermen with buckets of fresh fish get off the boat, while a few farmers haul baskets of ripe olives and grapes onto the steamer. He follows the lively to and fro on the pier, where buckets and baskets are loaded on carts drawn by donkeys. When the boat starts moving again, he looks up at the mountains surrounding the lake and behind the village. Right above him, on the highest peak, stand the ruins of an ancient castle. Further down, in the distance, is another fort and a tower.

What are these mysterious castles? Who built them? When? Against what enemies? Adrian shrugs—he doesn't know the answer. But Nina would. Or she would find out. She wouldn't rest until she found the answer. No historical detail or anecdote has ever escaped her. She would be passionately intrigued by the goings-on in those distant times.

Adrian takes out a pen and a small notebook and writes a note to himself. He stops: one more thing. What did these forts and castles look like in the past? How were they furnished and decorated? Nina would be dying to find out. This is her passion. More than literature and even history, architecture and interior design are the love of her life. She so much wanted to be an architect. But of course, that was not possible for a woman. Their home is full of magazines of architecture and interior design. It was she who designed the decoration of the apartment where they live now, and it was her idea to transfer the cartoon with the devil from the magazine to the windows of his office.

Adrian takes a deep breath and lights a cigarette. He makes a plan: he will tell Nina about the mysterious castles in the mountains, and make her curious about them. Also, to convince her to come to Lugano, he may have to tell her that he found the old villa, but that it badly needs redecorating and refurbishing. She may not resist this temptation!

When he looks up from his notebook, he sees that the boat has changed direction and is now crossing the lake, heading toward the Italian shore. The water is dark blue and indigo with small waves of white foam cresting around the body of the ship. In the distance he hears the beat of drums and the sound of a saxophone. "It can't be, I must be dreaming!" he tells himself. But the music grows louder. In addition to the drums and the saxophone he now hears a piano, trumpets, a bass, violins—a full jazz band playing modern American tunes. It is only now that he becomes aware of the elegant crowd of tourists who fill the boat: women in shimmering silk dresses, their bare shoulders covered by silver foxes, men in dark jackets, starched white shirts and black bow ties. The women wear high-heeled pumps, glittering jewelry and gloves made of transparent lace. The men's smooth and shiny hair looks pasted to their scalp. They're all going to dance in the afternoon and gamble the night away at the Casino of Campeone d'Italia.

And yes, here it is: as the boat docks at the foot of the pink stone columns, the large, inviting terraces overflow with guests having afternoon tea, or dancing to the frantic rhythm of the jazz band. There, right in front of him, on the terrace, a blond woman in lavender silk is doing the foxtrot with a gray-haired man, his face all red and puffy. Meanwhile, the saxophone keeps nudging them on.

Behind the terrace, the doors to the gambling halls stand wide open and Adrian is fascinated by what he sees. He would like to step off the boat and try his hand at the roulette. He is no gambler—although Nina accuses him of being one—but he believes that it is sinful not to try his luck when given the opportunity! During his first year of marriage he played roulette at the famous casino in Monte Carlo. He was lucky that night, and won enough money to buy Nina a gold necklace. But she refused to wear it, saying that she would never wear jewelry bought with money won at the casino.

Many people have left the boat, which is partly empty now. But the air remains heavy with the scent of expensive perfume. The ship blows the horn twice, and moves slowly away from the shore. The pink columns and the terraces of the casino become smaller and smaller and the sounds of the orchestra grow weaker, until they die in the distance.

The sun is more golden than earlier in the day, and the shadows grow longer over the lake. Its surface is flat, like a mirror. A single bird, large wings spread out, hangs motionless in the air.

Adrian smiles. This is bliss. Harmony. Perfection. Should he sing? The words of Goethe's Faust come to his mind:

> *"Werd'ich zum Augenblicke sagen:*
> *Verweile doch! du bist so schön!*
> ....

"If ever I should tell the moment:
Oh, stay! You are so beautiful!
Then you may cast me into chains
Then I shall smile upon perdition!"
The famous wager Faust himself proposes to Mephisto.

Adrian closes his eyes and whispers the words:

> *...Dann mag die Totenglocke schlagen*
> *Dann bist du deines Dienstes frei...*
> ....

"Then may the hour toll for me
Then you are free to leave my service

The clock may halt, the clock hand fall
And time comes to an end for me"

He smiles as he goes on with the poem: he does not believe in the power of Mephisto!

After a while there is a rumbling of engines and the boat changes direction again. Soon there is another rumbling like distant thunder. But as the lake takes a sharp bend at this point, nothing can be seen at the horizon. Soon, however, the roar grows louder, and a moving point advances toward them. Adrian watches it, and, after a short time he can see the whole picture. It is a motorboat carrying eight men in brown shirts, with military caps and heavy leather belts with holsters for their guns. As they come nearer he hears them singing at the top of their voices, and he can even distinguish the words of their song:

> *Salve o popolo d'eroi*
> *Son risorti i figli tuoi*
> *Salve o patria immortale*
> *Per la fede e l'ideale.*

And the refrain:

> *Giovenezza, Giovenezza*
> *Primavera di bellezza*
> *Del Fascismo*
> *La salvezza*
> *Per la nostra libertá!*

They sail full speed toward the steamer, interrupting their song with shouts of *"Viva Il Duce! Viva Fascismo!"* raising their right arms in the fascist salute. It looks like they're heading for a head-on collision. Adrian imagines them crashing into the steamer. The ship is destroyed. Bodies fly over the railing, plunging into the lake.

In the last minute the brown-shirts slow down and turn the boat around, sailing parallel to the steamer. Now they pull their guns out of the holsters and shoot straight into the sky, while others throw empty bottles of beer in the air, aiming their guns at them. Some shattered bottles fall on the deck. The men accompany this frenzy with shouts of *"Viva Il Duce! Viva Fascismo!"*

Adrian is watching them in horror. Are they drunk? Are they just celebrating? What will they do next? Climb on the ship and attack the passengers? Shoot them? Plunder them? Take them prisoners? He is petrified.

He never thought that the Fascists were so close to Lugano. Of course, he knew that Italy was just across the lake. Yes, Señor Pietrofino and many of his neighbors were Italians—but he never made the connection with Mussolini's Fascists!

He is even more troubled when he thinks of Nina. A scene like this would terrify her, would make her sick. (He never told her about the Nazi delegation who sang the German *"Deutschland, Deutschland über Alles"* at the Zürich hotel.)

Yes, indeed, Switzerland is squeezed between Hitler's Germany to the north and Mussolini's Italy to the south. But, on the other hand, is it safer to return home and continue living under King Carol's corrupt and reckless tyranny, and the constant threat of the Romanian Iron Guard? No, he thinks, as he watches the ship dock near the train station— finally free of attackers—Zürich and Lugano are safer, even though fascism is lurking at the borders.

He must have a long talk with Nina, as soon as he is back at the hotel.

DRAMA AT BREAKFAST

N EXT MORNING WHEN ADRIAN AND Nina come down to meet Sorel and Uncle Ariel, breakfast is served on the terrace restaurant, overlooking the lake. Sorel and the Uncle have already finished their meal and have pushed their dishes out of the way. They get up when they see Nina and Adrian, and embrace them.

"How was your trip?" asks Adrian. He is struck by their quiet and serious, almost solemn demeanor. Even though Sorel is wearing his white open-neck sport shirt, there is a somber air about him. The Uncle too has a grave look on his face. Even his black fedora seems faded and worn.

"Are you all right?" Adrian is worried. He thinks of the unexpected telegrams.

"Yes," says Uncle Ariel. "We're all right, but we don't bring you good news." He hesitates. "Remember Andrei, Nina's young cousin who moved to Palestine and lived on a farm in Galilee?"

"Yes," say Nina and Adrian. "What about him?"

"Well, there is bad news about him," says the Uncle. He stops. It is hard for him to continue. "He has been killed." He hesitates. "A gang... a gang of Arab militants who have then set the house on fire." His voice fades. He sighs. "His mother, your Aunt Becky, has hanged herself, and his wife is in a psychiatric hospital in Tel-Aviv."

"Why... Why..." Nina repeats. She is stunned. She can't speak. She stares fixedly at Uncle Ariel. "Why?... Why.....?" she keeps asking, as she covers her face with her hands.

Adrian too is shocked. His throat is dry, painfully so. "And where are the children?" he manages to ask with a rasping voice.

"They're all right. The two boys who are now 2 and 4 have been taken by friends—an Arab family who had a farm near Andrei, and who have now moved to Tel-Aviv."

For a few minutes it is silence again. Nobody speaks. Nina buries her face in a handkerchief.

"How did this happen?" Adrian asks. His voice is still hoarse, even though he tries to take control of himself. In spite of the pain, his mind refuses to take in the reality of Andrei's death. He cannot see him as the tragic hero he has now become. "Young and lively as life itself" everybody loved to describe him.

When they first got married, Adrian remembers Nina's youngest cousin as a wild kid with a head of blond curly hair, always in trouble with authority. He had an answer for everything, and had just been thrown out of school for drawing caricatures of the principal and of his teachers on the blackboard. He also wrote epigrams. He wanted to be a cartoonist and a writer, but his parents forced him to become a lawyer. Then he discovered Zionism, and decided to go to Palestine and live on a farm.

Everybody in his family was against him: his parents, his brothers and sisters—they all warned him not to go. But he left anyway. All he wanted was to build a Jewish home. He bought a patch of land in Galilee, married a woman who came from Morocco, and together they had two little boys. Six months ago his widowed mother came to stay with them, and help with the orange trees, the avocados and the chickens.

"Here are some old photos of Andrei and his family in the good days," says Sorel as he puts on the table a few snapshots of the whole family standing in front of a small van laden with baskets of oranges and avocados.

"They're all happy, as you can see. Andrei had just bought the new van and was ready to drive to the market."

"And here is the most recent photo" says Uncle Ariel, bringing out of his pocket a clip from a Jewish newspaper. It shows a badly burnt cottage and next to it a small truck without tires and windows, also badly damaged by fire.

Adrian looks up from the photo and sees that even though he is sunburnt, Sorel's face seems grayish, unhealthy, with dark circles under the eyes. Only his bald pate looks polished and tanned. The Uncle too looks older and frail. His salt and pepper beard is more silvery than a month ago, and his face looks tired and drawn.

"We don't have any details," says the Uncle. "All we know is that about two weeks ago a group of young Arab militants armed with guns and knives stormed into Andrei's house, took him out in the courtyard and shot him. Then they ordered the family to leave.

"How about Aunt Becky, Andrei's mother?"

"We don't know when and how she hanged herself. Was it before the wife and the children left? Was it immediately after the shooting? Or did she sneak back into the farm, after dark, when the others were gone, and hung herself in the attic? Maybe the others forgot about her in all that confusion!" The Uncle rubs the ivory tip of his cane with his fingers.

"Aunt Becky had arrived at the farm only six months ago and was still a stranger. I think Andrei's wife resented her—I heard they didn't get along. Aunt Becky wanted to be the head of the household and ordered Sharon around... But she worshipped the children, and now they were taken away from her. What was the poor woman to do without her son and her grandchildren? She didn't have much to live for anymore!" Sorel raises his hands and looks up, as if expecting an answer from above.

The waiter brings coffee and tea and a silver basket filled with hot rolls and croissants for Nina and Adrian. But nobody touches the food.

"There wouldn't be so much violence out there in Palestine if the Germans and the Italians didn't incite the locals by telling them that the Jews want to turn them into slaves!" The Uncle pounds the floor with his cane. "It's a shame, a real shame! Neighbors who were good friends until yesterday, don't trust each other any more. Now they're out to kill each other. This is why we have the urgent meeting: to see how we can stop the fighting!" The Uncle speaks with conviction and authority. He strokes his beard with his left hand.

Nina raises her silver spoon to get his attention.

"But Andrei's children—we should bring them back here? And his wife, wouldn't she get better treatment in Europe?"

"No, no," says Sorel. "They're doing all right in Palestine."

"But we're the family. We can't abandon them to strangers?"

"They're not with strangers. The children were born there. They're Sabras. That is their home. And their mother chose to live there. I doubt that she would like to move to

Europe. And, besides, it doesn't mean that we're not family and that we stop loving them." Sorel lights a new cigarette from the one he just smoked down to the nub.

"And, if you really want to help, you should pick up and move to Palestine," says the Uncle. "It's there that your help will be most appreciated!" He has interrupted Sorel, and is now quite animated. His eyes are shining, his cheeks are flushed, and his voice is strong and vibrant. "Yes, it's in Palestine that your presence is most needed!"

Adrian listens and thinks of the distant, rocky land, parched by the sun. He imagines the small, whitewashed Arab villages, and the Bedouins riding their camels. Here and there, lost in the moonlike vista, a few green oases—the new colonies with their lush orange groves and avocados. And, toward the East, on the Jordan River, Jerusalem with its crumbling Wailing Wall, worshipped over thousands of years by a handful of old Jews wrapped in their threadbare prayer shawls.

This is what he sees when he thinks of the Holy Land. And he cannot imagine himself and his family—Nina and the children—confined in a small colony lost in the desert. Nor can he see himself living in a shack built from the broken stones of Jerusalem's ancient walls.

Adrian looks at Sorel, the athletic young doctor, the enthusiastic pioneer, and wonders whether Sorel is indeed ready to practice his medicine by riding from village to village on the back of a camel or donkey like a Bedouin— with his stethoscope and his sterilized syringes. There are no good roads between the villages, and the camels and donkeys are the main ways to travel. He has heard that on moonless nights, lonely travelers have been attacked by hungry jackals or hyenas... or even stung by poisonous giant scorpions...

Will Stella really go with him? Will she follow him there? So many questions... And now the fighting, the violence...

"Young people who live there must have weapons and must know how to use them!" says Sorel. "And who will give them weapons? Certainly not the British!"

"No! No weapons! No fighting with the Arabs!" thunders the Uncle. "That would be the end. We have to make friends with our neighbors. The future is possible only in a peaceful society. Bringing weapons would mean suicide."

"And who will protect the new settlers?" Nina stares at Uncle Ariel, holding her cup of tea in a trembling hand. A few drops spill on the table.

"The British. The British must protect the settlers from their attackers. If our settlers are caught with weapons, they may be deported to their country of origin. So we must obey these rules!" The Uncle speaks with great conviction. He sits erect. His head is high. Adrian recognizes the Rabbi preaching at the *bima* of the Great London Synagogue. And he feels uneasy about the way in which Andrei's tragedy is being turned into a political theme!

Next to him, Nina puts down her cup. It is still full. She didn't take a sip.

When the bell from old Sankt Peterskirche tolls 9, Sorel and Uncle Ariel get up to leave for their meeting. They promise to be back for supper. Nina and Adrian watch them in silence, the Uncle walking with small, quick steps, Sorel with the vigorous, graceful gait of an athlete.

"What sad, heartbreaking news! Andrei's story is a real catastrophe! Surely if he hadn't bought his farm in the Galilee, he would still be alive today!" Nina wipes her eyes with her handkerchief.

Adrian takes her hand and strokes it gently. "It's sad, I know, but listen: I have other news. I couldn't talk to you when I came home last night, because you were asleep and had put up the sign DO NOT DISTURB on the mirror. I know that, if you wake up from your first sleep, you have trouble falling asleep again. So I tried to protect you. But I must tell you: I have found the villa in Lugano, and you must come and see it!"

"When?" Nina asks automatically.

"Now. As soon as possible."

"What do you mean, now? How can you talk about such things right now?"

Adrian bites his lips. "I mean now, before we go back to Romania. The villa is almost identical with the one we have visited on our honeymoon, but it needs you and your eye to decide how to refurbish it. We can go to Lugano if we only postpone our trip home by one day. But you must see the house."

Nina looks at him and frowns. She folds and unfolds the linen napkin in her lap. She squeezes a tiny crumb of bread between her fingers. "No," she says. "I can't do it."

"And if I told you that I bought the villa, would it make a difference? Would you change your mind?" He looks at her with a glimmer of hope in his eyes.

"I can't believe you did!" There is sudden color in her face. "You only told me you were going to see the villa. Did you know you were going to buy it?"

"No, when I spoke with you, before leaving, I wasn't planning to buy it. But then I realized that it was a unique opportunity. He sold it to me for half the price. What else could I do? It was a real bargain. But I implore you to come and see it before we leave Switzerland! It's most important for our future, and it would really be good for you. Here are the keys!" Adrian tries to place the keys in her hand.

But Nina shakes her head again. "I can't do it. I also have news to tell you. It's true, we didn't have a chance to talk last night when you came home. I'm worried about Nadia. I think we should go home as soon as possible. If we hadn't promised Suzy the trip in the Alps, we should go home right away. I'm too worried and too upset."

"What do you mean? I don't understand."

"Last night, Sorel brought me a card from Nadia and a note from Mathilda. I got worried after I read them. Here they are:"

Dear tata and mama,
The weather is good here, and we go to the beach every day. We play at Treasure-Hunters-Deep-Sea Divers, and we have found an old boat filled with the pirates' treasures. But when I dove down to get the treasure, a dolphin bumped into my ear and hit me so hard that I had to let go and come back to the surface empty-handed. Now I am fine, but Aunt Mathilda doesn't let me dive or swim underwater. Skender also had to return his boat to his father, so now all I can do is catch jellyfish with Theo and help him hunt for pink salamanders.
I miss you, much love.
Nadia.

"And then, here is Mathilda's note:"

Dear Nina and Adrian,
Everybody is fine here. Nothing unusual. Nadia was upset with her diving mishap, but now she is fine and in good spirits.
Love, Mathilda.

"So what's wrong?" Adrian has taken the letters from Nina.

"I don't like Nadia's tone. It isn't like her. That blow to her ear..."

"Did you speak to Sorel?"

"He said not to worry. She is O.K."

"Then why are you nervous?"

"He looked away when he spoke to me. He avoided my eyes."

Adrian rests his hand on her arm. "You worry too much. You always see the dark side of things. Remember, your brothers called you Cassandra?"

As they go on talking, a small flock of cardinals settles on the branches of a chestnut tree, making it glow. Adrian watches, and keeps stroking Nina's arm. "Let's make arrangements to go to Lugano and enjoy what we have. It makes much more sense! It's so beautiful and peaceful there, right by the water... the tall cypresses and the lemon trees— just what you need!"

But Nina bends her head and hides her face in her hands. "I can't. I can't do it now! It's too much!" She stops. They are silent.

Then she stands up and smoothes her dress. "It's getting late. I'll call Suzy to come down for breakfast."

PART III

DR. MILO'S BIRTHDAY

S ILVIA IS ALONE AT HOME and cannot decide what to do first: go out to the market and buy food, or press Eugen's green shirt for tomorrow's trip and demonstration? When she looks out the window and sees the gathering black clouds, she decides to hurry up and do the shopping before the rain begins. It is only ten o'clock in the morning, and she will have plenty of time to press the green shirts later on. She covers the typewriter with its black hood, takes her keys, her wallet and her net bag, and goes downstairs.

As she walks toward the marketplace, she sees gypsy women in colorful skirts huddled behind large baskets of flowers at almost every street corner. She admires the gladiolas and dahlias from a distance, without stopping near the flower baskets. When she looks up at the sky, she sees that the clouds have vanished and that it is a mild end-of-summer day, with golden sunshine in the tall poplars and chestnut trees.

Today is Eugen's birthday, and, since he is a great eggplant lover, she will surprise him (and Professor Georgescu, their only guest) with a homemade moussaka.

She is lucky at the open market. There are not many people—maybe because of the threat of rain—and she walks quickly from stall to stall. Within just about an hour she has filled her shopping net bag with ground meat, eggplants, onions, potatoes, ½-kilo tomatoes, a bunch of carrots, half a dozen eggs and a pack of cooking fat. Sour cream and milk she doesn't have to buy—since Stefan the milkman comes every morning to the house with his horse and buggy, and brings them a bottle of milk, a pound of fresh cheese and sour cream.

The net bag is heavy now and she can't wait to get home. Later, after she finishes preparing the moussaka and putting it in the oven, she will run to the Verdun pastry shop in the corner and buy a big chocolate cake which she will decorate with green pistachio cream.

Upstairs, inside the apartment, she puts down the shopping net with the packages and smoothes her blouse and her skirt. She is pleased with herself, and also with her life. She feels good since she has moved in with Doctor Eugen Milo. He makes her feel important with the special attention he gives her. He is always there, watching over her. She feels well protected and well taken care of.

How did it happen? She tries to remember. After being discharged from the hospital she stayed for a while at Doctor Eugen Milo's cousin's house on Calea Moşilor, and went twice a week for "booster" hypnosis sessions with Eugen at the hospital. But it was a very long trip, and then, one rainy day he suggested that they do the sessions at his apartment. That first time was a Sunday afternoon, and Silvia woke up in the doctor's embrace. After that, they kept doing the hypnosis booster sessions at his apartment. And then one day he asked her to move in.

She is happy here. She now has all her belongings, even her precious guitar—which has followed her first to the cousin's apartment on Calea Moşilor—and then here.

Her life has changed very much. Doctor Milo—Eugen, as she calls him now—has given her an old typewriter and has shown her how to type. He is a tough and demanding teacher. In the beginning, all she did was to practice and copy articles from the newspapers. But now she has started typing papers for the Iron Guard. Eugen has promised her that, if she continues to make progress, she might get a permanent job at the CASA VERDE, the Legionnaire headquarters, where a good typist is always needed. She has been there a few times, and she knows that she would like working there. It is an active and cheerful place with many enthusiastic young people coming and going, and always having meetings and conferences in which they sing their patriotic songs. They like to pray and sing together and on their large demonstrations they wear green shirts with revolvers tucked in black leather holsters and small satchels filled with earth strung around their necks. She herself has just received a green shirt, a black leather belt and a revolver, but no satchel of earth since she has not yet attained full membership.

As a matter of fact, tomorrow afternoon they will travel to Cernăuți for an important political demonstration in which everybody will wear their green shirts. This is why she has to take care of the uniforms before the end of the day.

Silvia leaves the net bag in the kitchen and goes to the bedroom to change into a housecoat and to put on an apron. When she comes back, she first makes the sign of the cross and mumbles a prayer as Eugen has taught her, then she lines up the things she has bought at the market and which she will need for the moussaka. Eugen has told her that it's a long time since he last tasted it, as it is such a complicated recipe. But it happens to be Silvia's specialty. She is a good cook, and she loves to prepare moussaka! She can't wait to see his surprise. She starts by cutting the eggplants in slices as thick as a finger, then dousing them with hot, salty water which must be thoroughly drained.

While the water is draining, she browns the ground meat, to which she has added two chopped onions, a grated carrot, and a thinly sliced potato. She lets the saucepan stand a while and cool off before adding one egg, two spoonfuls of sour cream, a sprinkle of salt and pepper. Then she returns to the eggplants, which she covers with flour.

Now the preparation is almost finished. From the kitchen cabinet she takes a deep baking dish, covers its bottom and walls with cooking fat and finely powdered bread crumbs, and fills it with alternating layers of eggplants and ground meat. Over the top surface she spreads slices of fresh tomatoes and pours a few spoonfuls of tomato sauce.

When she has finished, she steps back and wipes her hands with her apron. Yes, she thinks. Just in time! She places the pot in the oven.

She adjusts the timer for 50 minutes' baking time, then she unties her apron, combs her hair and, getting hold of her purse, she runs down to the Verdun pastry shop in the corner to buy the cake.

The store is decorated with French flags and reproductions of paintings and photographs from the battlefield of Verdun during the Great War. A large picture of Jeanne d'Arc armed with a spear and a heavy sword flanked by the Archangel Michael and a banner with the words *"Liberté, Égalité, Fraternité"* hangs over the counter.

"Oh! Les sales Boches!" cries Madame Françoise, pointing to a photo of Hitler in a newspaper which is lying on a small table.

"Laisse la dame tranquille!" answers her husband while he is packing up the chocolate cake and giving Silvia a beaker filled with green pistachio cream. Just before leaving she hears a record playing the song *"La Madelon pour nous n'est pas sévère..."* She stops to listen and becomes aware that she doesn't remember any of the songs she used to sing before she went to the hospital. Curious... curious she thinks, but she shrugs and hurries home with the cake.

Back in the apartment she is just in time for the moussaka. She turns the oven down to keep it warm and sets out to decorate the cake.

The pistachio cream is a light green and she imagines it standing out against the chocolate frosting like an emerald jewel pinned to a dark velvet cloak.

She spoons the pistachio cream into a small pastry bag fitted with a plain writing tip with which she carefully traces the words *"La Mulți Ani"* (Happy Birthday) in the middle of the cake. Then she traces a garland of roses and daisies all around the border.

When she finishes the last creamy petal she nods with satisfaction: yes, it is beautiful! A really artistic decoration. She tries to imagine Eugen's surprise when she will bring it to the table and set it in front of him.

After she hides the cake in the icebox behind tall paper bags filled with string beans and carrots, she prepares the ironing board for the green shirts. But before ironing, she plugs in the new iron. She is happy with it: she doesn't have to use the old iron, which was very heavy and which had to be filled with coals.

Also, at the same time, she covers the dining-room table with a hand-embroidered tablecloth, and she sets up the dishes, the glasses, the silver, the spoons, the forks and the knives.

She looks at the clock. There is still time for packing the bags for tomorrow's trip. She smiles as she walks by the mirror; she has been quick and efficient as Eugen, her new master and lover, wants her to be.

Professor Georgescu arrives at the house at seven-thirty, and parks his blue Citroen in front of the building. Before getting out he smoothes his graying hair, making sure that his long wisps lie neatly behind his ears. He watches himself in the car mirror and straightens his black bow tie. He gives a nod to the image in the mirror. He is satisfied with what he sees. It is the image of a distinguished French savant like Pasteur, or even more like Charcot, since the latter was clean shaven and had no beard or moustache. Yes, he tells himself, there is definitely a resemblance between him and Charcot. They have the same high, smooth forehead, the same full, sensuous lips, the same slightly unequal eyes. He is pleased to resemble Charcot, whom he deeply admires. (Besides, he is in the process of reading the correspondence between Charcot and Freud, and studying the influence the Frenchman had on Freud.) A last glance to the mirror, then he opens the car door, grabs his big leather bag with one hand and the basket with the potted orchid with the other, and steps out on the pavement. Luckily, the entrance door to the building is open, so he can easily balance the two packages while climbing the stairs. On the fourth floor he puts down the leather bag and rings the doorbell.

"Hello! Hello, and welcome back from your trip!" says Silvia as she opens the door. She has put on a turquoise dress which matches her eyes. Doctor Eugen Milo stands next to her, and they both greet the Professor warmly.

"*La Mulți Ani!* Happy Birthday!" he replies as he steps in.

"Good to see you back from the trip!"

Professor Georgescu embraces Eugen first, and gives Silvia a big hug.

"You look wonderful! Getting more beautiful by the day!" he says, stepping back, to better admire her. "You too—not bad at all." He nods toward Eugen. "Something is going right for both of you!" he adds. "I haven't seen you in four weeks, since before I went to Paris, and here you are, blooming like two prizewinning Catleyas!"

"Please sit down. You must be exhausted from your long trip." Eugen pushes a chair toward the Professor.

"Yes, it was long. Two nights and three days on the Orient Express." He wipes his forehead with a white handkerchief. "But it was worth it. Paris is still enchanting. *La Ville Lumière*—as the artists and writers have named her. Splendid! You must see it, you must travel to Paris without delay!"

Silvia and Eugen nod silently.

"Superb! Wonderful, I tell you. Paris is a special experience, and the orchid show was as exciting as the psychiatric conference!" His eyes are shining, and he opens his arms to an aerial embrace. "But my goodness, where is my head? I'm forgetting to give you the present!" He jumps to his feet, and picks up the basket he has left near the door. He plunges his hands inside and brings out a pink blooming orchid, with graceful flowers, like dancing ballerinas in their tutus.

"This is the oldest and newest French orchid. It's delicate looking, but hardy at the same time. Oh, those French botanists!" he says, shaking his head and smoothing his long wisps of hair. "They're always coming up with new species of plants and new techniques. They are now growing *Orchid Hybrids* from tissue cultures. It's very exciting, and this new technique can, one day, have applications for medicine. Let me just tell you that this one here is a historical hybrid, resistant to heat, dryness and insects. But you must go to Paris and see for yourselves. I'll try to make arrangements for you for the next conference..."

Eugen listens while looking for a good place for the plant.

"Put it on the table as our new, special centerpiece," Silvia tells him, as she brings in a tray filled with dishes of dried and smoked fish and black olives, *tarama salata* and feta cheese.

"Oh, my mind! My mind! When I think of Paris, I forget everything else!" The Professor opens the leather bag which lies on the couch and pulls out a large bottle of plum brandy, which he turns in his hands.

"Let's have some *țuică* with the fish and the olives! This is plum brandy from my brother's orchard in the hills near Cimpulung. To tell you the truth, he gave it to me last Christmas, but I kept it unopened, waiting for a special occasion. Well, I can't think of a better occasion than this."

Silvia brings in three jiggers, which are immediately filled with the brandy.

"Old *țuică* from the hills of Cimpulung is about the best you can find in the country today," says Eugen, smacking his lips. "Thank you for bringing it. Drinking this is the right thing to do. For the new madness and the many ads for foreign brandies and wines are killing our own industry. The Vermouth, Dubonnet, and the many Champagnes from France and the American whiskey advertised all over the city and served in the best restaurants are in no way any better than our own drinks. The 'foreigners'—the Jews—

make more money with that stuff and they are destroying our own wealth."

The Professor tries to interrupt, but Doctor Milo goes on:

"...And this is precisely what they want! And I can assure you that they do it with everything: books, records, fabrics, clothes, foods, cheeses, all kinds of things which are produced in this country and are just as good—or even better—than what they import. And it's all done for their own profit, and also to put us down, to undermine and to exploit us," he says with an angry voice.

"Let me read you a few lines from a book my good friend Moța has just translated." He turns around and takes a thin booklet from a shelf. The title reads "The Protocols of the Elders of Zion."

"This pamphlet will explain it much better than I can do..."

"Wait... wait... we can read this another time!" interrupts the Professor.

"Let's just enjoy what we have! It's your birthday! Forget politics. The fish, the olives, the caviar are so delicious! Let's savor the food and the brandy in peace." He pours more brandy in everyone's jigger and clinks his glass with the hosts'. He knows this book, he has read it some time ago in German or French. It is full of lies and hatred against the Jews, and he doesn't want to have an angry debate with his friends.

"To your birthday! To your health! *Prosit!* To your career!"

"To *your* health!" Silvia smiles at him, but she looks at Eugen as if expecting a silent approval from him. She seems so dependent, so dominated by him, the Professor thinks. Is she still under hypnosis? Will she ever regain her full spontaneity and individuality? He looks around the room and discovers Silvia's guitar in a corner, and her typewriter on the desk.

"Your guitar has finally reached you here, and I see that you are also typing! Maybe you'll type some papers for us? We can use expert help," he asks.

"Oh, yes, maybe. But now she is very busy typing work for the Casa Verde. It is quite urgent, and I don't know when she'll be through. She's still a beginner, you know!" says Eugen.

They take another sip of brandy and more fish and *tarama*, and, when Silvia goes to the kitchen to check on the moussaka, the Professor puts his hand on Eugen's arm.

"I'm thinking about your scientific work, your treatment of suicidal patients with hypnosis. You've been most successful with it. In addition to Silvia here, you had a number of good cases. Not since Charcot has anybody done such excellent work. You're very talented. But you must work harder at it, and publish your research. I can see you one day as Head of the Department, full professor of Neuropsychiatry, the Romanian Charcot. But you must tone down your other activities, and make your medical work your first priority. I hope you will think about it. ...*Prosit!* Let's drink to your brilliant career!" He raises his jigger and clinks with his host.

Eugen slowly turns the glass in his hand and keeps frowning.

"You don't understand," he finally says. "I can't just tone down or give up my other activities like giving up a sport or a hobby. I must fulfill my mission, a sacred mission from God for our people."

"What sacred mission? God gave you an unusually great talent. Your only mission is to live up to this gift, and fulfill your potential. If I use your mystical language, I must say that it is an unforgivable sin to act otherwise."

Eugen rests his head in his hands, letting his curls fall on his forehead.

"No. You're missing the point. There are larger, more important issues than scientific research. National issues. The fate of this nation and of this country, which is physically and spiritually robbed and destroyed by foreigners—by the Jews—and by our own foreign king and his Jewish mistress. The Jews are robbing us of our own spirituality, of the purity of our souls. We must all join hands and save our people from this catastrophe. My old school friends and I have joined the Iron Guard and have sworn to sacrifice our lives for this holy cause."

"I can't believe you! You're on the wrong track! There is so much violence in your Legionnaire movement!" The Professor cannot control his voice. "So many brutal attacks, beatings, even murders and assassinations! Nothing good can come of it. I can't understand you... This is the end of civilization, the end of the Enlightenment! ... I, for one, will always believe in democracy, not in murders and assassinations. Only democracy can assure the progress of a nation!"

"*You* are wrong. *You* believe in an illusion!" Eugen is getting up, pushing his chair back from the table. "The Western democracies are nothing but a thin veil of corruption, through which the Jews exploit and abuse Europe and the whole Western world. To counter it, a new man is needed. According to Nietzsche, this must be a dynamic new man who is not afraid of brutality and does not refrain from violence in his great Will to Power. Our Legionnaire movement is entirely composed of such Nietzschean new men."

"Sieg Heil! Heil Hitler!" The words come to the Professor's mind, but he swallows them, he doesn't say anything. He remembers that the Nazi theorists often quote Nietzsche and that Hitler refers to the German *Übermensch* in *Mein Kampf.* He is shocked and saddened by Eugen's passionate tirade. He looks at the young man and wonders when did the hardworking, studious physician change into this fiery militant? There must have been signs, but he must have overlooked them.

He is worried, too—for Eugen's sake. Because, with his hothead friends, they can easily get into trouble, be arrested, beaten or even murdered by the king's brutal militia. What a world! Yes, for sure, this is the end of the Enlightenment.

While Eugen opens a bottle of wine, the Professor continues his train of thought. Yes, the Enlightenment... Paris... His last trip to France... His French education... His mother who taught him French and taught him to love and admire the French philosophers—Voltaire, Rousseau, Montesquieu. Like Rousseau he always believed that man is born naturally good, and he could never accept the theory of a superior race meant to exploit and dominate other, inferior races.

His scientific work, too, reflects his admiration for the French thought and culture, for he is convinced that it was Charcot's Gallic genius which ultimately sparked Freud's creative imagination.

A few minutes later Silvia comes back from the kitchen. She is bringing a deep baking dish filled with steaming moussaka. While she is serving moussaka in the Professor's plate, Eugen is pouring wine in his glass. Then, between mouthfuls of eggplant and sips of wine, Eugen insists on reading aloud from a Legionnaire booklet he has just received as a birthday gift from Silvia. It is a very religious book and its main thesis is that, at the present time, the Western world is in a profound spiritual crisis sliding rapidly and dangerously into a dark abyss. And it is the role of Romania—precisely, the role of the Legionnaire movement—to save the Western world from its impending destruction by the Jews, and to lead it to new spiritual peaks. According to Legionnaire luminaries, the most ancient Christian center of Europe is located here. And it follows that the ultimate goal of the Iron Guard is to become the spiritual guiding light of the Western world. "...The aging Occident, which, until now, has made enough contributions to civilization and is now in decline, this leading Occident will now move to the Latin Orient of Europe..." The Professor has stopped eating, has closed his eyes and listens carefully to the pompous text of the book. It is full of big words and of such grandiose invocations that it sounds like a parody. It would make him laugh if it weren't so serious. Silvia and Eugen are sitting in awe. He is aware that thousands of intellectuals and students believe in this new gospel. He wants to say, How can anybody believe in such nonsense? The words are choking him, but he takes a deep breath and swallows them. It makes no sense to interrupt his hosts' ecstasy.

When the reading is finished and the book is back on the shelf the Professor gets up. He makes a few steps and stops near the window, by the cage of the yellow canaries.

The female sits in the nest on two eggs and the male serenades her with an abundance of trills. But he stops suddenly and blinks anxiously when the Professor stands near the cage. From here he has another view: the bedroom door is slightly open and he can see the large gilded icon of the Archangel Michael—the Patron Saint of the Legionnaires—with its red oil lamp, hanging from the wall. On the bed are two green shirts with their black leather belts and black pistol holsters. One revolver rests on the white down pillow.

How can one believe in such nonsense? The words are still sitting on the tip of his tongue, when Silvia and Eugen call him back to the table.

The dark chocolate cake with the pistachio cream decorations sits on a round platter. After everybody admires the birthday greetings and the green garlands of flowers, Silvia cuts the cake and places a wedge-shaped slice on everyone's plate. Even though he is not hungry any longer, the Professor wolfs down the creamy dessert, hoping to silence for good his angry thoughts.

But later, when Eugen tells him about the trip he and Silvia are taking tomorrow and invites him to join in their demonstrations, the words come gushing down like a waterfall.

"Me? Come to march in your demonstration? It's like joining a herd of wild pachyderms trampling everything underfoot! I don't' know how you can march with these hoodlums and believe all their lies! Where is your head? You must be drunk or drugged! Or bewitched! Time to wake up!"

"No," says Eugen firmly, as if expecting this outburst. "No, *you* must wake up. *You* live on a cloud of illusions which have ceased to exist!"

With great effort, the Professor takes hold of himself and nods. He mumbles something which is not very clear. Then he thanks them for the meal, gives a big hug to Silvia and steps out of their home.

Downstairs, at the wheel of his car, he sits motionless for a while. He takes a bottle of French cologne from the glove compartment, and sprinkles a few drops on his hands and on a white handkerchief. Then he wipes his hands and his face. "Yes, like a wild herd of pachyderms trampling everything in their way..." he mumbles and sighs. He feels shocked and saddened—like attending a funeral after a sudden catastrophe... No doubt, Eugen has joined the barbarians who burn books and destroy knowledge. And he—Professor Georgescu—has lost a precious son, a budding scientist whom he has lovingly groomed to continue his work. He shakes his head as he remembers how, after the devastation of World War I, he had sworn to stay out of politics and to devote himself to the alleviation of human suffering. He had come to believe that every educated man, every medical scientist was thinking like him. But now, to his surprise, he discovers that he is wrong.

But how about his other friends, Stella and Sorel? They do think like him and he feels close to them. But they are Jewish, and, with Sorel's passionate Zionism on one hand, and the situation getting progressively worse, will they eventually leave for Palestine? Stella has sworn never to abandon him. But he is not convinced. She is married to Sorel, and must think of her children. He shrugs. He doesn't know what the future will bring. Nevertheless, the thought of Stella makes him imagine her sitting next to him. He is suddenly hungry for her embrace. Soon... soon... very soon...

He puts the key in the ignition and starts the engine.

CERNĂUȚI: THE DEMONSTRATION

"I T's A LONG TRIP, IT will take us at least 11 hours by train to Cernăuți and there will be a full day of demonstrations," Eugen tells Silvia. "We'll need good walking shoes and plenty of food."

She prepares two backpacks with provisions—hard-boiled eggs, bread, feta cheese, sausages, BBQ-d chickens, apples, pears and two thermoses with hot peppermint tea.

"We're going to pay our last tribute to a young student who has fought for the rebirth of our nation. He is a hero who has lost his life in the struggle against our Jewish enemies."

Eugen adds that the man was a theological seminarian who was mortally wounded in the public park of Cernăuți, in a scuffle with a group of Jewish students. The students had been attacked by the seminarians a few days before. The main Jewish perpetrator had been taken into custody by the local police and fallen or jumped to his death from the fourth floor of the detention center.

At 6 o'clock in the evening they're in the railway station. The train is already there, and they climb in and settle in an empty compartment. This is a special train. All the passengers are Legionnaire students. Green-shirted guards are posted at every door and are turning away regular passengers. More and more students are boarding, and soon the compartment fills up. They're all wearing green shirts, black leather belts, and carry shiny revolvers in their holsters. Many of them also have small satchels of earth tied around their neck, in sign of their closeness to the land. And there are faces familiar to Silvia from the Case Verde.

At about 6:30 the train slowly moves out of the station. It leaves behind noisy vendors of *rahat locum*, of cheap cigarettes and sunflower seeds. Then it speeds along the dusty outskirts of the city and past small villages with houses shaded by mulberry trees. Soon it reaches the flat cornfields tended here and there by a solitary farmer in his oxen cart.

The setting sun is a blazing fireball at the horizon, and, after it disappears in a blood-red halo, everybody becomes restless and starts moving around. There is a rumor that Căpitanul Zelea Codreanu himself is on the train. Groups of people rush to the front, having heard that he is in the first compartment, while others run to the end, hearing that he is in the last car.

There are bottlenecks on the corridors as the two groups run into each other, with pushing and shoving, cursing, screaming and laughter. Only when there is an official announcement—through the loudspeaker—that Căpitanul is not on board, and only when the commanding voice orders everybody to return to their seats, does the pushing and shoving cease. A few minutes later, the Iron Guard anthem *"Garda, Căpitanul"* is heard over the loudspeaker and everybody joins in. Meanwhile, Eugen and his friends Valerian, Horațiu and Radu gather in a quiet compartment to discuss the last details of the demonstration.

Left alone with the other travelers in her compartment, Silvia watches them as they sing.

When the song ends a tall girl with long, stringy hair and dark rimmed glasses turns toward Silvia.

"You look familiar, and I think I know who you are. I have seen you at the Casa Verde. Your blond braids are not easy to forget. We've called you 'Gretchen' because of them. My name is Nicoleta," she adds, and she introduces her friends—Irina, Marilena and Aurel.

"We are all medical students, and we travel all over the country to organize the Frățiile de Cruce—the Legionnaire student brotherhoods and sisterhoods. We explain who we are, what we do, what we believe in..."

While Nicoleta is talking, Irina and Marilena pull out of their rucksacks packages of food—ham, bacon, tomatoes cucumbers, sheep cheese, butter and bread, all wrapped in wax paper.

"Won't you join us?" Irina asks, as she arranges the food on the table.

Silvia nods, and opens her own backpack to share her provisions with the others.

Nicoleta goes on speaking:

"...We teach the students everything: our credo and our philosophy, our strategies to vanquish the old, corrupt order. Many new members have joined us on this train, or will meet us in Cernăuți. They're all excited, it's the first public demonstration for many of them..."

Silvia is full of admiration for Nicoleta, for her devotion and her accomplishments. Eugen's words, "Be a leader of armies, a new Joan of Arc to the battlefield," resound in her head. Eugen would be so pleased if she became a leader in the organization!

Late in the evening Eugen returns to the compartment. His eyes are shining, his face is glowing with excitement. Silvia introduces him to her new friends, and gives him a few slices of sausage, some chicken and bacon which she has saved for him. He swallows quickly, almost without chewing. He also gulps down half a bottle of Bere Azuga which Aurel has shared with him. Then he slumps down on the seat next to Silvia, his long legs stretched out in front of him and falls asleep, his head resting on Silvia's shoulder. The others now speak softly, not to wake him up. Later, at 11, when the big overhead light is switched off, everybody has fallen asleep. Eugen's head is now cradled in Silvia's lap, and her fingers are entwined in his locks. Her left leg is tucked under her. Aurel is sprawled over his seat, an empty bottle of beer in his hand. Irina and Nicoleta rest their heads on each other's shoulders, as if sharing deep secrets in their sleep. In the luggage racks above them, the heavy belts and the pistols hit against each other with a metallic click whenever the train sways this way or that.

The whistle of the locomotive wakes Silvia early. She lifts a corner of the curtain which covers the window and sees that they are crossing a bridge over a misty river. The train has slowed down as it travels over the bridge. It is drizzling outside and she can see small fishing boats and flocks of wild geese and ducks floating on the water.

At the other end of the bridge, the train stops at a small railway station. While the engine is taking water, a group of young people in green shirts with black belts and revolvers accompanied by several priests with long beards and black robes are crowding the platform. The priests are carrying silver incense burners and holy water and are blessing the train. *"Doamne miluieşte! Doamne miluieşte! Doamne miluieşte-ne pre noi!"* (God help us! God save us!) Silvia can hear now, after she has opened the window.

At every station more young Legionnaires are boarding the train accompanied by the prayers of worshipping priests. And sometimes, in some stations, exalted mothers raise their babies above the heads of the crowd.

When they reach Cernăuţi, it is still drizzling. The whole place is an emerald sea of green shirts.

As they climb down, Silvia and Eugen are greeted by the mayor and the chief of police—both short and bald men, wearing wet green uniforms and carrying revolvers. Even the station master wears a green shirt, which is now stained by the rain.

The demonstrators form columns, and Silvia and Eugen march at the head of the column which he will be leading.

Eugen walks tall and erect, holding his chin high in the air—like a person of great authority. Silvia is proud to be with him at the head of the column. Everybody looks up at them, now that they are so important!

Nicoleta and her friends have joined them and keep pace with them. The columns formed by the demonstrators fill the streets around the station. New participants keep joining and several military bands are flanking the marchers.

The drums are beating, the trumpets are blowing, and just as they get ready to start, Radu and Valerian, Eugen's old buddies, join him from behind. Their faces are flushed and they're breathless. They bring important news. Soldiers, loyal to the king, are waiting for them in hidden places, ready to attack. The news spreads like wildfire across the ranks.

Eugen orders all demonstrators to check their guns. Everybody must carry a loaded pistol and be ready to shoot.

"We're not afraid. We'll fight them, even if we must die here, in Cernăuți! Besides, our pistols are better than theirs. We have modern Mausers, newly purchased in Germany, while the king's army still uses old weapons, remaindered from the Great War!" He then turns to Silvia and to his friends, speaking in a low voice. "This is Lupeasca's doing! She and her Jewish bankers have convinced the king to fight and destroy us and any other patriotic organizations!"

The students listen to their leader. They pull their guns out of their holsters and check the ammunition. Then, revolvers in hand, they start moving. At all important crossroads an improvised detachment of marchers is sent ahead to explore the terrain. The town has suddenly turned into a minefield of hidden and dangerous traps and ambushes.

They advance cautiously down the boulevard, toward the Public Park where they will pay their respect to the slain Iron Guard student.

The streets are empty. Only stray dogs and policemen add life to the ghostly town. All the stores which belong mostly to Jewish shopkeepers are closed, and their windows are shuttered.

Aurel, who is tall and thin with a sunken chest and looks as if he was dying of consumption, says that the Police have ordered the Kikes to close their shops and stay home, inside their houses. He is carrying a banner with the portrait of Căpitanul Corneliu Codreanu. The banner is too heavy for him, and he shifts it from shoulder to shoulder. Eugen's friend Valerian is carrying a national flag decorated with the Legionnaire symbol of "intersecting prison bars."

The gate to the Public Park is draped with black cloth, and has a large inscription with the words: KIKES NOT ADMITTED TO THE PARK. TRESPASSERS WILL BE PUNISHED.

"People say that children who couldn't read came to the park and were badly beaten!" says Irina.

"They must learn to respect the laws of the land," says Aurel, who is now holding a banner with both hands.

"Don't feel sorry for them! Compassion is not only a weakness, but a great weapon for the enemy!" adds Eugen. "Always keep in mind that a bleeding heart equals death."

They march through the gate and through well-kept alleys bordered by tall oaks and chestnut trees. It keeps drizzling and drops of water fall from the branches. Silvia's hair and shirt are drenched, and the rucksack feels heavier than before. Is it really waterproof, or will the bread and the sausages get soaked in the rain? She steps aside, avoiding a puddle. Then they all stop in front of the bench where the seminarian was killed.

The bench is wrapped in black cloth and has almost disappeared under a mountain of flowers. Candles are burning nearby, sheltered under a sheet of oilcloth. Four tall and muscular students wearing green shirts and holding their pistols ready to shoot stand guard by the bench.

Eugen falls to his knees, pulling Silvia and Nicoleta with him. The others follow suit.

"God bless your servant who has sacrificed his life for our victory against the Judeo-Communists!" he prays loudly so everybody can hear. "Silence! We'll keep two minutes of silence for his memory!" Nobody moves. A flash of lightning flares in the distance.

Eugen makes the sign of the cross, says, "Amen," and stands up, wiping the mud from his pants.

A clap of thunder follows the lightning. The demonstrators file out of the park, passing in front of other trees with the photo of the slain student and the words "This hero has given his life for our holiest cause." They march out through another gate—also wrapped in black streamers and carrying the same inscription prohibiting Jews from entering the park.

"We're heading now to the Church Sfîntul Niculae, where the student's body is lying in state," says Eugen. "We'll carry him to the cemetery after making a stop in City Hall Square."

The column of demonstrators has now grown to over 20,000 and is flanked by rows of peasants in national costume riding their black horses. The trumpets are blowing and the marchers are singing.

Again and again they repeat the same anthems and marching songs—*"Deșteaptă-te Române"* (Wake Up Romanian Citizen), and the Legionnaire anthem, *"Garda, Căpitanul"* (The Guard and the Captain) as if they were part of a sacred ritual. As soon as they finish one anthem, they start the other. With the drums beating and the trumpets blowing, a feeling of great excitement has taken hold of the crowd. Though they've been walking for many hours in the rain, they feel no hunger, no thirst and no pain. Silvia too could go on forever, so possessed is she now by the high mood of the rally.

And then they suddenly stop. A loud noise... the gallop of horses nearby... Silvia's heart pounds. Are we being ambushed? Are we under attack? A bloody scene of wounded horses and broken bodies appears in her mind. Eugen shot and wounded lying at her feet... Screams of anguish and pain... Automatically she raises her hands and covers her ears... but when she looks up, a different scene confronts her. Just around the corner new, steady arrivals are joining them. Other demonstrators, on foot and on horseback, are pushing into the crowded streets. And now they all sing loudly.

When they reach the Church Sfintul Niculae, the plain wooden coffin covered with garlands and wreaths is hoisted on the shoulders of strong youths who will carry it to the cemetery. Bearded priests wearing gold embroidered regalia and sprinkling holy water over the coffin and over the pallbearers are joining the convoy.

It has drizzled all the time they are marching, but the rain stops when they turn into the large square in front of City Hall—the last stop before the cemetery.

Silvia, joined by Nicoleta and her friends, stands in the first row by the speaker's platform which is draped in black cloth. A protective roof had been improvised on the platform by tying a blue oilcloth to four poles, but it was sagging and dripping so badly that it had to be removed. A big poster with the words "The Judeo-Communists are our deadly enemies" and a large photograph of the slain student framed by black, dripping streamers hangs on the wall behind the platform.

Anti-Semitic banners have appeared. There are banners showing cartoons of bearded Jews slaughtering Christian babies and using the blood for the ritual preparation of Passover matzos. Others show Jews with hooked noses, skullcaps and long temple locks holding the earth in their claws. They are perched on top of crowds, whom they trample to death. There are banners with Jews destroying religious monuments and Christian icons while clutching money bags, and pictures of a big Jewish star, dripping with blood. A youth next to Silvia carries a banner showing Magda Lupescu, the king's Jewish mistress, selling the Royal Palace for big bags of money.

As the City Hall square is filling with people, the mayor, looking like a wet balloon in his green uniform—has climbed on the platform and attempts to speak while the crowd is still singing and the bands are still playing. He tries to tell them about the Iron Guard leaders Moța and Marin, who went to Spain to join the army of General Franco. But his words are drowned by shouts of *"Trăiască Moța și Marin! Trăiască Francisco Franco!"* (Long live Moța and Marin! Long live Francisco Franco!)

When they are finally quiet, he tells them that the murder of the Legionnaire student here, in the Public Park, was similar to the murder of the German Nazi hero HORST WESSEL, who lost his life in Berlin, in his own flat, in a fight with a bunch of Judeo-Communists.

The bands start playing the "Horst Wessel Song," the anthem of the German Nazi Party. Immediately the crowd picks up the song and the words:

> *Die Fahne hoch, die Reihen fest geschlossen*
> *S.A. marschiertmit ruhig festen Schritt...*
> (Flag high, ranks closed
> The S.A. marches with poised, solid steps...)

Then they keep screaming *"Sieg Heil! Sieg Heil!"* raising their arms in the fascist salute. The mayor invites Eugen to the speaker's platform. Silvia watches him and notices that the thin, pink scar on his cheek has turned red and is bulging, a sign of great tension. She is worried about him, and, at the same time, filled with pride for being so close to a great man. She watches him climb on the platform, and, like a leader of people, raising his hands to silence the crowd. Next to the mayor he is a towering figure. His voice, too, is strong and commanding.

"...We all have a holy mission: we must make this country more beautiful than the sun, and, to reach this goal, we must vanquish and liquidate the Judeo-Communists who stand in our way. We must pledge the divine oath of allegiance and loyalty to our organization." He stops... clears his throat... and commands: "Repeat after me!

> ...For Christ and for the Legion
> For the Resurrection of my Country
> In every moment
> I am ready to die,
> I swear."

In one voice, the demonstrators repeat Eugen's words. Then he goes on.

"You must remember that in this struggle, in this crusade, each of us is a leader, a general, a Joan of Arc at the head of an army. And, for those who don't know it, I must inform you that our death squads are ready for action. They will punish all our enemies and all those who betray our ranks. There will be no forgiveness and no compassion."

He stops. He musters the crowd with a stern look.

"And from this day on we will call for the official banishment of all Jewish students not only from the Public Parks, but from all the Universities as well!"

An explosion of joy greets his last words. The people laugh, scream, applaud and sing at the same time. In the next minute all the anti-Jewish banners are thrown in a pile and burned.

Jewish newspapers are hurled on top of the heap. The demonstrators are delirious with joy. They howl, clap and dance around the fire. The Legionnaire anthem and the Horst Wessel song resonate with more power than ever: *"Wenn Judenblut vom Messer spritzt..."* (When Jewish blood squirts from the knife...)

Silvia too laughs and sings at the top of her voice until the sounds fade and hoarseness sets in. Around her, others are also getting hoarse from screaming and singing. But nobody cares. Silvia is filled with ecstasy. She now carries a banner with the image of the Archangel Michael, the patron saint of the Legion. She feels that she has turned into the true Joan of Arc in full armor, protected and guided by the saint. Now she will live up to the calling! When the banner flies in the wind, she knows that she is carried toward victory on the great wings of the Archangel.

WINTER 1937

O N HER NINTH BIRTHDAY IN January, Nadia has received a small photo-album from her parents. Today she is sitting at her desk and, instead of doing her homework, she looks at the pictures in the album.

Her parents have already pasted in a few photos. There is a picture of her as a small baby, one as a toddler, and one with Suzy and both parents. In the picture as a toddler Nadia sits in a big armchair, wears a silk bow in her hair and holds Hans, her favorite doll, in her lap. In that picture, Hans is still wearing his elegant, blue knitted costume and closes his eyes when she puts him to sleep. Not like today, when his eyes cannot move and stay always open—because, in her eagerness to see how they were moving, many years ago, she pushed them inside his head. Poor Hans had to be taken to the doll hospital and underwent a mysterious operation. His blue eyes were put back in their orbit, but could never move again.

And his elegant costume? Well, he can still wear the faded jacket, but the pants have become so threadbare that they had to be replaced with a child's real diaper.

But what Nadia is looking for now are pictures from last summer's vacation at the sea. She has collected a few of them—mostly from Anca Georgescu's birthday party.

But, since Fräulein Lilly also appears in them, Nadia doesn't care for them. There are a few photos of her with Theo and Corinna, but what she really wants is a picture of Skender in his boat. It would give her more hope for returning to the sea next summer! She only dreams of going back to the sea and searching for the sunken treasure. Even though Skender has promised to be there next summer, she would feel more hopeful if she had a picture of him and his boat. Maybe she is looking for magic, but she is convinced that this picture could bring her back to the sea.

Many nights she has the same dream: they're in the boat, sailing toward the rock with the sunken ship. They're going fast. Then Skender stops the boat. Nadia jumps, dives and slides inside the wreck through the narrow hatch. It is dark down there, only one ray of light reaches the treasure and makes it shine. She is close to it. She is touching it. Then, suddenly it gets very dark... The hatch closes on top of her. She is trapped.

Once or twice when she woke up she had a pain in her ear, like a very fine needle. But it vanished as soon as she opened her eyes.

She has asked her parents whether she will return to the sea next summer, but they said they didn't know. Her mother has even mumbled something about "the danger of diving." Only Uncle Sorel has laughed and said, "Yes, of course, we'll go to the sea and you'll swim and dive like a fish!"

Nadia keeps looking for her picture of Skender—she knows that she had such a picture with him standing in his boat, holding a big fish in his hands, smiling... She has looked everywhere, but she can't find it. Where did it disappear? Or has Fräulein Lilly stolen it or thrown it away? It is true that the photo was torn in one corner and had a yellow stain in another.

"You don't paste damaged pictures in an album!" the governess had warned her, and told her to throw it into the garbage. But Nadia didn't listen to her, and slipped the photo back in its envelope.

She will now check Fräulein Lilly's armoire, her drawers, and even her pocketbooks! Today Tuesday, is a good day to try: she's out today, it's her day off. But just as Nadia gets up on a stool and reaches the upper levels of the armoire where she knows Fräulein Lilly keeps her personal things, she hears fast steps approaching. Her mother walks in. She looks at Nadia with suspicion and asks, "What are you doing? Why aren't you doing your homework?"

Nadia blabbers, "What?" Something, a lame excuse her mother can barely hear. Then her mother tells her that the seamstress, Doamna Avramescu, is here for the Purim costume.

This is good news, Nadia tells herself—since she looks forward to her Purim outfit. How did she forget? It will be Purim soon, and she has persuaded her mother to let her wear the costume of a pirate ship's captain! Luckily, Joel had just such a costume from a show he had organized many years ago as a high-school student.

Of course, a few adjustments are needed: the shirt and pants are too big and need to be taken in and shortened. Otherwise, everything else—the black hat with the white skull and the crossbones, the red belt and the velvet vest—are O.K.

In the next minute, Nadia runs to the sewing room before her mother can catch up with her. This room is a sort of narrow alcove, squeezed between the master bedroom and the large bathroom. It has tall green closets built into the wall, reaching from floor to ceiling, and a big mirror which covers the door.

Doamna Avramescu—a fat lady with a big head of gray hair, thick glasses and a triple chin—sits by the Singer sewing machine sipping tea from a glass. She has already opened the seams of the shirt and the pants, and has secured them with many pins.

"Careful!" she says as Nadia tries on the outfit. "There are pins all along the sleeves and inside the pants!"

Nadia likes the costume, but hates the fitting. She has no patience—she cannot stand still. While the seamstress is busy with her measurements, Nadia discovers the pirate captain's black hat lying on a table within reach. She grabs it and puts it on her head, without any regard for Doamna Avramesu's pins. Next to the hat, she discovers the black eye patch which so many pirates wear over their blind eye. Left eye or right eye? She puts the patch on and takes it off, switching it from side to side.

This irritates her mother, who doesn't like the idea of the eye patch to begin with.

"Give me that piece of leather!" she orders. "You shouldn't wear it, we shouldn't make fun of people's infirmity! Besides, I am superstitious: nothing good can come of it!"

But the eye patch is Nadia's *"pièce de resistance,"* her most precious asset. She won't give it up, and their dispute turns into a fierce battle of wills. Nadia runs into the bathroom and locks the door.

"Come out of there immediately!" orders her mother as she tries to force the door open.

"I will not! I'll stay here as long as I please!"

But she finally comes out when her mother threatens to give the pirate costume away—perhaps to Theo. As for the eye patch, Nadia keeps holding onto it.

When the fitting is over and she is back in her room, she remembers the picture with Skender and his boat. Where can it be? It is quiet here and she is all alone. Fräulein Lilly is away on her day off, and won't be back before 8 or 9 in the evening. Nadia carefully opens the armoire and looks inside the pocketbooks—the brown leather one and the black alligator bag the governess wears in the winter. Then she examines the light-colored summer purses.

Afterwards she climbs on a chair and explores the shelves, looking under the lingerie—but she doesn't find anything. Everything there is carefully folded, and she forces herself to put it back just as she found it.

While she is doing it, she hears footsteps approaching and her mother's voice. The door handle turns, and the door is ready to open. Will her mother come in?

Nadia runs back to her desk, opens her book and pretends to be studying. She is ready now. But the handle snaps back, the steps go away, the door is closed again. She sits and waits. When all is quiet, she goes back to the shelves and finishes folding the nightgowns and slips. Then she opens the drawers, but she finds nothing there. Just some curlers, a few hairpins, and a bottle of sleep medicine.

Nadia closes the drawers and is ready to give up when she sees a fat book lying on the night table. She recognizes the romance novel Fräulein Lilly was reading at the beach in the summer. Inside the book is a card in the guise of a bookmark. She pulls it out, and there it is, the photo of Skender in his boat!

Nadia stares at the photo in disbelief. How did this happen? Why did Fräulein Lilly take the picture in the first place? Just because it was damaged? Did she hide it on purpose in the book? Nadia gets angrier and angrier. Now she can take her revenge: in her mind, she sees Fräulein Lilly captive on a pirate ship, where she is being force-fed and fattened like a goose. Then, when she becomes enormously fat, she is being sold to cannibals in Africa or in the South Seas. Nadia smiles with delight when she imagines Fräulein Lilly with her perfect little curls sitting in a boiling cauldron while the savages dance around the fire beating their drums and sharpening their knives.

Nadia gets up and marches to the bathroom. She opens the medicine chest and pours a few spoonfuls of mineral oil in Fräulein Lilly's bottle of sleep medicine.

THE VISITOR

I N HIS OFFICE, ADRIAN STANDS in front of the large windows, absentmindedly watching the picture engraved on the glass: the hairy, naked giant, covering, with his hand, the smoking factory chimneys, making the smoke billow out of the buildings through windows and doors and forcing a terrified crowd of people to run into the street. The scene is so vivid that Adrian can hear the screams of the mob.

This afternoon he is waiting for an important guest: Charles Kass of Switzerland is here for a short visit and has promised to meet him around 5. He telephoned last night and said that he was in Bucharest for two days and that he wanted very much to see Adrian. He said that he was invited by the king and Madame Lupescu to join them on a hunting trip in the mountains. But he didn't want to leave Bucharest without seeing his old friend.

Adrian remembers that Kass was a passionate hunter, that his office at Brown Boveri Company in Baden was lavishly decorated with the heads of stags and bears which he had shot, and he assumes that Kass has met the king and his mistress in the prestigious Zürich Jagdverein.

More than eight months have passed since Adrian has seen Charles Kass in Zürich, and he can't wait to meet him again. Unfortunately, there will be almost no time to talk to him alone, in the privacy of his office, since today is his brother-in-law Sorel's 40th birthday, and Adrian cannot miss the celebration. He has already told Sorel that he was bringing Charles along to the party.

As the stands near the window, he thinks of his trip to Switzerland, of the conversation they had in Baden, of Charles' generous offer, and of the house he bought in Lugano. He sees himself standing on the sunny terrace overlooking the water and the garden with the lemon and orange trees, and then sitting in the little boat, rowing along the quiet shore. It all seems so near and so far at the same time.

Almost without thinking he goes to the desk, opens the drawer, and pulls out the bronze keys of the villa. He holds them in his hand for a short while, then puts them back in the drawer and pulls out a pack of photos from the Purim party. He will bring these pictures to Sorel's house.

On the top of the pack is a photo of Nadia as a fierce pirate captain, wearing the black hat with the white skull and the crossbones as well as the leather patch over her left eye. She did get her way! Adrian chuckles, thinking of her fight with Nina over the eye patch. Good for her! She sticks to her guns!

He is still smiling while looking at Suzy dressed as the medieval knight Lohengrin, pulling behind her, on a leash, a wooden white goose-toy on wheels, which serves as a swan. But then he stops smiling. He turns very serious. In the picture there is a large window behind Suzy. He remembers clearly how it was smashed when a dead dog was hurled into the room. It was their own dog, Puck, now stiff and cold, his eyes fixed and glazed. His white, shaggy fur had been irregularly clipped with scissors, and around his neck he wore a blue ribbon. A small piece of cardboard was attached to it. Something was written on the paper, and when he read it, it said: *"Ciine jidovesc, la Palestina!"* (Jewish dog, go to Palestine!)

In the room, everybody was stunned. Nobody moved. Nobody spoke. Only Adrian and Sorel immediately started checking whether anybody had been wounded by the broken glass. Fortunately, nobody had been hurt, and everybody was in shock. Some children were crying and clinging to their mothers, and Nadia was particularly devastated by the death of her dog. For it was her dog, she had found it on her way to school, on an empty lot overgrown with nettles and poisonous weeds. It was a tiny, blind, newborn puppy which she brought home and bottle fed—very much against her mother's will. The puppy had grown into a dog with a fuzzy white coat. In the last year, it had often run away from home, but it always came back—sometimes with its coat shorn like today and sometimes with a silk bow around its neck. But it always came back clean and well fed, and announced its return with joyous barking.

But who was hating them so much and was so cruel as to take revenge on a dog? Who could it be? Somebody who knew them well? A neighbor? And how had they killed the dog? It looked like poison, since there was no cut, no bruises, and no trace of blood on his white coat.

The room was quiet. People were barely whispering to one another. Only Nadia was sobbing, while Nina and Suzy were trying to comfort her.

It was Adrian who then at the party remembered the story of Rabbi Loewe and the dog. In this old story, a dead dog was thrown inside the Jewish cemetery in Prague in order to desecrate this holy place. But the congregation gave the dog a full traditional funeral and buried him at the most sacred place in the cemetery, next to the tomb of Rabbi Loewe. On its small marble headstone they engraved a beautiful image of a dog. Now anybody who pays homage to Rabbi Loewe and places a stone on his tomb also pays homage to the dog and leaves a pebble on its gravestone. Adrian climbed on a stool in the middle of the room and told the story so that everybody could hear him. At the end he added that he was going to treat Puck like a beloved family member and bury him in the garden, under the linden tree. And he was going to order a marble headstone with the picture of a dog, just like the one in the cemetery of Prague.

The children calmed down. Even Nadia stopped crying after his talk. But people kept looking anxiously toward the broken window, wondering what else was going to happen.

Now Adrian gathers the photos and slips them into his briefcase. Then he returns to the window and notices that it has started to snow. Large snowflakes are hitting the glass, melting to water and running down the cheeks of the giant, like tears.

Adrian keeps thinking of Kass's visit and of the many questions it raises: first, the job offer he has received last summer, in Switzerland. He should have accepted immediately! Had he done so, he would now be settled and active in the new position at Brown Boveri, working at various innovative projects... And Nina's refusal to leave? He "should" have found a way to convince her! He should have tried harder, been more forceful, less accepting of her irrational arguments!

There are loud clamors outside in the distance, people shouting and singing, marching bands playing. This is a bad day to be out on the streets. Another big Legionnaire demonstration is taking place in the city. Today is the funeral procession of two major Legionnaire leaders who were shot dead while fighting for Franco, near Madrid.

Adrian can hear the beat of the drums and the songs of the demonstrators. He knows that even though he has sent Fritz with the car to fetch Kass from the hotel Athénée Palace, this short trip can take a long time; a large detour will be needed to get around the procession. But, to his surprise, the doorbell rings earlier than he expected. He hears voices in the other room, and Domnişoara Braunstein announces that Herr Kass has arrived.

"Grüssgott!" he says as he enters the room with a big smile on his face. He looks more tanned, his hair is lighter, his teeth shine brighter, and he seems taller, younger, and more athletic than Adrian remembers him. Under his open coat and his woolen scarf, he wears a navy blue blazer with a hunting horn embroidered on his chest pocket, just like the one he wore in Baden.

"So glad to see you! I was afraid I was going to miss you, with my brief stop in Bucharest... and I didn't want this to happen!" Charles Kass keeps smiling and gives Adrian a firm handshake.

"Sit down, sit down for a minute!" Adrian pushes a chair toward his guest. "So delighted to see you! ...And looking so good! You said you're going hunting with the king..."

"Correct. The king and Madame Lupescu have invited me to join them hunting in the Carpathian mountains." Kass sits down and takes a pipe out of his pocket and holds it in his hand, without lighting it.

"...I met them last summer, soon after you left. They were staying at your hotel, the Baur au Lac. They're members of the hunting club, the Zürcher Jagdverein, and we went hunting together. The king is an excellent sharpshooter and a witty raconteur, fluent in German—of course, since he is a born Hohenzollern. By the way, he told me about the hilarious incident at the hotel, when he ended up shooting the famous swans in the park... It must have been quite a scene! Also, the whole incident was later reported in the Zürcher Tageblatt, but, according to him, he was falsely accused of shooting without any provocation. It was the swans who attacked the dogs so viciously that they had to be liquidated!"

"This is a new Münchhausen story!" Adrian shakes his head. "I was there... The poor swans didn't have a chance. The dogs carried on like bloodthirsty beasts. Be careful, you don't know what a Hohenzollern-Münchhausen can do with a gun!"

They look at each other and start to laugh.

"I promise!" Kass puts his pipe on the table and covers his heart with his right hand. "I swear on my heart! But enough about me. How are you? How is your family? Things seem rather jumpy here."

"Yes." Adrian nods. He starts to answer, but the telephone rings. He picks up the receiver. A woman's voice can be heard through the telephone.

"Yes, yes, he is here. We'll be leaving soon. Yes, thanks, I'll tell him." Adrian nods a few times and smiles into the receiver.

"It was Nina. She asks us to hurry up and leave before it gets too late. Remember, we go to Sorel, Nina's brother-in-law's birthday party. We can talk more in the car." In a minute Charles Kass puts on his coat, his cashmere scarf, and his fine leather gloves, while Adrian takes his hat and tells the secretary to close the office for the day and go home.

When they're in the car, Fritz starts the engine and they take off.

"If we're lucky and don't get caught in the demonstration, we'll be there very soon."

Fritz follows the narrow back streets and stays away from the crowded boulevards. But he has to drive slowly because of the many potholes and the bumpy cobblestones. From a distance, they can hear the clamor of voices and the rumble of many marchers. When they take a turn on Brătianu Boulevard, they have to stop: they have come face to face with the funeral carts. Two simple peasant carts, each pulled by two oxen, carrying the wooden coffins covered by the national flag and a large wreath with green streamers. Black and green streamers are also draped over the oxen.

The funeral carts are followed by the old Mitropolit, the head of the Romanian church, walking slowly, bent over his wooden staff. Behind him are rows upon rows of priests in flowing black robes with golden chains and massive crosses on their chest, all chanting prayers for the fallen heroes. They are followed by a sea of green-shirted marchers carrying banners of the Archangel Michael, shouting slogans and singing Legionnaire anthems. Kass straightens up in his seat and watches the marchers with interest.

"I understand that your Iron Guard Organization loves these funeral processions. I heard that there was a big one a few months ago, in Chernowitz..." His words are drowned by the din.

The car is stuck. It cannot advance, it cannot go back and it cannot turn on a side street because of the crowd. The frantic, screaming marchers surround them on all sides, and then suddenly a young face with red cheeks, blonde braids twisted around her head and large, blue, steely eyes—Adrian recognizes Silvia staring at him. On her face, no sign of recognition. Only cold hatred. She is carrying a banner with the image of the Archangel Michael and is shouting "Death to the Judeo-Communists!" Next to her, Eugen Milo is marching in step, carrying a large cartoon with a fat old Jew with an enormous hooked nose grabbing a blonde girl.

But Adrian looks only at Silvia. He is dumbfounded, shocked. How can she! Somebody who has lived in his house, who was so close to the family, to the children, somebody he helped so generously when she was in need! And Eugen Milo, a doctor, an intellectual, Victor Georgescu's assistant!

Charles Kass, who has watched Adrian and the marchers, puts a hand on his arm.

"Are you all right? What's going on? Who is this woman?"

Adrian tries to pull himself together. He hides his face in his hands.

"Yes, I'm O.K. Just these people. She is our old governess. I've never seen her like this. She was sick in the hospital and we helped her for some time. But then we lost track of her."

The car is moving now. A sudden break in the column of marchers, and Fritz quickly steps on the accelerator.

"To tell you the truth, it doesn't matter who she is," says Kass. "But the hatred. I haven't seen such hatred in my life. This is dangerous. You must get out. You and your family. Get your pictures for a family passport tomorrow. You must go to the photo studio tomorrow with your wife and your daughters. I don't know why you didn't do it already!"

"I know, I know what you mean!" Adrian hesitates. "But the problem isn't me: it's Nina. She won't think of leaving without her sister, Stella, and Stella won't leave without..." Adrian stops, then clears his voice.

"Without?"

"...without Victor Georgescu."

"Who is Victor Georgescu?"

"How shall I tell you?" Adrian scratches his forehead. "Victor Georgescu, Doctor Georgescu is a special friend of the family, particularly of Stella's. He is a widower with two children. He is not Jewish. You'll meet him tonight at the party." He pauses. "As you see, this whole thing is quite complicated."

"I understand. Let me think." Charles Kass takes his pipe out of his pocket and rubs it with his thumb. Then he turns toward Adrian. "Maybe I can help—not only you, but also your family and friends. I'm an old member of the International Red Cross. I may be able to find a position for the doctors. And through Brown Boveri I could probably find something for your wife's brother who is an engineer."

Adrian thanks him, but wonders whether Victor Georgescu would really give up his position for an "unknown future" in a foreign country. He speaks fluent German and French, so the language is not a problem... But he is a full professor here, the director of a big hospital—a very prestigious position. He makes a good living and he will have a good pension. Also he is the private physician of the queen. And, he is not Jewish, so he has nothing to fear. Or? If the Iron Guard comes to power, could he too become a target of their violence? It could very well happen. He has so many Jewish friends.

So, where is the answer? Adrian wishes he was the kind of man who could have faith in a fortune teller and in her crystal ball.

The car turns into a narrow street and stops in front of a five-story apartment house decorated in Art Nouveau style. Today Adrian barely glances at the façade with the colorful stained-glass windows and the gold-covered floral reliefs. It's the house where both couples—Sorel and Stella, Nina's sister, and Dora and Emil, Nina's brother—live with their children. Adrian loves this house. He built it with the help of a French architect in the early '20s, soon after the war, and it still belongs to him. It is in good condition, and, should he decide to sell it, he could make good money from it. But he won't sell it as long as Nina's siblings live there.

Adrian and Charles Kass take the small, ornate elevator to the fifth floor. Upstairs, Stella opens the door and gives Adrian a big hug, while Kass bows and kisses her hand, making her blush with pleasure. She wears a black silk sweater with a low-cut neck, a red carnation in a corsage, and a black pleated skirt. Her dark hair is gathered in a bun at the back of her neck and she holds her famous fan of black lace and feathers in one hand. She puts down the fan, unfastens the red carnation and pins it to Charles' lapel. Sorel stands next to her, and the two guests try to hand him the gifts they have brought—Adrian a bottle of French cognac and Kass a box of Swiss chocolates—but they are assailed by the other guests, who have all rushed to the door. Adrian sees Nina standing at the back of the crowd, but he cannot join her because of all the people. Innumerable questions are hurled at them.

"How are things outside?"

"Are those thugs still marching?"

"Have you seen beatings? Violence?"

"Can the cars still get around?"

"Are there police on the streets? Or armed troops?"

Using her fan as a weapon, Stella succeeds in dispersing the assailants and leading the two guests to the dining table, which is laden with mountains of fragrant appetizers and mouth-watering entrées. Watching her fill his plate with slides of *pâté de foie gras* and a salad of endives with walnuts, followed by a tender *filet mignon aux champignons*, Adrian remembers that Stella's dream was to open an "authentic" French restaurant in Art Nouveau style in the heart of the city, near the hotel Athénée Palace. She talked about hiring Parisian *chansonniers* and serving exclusive French wines and liqueurs, thus making it into a unique attraction in the capital.

But now he can barely savor his food since the excited guests have followed them in the dining room and keep bombarding them with questions. They stop talking for only a brief moment, to admire the huge chocolate dessert—a dark soufflé surrounded by four rows of burning candles—which Stella brings to the table. Then, after Sorel has blown out the candles and the guests have applauded, the loud chatter starts again.

Suddenly the maid bursts into the room, her round face crimson with excitement. She runs to Stella and whispers rapidly into her ear. Stella's eyes widen as she listens. Then she claps her hands to get everybody's attention. She announces that, according to a "well-informed" neighbor, tonight the demonstrators are planning to raid the streets of the Jewish section of the town.

In the next five minutes all the guests who live in that part of the city or have to cross it on the way home are gone. Nobody wants to be caught on the street.

Now, after everybody has left and only the family and their close friends Victor Georgescu and Charles Kass remain, Stella invites everybody into the living room. Turkish coffee and cognac is served on silver trays. A fire is burning in the Art Nouveau fireplace. It is richly decorated with a forest of curved and flowing orchids and water lilies thriving in the warmth of the flames.

Adrian is watching Sorel place a heavy log on the hearth. He has taken Nina by the hand and has led her to a red and blue striped loveseat in front of the fireplace. They are both listening to Emil, who is speaking to Charles Kass and asking him about the king's position toward the Jews in Romania.

"The king says very little. He doesn't want to commit. But the signals are not reassuring," says Kass.

"What do you mean the signals are not reassuring?" Emil looks incensed. "Carol is Queen Victoria's great grandson and first cousin of Britain's King George the V. And he also has a Jewish mistress. It is very clear to what side he should commit!"

But Charles Kass shakes his head and explains that, as the King's rule is threatened by the Iron Guard, he needs to rely on other anti-Semitic politicians and will not oppose their programs.

"So what will happen?" asks Emil.

"I don't know." Kass shrugs and arranges the carnation in his lapel. Then he goes on to say that, as in Germany after the institution of the racial laws, here too the Jewish population will lose their civil rights and will be excluded from the economic, professional and cultural life of the country.

"So, what shall we do? Commit suicide en masse? Convert by the thousands on Sunday afternoon in the soccer stadium? Dive into the stinking waters of the Dîmbovița River to receive the malediction of an anti-Semitic priest? What shall we do?"

"No, neither is a practical solution." Charles Kass looks at him seriously. "It is too late to convert to save one's skin. And mass suicide has never been practical."

"Then what?" In his excitement, Emil gets up and stands in front of Kass. "What should we do? You forget that this is Romania, not Germany. Here, in this country, people have always survived with *backsheesh* and other arrangements. There have been pogroms in Moldova with synagogues set on fire and other violence, but we have survived and even made a good living. And you forget that all of us here are full Romanian citizens. *We are Romanians*, not simply Jews! And those of us who have fought in the Great War have received special privileges and important decorations."

"I know, I know," says Kass as he keeps rubbing his pipe with his thumb. "I know because I was here, as a German ambulance driver with the Red Cross during the war. I was stationed in Predeal, in the mountains with my ambulance. And that's where I learned to know and to love your mountains and forests full of wolves, stags and bears... I was born in Germany, but after the war I studied in Switzerland and then settled there. But I am still an active member of the International Red Cross. I never gave that up! But speaking about veterans' decorations and privileges: yes, they exist, but they can always be revoked under one pretext or another. Just watch what happens in Germany!"

"So what should we do? What is the answer?" asks Adrian.

Charles Kass takes a long sip of cognac and closes his eyes in ecstasy. He stays like this for a moment, then he opens his eyes.

"I think that the only solution is to leave as soon as you can." He takes another sip of cognac. "Yes, leave as long as you still have complete control of your assets and as long as you still can take them with you. Besides, the king is in favor of emigration now. This makes the situation much easier."

Everybody sits quietly for a moment, watching the fire. Then Stella closes her fan with a click and turns toward Charles.

"I have a short and very simple question: you say we should all leave, emigrate, as soon as we can. But where should we go? How should we do that? What should we do first?" She stares Kass straight in the eyes. He sits up, ready to answer.

"It's very simple: I think I can help all of you come to Switzerland. Adrian has no problem: he has a position assured at Brown Boveri Company. For the doctors—Sorel, Liviu and Doctor Georgescu—I could probably find positions through the Red Cross. And Emil, as an engineer, is always interesting for Brown Boveri. I know that you specialize in railroads and railroad bridges. So you probably know that railroads, railroad bridges and tunnels through the mountains are constantly being built and renovated in Switzerland. Adrian told me that you have an unusual record of excellence. It shouldn't be difficult to find a good position for you!"

"So, then: what should we do first?" asks Victor Georgescu. He has been very quiet the whole evening. Adrian catches Stella looking at Victor with surprise.

"First you must have your family passports ready. You must go to a photo studio and take family pictures with your children. You should do this immediately, before the end of the week. Then you must get the new passports—the family passports, I mean. And in the meantime—prepare for departure."

When he stops talking, everybody is silent. Adrian looks from person to person, trying to read their thoughts. He then turns to Nina, who is watching Stella and Victor. He is the first to speak again.

"So, when shall we meet?"

"Thursday afternoon at 4, with all the children," says Stella. "Where shall we meet?" she asks Nina.

"I think at Studio Riviera, on Calea Moşilor," Nina says hesitantly, glancing at Adrian for approval. He nods and turns toward Emil and Dora.

"How about you and your children?"

"I don't know. I'm not ready yet," Emil says with a shrug, while Dora gets up and throws her cigarette into the flames.

It is late when Adrian, Nina and Kass leave the party. They are heading toward the Athénée Palace, to leave Charles at his hotel.

Outside it keeps snowing, and the streets are quiet now. Broken banners from the demonstration litter the sidewalks. The cartoon of a fat, ugly-looking Jew, a Star of David dripping with blood, a fragment of a black swastika or a torn picture of the Archangel Michael with his sword and his large wings.

Inside the car they speak very little. But when they reach the hotel, the two men step out of the car. They stand on the sidewalk and Charles Kass takes Adrian's hand. He speaks to him in a low voice.

"Before I leave I want you to know that I have a good friend here in Bucharest. His name is Stiller, Edward Stiller, and he works for the International Red Cross. If you need any help with your preparation for departure, or if you need to send money to Switzerland, just call Edward Stiller and say that I've sent you. I will also tell him about you. And he'll help you, when he learns who you are."

"I don't know how to thank you," Adrian says. "You've done so much for us..." But Kass doesn't let him finish.

"You'll thank me when you come to Zürich. I see you at the Baur au Lac! And keep well until then!" He shakes Adrian's hand and salutes Nina by lifting his hat. Then he disappears in the revolving doors of the hotel.

PHOTO RIVIERA

A T 4 O'CLOCK ON THURSDAY afternoon they all meet at Studio Riviera, on Calea Moșilor. Fritz stops the car near the entrance to the studio, where there is a narrow passage between two mountains of snow. It has been snowing for the last three days, and it's still coming down. The city has vanished under a white, fluffy blanket, and even the large display window of the photo studio is now framed by a thick border of snow.

From inside the car, Nina can still recognize the portraits of the actresses Lucia Sturza Bulandra and Marietta Sadova, of the handsome actor George Vraca and of the great musician and composer George Enescu. Dominating these portraits are the gold-framed pictures of the King and of the Queen Mother, wearing her tiara of diamonds. The space around them is crowded with wedding and baby pictures printed in sepia, dark blue, or simply in black and white. In the furthest corner, under the picture of a military parade, are a few passport photos. Above the window is a large neon sign with the words STUDIO RIVIERA, and underneath, in smaller print, Martin Weissman, Photographer of the Royal Court.

As she reads these words, Nina wonders whether the king or the famous actors and actresses ever come to be photographed in this small studio with the cluttered window. But then their visit today is not motivated by their aspiration to fame: Martin Weissman is a good photographer, a friend of Sorel's, a discreet and reliable man who, according to Stella, is also planning to emigrate. His children are Sorel's patients.

They step out of the car and they are barely inside the store when the others—Sorel with Stella, and Doctor Georgescu—all with their children, also arrive.

The photographer, Martin Weissman, a very short man who looks like a weasel, with a sharp, pointed nose and penetrating eyes, plays host to the visitors. His wife Bertha, who, to Nina's surprise, is also short and looks very much like her husband, joins him in taking care of the guests' coats, hats and gloves, wiping the snow from their boots and sweeping it from the door.

In the now-crowded room, the air has a pungent odor of film developer, a smell reminiscent of burning chemicals, which is vaguely familiar to Nina. Here it seems mixed with an odor of garlic and pickled cucumbers which irritates her throat and makes her cough. She is afraid she will end up with a migraine, particularly since she hasn't slept well during these last nights. For the news is not good. There are rumors of an impending Legionnaire coup: following the funeral celebration of the two fascist leaders Moţa and Marin, the capital is still filled with heavily armed high-level militants. In addition, the dean of the University of Iaşi, a friend of the family, an outspoken antifascist, has been gravely wounded in an assassination attempt by Legionnaire students.

Nina wants to speak to Stella, to learn more about this, but she cannot reach her, since she is busy with Sorel and the children.

Everybody in the room is excited about today's meeting. They all greet and hug each other as if they hadn't seen one another in a very long time. Then they line up in front of the two mirrors in the waiting room.

Nina, who wears the Marlene Dietrich brooch which Adrian has given her last summer in Zürich, carefully takes off her pillbox hat with the black voilette and the silver fox wrapped around her shoulders, and then rearranges the pin on the lapel of her suit. It was Adrian who insisted that she wear the brooch as a good-luck talisman for their forthcoming trip. But Nina has dark memories of another voyage, during another winter, in the middle of the Great War, when she was forced to flee this same city ruined and devastated by German bombardments. And then came hunger, illness, and the death of her mother in exile.

Nina stares into the mirror absentmindedly while she adjusts the "magic" pin. She's interrupted by her two daughters, who join her in front of the mirror. Suzy wants to admire her new outfit, a hand-knit blue sweater and a pleated skirt. Nadia wants to make sure that her white silk bow sits well in her hair and that her red nose and swollen eyes look more normal. For, before leaving the house, she had a fierce battle with her mother, who insisted that she wear a hat in this cold weather.

"I'm not wearing a hat! It will upset my hair and my silk bow!" she declared as she grabbed the woolen cap Fräulein Lilly had prepared for her and threw it on the floor. All of Nina's coaxing and threats that if she got sick nobody would take care of her were for naught.

"If you keep pushing that hat I'm not going!" she kept screaming, and, since this was not acceptable, Nina had to give up the fight, but not before Nadia had burst into tears, ending up with a red nose and swollen eyes. Now, Nina is watching her, worried that she might refuse to have her picture taken because of her "ugly face." Is she too nervous, too harsh with the children? Nina asks herself. She knows that Adrian would say yes, she is, and she should change.

Finally, Stella has reached her. She stands in front of the mirror fixing her hair and adjusting her dress. "There was another death threat against Victor," she whispers to Nina.

"When?"

"Yesterday!" Stella has just time to murmur before they are joined by the children.

In the corridor hangs another mirror which is used by the men. Nina watches Doctor Georgescu arranging his bow tie and smoothing his long wisps of hair behind his ears. She thinks that his face looks more tense and that there are deeper lines on his forehead.

"It all seems like a big stage production!" he says to the men who have joined him.

"Indeed, you're right!" says Sorel, who, today, has replaced his open sport shirt with a white starched one and a silk tie. "What are we playing?"

"My choice is an operetta with a happy ending," says Adrian.

Finally, the studio is ready for shooting. Nina, Adrian and the two children are the first to go in. The bright lights make them feel hot. The photographer asks them to hold still, and particularly not to squint while he is taking the pictures. Nobody stirs. The camera clicks. Once. Twice. Three times. And twice again.

When he has finished, they all stretch as if they had been in restraints.

Nadia is now exploring the room, and it is she who discovers the "scenic" background which represents snow-capped mountains, dark forests, and a fairy-tale castle with tall, pointed towers. "Oh! Look at Snow White's castle! Where are the Seven Dwarves?" she asks.

"My God! I didn't notice! I was too busy with the lights and the camera!" says Mr. Weissman. He turns red with embarrassment. "I apologize. We need a white background for the passport photos. I'm sorry, we have to take the pictures again!" He bends toward Nadia and thanks her for being so observant. "Without you, it would have been all wrong!"

Nadia is beaming. She makes a pirouette in the middle of the room and looks triumphantly at her mother, who tries to suppress a smile. Then, after the background has been changed and the new pictures have been taken, Nadia declares that the white sheet is boring, and that the fairy-tale background was much more exciting.

"Yes, you are right," says Mr. Weissman as he loads the camera for the next session. "But *you* and your family are the exciting subjects in the picture, not the background!"

Nadia looks at him, doubtfully, and shakes her head. She is not convinced by his words.

Next in line in the studio is Dr. Georgescu with his children, followed by Stella, Sorel, Corinna and Theo. The photo sessions run very smoothly, now that Mr. Weissman uses the same technique as with the Stein family. All the children are quiet and well-behaved—they seem intimidated by the bright lights, the heavy equipment and the unfamiliar place. Only Anca Georgescu insists on having her picture taken with the photographer's cat in her lap.

"Cats don't need passports, and you won't qualify for a passport if you have a cat in your lap," says her brother Paul with authority.

When the photo sessions are over and Martin Weissman has switched off the lights in the studio, his wife opens a narrow door hidden in the floral wallpaper of the waiting room and invites everybody to a cup of tea with cake and preserve.

The steaming brass samovar dominates the round table, while the pungent smell of film developer mixed with the odor of garlic and pickled cucumbers still floats in the air and gives Nina a headache. She knows that she won't be able to eat since everything will taste like chemicals mixed with garlic, and she knows that she will be sick if she does. But she watches Ms. Weissman tie a pink apron embroidered with blue daisies around her waist and pour hot tea in crystal glasses supported by silver glass holders. Her husband stands next to her and helps her pass the sugar and the small dishes filled with apricot preserve around the table. They both move very quickly, with short, rapid gestures, and Nina marvels again how much they resemble each other—Are they related, by chance?—and how much they look like a couple of weasels. She wouldn't be surprised if they would suddenly grow a big, fluffy tail.

She watches Mr. Weissman get up and raise his glass in a toast.

"I understand that you are all preparing to go to Switzerland. I was there, in Zürich, a few years ago. That's where I bought my cameras, my lenses, and my studio lights, and that's where I got my special cuckoo clock with its little bird," he says, pointing to the clock on the wall, which looks like a mountain chalet covered with snow. "We had a wonderful vacation there, we did so many things... but now we're preparing to go to France, since we have a son in Paris. And then, isn't Switzerland somehow unsafe—so small and wedged between Germany and Italy? I've heard that the Gestapo and the SS have quite a few people there."

"Not at all," says Adrian. "We've been told that it's not less safe than France or any other place. Besides, I'm sure that everybody here has already made plans what they will do when they arrive in Switzerland!"

"Yes, I'll buy ten large boxes of chocolate and finish them all at once," says Theo with shining eyes, as he licks his spoon of preserve.

"Me too," says Nadia. "I'll buy the biggest box of chocolates in the world. I know where to get it. I saw a picture of it in a magazine. It is as big as a house... and I'll eat it all by myself."

"Then you'll be sick, both of you!" says Suzy with contempt. "I'll take a walk on the *Bahnhofstrasse* and buy myself a new dress and high-heel pumps."

"I'll rush to the Botanical Garden to check out their Orchid Collection. I want to see their rare and unique specimens," says Doctor Georgescu. "Of course I plan to bring my orchid collection with me to Switzerland..."

Nina thinks, he can't be serious. Yesterday the death threats, and today all he cares about is his orchid collection. He can't mean what he's saying!

Her head throbs. The acrid smell is burning her throat. It makes her think of fire, of burning chemicals, melting iron... She's smelled it before, but where and when?

She hears Adrian say to Nadia, "Won't you come to Lugano and ride in my little boat?" but she misses Nadia's reply. She's completely overwhelmed by the odor, and she knows why it's so familiar. It brings back a clear image— the bombed city, the burning house, the Zeppelin dropping bombs all around them, the bodies of dead and dismembered horses in the street, then the train station filled with smoke, the friends who couldn't get on the train and who suddenly vanished in an explosion of fire and flames as soon as the train cleared the station. It could happen again! It could happen again!

Then she hears Adrian speaking to her:

"How about you? What will you do? Won't you come to Lugano and join me on the little boat?"

"That's not the point!" she says in a low voice. "We should, first, all be on that train, beyond the borders, *all* of us."

Adrian looks at her with surprise. "Of course we'll all be on the train! What a question! Just trust me for once." He takes her hand, under the table, and squeezes it hard.

For a moment, everybody is quiet. Then somebody coughs. The conversation resumes. And Mr. Weissman promises them that the pictures will be ready before the end of the week.

A NEW FRIEND

T HE PASSPORT PHOTOS ARE INDEED ready on Saturday, and Adrian takes them to Stella and Sorel's apartment. He then wants to hurry to his office to prepare his papers for the new passport. As a matter of fact, all the necessary documents—birth certificates, marriage licence, proof of citizenship, receipts from tax payments—are locked in the big safe and must only be pulled out of their folders. Nevertheless he wants to make sure that everything is in good order. But the thought which is haunting him is how to dispose of his apartments, how to sell his properties and to whom to sell.

The first to go should be the two apartments from this house, the ones occupied by Stella and Emil and their families. He thought about selling them in the past. He had many tempting offers and could have made good money even six months ago, but he didn't want to make trouble for Nina's brother and sister. But now, of course, everything is different.

He takes the elevator to the ground floor, and as he steps into the lobby he runs into Emil, who is returning home with a newspaper. Emil is not working today, and Adrian sees that his face is red from the cold. His gold-rimmed glasses are now getting blurred by dampness. He is wearing a gray astrakhan hat which matches perfectly his thick fur collar, while his navy-blue mittens match his woolen scarf. Adrian is glad to meet Emil, whom he hasn't seen in a while, and invites him to a quick cup of coffee. He takes his arm, and they step out of the building. They walk toward Capşa, the elegant coffee house and restaurant on Calea Victoriei.

Since it is a sunny winter day, Adrian tells Fritz to pick him up in front of the restaurant by 11.

They try to walk quickly, but progress is not as easy as they thought. The streets and the sidewalks are still covered with ice and snow, which is stained with oil, soot and horse droppings. Packs of errant dogs urinate on the mountains of snow, staining them yellow. In the middle of the street, black crows are nibbling at the fresh horse droppings. In front of the restaurant, gypsy girls in bright skirts wearing flimsy sandals accost them with bunches of violets and snowdrops.

When they are comfortably seated on the banquette covered with Viennese floral cretonne, it is Emil who speaks first. He wants to know the latest news, since he and his family have not been at Mr. Weissman's photo studio. Are they all still sticking to their decision to leave the country? And how about Nina? Is she really willing to emigrate?

"It looks like this time she keeps to her decision. The whole secret is Stella," says Adrian. "Where she goes, Nina goes."

Emil nods. "They've always been like this. Ever since Stella was a little girl. Even at five, Nina had taken Stella under her wing. Then, after the war and after our mother's death, everything changed, and Nina started clinging to Stella like a baby to her mother's apron strings."

Emil takes a cigarette out of his gold case and offers one to Adrian, who lights both cigarettes with his Swiss lighter.

As he draws a few puffs and watches the rings of smoke in the air, Adrian wonders whether Emil is still as firm in his decision to stay put. "Won't you even consider getting a family passport as a precaution?" he asks.

Emil shakes his head. "No. Dora and I are not leaving." He takes a long sip of Turkish coffee. "You talk so much about your preparations for emigration. But what will you do with the apartments you own? I mean the apartments you rent to Stella and me?"

Adrian feels uneasy. He dislikes talking business with relatives. "Don't discuss business with family!" his father has warned him. But now he has no choice.

"I must sell," he says. "Both apartments." He takes the Swiss lighter out of his pocket and puts it on the table. "Will you buy?" he adds as an afterthought.

Emil looks surprised. He puts down his cup of coffee. He didn't expect this question. But he thinks quickly.

"Yes," he says. "I'll buy. Both apartments. As a matter of fact, I could buy, at some point, the entire building. I have money coming in next week from the repairs of a big railway bridge over the Danube. It was a big project, and we'll get loads of money. I'm thinking that after I buy our building I could modernize it, or maybe I'll sell it and build a new one, a high-rise apartment house." His cheeks are flushed. His eyes are shining.

"Isn't it risky to build an apartment house today? The way they're talking, they may take it away from you one day!"

"I don't think so. It's not riskier than what you're doing."

He finishes his coffee and gives the empty cup a spin with his finger. Then he turns it upside down on its saucer to read the coffee grinds. "It would be good to know the future!

But can you trust the coffee grinds? Seriously speaking, I don't believe that anything bad will happen here!"

Adrian watches him quietly. He thinks that Emil is naïve, too credulous and unrealistic. But he doesn't want to challenge him further. "All right," he says after a moment. "Then let's drink to our agreement! It is still early in the day, but our contract calls for a libation!" He makes a sign to the waiter, and asks for the best French cognac in the house. When the waiter returns, they clink their glasses and Emil looks thoughtfully at his transparent beaker. "The new high-rise will be a beautiful, modern construction... A smaller version of the skyscrapers in New York!"

A few days later, carrying the money he has received from Emil for the apartments, Adrian hurries to see Kass's friend Edward Stiller, the representative of the International Red Cross in Bucharest. He follows Kass's suggestion to bring all significant new money to the friend, Stiller, who is going to dispatch it to Zürich via courier. Charles Kass had assured him that Stiller was his oldest, most reliable friend, and Adrian has trusted him. However, he hasn't yet shared his decision with Nina, nor has he told her about the sale of the two apartments. He will certainly tell her everything, but not yet—it is too early: something holds him back, an irrational belief that if he tells her the plan it will be hexed.

As he sits in the car with the attaché case filled with money on his knees, he shakes his head, scolding himself for thinking such nonsense.

They drive along Embassy Row on Boulevard Dacia, since the office of the International Red Cross is housed inside the Swiss Embassy. They stop in front of an elegant mansion set in a park with old trees which belongs to Prince L, the ex-majordomo of the Royal Court. But the Prince and his family now live in Paris, and they have rented the mansion to the Swiss Embassy. (Adrian remembers an old picture showing the king and the queen presiding an official ball in this mansion.)

After giving his name to a uniformed clerk who stands by the door, Adrian climbs the marble stairs covered with a soft blue carpet and is welcomed by Ed Stiller on the first landing.

He is a tall and very thin man with a long face and neck, narrow shoulders and a slight stoop. He shakes Adrian's hand and clicks his heels as he introduces himself. Then he leads him along a winding corridor which ends in a light painted room with a high ceiling and a large window. Two maps, one of Europe and one of the whole world, hang on the wall.

"I was waiting for your call," says Stiller as he guides Adrian to a leather-upholstered armchair. "Charles has told me a lot about you and your family. We are old friends. We both fought in the war. We went to school, even to kindergarten together. We were like brothers... even closer, because Charles saved my life during the war, when a shell almost blew off my head... He rescued me in spite of the danger! And I'll do anything for him now."

Adrian has put down the briefcase and, as he listens to Stiller, he wonders what Nina would think if she were in his place. He can almost hear her asking: Who is this man? How can you trust him? How do you know he is telling the truth or that he will keep his promise? Isn't the temptation too great? And isn't it foolish to entrust all the money to him? Instinctively, Adrian grabs the attaché case and lifts it on his knees.

But it is as if Stiller has read his mind, for he turns toward him and asks him how he feels about handing so much money to him. "After all, you don't know me, and I have no way of assuring you that the money will indeed reach Charles and will be deposited in your account. But what I can do is give you a note attesting that I have received from you today a certain sum of money which I will hand over to Charles."

As he is speaking, Stiller goes to his desk and, using official stationery, types out a note which he signs. He hands it to Adrian, who takes the sheet of paper and reads it. With a handkerchief he wipes a few drops of perspiration from his forehead. Then he folds the paper in four, and slides it in his pocket. When he raises his head, he sees Stiller watching him closely.

"You have an office in a building nearby. And a modern, beautiful home. Do they belong to you too?"

Adrian nods.

"I was wondering," Stiller says in a soft voice. "What are your plans?"

Adrian fidgets in his chair. The seat, the armrests, even the pillows feel suddenly uncomfortable.

I must sell. I know," he says. But I don't know when and how. Certainly not yet," he adds quickly with a sigh.

"I can make a suggestion, if it's all right with you. We, the Red Cross—or actually, the Swiss Embassy—could buy your house and your office when you're ready to leave. And we could deposit the money directly into your Zürich account."

Adrian chokes with emotion. His hand trembles, and he spills the ashes from his cigarette on his lap. This is more than he can take, more than he had expected. He feels like laughing and crying at the same time. How could this happen so suddenly? For the problem of how to dispose of his house and of his office was haunting him for some time; he couldn't figure out how to coordinate the sale of their home and the transfer of the money with their still-unknown date of departure. Where were they going to stay after the apartment was sold and cleaned out of furniture? And for how long?

"We may even help you with the transportation of your furniture and household goods to Switzerland!" Stiller adds as an afterthought.

For a moment, Adrian imagines himself with Nina and the two girls sitting in the Orient Express. They're passing through a dark tunnel. Then the train stops in the elegant Zürich station. So they're going to leave!

He sees his host standing up. He too stands up and hands him the briefcase. He is still choked up and can barely thank Stiller for his "life-saving" help. Then they slowly walk to the door, after promising to touch base again in a couple of weeks.

THE EARACHE

T HE PAIN HAS STARTED EARLY. It woke her up. First she thought it was going to be just a few stabs in her ear like in the past, and then she would go to sleep again. Like other times, this morning too Nadia dreamt that she is in the boat with Skender and Theo, then jumping into the water and floating, hovering over the wreck of the pirate ship. She is diving deep into the sea to grab hold of the sunken treasure—but the moment she is ready to touch it with her fingertips, a dolphin bumps into her ear—as it really happened—provoking a sudden, stabbing pain. It cuts like a knife deep into her head.

She clenches her teeth and doesn't say anything. She is afraid Fräulein Lilly and even her mother will scold her for running around in freezing weather without a hat. But the pain gets sharper and sharper. She is bathed in sweat, then it's cold. She shivers under the blanket.

Now the pain takes over. It is stabbing and drilling inside her ear like needles. It swallows her like a big wave. It is unbearable, and she hears herself scream.

Nina—her mother—Sorel and Joel, the two pediatricians, stand by her bed and watch her. Then Sorel lifts her, and, with Nina's help, wraps her tightly—her arms along the body—in her own pink blanket. She is then passed on to Joel, who sits on a chair and holds her in his lap.

"I won't hurt you, I only need to look," says Sorel, trying to insert a shiny instrument into her ear. But she yanks her head away and gives another scream. Nina has to come to the rescue, to immobilize her head.

Sorel is quick with the examination: the otoscope is inside her ear in a second. "It is what I have expected: a purulent infection which must be drained immediately," he whispers.

In the next minute, while Nadia continues to cry, he picks up a pair of scissors, and trims her hair on the right side of her head. Then he wipes her ear with a cotton swab dipped in iodine, and inserts a long needle attached to a syringe into her ear. The time between the iodine swabbing and the insertion of the needle is so short that Nadia cannot pull her head away. But she keeps screaming, while the yellow pus spurts into the syringe.

When the syringe is full, Sorel, who seems unaffected by her cries, pulls out the needle and replaces it with a thin cotton drain, which he covers with thick layers of cotton. Then Nadia's head is wrapped in a big, white bandage.

"You are not allowed to touch your head or the bandages!" Sorel orders, while Joel helps Nina unwrap Nadia from her pink cocoon. Tears are running down her cheeks, but she is exhausted and her screams are turning into sighs and moans.

For the next ten days, either Sorel or Joel come every morning to change the bandages and replace the drain. After the first few days, the fever goes down. The pain too disappears. Only in the mornings, when the old drain is pulled out and a new one is inserted into the eardrum, Nadia cries out and has to be held, her hands secured behind her back, so as not to hinder the treatment.

It is merely the promise that she will soon be able to get out and enjoy the last days of ice skating before the weather gets warm which makes her cooperate with her doctors.

Finally, on the day when the big bandage is removed for good, Nadia looks in the mirror and breaks into tears. "This isn't me! A girl on the left side, and a boy on the right! I won't go to school like this, or any place! Nobody should see me! And I won't step out of the house." She picks up a hiking boot and aims it at the mirror. But Joel stops her in time.

"I can't believe you throw a fit for such a trifle! Your mother can ask the hairdresser to come to the house and give you a modern haircut. You don't need long hair like the old-fashioned ladies! Don't you know that the Olympic swimming champs all have short hair? You'll look just like them and everybody will envy you!"

Joel's words do the trick. Nadia puts down the hiking boot. Then she makes Joel promise that he will convince her mother to get her an Olympic swimmer's haircut.

The day after the hairdresser's visit, Adrian watches Nadia, who sits across the dinner table. He shakes his head. Nadia doesn't look like the girl in the passport photo. Now she looks like a little boy with very short hair, while in the picture she looked like a girl with a white bow in her long, wavy hair. Is this important? Should he worry about it? Must he do something about it? And what could he do?

He decides to discuss it with Nina, but he'll wait until after dinner, when they're alone in the bedroom.

Two hours later, Nina is slipping into her nightgown when he asks her advice. She stops to think, then she shrugs and says that she doesn't know. "This is more than I can handle. Nadia's illness has worn me out. I hope she'll be all right. Why don't you speak to Sorel or to Stella? They know more than I do. Or, even better: talk to Edward Stiller. He'll give you the best advice!"

What a good idea! Adrian remembers that Nina knows about his connection to the International Red Cross and the Swiss Embassy. He confided in her soon after he had delivered the money, when he made up his mind not to keep it a secret. To his surprise, Nina didn't get as upset as he had feared. She seemed calm, almost detached, as if she didn't care. How was this possible? He was sure that she was going to be very angry and scold him for taking too many risks.

He now realizes that it was just one day after Nadia had fallen ill with her ear infection. He thinks that while he was obsessed with passports, Stiller and money, Nina was overwhelmed with Nadia's illness. Indeed, she isn't looking good. Her face is pale and drawn, and she has dark shadows under her eyes. She doesn't eat properly either. At dinner, she ate only half of the ham omelette and didn't touch the cherry pie. This wasn't like her. Nina always likes omelettes, and she usually has two helpings of cherry pie. Is she also losing weight? He can't tell, but he is worried about her.

In the dark, he snuggles up to her, and holds her tightly in his arms.

BUTTERFLIES

F OR ADRIAN, BUSINESS IS NOW better than ever: two new
electrical turbines have been installed at Grozăveşti, and
Emil, in association with a friend, bought the entire building
where he lives. Both projects—the electrical turbines and
the sale of the apartment house—have been fully paid, so
Adrian is in a hurry to bring the money to Stiller. A letter
of confirmation regarding the previous transfer has arrived
from the Zürich bank, as well as a friendly, encouraging note
from Kass. Adrian has shown these letters to Nina, who is
now more relaxed and more accepting of these transfers.

But it is the question of the family passport with the
photo in which Nadia appears so different from the way she
looks now with her short hair—instead of her long hair and
the white bow—the question of what to do with this photo
torments him. As Nina has suggested, he will ask Stiller's
advice.

On the day he goes to the International Red Cross at the
Swiss Embassy, he carries with him a new briefcase filled
with money. He also makes sure that the family passport
photo is in his wallet.

Then, when he arrives at the mansion on Boulevardul
Dacia, he finds his host seated at his desk buried under big
books with colorful pictures and maps. He can see that

the pictures represent all kinds of butterflies. Adrian is surprised, almost shocked to see a man so strict and reserved, almost severe, devote his time to things as frivolous as... butterflies!

As he walks in, Stiller gets up and shakes his hand. "I apologize for this," he says, pointing to the books, "but I get lost in this passion of mine. Butterflies bring a sense of harmony and beauty to a chaotic world. I am reading this book about the butterflies of Eastern Europe, because I want to take a trip to the Danube Delta and study the species who live there. I have followed the butterflies all along the banks of the Danube, from its source in the Schwarzwald in Germany, through Austria, Hungary, Czechoslovakia, Yugoslavia, Bulgaria, Romania, up to the Delta—but there only from a distance. I was in that part of the country during the war. We were camping by the river, and just as I was about to take a trip into the Delta where the most gorgeous butterflies dwell, the Armistice was signed and we got orders to leave. Now that spring is coming, I don't want to miss this opportunity again!"

"Of course not." Adrian has sneaked a few impatient looks at the grandfather clock near the wall. "If you allow me, I can help," he says. "I can introduce you to a friend of mine who knows the Delta like the palm of his hand. He is a doctor, his name is Victor Georgescu. He studies the wild orchids of the Delta. He'll take you along and show you all you want to see!"

They sit comfortably in the big leather chairs, and Stiller thanks Adrian for his offer.

"Speaking of doctors, I have an urgent question to ask you," Adrian says, squeezing the handle of his briefcase. "It is about my daughter Nadia and the family passport photo." He tells Stiller about Nadia's ear infection, about the surgical intervention and about the "radical" haircut which left her looking like a boy.

"Now she is very different from the little girl with the white bow in her long hair, which you see in this family picture." He pushes the passport photo under Stiller's nose. "Will this be a problem with our passports and visas? Will they—I mean the authorities—make a fuss about it? Should we take another picture with Nadia's short hair? Or... am I fussing too much about nothing?"

Stiller examines the photograph without saying a word. He frowns slightly and taps the table with his bony fingers. "I don't know what to tell you," he says. "They may accept this picture and look the other way, or they may be difficult and reject it. Your luck depends on who sits at the desk on that particular day."

"That's too risky!" says Adrian. "I won't play roulette with the passport!"

Stiller fumbles with his blue tie which is decorated with tiny red and gold butterflies. "Did you receive your passport yet?"

Adrian shakes his head. "Not yet."

"In that case you could take a new family photo with your daughter's short hair and ask the passport department to replace the old picture with the new one. It shouldn't be a problem. I think this is the safest, and this is how it would be done in Switzerland!"

"I wish we were in Switzerland! Everything seems possible there!" Adrian sighs.

Stiller starts to answer, but is interrupted by the young secretary with high heels, who brings them two cups of steaming hot chocolate with whipped cream and freshly baked scones on a silver platter.

"Good luck!" says Stiller, raising his cup.

"Thank you. I need all the luck I can get!" Adrian takes a sip of hot chocolate, but his throat is tight, he coughs after swallowing.

Later, before leaving, Adrian exchanges briefcases with Stiller: he gives his host the new case, which is filled with money, while the latter hands him the old, empty one he had brought the first time. Then they walk downstairs together, and Stiller accompanies him to the door of the building.

"Don't worry so much!" he says as he rests his hand on Adrian's shoulder. It really shouldn't be a problem."

Adrian nods and tries to smile.

Outside, when he steps onto the sun-drenched boulevard, he sees a small piece of paper fly up as if a butterfly. He follows it getting lost above the branches of the naked trees. Ah! To be a butterfly!

For a moment he stands still on the sidewalk. Then he starts walking toward his office.

THE MEMORANDUM

A S SOON AS NADIA IS allowed out of the house, the whole family goes to Studio Riviera for a new passport photograph.

Nadia is so happy that she can finally get out that she doesn't object to being photographed with short hair. As a matter of fact, to console her for her long illness and suffering, Nina surprises her with a new dress of red velvet with gold buttons and a white lace collar, which Nadia had admired in a shop window. She is so excited with the new dress that she even forgets about her swimming ambitions. Besides, Adrian tells her that she looks ravishing, and Mr. Weissman, the photographer, promises to put her picture up in his display window.

By the end of the week Adrian prepares a memorandum regarding the passport, and, with the new family photo in his pocket, rushes to the Passport Department at Police Headquarters. The Memorandum section is located in a dim corridor, at the back of the building.

As he hurries on, he pays no attention to the grimy windows nor to the stains and watermarks on the walls and on the ceiling. He rushes along a row of small cashier windows protected by metal bars—some of them closed and boarded up—and avoids tripping over a large spittoon. He forges ahead, compelled by a burning urge to have the new picture placed on the passport. But he has to stop when he reaches a group of people waiting in line in front of an open cashier window.

He is tired and restless; this night again he slept very little. Nina has tried to calm him down by telling him that it makes no sense to hurry, that they will get the passport sooner or later, and that they may very well wait for Nadia's hair to grow longer before applying for visas. Besides, Sorel too has problems with his passport: he has to travel to Iaşi, where he was born, to get a new birth certificate. And they will have to wait for Sorel and Stella anyway, since they have vowed to apply for visas together.

Even though Adrian agrees with Nina in principle, he still feels compelled to take action now. He is so impatient and agitated that he wishes to run to the window and push everybody out of his way. But since he has to wait, he plops himself on a wooden bench, and tries to read the newspaper.

But he has no success. Just as he realizes that he is reading the same sentence over and over it is his turn at the window.

Behind the metal bars, a middle-aged clerk with sleepy eyes and shoulders powdered with dandruff yawns while Adrian hands her the new family photo and the official memorandum. He waits until she stops yawning, and discreetly slips into her hand a small envelope with cash and says a few words about his situation. The clerk takes the envelope without blinking and, after another yawn, she gets up and disappears from the window.

Where did she go? Why did she leave? What will happen next? he wonders. But then, to his relief, the sleepy-eyed clerk unlocks a door next to the window, and signals him into the office.

Adrian finds himself inside a windowless room with a high ceiling, lit by a naked bulb. There are two wooden desks near the walls. A large portrait of the king in military uniform hangs on one wall, and a silver crucifix hangs on the opposite wall. Adrian recognizes his papers lying on top of one desk—between a gold-trimmed police cap and an ashtray overflowing with cigarette butts.

As he enters, a policeman who stands guard by the door and is armed with an automatic rifle topped by a bayonet pulls a chair to the middle of the room and tells him to sit down. Adrian feels nauseous and sick, seated in the middle of this windowless room, under the naked light bulb. Is he a prisoner suspected of a crime? Has the clerk denounced him because of the bribe? Nina had warned him not to bribe government clerks, it could be dangerous, but he knows, and he has learned from this father that nothing gets done without *"baksheesh."* Maybe the bribe was too small! Or are they taking him for somebody else?

He is racking his brain trying to understand what is going on when the door opens and a police captain—a giant of a man—walks into the office. His heavy boots make the floor tremble, and, when he sits down, the chair creaks dangerously. With a roaring voice he orders Adrian to sit by his desk, facing him. Adrian complies, and keeps staring at him. He is mesmerized by the captain. His thunderous voice and his heavy boots remind him of the principal he had in grade school. That man too had a deafening voice and wore heavy boots. He also carried a leather whip, and, when he caught a student talking in class or not paying attention, he lashed him with his whip.

Now the officer puts on his gold-trimmed hat and examines the documents. Then he stares at Adrian with his shrewd eyes, hidden behind bushy eyebrows. "Why are you here?" he asks.

"I am here to replace my original passport photo with a new one," says Adrian. "Let me explain: my daughter was very sick with a severe ear infection just after we submitted an application for a family passport. She needed surgery, so her hair was cut short, and she looks very different than in her first photo. She actually looks like a boy." He whips both pictures out of his pocket and arranges them side by side on the desk. "She doesn't look like the same child anymore, and this is why I want to replace her photo with long hair with the new one with short hair. It's a small thing," he adds, trying to smile, "but it can make all the difference. I am sure you understand!"

The policeman takes the two photos and examines them closely, as if he wished to remember them forever. He reads Adrian's memo, takes his hat off again and polishes the gold trimming with the cuff of his sleeve. Then he looks at the pictures again. He lights a cigarette and slowly arranges the match on top of the full ashtray.

Adrian sits at the edge of his seat watching the captain's every move. He wishes he had magic power to control the officer's thoughts.

Finally the policeman takes the memorandum, reads it for the third time and scribbles something on it.

"No," he says in the end. "We don't tamper with passports and photographs." His voice swells as he speaks. "A passport is a unique and *sacred* document which needs to be respected. Tampering with it is sacrilege."

With these words he turns toward the crucifix on the wall and makes the sign of the cross.

Adrian can barely breathe. He wonders whether the policeman will fall to his knees in front of the crucifix.

But the captain stands up and hands him the pictures. "Go home," he says, "and wait for the passport. There is nothing you can do." He takes the overflowing ashtray and empties it in the spittoon at the foot of the desk.

The guard opens the door, and Adrian is back in the corridor.

SCHOOL TIME

N ADIA'S SCHOOL—A SQUAT, WHITEWASHED BUILDING with a walled-in courtyard dominated by a solitary linden tree—is only two blocks from Adrian's office, so that, when she is finally ready to resume classes, she is driven there by Fritz.

Nadia has always felt awkward about being driven to and from school, so she asks to get off a block before reaching her destination. Now, after an absence of more than three weeks, and with her short hair, she feels self-conscious. Most of the other girls have braids, and she dreads their nasty comments about her boyish looks.

Also she worries about being up to date with her lessons, particularly in math. Her teacher, Doamna Moisescu, is a short, fat woman with gray hair pulled into a bun and small, piercing eyes. She never smiles, and her round glasses perched on her long nose make her look like a bird of prey. She has a high-pitched voice which can be painful to the ear and she carries a wooden rod with which she pounds her desk to keep silence in the classroom. Even though she is a good student, Nadia has always been afraid of this teacher who succeeds in cowing into silence the 65 girls in her charge.

Nadia knows that she will be called to the blackboard on her first hour to demonstrate a complicated multiplication operation. She is afraid, because in contrast with her sister Suzy, who is a mathematical whiz, she, Nadia, is scared of numbers. They look to her like threatening beings from an unfriendly planet. And she worries that the girls in her class will snicker if she makes a mistake at the blackboard. Nina and Mathilda—who have tutored her during her absence from school—have assured her that she is well prepared for her return to class. But yesterday, before going to bed, Suzy gave her a mathematical quiz, and when Nadia didn't find the answer, Suzy mocked her and told her that she has a head like a *"bostan"* (pumpkin), filled with seeds, and without any brain. "Everybody can see this now that your hair is so short. It makes your skull transparent, and everybody can see that there is no brain inside." Suzy's words cut like a knife. Nadia tells herself that Suzy is jealous that she, Nadia, has received so many gifts like the red velvet dress and boxes of chocolate, while Suzy hasn't received anything.

Still, the words burn like hot iron.

But, when she arrives in school and is welcomed by the familiar smell of creoline disinfectant—phenol and choramine—things work out differently than she expected.

True, Doamna Moisescu, who perches on her raised platform and dominates the classroom, calls Nadia to the blackboard and makes her write and calculate at complicated multiplication exercise. Even though Nadia's heart beats fast and she feels hot and flushed, she performs well, and gets the right answer. Her homework, which Doamna Moisescu checks while Nadia stands in front of the blackboard, is also correct and up to date. Now, as she returns to her seat, she can finally relax.

During the break, her friends Liudmila, Simona and Adina share their snacks with her, as they always did before her illness. Liudmila even gives her a piece of *"halvița"* (nougat) she has bought from a gypsy boy at the corner of the street. A few girls start to tease her and call her "Mickey Mouse" or "Funny Face," but she sticks her tongue out at them, and they stop teasing.

But the high point of the day arrives after the break, when the music teacher, Domnișoara Valentin, a young, athletic woman who is also their gym teacher, tells the girls that the class will perform a play adapted from a folktale, and that Nadia, who is the only one here with short hair, will play the role of Făt Frumos, the prince charming who saves the princess in distress.

"Your short hair is a blessing for us!" she tells Nadia. "Everybody here has braids, while you're our only authentic boy! I was ready to hire—or even kidnap—a student from the boys' school next door, but now I don't need to do that since we have you! Just keep your hair nice and short for another few weeks! And since the play is going to be a surprise, all of you must hold your tongues and don't spill the beans at home!"

Nadia is very proud of the new assignment. Her friends Liudmila, Simona and Adina look at her with admiration, and some envy, too, since they haven't been chosen for the play at all.

"See, you're the chosen one, the special one—the one with short hair!" they keep repeating like a refrain for the next several days.

318

The family passport with the "old" photograph arrives on a Sunday morning in May.

As always when he has to deliver an important letter or package, the mailman waits for Sunday morning, when he climbs the service staircase and knocks at the kitchen door. He knows that Adrian and Nina are at home, and will give him a cup of coffee, an extra tip, and a piece of cake for his children.

As soon as Adrian opens the envelope, he is all smiles. He takes Nina in his arms and kisses her, happy that "things are moving along" even if only an inch at a time.

"We should decide now what we're taking with us and what we'll leave behind," he says. "Time is getting shorter and shorter. You must start by making a list. We should be prepared—Nadia's hair is getting longer... We really should be prepared!"

They can hear quick steps, small feet running in the corridor, and Nadia walks into the kitchen. She is wearing her pink pajama with blue polka dots and matching pink slippers. She is yawning. Her hair is unkempt and her eyes are still puffy with sleep.

"Good morning, Struwelpeter," Adrian says and kisses her on the cheek. "We were just talking about you. Let me look at your hair."

He gently pulls her toward the window and strokes her hair. Then, turning toward Nina, he says, "I was right. See that wave? It is new. Her hair is definitely growing. Soon we will be able to tie it in a bow! Good girl. Just keep it up!" He gives her another kiss, while Nina pours a cup of hot chocolate for her.

"A new wave?" Nadia asks with a frown. "It shouldn't be! It shouldn't happen!" she mumbles under her breath. But her parents are too busy to pay attention.

From that Sunday on, Adrian is actively preparing for departure. He will definitely leave behind the office furniture which Stiller assures him he can use when he takes over the office.

He decides that the home furnishings are Nina's domain, but he checks with her every day, reminding her how important it is to choose what goes with them, and what stays behind. And, even though Stiller has assured him that everything will be taken care of, he has already contacted two companies which could pack and transport their belongings to Switzerland.

But Nina is slow in her actions. Whenever she sets out to make the list, she starts thinking of Stella: their family passport has not yet arrived, and Sorel has left again for Iași for his birth certificate. How long will this go on? She is afraid that, if it takes too long, Adrian will pressure her to leave without her sister, particularly now, when Nadia's hair is growing so nicely!

In the meantime, while Sorel is away, a meeting is arranged between Stiller and Doctor Victor Georgescu at Adrian's house.

It is a beautiful spring day. They all sit on the terrace, under the blooming wisteria, sipping *"Salep"* prepared by the doctor from his wild orchids, and listening to the cooing of turtledoves. Stella sits near Doctor Georgescu, and holds a red fan in one hand, which matches her silk dress and crimson cigarette holder. She has introduced the two men to each other, and they immediately connect, as if they were old friends. The doctor has brought a map of the Danube Delta, and Stiller shows him where he was posted during the war. They toast to peace, to the Delta, to butterflies, to orchids, and they discuss the role of butterflies in the pollination of orchids. Doctor Georgescu invites Stiller to see his orchid collection, and before the last round of *salep*, they set a date—May 20th—for their expedition in the Delta. Stella will be part of the group.

She thanks them and says that she is delighted with the invitation. But there is worry in her big eyes and she chain-smokes nervously as she watches Doctor Georgescu. Is it safe for him to take this trip? Is he taking too many risks? Not too long ago there were threats against him. But he shrugs them off and treats them like a joke, while she thinks that he is wrong. With a shaking hand she takes the doctor's lighter from the table, and lights her 12th cigarette this afternoon.

Suzy has fallen asleep in her room, and she is late joining the guests. While they are gathered on the terrace she is getting dressed, choosing her best spring blouse.

Before getting ready, she sees that a button needs fixing and she looks for the scissors—but they are not in their regular place. She looks everywhere: in drawers and boxes, and on the top of shelves, but the scissors have vanished. Where can they be? When she cannot find them, she goes to the kitchen to get a knife. But on her way, she catches a glimpse of light in the bathroom, and hears a noise, like somebody speaking. She opens the door, and sees Nadia, perched on a stool in front of the mirror, with the scissors in her hand. She is clipping her hair while reciting a poem about *"Făt*

Frumos" (Prince Charming) and Ileana Cosînzeana (the Fairy Princess).

Suzy tries to wrestle the scissors out of her hand. But it is too late: several locks of hair—the "new wave"—lie at the foot of the stool. "Why did you do that?" Suzy screams. "Tata will be furious. He will never speak to you again!"

Nadia's eyes fill with tears. She bites her lips, trying hard not to cry. "I can't tell you!" she says. "It's a secret and I've promised to keep it a secret. I can't tell you why!"

With these words she throws down the scissors and runs out of the room. Suzy watches her, speechless. "This isn't good. Nadia looks again like a little boy. There will be trouble," she whispers. She bends down and gathers the scissors from the bathroom floor.

THE TEA PARTY

IT IS AN UNEXPECTED LETTER from Kass to Adrian which calms Nina down and makes her more accepting of Adrian's project. The letter tells them that, in a very short time, emigration will be encouraged in Romania and will proceed smoothly. Nina trusts Charles Kass because she has discovered that he knows history, particularly French history. He knows many details about Marie Antoinette and the French Revolution. In Nina's mind, in order to understand and cope with the present situation in Europe, it is essential to know the history of France. "The development and history of France actually represents the development and history of Europe," Nina loves to quote a famous French writer, whose name she has forgotten.

This Sunday afternoon Nina's brother Emil and her sister Stella, with their spouses, will meet again for tea at her home. Nina has decided that, for a change, they will sit in the garden, under the pergola. From here they can admire the pink and red peonies in full bloom.

It has rained in the morning, and the air is fragrant with the perfume of jasmine.

Before the arrival of the guests, the garden table has been set up under the bower, and Fräulein Lilly has covered it with the linen tablecloth embroidered by Nina when she was a teenager. This tablecloth was part of her dowry.

Marish, the maid, brings down the green and gold majolica tea service which Nina and Adrian bought in Venice during their honeymoon. Nina arranges the cups and saucers with great care: both she and Adrian love this service which carries many happy memories, and she knows that Adrian would never forgive her if she left it behind.

This Sunday the family gathering is small: Nina's sister Stella with Sorel and her brother Emil with his wife Dora are the only guests. As soon as they are seated around the table and start sipping their tea, Adrian reads them Kass's letter. His voice is lively and excited, and he smiles while he reads.

"There couldn't be better news!" he says in the end. "Charles is always perfectly informed about the political events in our country—due to his friendship with the King and with Magda Lupescu. And his political judgment and insight are excellent! Even Nina thinks so. Am I right?"

Nina nods. She feels ill at ease and she blushes as everybody turns toward her.

"So what does this really mean for us?" asks Emil. He is wiping his gold-rimmed glasses with his monogrammed handkerchief.

"Well... I think..." Adrian closes his eyes thoughtfully. "I think it means that Sorel will finally get his family passport. And it means that Nadia's short hair won't be a problem any longer, and we could go and apply for our visas any time soon. What a relief!" he adds after a moment of silence.

Everybody cheers and applauds. Only Stella remains serious and frowns. "We must tell Victor to hurry up and make his preparations," she says as she lights a new cigarette.

Nina throws a worried look at her sister. She understands her concern: if Sorel gets the family passport, he may not want to wait for Doctor Georgescu. But Stella won't leave without Victor. And what about them, Nina and Adrian? Adrian will want to leave immediately, but she, Nina, won't leave without Stella. It's the old problem, all over again! Nina remembers the painful days when, after their mother's death and her own attempted suicide, her younger sister Stella who was only 16 at that time devoted herself entirely to Nina's recovery and well-being. They have been inseparable ever since. Also, Stella is the only one whom Nina has told about cousin Arnold's shameful attack. She couldn't imagine life without Stella. Leaving her behind would be unbearable.

Nina's thoughts are interrupted by Emil, who asks more details about their plans.

"How about you? Any change of mind? Any decision to join us?" Nina asks, as she pours him more tea.

Emil throws his head back as he laughs. "No! How could I? Somebody has to stay here and take care of Liviu's parrot, Coco. Have you forgotten that our brother has abandoned the poor thing in my care?"

Nina remembers that, indeed, their brother Liviu left for Paris a few months ago. Before leaving, he told everybody that he was going to work at the Institut Pasteur for about three months. But then he made his wife, Bea, join him. And last month, their daughter Lillian had also left for France. She was going to enroll in a boarding school at La Rochelle for the next year.

Both Nina and her sister Stella suspect that Liviu isn't coming back to Bucharest so soon... maybe not at all. He must have planned this trip in secret with his wife.

Nina has mixed feelings toward him: she misses him and she worries about his long absence. But she is also angry about his secretiveness, about the hidden way in which he organized this trip. At the same time she feels liberated from the old vow, relieved from the promise made to her dying mother to keep all the siblings together. With Liviu's departure, the vow is broken. She is now free of any obligation. A burden has fallen from her shoulders. But it is this sense of freedom which also frightens her. "Will you really stay behind all alone?" she asks.

"Yes," Emil nods. A drop of raspberry preserve has fallen on his expensive, custom-made shoes, and he bends down with his napkin, trying to remove it.

"You can't be serious!" says Adrian.

"But I am. I have already dreamt that I'm sitting alone in a deserted island!"

"Then join us! Don't stay behind!" Stella, Adrian and Sorel cry out. But Emil shakes his head. "I can't. You must understand: somebody must stay here and take care of Coco, Liviu's parrot!"

MORE PAIN

As predicted by Adrian, Sorel and Stella indeed receive the family passport during the next week. Stella immediately calls Doctor Georgescu and Nina, and a date is set for all of them to meet at the Swiss Embassy and apply for their visas.

"We must go now and take this opportunity! We can't wait for Nadia's hair to grow!" Adrian tells Nina and Stella. As the day of the audience approaches, everybody is excited. No one can eat or sleep. But it is Suzy who, the night before the designated Thursday, hears Nadia moan in her sleep. Suzy gets out of bed and tiptoes, barefoot, into her sister's room. Fräulein Lilly is fast asleep and snores so loud that she cannot possibly hear Nadia's moaning.

"What's wrong? Are you having a bad dream?" Suzy whispers. "Are you in pain? Wake up! Wake up! If it's a bad dream you'll be better off if you're awake!" She would like to shake Nadia. But she doesn't dare.

Her sister's response is a loud moan. Then she turns on the other side and goes on sleeping.

But in the morning she wakes up crying in pain, drenched in sweat, with high fever. She has dreamt again that she is trying to recover the hidden treasure from the sunken ship while a giant fish bumps into her head so hard that her left ear gets terribly painful. She is pressing her hand tightly over her ear in an attempt to stop the pain.

Nina immediately calls Sorel and Joel. They confirm her suspicion as they recognize a serious infection of the ear. Sorel promptly sets up the syringe and the long needle. This time Nadia fights with all her strength, she even bites Joel's finger until she draws blood. But he goes on with the process, in spite of her battle. Then, like the previous time, one of the two doctors comes in every morning to change the dressing and to check the ear.

Nadia's hair is clipped again, which pleases her. As soon as she can get out of bed she runs to the big bathroom mirror and rehearses her lines for the school play. Even though she cannot yet return to class, she vows that she will not give up her role in the play. But she keeps her secret to herself.

Days go by, and another date set for the audience at the Swiss Embassy comes and goes. Nina, who is full of anxiety, watches every sign of illness in her daughter. She sleeps poorly, eats next to nothing and her hair turns more gray every day. She would like to move Nadia into their bedroom, but she knows that Adrian wouldn't like it. He too is distraught by Nadia's illness. But he tries to keep calm and not let Nina lose hope. "Nadia will recover soon and you'll forget these hard days! Try to sleep and don't run yourself down!" he tells her every evening. At the same time he repeats to himself the plans he has made: upon their arrival in Zürich, they will move into a pension close to the Opera House. They will watch Wagner's masterpieces—*Tristan and Isolde*, *The Meistersingers* and *Lohengrin*, Suzy's favorite. They will listen to Enrico Carusso and Amelita Gallicurci. He is happy that the pension is so close to the Opera. He has already written to Hotel Europa, telling them that they'll be arriving soon. Also, he can't wait to start work on the new electrical turbines. He has many fresh ideas which he is eager to share with Kass. They will invite him and his wife Brigitte to a festive dinner at the exclusive Hotel Baur au Lac, overlooking the lake with the colorful sailboats and the many swans. And then they'll travel to Lugano. In his mind, Adrian can see the quaint, old villa, the lemon and orange trees in the garden, the lake and the little red boat. He takes the brass keys of the villa in his hand and holds them tightly, to reassure himself that all this is true.

In a few weeks Nadia starts recovering. Another date is set for the Embassy audience. But this too has to be canceled because, before the fever has totally disappeared, the other ear is acting up again.

During the next months, from June to the beginning of the next year, Nadia has repeated ear infections: five in one side, six in the other. There is a cyclical character to these episodes: as soon as one ear is healing, the other becomes painful again. The whole family watches the unfolding of her illness: when the pain and the fever go up, everybody is discouraged. But when the signs of health reappear, they all become hopeful again.

The cycles follow each other like clockwork, resembling an uninterrupted *perpetuum mobile*. Then, one morning in January, Nadia wakes up with unbearable pains in her ear and her head. The pain shoots deep into her brain. She lies in her bed, pale and shivering, crying, beating her head with her fists. Nina calls the two pediatricians, Sorel and Joel. They examine her, and, as their faces turn very serious, they tell Nina that the infection has grown into mastoiditis.

"She needs surgery right away! I'll take her to the hospital myself and I'll speak to the surgeon!" says Sorel. He helps Nina wrap the child in her heavy pink blanket, and carries her down to the car. Joel telephones Adrian to meet them at the hospital, while Nina follows Sorel into the car. With frightened eyes she watches Nadia shaking with fever in her arms.

All Nadia remembers from that day in the hospital is the sea of white light. Blinding, painfully bright light. She is placed on a stretcher and wheeled into a large room, with walls covered with white tiles reflecting the lights from the large ceiling lamps.

"Die weisse Küche!" (the white kitchen) she is calling it later on. Curiously, there are no shadows in this room. Masked men and women wearing white masks, white coats, bonnets and gloves tiptoe silently about.

"The mastoid! We have to break and remove the infected bone! And no anesthesia: she is too weak for it!" are the only words whispered by these white phantoms.

Nadia is strapped to a table with leather thongs, and when she looks up, she meets Sorel's clear blue eyes hovering between her and the lamp suspended from the ceiling. He too is wearing a white coat and mask, and his bald scalp is reflecting the bright lights of the room. His eyes are protecting her.

Then, the loud hammering starts. The blows which land on her skull are so deafening that her head feels like exploding. It goes on and on... Until it peaks into a scream which reverberates from every corner of the room . Then it all vanishes.

When she comes to, Nadia lies in a big bed, in a hospital room with a high ceiling. Another bed is next to hers. Her mother is there, wearing her cream-colored satin and lace nightgown. Her hair is unkempt and her face is pale. She has purple shadows under her eyes.

Even though it is winter, sunshine is streaming through the tall windows hung with yellow, flowery draperies. Nadia hears voices and footsteps. She opens her eyes and tries to lift her head and look around. But her head is so heavy, she can't raise it. She closes her eyes, she is too weak to keep them open.

The next day she is up a little longer and she can sip a few drops of water. Later—she doesn't know when—the surgeon, followed by a young nurse dressed all in white and pushing a small trolley laden with scalpels, syringes, scissors, bandages and bottles of disinfectants, walk into her room. The tall surgeon wears a dark hospital coat which reeks of carbolic acid. He has a long nose, bad teeth and small, piercing eyes. His features seem chiseled in stone. He never smiles. As soon as he touches Nadia's bandages, she starts to cry and raises her hand to protect herself. The doctor orders Nina to place Nadia in a chair and hold her still. Then, shaking his finger in Nadia's face, he tells her that if she touches her bandages and doesn't obey his orders, the devil will come and take her away. "The devil is watching you. And, if you are a bad girl, he will come at night, when everybody's asleep, and take you away. Now, I don't want to hear a sound while I'm cleaning the wound."

Nadia is stunned. She doesn't say a word. Tears run down her cheeks.

From that day on, she has trouble sleeping. As soon as she closes her eyes, she sees the surgeon bending over her, holding a shiny scalpel in one hand and a hammer in the other. He grins, showing his stained, pointed teeth and fixing her with his fiery eyes. He smells of an unpleasant chemical mixed with sulphur. She screams when he reaches out to grab her, and she has a glimpse of two black horns sticking out of his head just before she wakes up. Nina, Adrian and Sorel talk to her and try to calm her down. But nobody can convince her that the surgeon himself is not the devil.

Nadia's recovery is slow and not without pain. She has no appetite, and, as the surgeon comes every day and goes on threatening her with the devil, she cannot forget him, and keeps having trouble sleeping.

But every morning her mother gives her a sponge bath. Nina has a gentle touch, much softer than Fräulein Lilly's harsh and hurried scrub. Nina's hands are delicate, with long, graceful fingers, and her skin is smooth, so that, whenever her mother gives her a sponge bath, Nadia lets go of her fright of the evil surgeon. She closes her eyes, lets her body go limp, and wishes to remain here, in this room, as long as possible and have her mother all for herself.

Among the relatives who come to visit her, the one Nadia likes best is old Aunt Josephine, Joel's mother. She is Nina's aunt, Uncle Ariel's youngest sister.

Aunt Josephine lost most of her hearing in childhood. She has suffered the same infections Nadia is suffering today. Now Aunt Josephine uses an ivory horn suspended from her neck with a silver chain. But in spite of the ivory horn, people must shout to make themselves heard.

Aunt Josephine comes to the hospital every day, and she brings Nadia the most beautifully illustrated adventure books: *Treasure Island*, *Robinson Crusoe*, Jules Verne, Karl May's books about Indians, *Tom Sawyer* and *Huckleberry Finn*. She sits by Nadia's bed and reads to her. Then, after she leaves, Nadia keeps looking at the pictures and reads the stories again.

But then one morning Aunt Josephine surprises everybody with an unexpected gift: as Nadia wakes up she hears the most melodious trills. When she opens her eyes, she sees a tall silver cage standing in the middle of the room, and a yellow canary perched near the top of it. He turns his head toward the window and greets the day with a cascade of trills.

Aunt Josephine stands near the cage and watches Nadia's delight.

"I cannot hear the song and chirping of warbles, canaries and nightingales which I love so much! It's a miserable life to be locked in a tower of silence," she tells Nina and Adrian. "But Nadia must be able to hear and enjoy many songs for the rest of her life. You must do everything possible not to let her go deaf!"

THE DECREE

TOWARD THE MIDDLE OF JANUARY, four weeks after Nadia's operation, she is finally going home. The surgical wound has closed, the fever is almost down to normal, but she is still very weak. She has lost a lot of weight and she can barely eat. But when they arrive home, it is Nina who has a great shock. Nobody is there, neither Marish, nor Ilona the cook, nor Fräulein Lilly. Only Suzy is there, sitting at her desk and doing her homework.

"Where is everybody? Why aren't they here?" Nina asks Adrian, after helping Nadia take off her coat.

Adrian sets down the cage with the canary, puts his arm around Nina and tells her about the new governmental decree issued a few days ago, which prevents all Jews from employing household help younger than forty.

"We have been called white slave traders," he quotes from the governmental decree. "I didn't tell you earlier because I didn't want to upset you at the hospital."

"How will I manage with a sick child and no help? Who will do the shopping, cooking, cleaning, washing, and who will look after Nadia and Suzy? Even though she is older than Nadia, Suzy is still a child who needs some looking after. And I can't do all this by myself!"

Nina's thoughts turn to the past, to the war, when she and her family were forced to take refuge away from Bucharest, in a small city—and when her mother was dying from the Spanish flu. Then, too, they had no maids, nobody to help carry firewood. It was so cold, the water froze in the kettle on the stove, and Nina got frostbite from standing in line for bread. Maybe it's not quite so bad as back then, but with Nadia sick and no help...

"What am I going to do now?"

"Don't panic! This won't be for long. We'll find a solution. I'm sure Stella or Mathilda or some other friend will find help for us. But remember, this won't last long. I promise you that we'll be out of there in less than a month."

Nina gives him a doubtful look. She has heard this promise so many times.

The following day, Ilona, the cook, Marish, the maid, and Fräulein Lilly come to say goodbye. Ilona carries a pocketbook Nina and Adrian have brought her from abroad, and Marish wears a sweater they gave her last Christmas. They both cry as they sit down for tea in the dining room. They were very young when they came to Bucharest. They lived with the Steins for more than ten years. This household became their family.

"This new law isn't good for us either," says Fräulein Lilly. "If we can't work for Jewish households, it will be hard to find jobs. And nobody wants to work in factories or go back to the country and work the land!" The cook and the maid sigh at these words. Then, before leaving, they promise to keep in touch and to come visiting.

As soon as they are out on the street they run into Doctor Ionescu, the neighbor from across the street. He is wearing the badge of the Iron Guard on his lapel and he's grinning.

"Congratulations! The kikes finally get what they deserve!" he says. "Do come by to the Casa Verde and say that I invited you. I am sure we will find decent work for you, certainly more dignified than toiling for these greedy slave traders!"

The women barely listen to the doctor and hurry on their way.

"I'll stay away from the Casa Verde even if they offer me the best job in the world! I don't like the Green Shirts!" Marish says when they're out of the doctor's earshot. The others nod in agreement.

Nina's household crisis is short-lived. Fritz the chauffeur has a sister, Alina, who turned 41 in the summer. She's a skilled cook and is willing to work for the Steins. And Ilona's older cousin, Regina, is eager to be their cleaning lady.

But how about a new governess? Nina keeps pressing Adrian about this.

"It's not necessary. We'll be out of here in less than a month!"

There is, indeed, a visa appointment at the Swiss Embassy set for Wednesday, January 26. But it is on January 25th, one day before the appointment, that a wave of panic shakes the entire Jewish community: a new governmental decree suddenly requires that all Jews' citizenship must be reevaluated. The head of every Jewish household must report urgently to the police or to a specifically designated center to obtain the necessary forms and applications. Without this proof of citizenship passports become invalid and no foreign visas can be obtained.

Adrian can barely contain his anger. "I was born in this country and so were my parents, my grandparents and great-grandparents. What is there to prove? Not to mention that we fought in so many wars! This is terrible! The person who loses his citizenship loses everything: his right to work, his right to own a store, a house, a business, a car, or even a horse or a cow. He may lose his right to travel or not be allowed to live in the city! Our passports are now invalid and we can't apply for a foreign visa!"

He keeps pacing furiously back and forth in the living room. Then, as he realizes, that the lines at the police headquarters will be very long, he asks Fritz to drive him there at 5 o'clock next morning.

Even at that time the line spills out of the courtyard and winds around the block. It is a very cold day, a strong wind is blowing. Later it starts to snow. Adrian shivers and his feet are freezing. In his rush he has forgotten to put on warm boots and woolen socks. Also his imported leather gloves have no lining. He buries his hands in his coat pockets and keeps stamping his feet.

But he is lucky: at eight o'clock, when she comes to work, a woman wrapped in a woolen scarf taps him on the shoulder. It is the clerk with sleepy eyes from the Memorandum Department, who recognizes him now. She takes him inside the building with her, hands him the papers he must complete and tells him to return them urgently with other documents.

Adrian leaves the building before most offices have even opened. He is pleased that the clerk has not forgotten him. "There is always hope, if you know your way around!" he tells himself as he returns to his office and sits down with the papers.

NADIA

F OR SOME TIME AT HOME Nadia is doing well. She has a good appetite and gains weight, her cheeks are rosy and she prepares to go back to school.

But suddenly one morning she is sick again, and this time it is worse than ever before. It is so bad that Adrian himself is frightened. She lies in bed barely moaning and doesn't recognize anyone. Her fever is high, and she is shaken by convulsions. Her hands are moving incessantly and her eyes are closed.

Adrian would like to call Sorel, but he is in Iaşi, for his citizenship papers. So he calls Joel, and they rush Nadia to the hospital.

The surgeon with the bad teeth and the gold-rimmed glasses examines her, and after he finishes, he calls Nina and Adrian to his office. Standing behind a massive desk strewn with anatomical models of ears in different sizes and colors—which all can be taken apart and put back together—he tells them that this time he will not operate. He avoids looking at them as he speaks. "She is too sick. Her illness is too advanced. It is too late," he says. "She will die on the operating table, and I don't want to be known as my patients' executioner." He sits down and picks up a few small fragments of an artificial ear and stares at them, avoiding Nina and Adrian's eyes. "The new mastoiditis which has now developed on the left side is turning into meningitis, for which we have no treatment. A time comes when we have to let go, and allow God and nature to do their handiwork!" He looks up briefly, then concentrates again on the pink and blue anatomical fragments resting in his hand.

Adrian cannot believe his ears. Does the surgeon really mean what he says? Is he going to abandon a patient consigned to his care? Let Nadia slide into death without trying to save her? And all this because of his own pride and selfishness! Adrian is full of angry doubts. "You're not going to let my daughter die!" he shouts. He makes a step toward the doctor. His face is crimson and a vein is bulging on his forehead. "You will do whatever is necessary to keep her alive!"

They stare at each other. "If this were your daughter, what would you do? Let her die?" Adrian still stares at the surgeon.

The doctor hesitates, caught off guard. "I... may not... operate!" he says without conviction. Then he puts down the pieces he holds in his hand, stands up and leans forward on his desk. "Since you insist, have it your way. I'll operate on condition that you sign a release stating that you don't hold me responsible if something goes wrong or if she dies on the table." He pulls a sheet of paper from a drawer, scribbles a few lines and hands it to Adrian. His face is still red and the vein on his forehead pulsates rapidly. He takes the paper, signs the bottom of the page and returns it to the surgeon. Nina, who stands next to him, is very pale.

The doctor opens the door and lets them out.

When they step into the corridor, Nina and Adrian look like two walking ghosts. Nina is ready to collapse, and Adrian supports her with trembling hands. But three people are there, waiting for them: Aunt Josephine, her husband, Leon, and Joel. When they see them, they take them in their arms.

"Tell me quickly, what's going on?" asks Aunt Josephine.

Adrian bends toward her, and shouts into her hearing device, telling her that the surgeon will do the operation now, but that he thinks that Nadia doesn't have a chance and that she may die on the table.

"How terrible! We must do something immediately! We must save Nadia!" cries Aunt Josephine with her high-pitched voice. "Come! We have no time to waste! We must act quickly and leave immediately! I know what we have to do—just come with me!"

"Where to?" asks Adrian.

"To the temple! To the Geller Temple. I spoke to the Rabbi and he knows what to do. He promised to conduct a special service aimed at saving a dying child! We must go *now*. The Rabbi is waiting for us!" She turns around and starts running down the stairs, followed by Adrian, while Uncle Leon is trailing behind, helping Nina walk down the stairs. Only Joel is left behind in the hospital. He hastens toward the operating room, to keep up with Nadia's surgery.

15 minutes later, the car stops in front of the Geller Temple. It is a rainy weekday morning, and the deserted sanctuary is dark and cold. Adrian can hear the rain falling outside. A smell of stale air, smoke and burning candles pervades the room. There is only a small light on the *bima*.

The dark, empty sanctuary and the small light in the distance remind Adrian of a scene in Kafka's book *The Trial*. It is the scene when, in the dark and deserted cathedral of Prague, K is confronted by the mysterious "prison chaplain" whom he can barely see. The clergyman tells him the story of a man who comes a long way from the country, driven by the wish to be admitted to the Law. But when he reaches the entrance to the Law, he is confronted by a lowly gatekeeper who stops him from entering "at this time." He gives the man a stool, and allows him to sit by the gate. The man from the country spends the rest of his life at the doorstep of the Law, waiting for permission to go in. He gets older and older, and, finally, at his death, the gatekeeper tells him that he must now shut the gate, since this particular entrance was built especially for him.

In the book, K is left confused by this strange tale, the meaning of which he cannot grasp. Neither does Adrian, who finds the story sad and haunting. When he tries to understand it, he only concludes that man is small and powerless in front of the Law. All his life he strives for admission into the radiance of the Law. But a lowly and cruel doorkeeper has the power to stop him from access to the spiritual space to which his whole being aspires. Adrian feels a deep bond with the poor man from the country who spends his entire life waiting in vain for the gatekeeper's permission to enter the brilliance of the Law... He, Adrian, has never been religious or given to spiritual meditations. But now, with Nadia's plight, everything has changed. Sometimes he doesn't recognize himself.

Suddenly, a light switch is turned on in the temple, the darkness vanishes, and Adrian is jolted out of his ruminations. The Rabbi with his dark beard, his tall headgear and his long robe is standing on the *bima*. He is wrapped in his white *tallit* with its thin blue stripes which represent the divine thread of life. A thick chain of gold dangles from his neck. (Adrian remembers that he was nicknamed the "Jewish Pope" because of his love for jewelry.) With a small flutter of his hand, he invites Adrian and Uncle Leon to join him on the *bima*.

"We should be ten men, a real *minyan* for this service. But since it is a matter of life and death, the three of us will suffice. The ceremony in which you are about to participate consists of a symbolic transaction. To save your daughter's life you must sell her to another couple who will now be her parents and who *must* change her name. She will become somebody else's daughter and will be known by another name. In this way the Angel of Death will not be able to find her."

The Rabbi turns to Uncle Leon.

"I should add that the new parents must pay for this sale, here in the temple, and the money must be blessed by the Rabbi."

Adrian nods as he stands to the left of the cleric, while Uncle Leon stands to his right. Nina and Aunt Josephine, their heads covered with scarves, watch from the narrow balcony, where they cannot be seen by the men. Then, on the *bima*, the Rabbi and the two worshippers turn, facing the ark where the Torah scrolls are kept.

"BARUCH ATA ADONAI, ADONAI ELOHEINU, ADONAI EHAD. BARUCH SHEM KEVOD" prays the Rabbi. "I inscribe TOVAH, daughter of Leon and Josephine Gold, into the Book of the Lord. And I pray to strike out of the Book of the Lord Nadia-Haia, daughter of Adrian and Nina Stein." The three men bow deeply in front of the ark. Then the Rabbi takes a gold coin from Uncle Leon and recites a special blessing over it, bowing repeatedly as

he prays. When he finishes, he hands the coin to Adrian, who looks at it, but doesn't know what to do: should he put it in his wallet like any other coin? Should he handle it differently? The gold coin was blessed by the Rabbi, but what does this really mean? Adrian never believed in "magic" amulets, talismans, or wondrous stones, blessed by "holy men." But he cannot put the coin in his wallet and let it mix with his regular money. So he wraps it in a clean white handkerchief and slides it in his breast pocket.

Afterward he looks up at the balcony, trying to get a glimpse of Nina and Aunt Josephine, but instead he meets the Rabbi's eyes, looking at him sternly.

He touches Adrian's shoulder, as they descend from the *bima*.

"The power of God is great," says the Rabbi. "He performs countless miracles. And the Angel of Death is His servant, like the entire Creation!"

Adrian listens in silence and sighs. He wishes to believe in these words of wisdom.

A few days after the surgery, Nadia lies in her bed without moving. Her eyes are closed and she doesn't speak, nor does she eat. An intravenous needle is inserted at the base of her neck, and the clear liquid which contains sugar and salt runs into her body. Sometimes her hands move without any order or goal, sometimes her feet twitch, and sometimes a shiver runs through her body. However, her breathing is deep and regular.

The surgeon with bad teeth and gold-rimmed glasses and the young nurse come every day to change her dressing. But Nadia gives no sign of recognition, no start to pain, or any response to their ministrations. In their hands her body is like a rag doll.

The doctor never talks to Nina or Adrian, even though they are always in the room. He turns his back on them and avoids looking at them. He only speaks to the nurse, pretending they're not there.

Every morning Nina gives Nadia her regular sponge bath. She knows already that the child will not react even if the water is cold.

For most of the day Nina sits by the bed watching her, or simply staring into space. At mealtime, she frowns and pushes away the bowl of lukewarm potato soup and the plate of *mămăligă* with *brînză* provided by the hospital. When she returns the food without touching it, Adrian scolds her, pointing out that Nadia's color is improving, and that her breathing is steady and deep.

Sorel, who is back from his trip to Iaşi for the citizenship application, tries to speak to the surgeon about Nadia's illness and prognosis, but is politely dismissed. Even Doctor Victor Georgescu, who went to Medical School with the surgeon and has known him for many years, is ignored when he mentions Nadia's name.

Then, one morning, the sound of a barrel organ comes right from under the window. It plays a slow waltz, a popular tune—"Estudiantina"—a waltz regularly played at the skating rink. Nina is angry at the organ grinder, who may disturb Nadia's sleep. She gets up to open the window and tell the musician to go away. But before she reaches the window, Nadia opens her eyes, turns her head as if listening to the music, and smiles.

"I'll be damned!" Adrian whispers. "Look at the magic cure! Whom should we credit with Nadia's improvement:

the Rabbi's prayers, the surgeon who didn't want to operate, or the street musician with his barrel organ?"

"Don't be so quick to cry victory!" Nina answers. "We still don't know whether Nadia has a meningeal reaction to the infection, or whether she has true meningitis as the surgeon thinks. In this case, the noise can really harm her." As the organ grinder is still playing, Nina tries again to reach the window. But Adrian stops her when he sees Nadia yawning with open eyes and stretching in bed, like a person who wakes from a deep sleep.

From that day on, everything changes: Nadia is on a slow but definite road to recovery. As she starts eating, the intravenous needle is removed from her neck, and she gains strength every day. Still, she has to stay in the hospital for a few more weeks until the surgical wound is completely healed.

FOUR WEEKS LATER

W HEN THEY RETURN HOME, NINA has no time to relax: Adrian urges her to inspect the whole house and make a final decision what to take and what to abandon. "When we get the citizenship papers, we should be ready to leave. The papers will be here soon! People have started receiving them. When we get them, we won't have time to make decisions." Then he reminds her again to inspect the entire house, including the basement and the attic.

He hands her the keys to the basement and gives her his woolen cardigan so she shouldn't catch cold there. Nina wraps the sweater around her—it is so big, it fits her like a coat—and walks down to the basement.

She has been here only a few times since they moved into the house, about ten years ago.

The door creaks when she opens it. She switches on the light in the dark room where the air is stale and musty. She takes a few steps and stops in front of a tall armoire made of blonde rosewood with dark inlays. The lock is rusty, hard to open, and Nina worries that the key will break in the lock.

When the door opens, she inhales the stuffy air with a faint tinge of old lavender. In front of her, on the left, are shelves filled with neat piles of embroidered and monogrammed bedsheets and pillowcases and old-fashioned petticoats trimmed with lace. Everything here was made and belonged to her mother and grandmother and was embroidered and used by them.

After she looks at a ruffled petticoat, Nina turns to the right side of the armoire, which is reserved for dresses and gowns. She pulls out a long white organza chiffon dress embroidered with beads. It is her mother's wedding dress, made by her grandmother and embroidered by her mother. Nina herself wore this dress at her own wedding: she didn't have to make any adjustments—it fit her perfectly.

Next to it hangs her grandmother's wedding gown, made of silk satin, with a corsage of re-embroidered lace and a long train of white tulle. This too was made by her grandmother.

On a top shelf above the dresses, Nina sees a large cardboard box tied with a ribbon. She wipes the dust off its lid and opens it. Inside she finds rolls of fine lace imported from France, Spain and Italy, all packed in rose-colored tissue paper. And in another box she sees lace bobbins and crochet hooks. Next to them, also packed in rose tissue paper, lies a pair of unfinished white gloves, made in a pattern of lace created by her mother.

Nina still remembers her working at them. The white gloves were her last handiwork. She made them during the war, in refuge, just as she started to get sick, shortly before her death. Even though she was running a fever and even though her vision had become blurred, forcing her to bend deep down over the lace bobbins, Nina remembers her struggling to finish her work.

"These gloves are for you, for your wedding day," she had told Nina. "You must wear them. You'll be beautiful. You will dance, and you'll be happy on that day!"

Nina's mother and grandmother were skilled artisans. Even though they were not professional dress and lace makers, friends and neighbors asked them to make and embroider their wedding gowns, or even to embroider or add lace to a trousseau. Nina's mother had even taught embroidery and lace making at a Jewish school for girls.

Nina strokes the gloves while she stares at the cardboard boxes and the dresses hanging in the closet. She knows that she cannot take them with her, but she cannot leave them behind and abandon them either. It would mean a cruel betrayal, a painful desertion of her mother and grandmother's, love and devotion. What should she do? What is the right thing to do? Or, is there a right thing to do? she asks herself as she puts the boxes back in their place, and picks up, from the shelf, a white bonnet embroidered with beads, which both her mother and herself had worn on their wedding days. It is a most delicate work, with the white small beads still shimmering in the basement light.

What should she do? She cannot find an answer as she contemplates the lacework of the bonnet, and then puts it back on the shelf.

She finally decides to ask her sister Stella for advice. She is more practical. She may come up with a solution.

Back upstairs Nina has to attend to other chores. Nadia has grown out of her red velvet dress and needs a new one. And Suzy keeps asking her for a bra. All her girlfriends wear bras, she says. She is the only one without a bra! She doesn't really need it, Nina thinks, but she doesn't want Suzy to feel different from other girls. How fast will Doamna Avramescu be able to sew one for her? She must hurry up.

This afternoon, when the girls come home from school, she will take Suzy to Doamna Avramescu for measurements. She will telephone Adrian at the office that she needs Fritz with the car in the early afternoon, right after lunch.

The girls also need new shoes—Nadia has grown so fast she can only wear her black patent leather shoes. The children should have everything they need as clothing goes when they arrive in Zürich, Adrian has told her. He has made a subscription for her at MARIE CLAIRE and LE JARDIN DES MODES for children so that Nadia and Suzy should be dressed like the girls in France and Switzerland.

Nina will have to hurry now. With luck she will be able to go to Doamna Avramescu for Suzy, and then get the new velvet dress for Nadia and shoes for both girls at Galleries Lafayette.

She hopes to do everything this afternoon.

She feels relieved after she makes this decision as she goes to the telephone: it will prove to Adrian that she is making a real effort to be ready for the trip.

If only Stella and her family would get their citizenship papers in time!

ON A BEAUTIFUL MORNING IN MARCH

I T IS A BEAUTIFUL MORNING in March. The sun is shining, little white clouds float in the sky, and furry buds adorn the willows in the gardens. Adrian rides to the office and when he is two blocks away, he asks Fritz to stop the car and let him out.

He has to step carefully over the rivulets born from the melting snow, which now crisscross the sidewalk.

Adrian stops at the newspaper stand near the corner and, as he reads the headlines, he cannot believe his eyes.

"AUSTRIA UNITES WITH THE GERMAN REICH" says the bold print on the first page. Even though this is not totally unexpected, Adrian is shocked. His heart beats like a hammer and there is a choking sensation in his throat. But in the next minute he buys the paper, folds it under his arm, and rushes to his office. Without taking off his coat he sits at his desk and reads the main article, which says that yesterday Austria was united with the German Reich, according to Hitler's plan. A great number of German troops were amassed at the border, and Chancellor Schuschnigg ordered the Austrian Army not to resist, in order to avoid bloodshed. A plebiscite which would have allowed the Austrian citizens to vote either for resistance to Germany or for unification had been cancelled by the

Chief of State. A short note at the bottom of the page says that Hitler is already on his way to Vienna, and that many people, including many artists and intellectuals, are trying to flee the country.

Adrian is so deeply immersed in the article that he doesn't hear Domnișoara Braunstein walk in with a cup of Turkish coffee and give him the mail. He stops reading and raises his head only when she stands next to him and sets the cup on the table.

"Terrible news!" he says, pointing to the paper. "Did you read the article?"

"Yes, of course!" she says. When Adrian looks at her, he sees that her face is pale and her eyes are swollen and teary.

"Any news from your brother in Vienna?" he asks.

The secretary shakes her head. "No, we hope he'll come back to Bucharest with his wife and baby! We'll go to the train station today, after work, my mother and I," she adds with a trace of hope in her voice. "But I almost forgot: here is the mail. You have a letter from Switzerland, from Mister Kass, right here, on top!"

Adrian tears open the envelope and quickly reads its contents. After inquiring about his wellbeing, Kass invites him to come urgently to Switzerland, since a new electric power station is about to be built close to Baden, and Adrian's expertise is badly needed. "Come immediately, or as soon as you can," he writes. "The new power station is very much like the one you have designed and built in the Romanian mountains, and we want you to direct our project. We have the funds, and all the preliminary work has been done. All we need is your physical presence."

Adrian is mesmerized by the letter. In the next minute he sees himself in Baden, with Charles, inspecting the site of the electrical power station, some place in the mountains, near a waterfall. Is there already a sketch of the plant? Is he expected to draw one? Kass didn't mention it. Adrian will certainly have to take along the diagrams of the station which he has built here, and he may have to look for newer, more modernized turbines and generators. All this makes him feel hopeful. This is a good omen! They will soon receive their citizenship papers, and then the road to freedom will be open.

He calls to Nina to tell her about the letter of invitation to Switzerland. She is startled by the news and remains silent for a moment. Then she tells him that their citizenship papers have been approved—the notification has just arrived in the mail. She was going to call him, since he must go to Police Headquarters and collect the papers as soon as possible. Stella and Sorel have also received the approval.

Adrian doesn't waste any time. He has Fritz pick up the official notification from home, after which they rush to Police Headquarters.

Two hours later he holds the affidavit of citizenship in his hands. All they have to do now is apply for the visas at the Swiss Embassy.

When he returns to the office, Adrian unlocks the big metal safe to check the engineering publications he will need in Switzerland. The first objects he sees when he opens the safe are the bronze keys to the house in Lugano. (One set of keys he has given to Charles before leaving Zürich.) In his mind, he recalls the villa with its flowery balconies, and the walls covered with blooming wisteria. The entire house and the trees which surround it are reflected in the quiet lake. It is a vision of great peace and serenity.

Then the memory fades, as he picks up the blue folder with the plans of the power station in the mountains which he had projected, and where he had first used the alternative current generators and turbines invented by Tesla. He opens the folder, flips through the pages, decides that he will need it, and puts it on his desk.

Next to this dossier are many publications by and about Nikola Tesla, the mysterious scientist who has revolutionized the field of electricity and has masterminded the electrification of America. Adrian has always admired this man. Ever since his student years he has been fascinated by him and has collected his publications. He has been impressed by the fact that, even though he was born in a small village in Croatia, he has succeeded in becoming an engineer—very much against the will of his father, who wanted him to be a priest like himself—and he has succeeded to travel to America, where he became the most famous inventor of his time. It is precisely the richness and the originality of his mind which has so awed Adrian. Now he makes sure not to leave behind any of the Tesla publications he has collected.

As he rummages through his files, Adrian thinks that today Nikola Tesla is an old man in his eighties, but he remembers the scientist many years ago, when, still in his student years, he attended a conference in Zürich given by Tesla. He was a tall, elegant man with dark hair, a black moustache and penetrating blue eyes. He always wore spats and he spoke with passion about his discovery of alternative current. Everybody in the audience listened in awe.

At that time, Tesla was known as the dark "Prince of Light," or the "Mephisto of Light." At the end of the conference he gave Adrian an autographed picture of himself: it shows him sitting in his lab and reading, while next to him his huge electrical transmitter spews out into the room a cascade of sparks and streamers—a supernatural storm of lightnings. Indeed, Prometheus unbound! Adrian thinks as he carefully places the photo on his desk.

Adrian handles the stack of papers on his desk as if they were a cache of gold and diamonds, while he selects those which are essential for his work. He will pack them in a briefcase and will carry them, by hand, on the train. These papers are as important to him as his eyes. The less significant but still valuable publications he will bring to Stiller and ask him to send them to Zürich by diplomatic order.

The only objects left in the safe are two manila envelopes. He opens them and pulls out two cartoons identical with the engravings of the devil and the smokestacks on his windowpanes. They are the source of the engravings. To him they represent the condemnation of the burning of coal in industry. It's the end of an era and the beginning of the new age of electricity. The engraved windows of his office are precious to him but since he is forced to leave them behind, he will take the cartoons with him. Then, as soon as he'll have his own room in Baden, he will ask an engraving artist to transfer the drawings on the new windows. Also, he will frame Tesla's autographed photo with the torrent of sparks, and hang it on the wall. In his mind, he is already busy decorating his office in Baden.

The telephone call from Stiller comes early next day, minutes after Adrian has walked into the office. It's short, but precise: "Do not come to the Swiss Embassy for visas. The Swiss border is closed to all Jews. It's too late. Immediately after the Anschluss—which took place a few days ago—thousands of Jews from Austria have attempted to flee to Switzerland. Because of the fear of such a massive invasion of Jews, the head of the Swiss Police, the anti-Semitic Dr. Rothmund, has closed all the borders to them, and is expelling all those who have entered the country after the Anschluss. Besides," Stiller continues, "I am being recalled to Zürich immediately. I am very concerned about these developments, and I promise to keep in touch as much as I can!"

After he hangs up the receiver, Adrian sits in his chair without moving. He doesn't notice when the folder with the citizenship papers and with the now useless family passport slips from his hands. After a while he picks it up and, looking at the picture, he sighs and thinks that at least Nadia is well now, and this is what matters most. But, is this the end? Can this be all? With the borders closed and Stiller gone, are they really trapped here for good?

He goes to the window and, as if waiting for an answer from the giant, he stares at the naked devil engraved on the glass. But there is no answer. Silence prevails.

Adrian returns to the desk, and, very slowly, he starts putting the folders back in the safe: the Tesla file with all the original articles he has collected. The plans for the power station he has built in the Carpathian mountains. Important publications in the field of electrical turbines and transformers. His correspondence with Kass. And finally, the two manila envelopes with the cartoons of the giant and the smokestacks. Everything is back in the safe, except the bronze keys to the house in Lugano. He picks them up—and hesitates. He holds them tight—he cannot bring himself to lock them in the safe. Instead, he slips the keys into the uppermost drawer of the desk, the one he opens and shuts many times every day.

THE END